A Plague of Emperors

Sempronius Scipio and the Emperors of the Gothic Wars
CE 251 to 253.

By Gordon Anthony

Copyright © 2025 Gordon Anthony
ISBN : 9798281918824

Part 1

Barbarians at the Gates

Chapter 1
Letter Of Introduction

"There it is," I said as I reined in my horse at the crest of a rise. "That's the border of the empire. Beyond the Danubius, you'll find your people again."

Aoric pulled up beside me, shading his eyes against the afternoon sun and gazing down the gentle slope of the hill to the wide, muddy brown river which flowed away to the east. A couple of miles downstream was a small settlement of wooden huts with thatched roofs, and beyond that was our destination. It was a Roman fortress, with high walls of stone, and several square towers. Pennons fluttered from tall flagpoles, and the place gave an impression of permanence and solidity. It sat perched on a steep hill, the walls climbing from the river bank to the summit of the hill, giving the place a lopsided look, but it was clearly well defended, with deep ditches dug all around the perimeter.

On the river were a couple of ships of the Danubius Fleet, their many oars propelling the vessels as they patrolled the waterway which marked the limit of Roman civilisation.

Aoric had still made no comment, so I pointed to the distant fort.

"That must be Novae," I said. "You don't need to come in with me. You can cross the river and go in search of your people."

His horse shook its head and snorted. Aoric's own grunt was almost masked by the sound.

"I am half Roman," he reminded me. "I am still not sure I want to go back."

"It's your choice," I told him. This was a conversation we had held several times, but now the chance for him to return north was close at hand, and I could see he was suffering from some internal conflict. He had never revealed very much about his early life, but I had the impression that his youth had not been easy. He claimed to be the son of a Gothic tribal leader, but his mother had been a Roman woman who had been taken as a slave in a raid. As a result, I guessed that he had probably had to endure some discrimination from other boys while he was growing up. His unwillingness to talk about his early years, and his obvious reluctance to return to Gothic lands told me that he had been deeply affected by his upbringing.

After a moment, he asked me, "Are you still planning to cross the river yourself?"

"Those are my orders," I nodded. "But you don't need to stay with me. That might look bad for you when we encounter your people."

He gave a nonchalant shrug, then decided, "I'll stick with you a bit longer. Life is interesting around you."

I smiled my thanks. Aoric was young enough to be my grandson, but we had developed something like kinship over the past year or so.

"You can leave any time you like," I reminded him. "But I will admit I feel safer with you around."

He gave a grin, one hand tapping the hilt of the long, straight-bladed sword which hung from his saddle.

"Just tell me who you want me to kill," he chuckled.

"Nobody," I laughed. "Especially not in Novae. I'll need the Governor's help."

"You'll need the help of several gods," Aoric muttered in response. "You won't last long if you go north on your own."

That was a grim reminder of the task I had been set. I would have liked to argue with him, but I had a horrible feeling that he might be right.

"Let's go and talk to the Governor," I said as I nudged my brown mare into motion.

We clopped along the cobbled roadway which ran straight as an arrow towards the fortress. We attracted a few glances from some of the inhabitants of the cluster of huts which crowded near the river bank, but nobody paid us more than passing attention. This may have been an outpost at the edge of empire, but travellers were not uncommon. The only thing which might have marked me and Aoric as unusual was that we were both wearing trousers beneath our tunics, jerkins and cloaks. Winter had not long turned to spring, and I was accustomed to the heat of Italia, so I had adopted the barbarian habit of wearing trousers in winter. My old bones felt the chill more than they used to, so trousers, thick socks and stout boots helped keep me warm. Not only that, if we were to cross the river, travelling in Roman garb might provoke some hostile reactions.

I studied the fortress as we drew nearer. The walls were massively thick and very tall, with soldiers patrolling the high ramparts. The towers bore *ballistas* and catapults, and even the deep ditches were lined with row upon row of sharp wooden stakes to impale anyone who fell into them.

There was a small group of soldiers at the open gateway, all wearing chainmail, and armed with sword and spear as well as curved, oval shields. Iron helmets with cheek flaps protected their heads and faces. They looked more than a little tense, which I took to be a by-product of living on the very frontier of the empire.

One of them stepped towards us, holding up a hand.

"Stop there!" he ordered. "What is your purpose here?"

"I have a letter for the Governor," I explained.

"Then get off your horse and hand it over."

I dismounted, then dug into my satchel, pulling out a small, cylindrical sealed scroll case which I handed to him.

"Here is my letter of introduction," I said.

Frowning, the soldier examined the seal, then glanced up at me.

"By order of the Emperor?" he asked in surprise.

"That's right."

He pursed his lips, then announced, "I'll fetch an officer."

"Good idea," I smiled.

Aoric and I waited while a Centurion was fetched. He, too, examined the seal, then invited us into the fortress.

"I'll take you to the *Principia*," he told us. "Leave your horses here. I'll see they are taken to the stables and cared for. Your bags will be taken to one of our guest rooms. Eyeing Aoric, he added, "Your sword will be placed with your baggage."

He made it sound as if the fort was a *mansio* where travellers could find lodgings while on the road, but two more soldiers fell into step behind us as we walked, giving the lie to that impression.

The Centurion led us up the hill, moving along gravel paths between dozens of long, low buildings. This was a permanent base, so the soldiers had fixed barracks. There were also granaries, a bath house, armouries, an infirmary, workshops and stores. Because of the steep slope of the hill, terraces had been cut into the hillside to provide flat ground for the buildings which rose in steps as we climbed. And everywhere I saw the boar insignia of *Legio I Italica,* the legion which was permanently based at Novae.

Many of those soldiers were practising battle drill in the open spaces of the fort, and the entire place had the feeling of being at constant readiness for trouble.

The *Principia* was a large, imposing building, and a busy one too, with men coming and going all the time. The Centurion handed us into the care of a clerk, giving him the sealed scroll case. The clerk, in turn, passed us on to a Tribune who said he would guide us to the Governor's office.

Clutching the scroll case in one hand, the red-cloaked Tribune informed us, "You've arrived just in time. The Governor always spends a few hours working in his office each afternoon before retiring to his private quarters in the *Praetorium* next door. As long as you don't delay him from his dinner, I'm sure he'll welcome you."

The Tribune led us through a maze of corridors until we reached a large ante-chamber where three scribes sat at desks, scribbling with quills and ink or reading parchments and tablets, sorting them into piles. At the far end of the chamber was a wooden door which was guarded by two armed soldiers who eyed us intently when we entered the chamber.

"I shall inform the Governor of your arrival," the Tribune said. "Take a seat."

He gestured to a long, wooden bench which sat against the wall opposite the three busy desks.

The Tribune knocked on the door, went inside, and we waited.

And waited.

I unlooped my satchel from around my shoulder, placing it on the bench beside me. Then I unfastened my brooch, taking off my cloak and folding it before placing it on top of the satchel. My every move was watched by the two guards whose faces were anything but friendly.

Eventually, the door opened again, and two scribes emerged, each carrying a satchel full of their writing implements. I could tell they were scribes because of the ink stains on their fingers. Our guide appeared next, nodding to me.

"Sempronius Scipio? The Governor will see you now."

I rose to my feet, gesturing to Aoric to remain seated.

"Wait here," I told him. "And try not to start any fights."

Grinning hugely, he nodded, stretched out his long legs and leaned back against the wall as if to show that he was entirely relaxed and comfortable. It was an impression I wished I could share, but my heart was beating a little faster as I moved towards the door.

One of the guards stepped out to intercept me.

"Leave any weapons out here," he stated gruffly.

I took my small eating knife from my belt, handing it over.

"That's all I have," I told him.

The look he gave me suggested that he thought this unlikely.

"I'll need to search you," he told me. "Put your arms out."

I held my arms wide while he patted me down. It was expertly done, and very efficient. Once he was satisfied that I had no concealed weapons, he stood aside, gesturing for me to pass. His companion pushed the door open for me.

I stepped through into a surprisingly compact office which was sparsely furnished. There were a couple of chairs, some storage chests and a large desk. Open windows provided a magnificent view over the interior of the fort and, because the *Principia* was at the top of the hill, I could see across the mighty Danubius all the way into the lands of the barbarians.

Most importantly, I quickly took in the two men who waited for me. One was standing against the wall to my left. He was a tall, broad-shouldered, athletic character who looked very tough and competent. His hair was trimmed short, although his beard was full and a little untidy. He was wearing a military tunic and had a long dagger hanging from his belt. He wore no armour or insignia of rank, but I guessed he must be either a senior aide or possibly the Governor's personal bodyguard. From the icy way he was staring at me, with his arms folded across his chest, I was leaning towards the bodyguard idea. Either way, though, he was not the man I had come to see.

The second man was sitting behind the desk. He was a fairly short, plump character with a round, pleasant face, neatly trimmed hair and a fuzz of beard. His tunic bore the wide purple stripe which told the world that he was a man of senatorial rank. On the desk in front of him lay the scroll I had brought. The seal had been broken, and the parchment was held flat by a pair of stone weights.

"Sextus Sempronius Scipio?" the man asked, his tone welcoming and relaxed. "I am Gaius Vibius Trebonianus Gallus, Governor of Upper and Lower Moesia."

Gesturing to the man standing to the side, he went on, "This is Fabius Successianus. He is Camp Prefect of *Legio I*."

Successianus gave me a slight nod of acknowledgement, but his impassive face betrayed no emotion at all. I felt slightly embarrassed that I had mistaken him for a bodyguard, because he was almost certainly one of the most senior officers in Novae. Not only that, to attain the rank of Camp Prefect, he had probably risen through the ranks, a fact which meant he was very tough indeed.

The Governor went on to clarify, "Successianus is second in command here. The Legion's Legate died of fever during the winter, and I have sent the Senior Tribune away with despatches for the Emperor."

Gallus did not explain any further, but I guessed he had sent the Senior Tribune away in order to get rid of him. Senior Tribunes were generally young nobles who were appointed by the Legate to provide them with some experience of military life before they returned to Rome to take up a political career. This often meant that the Tribune, nominally second in command, was younger and less experienced than any of the men in the legion. Successianus, on the other hand, had clearly spent years as a soldier. Gallus obviously placed great trust in him.

Having completed the introductions, the Governor smiled, "Welcome to Novae."

"Thank you, Governor," I nodded.

For all his apparent friendliness, he did not indicate that I should sit down, so I remained standing, facing him across the desk and chairs, with my hands clasped behind my back.

"You have travelled from Rome?" the Governor enquired.

"Yes, Sir."

He tapped the parchment with one finger as he said, "Publius Licinius Valerianus speaks very highly of you."

"Thank you, Sir."

"He is close to the Emperor," Gallus said.

It was a statement rather than a question, but I replied, "Yes, Sir."

"He is also a very clever man," Gallus went on.

"Yes, sir."

Privately, I felt that there were other words to describe Licinius Valerianus. In my opinion, he was a cunning, ruthless, manipulative bastard.

I kept those thoughts to myself because, since Gallus was also a Senator, he must have known Valerianus personally. Given the mission Valerianus had assigned to me, I suspected the two of them were not on good terms, but you never could tell when it came to Rome's leading citizens.

Gallus' smile gave the impression of an affable uncle as he regarded me, but I knew better than to be fooled by that. He had been a Consul of Rome only a few years earlier. Some men did achieve that high status thanks to family connections or suitable grovelling to the Emperor, but I had made a point of asking about Gallus before we had left Rome, and the general view was that he was a clever and capable man.

"Don't be fooled by his charm," my friend Fronto had warned me. "He's as devious as any Senator. That lot spend their entire lives plotting and scheming, making and breaking private alliances, and metaphorically stabbing each other in the back."

Gallus tapped the letter again, still smiling as he said, "Licinius Valerianus has asked me to assist you in a special mission."

"So I understand, Sir."

"He writes that you intend to cross the river and spy on the Gothic King, Ostrogotha, in order to learn his intentions."

"That is what I have been instructed to do," I acknowledged, doing my best to sound as if the task were a simple one rather than the potentially fatal mission Aoric believed it to be.

With a slight frown, Gallus asked me, "Does Licinius Valerianus not appreciate that we have our own agents, informants and spies?"

"I'm sure he does, Sir."

"Then why has he sent you here?"

"I have carried out similar tasks in the past," I replied, knowing it was an inadequate response.

With a grim smile, Gallus sighed, "It strikes me that Valerianus intended to send you on a suicide mission. Perhaps you have displeased him in some way?"

"Not that I am aware of, Sir. But I do speak Gothic, and I have visited barbarian tribes before now. I intend to go as a trader."

He smiled, "Well, forgive me for saying so, but you could hardly expect to pass for a Goth."

I gave him a smile of my own in return. I knew what he meant. Although I had been born in Rome, I had inherited my dark hair, which was now tinted with grey, and my olive skin from my Syrian mother. It would be hard to imagine anyone who looked less like a tall, fair-haired and pale-skinned Goth.

Still smiling, Gallus went on, "As you say, travelling as a trader might help. Valerianus has asked that I provide some mules and trade goods for you. I don't suppose he provided you with the means to pay for them?"

I nodded. Like every Governor, Gallus was acutely aware of the finances of officiating over a province. Some Governors could become immensely wealthy by exploiting the regions they controlled, but out here on the northern border, expenses needed to be controlled because the opportunities for making money were scarce.

I said, "I have been given a bag of gold coins, Sir. All newly minted with the head of Emperor Decius on them."

Gallus nodded, but he gave the impression that there was something else on his mind. Placing his elbows on the desk, he clasped his hands together and gave me a serious look.

"I'm not sure I like the idea of Valerianus sending his own spies here," he said. "I cannot understand his thinking. Perhaps there is more to your mission than you are letting on. Did he send you to spy on me, perhaps?"

He'd hit the mark with that one, and I knew now that Fronto's warning had been accurate. Trebonianus Gallus was a very shrewd character indeed.

I decided there was little point in trying to bluff my way past his question.

"Of course he did," I admitted readily. "Although I'm not sure it makes much difference, Sir. After all, I'm sure the Emperor has spies of his own watching you already. Some of your aides will no doubt be *frumentarii*."

The fact that Gallus did not argue told me that he understood only too well that every Governor would have spies watching him. Sometimes, a *frumentarius* could even be ordered to assassinate any provincial official who showed signs of wanting to raise a rebellion against the Emperor. It was necessary for Governors to control armies because they defended Rome from the barbarians, but plenty of provincial Governors had used those armies to back their own bids to become Emperor. Our current ruler, Messius Decius, had gained the imperial throne precisely that way.

My reply had clearly surprised Gallus. He sat back on his chair, then permitted himself a soft smile. I saw him cast a look at Successianus, but the Prefect's only reaction was a faint tightening of his jaw muscles as he continued to stare coldly at me.

Returning his attention to me, Gallus asked, "Do you know why he wanted you to spy on me?"

"No, Sir. But Licinius Valerianus has spent his entire life trying to discover other people's secrets so that he can blackmail them into doing what he wants."

Gallus actually laughed.

"You know him well, then? And is that why you are doing his bidding?"

Bitterly, I nodded, "Yes, Sir."

"He has a hold over you, then?"

"I'm afraid so," I confessed, unwilling to dwell on this difficult subject.

Gallus had the good grace not to ask what sort of blackmail Valerianus was using against me. Instead, he pointed out, "You probably shouldn't be telling me this."

"It makes little difference," I shrugged. " I suspect Valerianus wants to ingratiate himself even more with the Emperor. He wants me to find out what the Gothic King plans to do. That's my main reason for being here. But if I can also give him some scandal or other about you, he'd regard that as a bonus."

Gallus nodded, still seeming amused. Then he leaned forwards again and said, "It does not matter at all, Scipio. I'm afraid that events have overtaken Valerianus' plans, so your journey has been wasted."

"Wasted?" I echoed.

With an expansive gesture, he explained, "I told you we use our own spies, scouts and agents. King Ostrogotha is dead. He has been succeeded by a man named Cniva, and I know his intentions only too well. He has already gathered a vast army, and he intends to launch a massive raid across the Danubius. The only question is when and where they will make the crossing."

While a part of me was shocked to hear this news, it actually relieved some of the pressure I had been feeling. Venturing into barbarian lands was dangerous enough, but if the Goths were about to launch yet another war, travelling north would be a suicidal move. My mission was over before it had begun.

Gallus continued, "That is why I sent our senior Tribune to warn the Emperor, and to ask him to bring his main army to help counter the invasion. I have only one legion here, plus some auxiliary units and several hundred cavalry, but the reports I have received suggest that Cniva has over fifty thousand men in his army. That is too great a force for me to defeat. I have sent all our ships to try to block any attempts to cross the river, but the Danubius Fleet is not nearly as strong as I would like. Most of it is down near the Black Sea where Gothic ships are already attacking our trading vessels."

I was more than a little shocked by these revelations. Far from being able to carry out the spying mission my patron, Licinius Valerianus, had given me, it seemed I had arrived in what could soon become a war.

I said, "In that case, Sir, I may as well return to Rome. I would not be much help to you when the fighting starts."

"What about your secondary mission?" he asked with a grin which was almost like that of a mischievous young boy. "Are you not going to spy on me?"

"No, Sir. Spying on the Goths might serve the empire, but spying on you only serves Licinius Valerianus. I have no desire to make his life any easier."

"You don't approve of his actions, then?"

"No, I do not."

Gallus smiled, "I think I like you, Scipio. But, as you say, you may as well return home. You can spend the night here in our guest quarters, but I'd recommend you leave at first light tomorrow. The Goths are on the march, and we will have a war on our hands any day now."

Chapter 2
Invasion

Aoric and I were allocated a room in one of the long, low buildings on the terrace one level below the *Principia*. Our travel bags, along with Aoric's sword, had already been left for us, and a slave delivered a tray which held plates of food and a jug of wine. The food was fairly basic army fare, but it was nourishing enough. The room itself contained two beds, two old but reasonably comfortable chairs, a table and little else apart from the rugs on the wooden floorboards.

"I suppose they get quite a few visitors coming to check up on things at the frontier," I said to Aoric. "At least that means we have a room to ourselves."

He grunted, "Do all their visitors have soldiers on guard outside their door?"

When I looked puzzled, he waved towards the wooden door, telling me, "There are two of them out there. Why is that, do you think?"

I shrugged, "Trebonianus Gallus thinks I'm going to snoop around and report back to Licinius Valerianus. I expect he's just taking precautions."

"So what happened?" Aoric asked. "You were very tight-lipped when you came out of the Governor's office."

I explained the situation while we ate. Aoric listened attentively, especially when I mentioned that the Gothic king I had been sent to spy on was dead.

"Gallus already knows that the new king is planning to invade," I told him. "Our journey here has been a waste of time."

Aoric nodded his understanding, then asked me, "Did he mention the new king's name?"

I frowned, searching my memory, then nodded, "I think he said the man is called Cniva."

My words seemed to hit Aoric like a physical slap. He sat very still, a slice of honey-smeared bread held half way to his mouth.

"Cniva?" he asked slowly. "Are you sure?"

"That's what the Governor said. Why? Do you know him?"

Carefully and deliberately, Aoric placed the bread back on his plate. He sat back in the chair, putting his hands on his cheeks before letting out a long, slow breath.

"Yes," he said. "I know him. He's a dangerous man. We need to leave here as soon as possible."

"We'll go at first light," I assured him. "Our horses will be rested by then. But what can you tell me about Cniva?"

Aoric frowned, lowering his head as he sat deep in thought. After a long pause, he said, "He was always a clever and calculating man. He was a strong leader of a sizeable tribe, but I never expected him to become king."

"So he wasn't related to the old king?" I probed.

Aoric shook his head.

"No, but that's no reason for him not to be elected. You know that the Goths are not really one tribe but a collection of related groups with a common language and culture."

"Yes, I remember you telling me that before."

"So when a king dies, the various leaders often argue about the succession. Cniva must have been very persuasive."

"Perhaps he resorted to bribery," I suggested. "That's what a Roman would do."

Aoric did not find this funny. He said, "I'd guess he's promised them a lot of plunder. That will be why he's gathering an army. Attacking Rome is always popular with the young warriors."

I shrugged, "Well, it saves me the bother of setting out to spy on the Goths. It wasn't something I was looking forward to in any case."

Aoric remained silent, so I asked him, "What about you? What do you want to do?"

Speaking fervently, he repeated, "I want to get away from here as soon as I can. I don't want to be here when Cniva arrives with his army."

"That suits me," I agreed. "Like I said, we'll leave first thing tomorrow."

"We should leave now," he insisted.

"There's no point," I told him. "Not unless you want to camp out overnight. It will take us most of a day to reach the nearest waystation where we can find lodgings and stables."

Aoric reluctantly accepted my argument, but he remained on edge for the rest of the afternoon.

As dusk approached, there was a knock on our door. It opened before I could reach it, and a red-cloaked officer strode in. He was in full military garb apart from his plumed helmet which was being respectfully held for him by one of the guards who stood outside the door.

I instantly recognised him as Fabius Successianus, Prefect of the First Legion. Now dressed in his chainmail, with a short sword at his hip, he retained his cool, hard expression as he cast his eyes over us.

"Good evening, Sir," I said, bobbing my head in acknowledgement since he had not bothered to extend a hand in greeting.

Gesturing to Aoric, I informed him, "This is my grandson, Auricus."

This was the story we had decided to use to cover Aoric's true origin. He hated the Romanised version of his name, but he had grudgingly conceded that it made sense not to use his Gothic name while he was in the fort. Rome had fought several battles against the Goths in recent years, so feelings among the soldiers would already be running high. With an invasion imminent, there was no point in making Aoric a target by revealing his Gothic ancestry. Fortunately, his hair was dark, so there was little chance of him being mistaken for a fair-haired barbarian.

Successianus accepted my explanation, then fixed me with a cold stare. I was beginning to wonder whether he was capable of any other facial expressions.

He said bluntly, "I do not like spies."

When I made no reply, he added with a grudging admission, "But I understand they are necessary. What is not necessary, though, is for you to spy on Trebonianus Gallus."

"I have no intention of doing so," I assured him.

From the look in his eyes, I didn't think he believed me.

Speaking firmly, he went on, "Governor Gallus is a true Roman. That is all you need to know. He serves Rome with considerable energy and skill."

He was expecting some sort of comment so, for want of anything better to say, I put in, "I'm sure he does."

There was another long pause while he continued to stare at me, then he said, "I suggest you follow the Governor's advice. Leave here as soon as you can."

"We will leave first thing in the morning," I told him.

He gave a nod of satisfaction.

"Good. When you see your patron, Licinius Valerianus, you can tell him what I have said."

"I will be sure to relay your message," I promised.

Successianus stared at me a moment longer, nodded again, then spun on his heel and marched to the door. He retrieved his helmet, placed it on his head, then stalked off into the gathering gloom.

I went to the door, pushing it shut until the latch clicked into place, then I moved back to sit on my bed, facing Aoric.

"What was that all about?" he asked me with a frown.

"I'm not sure," I shrugged. "But Successianus is a veteran soldier, and he's probably a good judge of character."

Aoric grinned, "Or it could be that Trebonianus Gallus has duped him. After all, a man like Successianus won't know much about political life. If the Legate is dead, and the Senior Tribune gone, Gallus is very firmly in control."

"True enough," I conceded, "although I don't think Successianus is the type to fall for political propaganda. He's too long in the tooth for that."

"But why did he bother coming here to talk to us?" Aoric frowned.

I shrugged, "That's a mystery. On the face of it, all he was doing was backing Gallus, but you'll notice that he never mentioned the Governor's loyalty towards the Emperor. All he mentioned was his loyalty to Rome."

"Was that deliberate, do you think?"

I shrugged again, "I have no idea. Not that it matters. I'll need to tell Valerianus something, and being able to report a Prefect's backing for the Governor might convince him I've done enough."

Aoric scoffed, "From what I know of Licinius Valerianus, you'll never have done enough to satisfy him."

I had no answer to that, so I announced that I was going to get some sleep.

"I need a decent rest," I sighed as I lay down on the bed.

I was to be disappointed. I did manage a short spell of deep sleep, but I was woken after only a couple of hours when I heard Aoric fling the door open and demand that the guards tell him what was going on.

Blinking awake, I clambered from the bed and hurried to the door.

"What's happening?" I asked.

"There's some sort of panic," Aoric told me. He was standing in the doorway, his exit blocked by the two armed guards, both of whom looked as confused as I felt.

"You're to stay here," one of them growled when Aoric attempted to push past him.

I laid a hand on Aoric's shoulder, easing him away from a potential confrontation.

"We'll find out soon enough," I said.

That, at least, was an accurate prediction. Word soon arrived when our guards were called away by an Optio who hurried over to give them new orders.

"Everyone to defensive stations!" he ordered them.

When I asked what had happened, the Optio told me savagely, "The bloody Goths are crossing the river a few miles upstream from here. Our patrols have all been chased away."

The soldiers hurried off, leaving me and Aoric standing in the open doorway, regarding each other with one common thought.

"Upstream," I murmured. "That cuts us off from heading back to Italia."

We were not the only ones with problems. Throughout the night, civilians from the nearby settlement were brought into the fort, along with any livestock and supplies the soldiers could round up. By the light of flaming torches, tents were erected on the parade ground to provide shelter for the civilians, but there was an air of near panic from the displaced men, women and children.

As dawn began to lighten the sky, the Governor sent out a strong force of cavalry to keep a track of what the Goths were doing. We watched them ride out of the fort, the men's faces set in masks of grim determination.

"If it's a full invasion, a few hundred riders won't stop Cniva," Aoric muttered as he watched the horsemen leave.

"They aren't going to fight them," I replied. "Their task is to find out what the Goths are up to."

Aoric said, "If Cniva really does have tens of thousands in his army, they'll be lucky to get anywhere close to the main Gothic force. Cniva will have thousands of his own cavalry protecting his flanks."

He was probably right, but all we could do was wait for news, so with no guards to stop us, Aoric and I wandered down to the foot of the hill where we found quite a commotion on the wooden docks which lined the river bank just beyond the fort's northern wall. A couple of boats had arrived, their oarsmen streaked with sweat, and the marines babbling about what they had encountered.

"The Goths have built a bridge of boats," one of the marines informed us. "The Captain tried to get close enough to use our catapults against them, but they had lined both river banks with archers. We lost a couple of men, and the Captain took an arrow in his arm."

"Will the Governor send more ships?" I asked.

"If they get here in time," the man shrugged. "Most of the Danubius Fleet is spread out all along the river, trying to find where the bastards were planning to cross. It will take a day or two to get enough ships together, and by that time, I expect they'll all be across the river. We could see another bridge of boats further upriver, so they're not using just one crossing."

The marine's tale was confirmed when a second boat docked, its crew bringing tales of yet another crossing several miles downstream from Novae.

"The bastards can come at us from both directions," one sailor muttered darkly.

The mood among the naval crews was bleak, and although I knew reports often exaggerated the size of enemy armies, it seemed that there were indeed tens of thousands of Goths crossing the river at various points. Cniva had clearly been studying the patrols, and he had timed his invasion to perfection, splitting the river fleet in two, and taking precautions to prevent the ships from attacking his bridges. And once the first Gothic horsemen were across the river, they could travel very quickly, securing a bridgehead for the invasion.

While we watched the crews of the ships carry out running repairs, hauling out arrows which were embedded in the wooden hulls, Governor Trebonianus Gallus arrived with a gaggle of officers and aides accompanying him. He slowed when he caught sight of me.

"Sempronius Scipio!" he smiled. "It seems you will be our guest for a while longer. Cniva has begun the war even earlier than I had anticipated."

"Do you plan on going out to fight him?" I asked.

"Hardly!" he exclaimed. "I have one legion here, and it's not at full strength because various detachments are based at several other forts along the river. Those forts are themselves faced by thousands of Goths, so we cannot expect them to join us. I called in our Auxiliaries some days ago, but even with them bolstering our numbers, we have fewer than seven thousand men. Trying to battle it out with Cniva would be pointless. He could easily surround us if we venture out to face him."

"I thought there were other legions available?" I frowned.

"There are," Gallus nodded. "But we had no idea where the Goths would cross the river, so our forces are spread all along the frontier. I have sent messages to summon the other legions, but it will be several days at the very least before any of them can reach us. That is assuming that our messengers get through, and that a relief force can get to us at all. So I'm afraid we will need to sit tight for a while."

The following day, Gallus' cavalry returned to Novae on sweat-lathered horses, some men bearing injuries as evidence of a clash with the Goths. Their return caused a stir in the fort because it was plain to everyone that they had been driven back by the marauding barbarians.

"There were thousands of them," I heard one trooper tell a group of legionaries. "They are swarming everywhere, burning farms and looting anything they find."

To his credit, Trebonianus Gallus made a point of being very visible to the garrison of the fort, as well as to the hundreds of civilians who had fled to Novae for sanctuary. He spent hours walking the ramparts, striding through the camp with aides in tow, speaking to as many people as he could. This provided me with another opportunity to talk to him, and I approached him when I saw him coming our way.

"Good afternoon, Governor," I said. "Is there anything we can do to help? I'm no fighter, but I don't like sitting around doing nothing."

Gallus glanced at Aoric, a questioning look on his face, so I made the same introduction as I had given to Fabius Successianus. Gallus gave Aoric a curt nod, then turned back to me.

He asked, "You speak Gothic?"

"Yes, Sir. We both do."

"And you've been among them before?"

"Yes, Sir."

That was a bit of an exaggeration as far as I was concerned. Aoric may have been raised among the Goths, but he was the only member of that tribe I had ever met in person. I had, though, spent a few years trading among other barbarians. I didn't think the distinction would bother an upper class Roman like Gallus. To him, one barbarian was probably much like any other.

Gallus considered for a moment, then said, "I'm not sure how much help you can be, but why don't you join my staff? At the very least, you can act as messengers, and you may be able to advise me on what the Goths are up to."

"It would be a pleasure, Sir," I assured him.

So we became messengers, carrying scribbled notes or verbal communications around the fort. Gallus had an entire legion, plus his own household, to support him, but he wanted as many soldiers as possible bearing arms and not being burdened with administrative duties, so two extra pairs of hands could always be found work to do, and our new duties were not confined to carrying messages. We also spent some time distributing food to the civilians, rations being doled out from the fort's stores. That was a harrowing experience, because the fear among the women and children was palpable. These people had been forced to abandon everything when they fled to the sanctuary of the fortress.

On the evening of that second day, word came to us that Gothic scouts had been seen. Aoric and I accompanied Gallus to the western wall where, from the top of the ramparts at the highest point on the fort's slope, we had an excellent view along the river.

"There's only a few of them so far," a grizzled Centurion reported. "They're still a long way off."

Far to the west, we could make out a group of horsemen who had stopped on the same spot where Aoric and I had first come in sight of Novae. Even as we watched, though, more came up behind them, spreading out along the crest of the ridge.

"Just a few scouts so far," Gallus remarked. "But the big question is whether their main army is coming this way, or whether that is merely a screening force to keep watch on us while Cniva rampages elsewhere."

After a moment, he asked me, "What will he do? Will he attack us here, or will he simply leave a holding force, then move on to easier targets?"

That was a difficult question to answer, and I shot Aoric a glance to see whether he could provide any insights, but he gave the slightest of shrugs.

I told Gallus, "I've never met Cniva, but from what little I've heard, he's a clever and cunning tactician, as well as a hardened warrior. I think we can be fairly sure that his men will want plunder, but they'll probably look for easy targets."

"That's what I thought," Gallus nodded. "So we need to convince them that we are weak. That might persuade them to bring their main army against us. They will know we have a lot of valuable supplies here, and that might tempt them to waste their time trying to storm our walls. In turn, that will allow the Emperor time to reach us. With luck, we can catch the Goths between us."

He turned to his aides, snapping out orders.

"I want only every third Maniple on the walls, with the men spread out as thinly as possible. The rest of the men are to return to barracks and stay out of sight. Let those riders believe we are short of troops."

Several of his aides hurried off, shouting commands as they went. As usual in the Roman army, discipline was superb, and soon the ramparts were far more sparsely populated.

"So you want them to attack us?" I asked the Governor.

"That's right," he confirmed. "As I said, the longer we can delay them here, the more chance there is of the Emperor arriving with his main force."

"Are you sure he is coming?" I asked.

Gallus gave me a confident smile as he said, "Of course he is. If he received the message I sent last month, he knows that an invasion is imminent. He will come."

I wasn't sure how much of his apparent certainty was for the benefit of the troops, but Gallus remained adamant that the Emperor would bring his army to our rescue.

Aoric muttered, "I wish we'd met that bloody messenger on our way here. We could have turned around and stayed in Rome."

"It's too late now," I sighed. "The Goths are all around us, and it looks as if they are coming for a closer look."

We watched as around fifty of the Gothic scouts began to descend the slope. Once on level ground, they broke into a canter, heading towards Novae in a long line. Behind the first group, more riders soon appeared on the crest of the rise, but they maintained their position on the ridge.

The Centurion asked, "Should we fling a few boulders at them? They'll soon be within range of our catapults."

"No," Gallus replied. "I want them to think we are short of ammunition. No catapults, and no arrows unless they come very close."

But the Goths did not come close. They maintained a safe distance from our arrows, then began circling around the southern wall of the fort.

"They're checking our defences," Gallus nodded. "Let them."

After a moment, he observed, "They do seem well equipped. I think most of them are wearing chainmail and iron helmets."

He looked at me as he said this, but it was Aoric who informed him, "The cavalry are the elite of Cniva's army. They will have the best equipment. But his foot soldiers won't be so well armed. They come from the poorest among the Goths, and some will probably have no armour at all."

"That's right," I put in, pretending I had more expertise than I did in reality.

"They'll be easy pickings for our archers, then," Gallus nodded. "If Cniva wants to breach our walls, he'll need to send men on foot."

Aoric continued, "You should also remember that other tribes will have been invited to join the invasion. The Carpi and other Sarmatians may have joined the Goths."

Gallus nodded, "That is why I do not expect much help from other provinces. They will have their own problems to deal with. So that makes our task even more vital. We need Cniva to waste his time besieging us."

We watched the Gothic scouts while they completed their ride. Once they had reached the river on the eastern side of the fort, they turned around and retraced their steps, rejoining their fellow barbarians who waited on the top of the distant ridge.

"It will be dark soon," Gallus said. "I expect they'll stay well clear. Tomorrow, we will probably see their main force."

He waited until we saw the bulk of the Gothic horsemen ride back over the ridge, only a few dozen remaining to keep an eye on the fort.

"Very well, gentlemen," Gallus said as he rubbed his hands together. "I think it is time for dinner. We can relax until tomorrow."

And tomorrow, I thought glumly, we would see the full might of the Gothic army. I could understand Gallus' tactics. From a military perspective they made perfect sense. What troubled me was that the plan required us to be the bait.

Chapter 3
Negotiations

The following day brought dark clouds and showers of rain, and in their wake came the Goths. There were, as the reports had suggested, thousands upon thousands of them. The horsemen came first, spreading out all across the plain on the southern side of the river, with more coming from the east to complete their cordon. On the north bank of the Danubius, we could see many hundreds of men on foot who set up camp opposite the fort, effectively completing the encirclement.

Aoric and I stood with Trebonianus Gallus and his aides while we watched the besieging army grow and grow. Some of the Goths plundered the civilian settlement which lay outside the fort, while others began cutting down trees for firewood and also, we suspected, to form into battering rams or ladders. Many small tents were erected, but most of the Goths seemed prepared to shelter from the rain by huddling under their cloaks.

"Cniva must be among them somewhere," Gallus observed.

I glanced at Aoric but he gave a shrug of ignorance. The Goths carried no flags or banners to mark out their units. Their army was formed by tribal groupings, not into organised units of similar size. Some of their war bands consisted of only a few dozen riders, while others numbered in thousands, but none of them had any displays to show where their leader might be.

As the day progressed, their foot warriors came into view, marching in high spirits and spreading among the horsemen to find their own places to set up camp. There must have been someone organising things, though, because we soon saw that the unmounted warriors would form the front line of the Gothic siege. They were arranged in a long arc all around the west, south and east of the fort, with the mounted warriors camped behind them. As Aoric had predicted, we could see, even from a distance, that the bulk of the men on foot were not nearly as well equipped as the horsemen. Few of them had armour, and some even went barechested. Their weapons were a motley collection, although most of them seemed to carry spears, the weapon of choice of men who could not afford a sword.

By late afternoon, Novae was completely surrounded. Our boats might still be able to row away, although the crews would need to run a gauntlet of arrows from the Goths on the northern bank, but there was no way anyone could leave on foot.

Fear was palpable within Novae, especially among the civilians, although the troops were not immune to its grip. Gallus called a parade, summoning all but a handful of sentries to the main parade ground. Since there were many tents now set up here to house the refugees, virtually everyone in Novae could witness Gallus' demonstration of his confidence. He had a small altar brought, and he stood before it, wearing a formal toga, with the folds draped over his head as he assumed the position as the city's senior priest and augur. There, he sacrificed a chicken, carving it open to examine its innards. Then he raised his blooded hands high.

"The omens are favourable!" he called in a loud, strong voice. "The Gods are with us! If our hearts remain as strong as our walls, and if every man does his duty, the Goths will perish when they attempt to attack us."

The troops cheered loudly, reassured by this augury, and Gallus went on to deliver a short but rousing speech, promising rewards for men who fought well. Then he dismissed the parade, ordering the soldiers back to their positions, while he went to change into his armour and plumed helmet. When he returned, he led his aides back up to the wall to observe the Goths once more.

"There certainly are a lot of them," he remarked casually. Then, glancing up at the sky, he added, "But I doubt they will attack us today. Their foot soldiers have marched a long way, so I expect Cniva will want them rested before they make any attempt to storm our walls."

He seemed to be right. There was a great deal of movement and noise within the Gothic camp, but no obvious signs of preparation for battle. They had set picquets to watch us, so those men could raise the alarm if we ventured out, but the rest of the Goths were more intent on setting up camp and cooking food. And still more of them streamed into view, but the latecomers were mostly women and children who plodded along beside dozens of ox-drawn wagons which were piled high with supplies. Flocks of goats and sheep, along with a herd of cattle, were driven into a makeshift pen.

"That's their evening meal arrived," Gallus observed.

He paused, then smiled cheerfully as he said, "Ah, it seems they wish to go through the formalities before they eat."

I followed his gaze to see a small group of horsemen coming along the paved road towards the western gate. They came at a slow walk, one of them holding high a leaf-covered tree branch as a signal that they came as emissaries.

Gallus immediately turned to me.

"Go out and talk to them, Scipio. Stall for time as much as you can, but make no concessions."

"Me?" I gaped. "Are you sure?"

"You speak their language," he replied. "Licinius Valerianus sent you here to discover what the Gothic king plans to do, so you may as well complete that mission."

Then, with a disarming grin, he added, "Besides, I don't want to lose anyone valuable if they turn hostile. I do like you, Scipio, but you are expendable."

Even though his words were softened by his encouraging smile, his open admission left me momentarily dumbfounded. I stood there, staring at him, but I quickly realised that, even though he was sending me into grave danger, I could hardly refuse a direct order from a provincial Governor.

Still smiling, he added, "I'm sure you'll be fine. They will want you to relay their demands. You can't do that if you're dead, can you? And I'll give you an escort of good men."

I felt trapped, not at all reassured by his blithe confidence, but there was nothing I could do to avoid this. While he allocated a couple of junior Centurions to accompany me, I turned to Aoric.

Speaking in Gothic, I hissed, "You stay here. I don't want to take a chance that one of them might recognise you. There must be someone in that host who knows you."

He looked conflicted, wanting to support me, but he knew I was right.

"Be careful," he said as I turned to go. "You can't trust Cniva."

"That's not very reassuring," I murmured.

We held each other's gaze for a long moment, then I smiled and said, "I'll be back soon."

I silently prayed that was a promise I would be able to keep.

Gallus had chosen two Centurions to act as my escort. Both were tough-looking men who wore their plumed helmets with pride. Neither of them seemed at all put out by the prospect of walking out to face a horde of barbarians. Stolid and impassive, they followed me down the steps to the western gates. The huge locking bar was heaved aside, one gate swung open just enough to let us pass, and then the gates were closed behind us as soon as we had stepped beyond the gateway.

The Goths had come to a halt some three hundred paces away, far enough to keep them relatively safe from any arrows.

"Let's go and see what they want," I said to my two companions, trying to sound a lot more confident than I felt. Silently, I cursed Trebonianus Gallus, knowing he had chosen me for this dangerous task because Licinius Valerianus had sent me here to spy on him. As he had told me, it would be no great loss if I failed to return.

The two Centurions looked at me expectantly, so I took a deep breath and set off at a brisk walk, striding confidently as if I had nothing to fear. I had met emperors and kings before, although never in a situation quite like this, but I knew that we could not afford to display any fear. I was a Roman, and Rome had conquered most of the known world. I needed to act as if I implicitly believed I was superior to these barbarians.

Even so, I was acutely aware of the thousands of eyes upon us as we marched along the cobbled road towards the waiting horsemen. An eerie silence fell over the entire plain as men watched us, and I knew some of them would be wondering why the Governor's spokesman was an ordinary civilian wearing a plain tunic and cloak. I hoped that the presence of two men wearing armour and plumed helmets would add some weight to my authority.

"Do either of you speak any Gothic?" I asked the two Centurions.

"A few words," one of them admitted. "Nothing more."

"The savages should learn Latin," the other growled.

"I expect some of them do speak our language," I remarked. "We'll soon find out."

As we drew closer, I studied the men waiting for us. There were six of them. The one holding the tree branch had moved aside when he saw us coming, taking up his position at the end of the line. All of them wore chainmail and iron helmets. Swords hung from their waists, and some also carried long lances in gauntleted hands.

I stopped barely ten paces from them, close enough to hear the breathing of their horses, and to smell the rank odour of sweat and damp horseflesh. The rain had relented for the moment, but the ground was wet, and so were the Goths.

"I am Sempronius Scipio," I announced, my eyes scanning the six men. "Trebonianus Gallus, Governor of Upper and Lower Moesia, has sent me to talk on his behalf."

One or two of the riders looked amused, but it was the third man from the left who nudged his horse forwards a few paces.

"Where did you learn our language?" he asked me. "Your accent is atrocious."

I gave a shrug.

"We can speak in Latin if you prefer," I told him.

He made no reply, so I assumed his Latin was even worse than my Gothic. Or perhaps he didn't want me to know that he understood our language.

I asked him, "Do you speak for the king of the Goths?"

He sat up straight in his saddle, his blue eyes sparkling. It is always difficult to get a full impression of a man who is wearing a helmet, but he looked to be around fifty years old, yet still strong and athletic. He was, I guessed, quite tall, with broad shoulders. Most importantly, though, he had a very fierce demeanour, his blue eyes glaring at me from above a blunt nose.

He tapped a hand to his chest as he informed me proudly, "I am Cniva, king of the Goths. I speak for myself. Why does your Governor not come out to talk to me? Is he afraid?"

"He is merely being cautious," I replied.

"So he is a coward?" Cniva snorted derisively, bringing some chuckles of scornful laughter from his followers.

I said, "If you wish to enter our fort with only two companions, I'm sure he would be prepared to talk to you."

He bared his teeth in a savage grin, then began chuckling.

"I take your point," he said. "But I trust you Romans as much as your Governor trusts me."

"So what is it you wish to discuss?" I asked him. "Are you offering to surrender?"

He blinked in surprise, then began laughing again, but there was little real humour in the sound. The cruel edge to his laughter was plain to hear. As with most rulers, he was putting on a performance for the benefit of his followers, making sure they saw how tough he was, but I had a horrible feeling that this was not all an act.

After a moment, he answered my impudent question.

"Surrender?" he growled menacingly. "I think not. But I will offer you the chance to open your gates to us. Your men may march out and leave unharmed. I'll even let you keep your flags and banners."

I was sure he knew I would never agree to such a thing, but I said, "There are civilians in the fort, women and children among them. Will they have safe passage as well?"

"Of course!" he nodded, waving a hand magnanimously. "But you leave everything behind except what you can carry on your backs."

"That is a generous offer," I said, putting on a show of actually considering it. "I will relay your message to Trebonianus Gallus. But I'm sure he will need time to consider it."

I glanced up at the cloud-laden sky as I added, "There are only a few hours of daylight left, and I know the Governor will need some time to think about it. If we open our gates at dawn, then that will signal our agreement, and we will leave as soon as we can after that."

"You have one hour," Cniva shot back. "And tell your chicken-livered Governor that if he does not agree, I will kill every man, woman and child in your puny fortress."

"I will tell him," I nodded. "But you ought to know that he is a stubborn man. He is a Roman Senator, so I doubt he will agree. Perhaps you could offer hostages as a token of good faith?"

"Perhaps I could wipe my arse on your Governor's purple tunic," Cniva scoffed. "There will be no hostages."

His eyes flicked to take in my two companions, and I knew he was thinking of taking us prisoner as a demonstration of his power. Despite Gallus' assertions, Cniva could have us executed in full sight of the fort's garrison to show them what fate awaited them.

I said, "I understand. I will do my best to persuade him to agree to abandon the fort."

There was an aura of cruel savagery surrounding Cniva, and I could feel cold sweat breaking out on my back. I was convinced that he was on the point of ignoring our supposedly sacrosanct status as heralds. If he did tell his men to take us captive, that would be the end of us.

Thinking desperately, I spoke before I had fully formed my idea of what to say.

"I am not a soldier," I told him. "I am one of the civilians caught here by bad luck. So I have no loyalty to Trebonianus Gallus. That is why I will do my very best to persuade him to agree to your proposal. I might even be able to open the gates in any case. I know I am not alone in dreading the thought of a siege."

Now Cniva stared at me as if trying to read my mind.

"You could open the gates for us?" he asked suspiciously.

"Not until after nightfall," I said, not needing to put on too much of an act to appear terrified. "If you send a small force of men close to the western gate at midnight, I should be able to let them in. I can get a gang together who could overpower the guards, but your men will need to hold the gateway until the rest of your army arrives."

"And why should I believe you?" he demanded, his growl full of dire threat.

"Because I want to live," I told him "I'll open the gates in exchange for being allowed to leave. Me and one companion."

Now he hesitated, the prospect of gaining an easy entrance to Novae outweighing his desire to terrorise the garrison by executing us. His army might outnumber us by ten to one, but Novae was a strong defensive position, and he could lose a lot of men if he attempted to take the fort by storm. A stealthy attack, aided by a traitor, would make his life much simpler.

He stared at me for a long time, then he broke into another soft laugh.

He snorted, "If you are the best Rome can produce, then I have little to fear. All right, little man. Go and try to persuade your Governor to open the gates. And if he disagrees, I will spare your miserable life if you let us in anyway. Do we have a bargain?"

I forced a smile as I nodded, "We do, Lord King."

He held my gaze for a long moment, perhaps hoping I would betray my insincerity, but I had long ago mastered the art of masking my true feelings.

"Go then!" he snapped at last, gesturing for us to return to the fort.

I turned, signalling to my escort to follow. Then I set off at a fast pace.

One of the Centurions snapped, "Slow down! He'll think we are frightened of him."

"That's what I want him to think," I replied.

"Why?" the soldier frowned as he increased his pace to keep up with me.

"Because I've told him I'm so afraid that I'm prepared to betray the city. That's the only reason he let us go."

Neither of the two Centurions was pleased about this, but Trebonianus Gallus laughed when I reported back to him.

"You did well, Scipio," he chuckled. "I must admit I was afraid he would not let you come back. Does he really believe you will open the gates for him?"

"I doubt he truly believes it," I shrugged. "But the slight chance that I might betray you was enough for him to let us go."

"Well done!" he beamed. "You've bought us a few more hours, and every moment counts. And your offer of betraying the city has given me an idea. I think we can prepare a little surprise for Cniva."

He refused to say any more, but dismissed me as he went to talk to his officers.

I turned to find Aoric giving me a very worried look.

"You met Cniva?" he asked.

"I'm afraid so. I see what you meant about him. He's a dangerous character."

"He won't take kindly to you deceiving him," Aoric warned. "If he gets hold of you, he'll take revenge."

"That's not a pleasant thought," I sighed. "But if he gets into the fort, I don't expect many of us will survive."

"There is that," Aoric agreed solemnly. "But there are many ways to die. I'd prefer a quick death to the one Cniva will reserve for you."

Chapter 4
Trapped

Trebonianus Gallus invited me to join him for dinner that night. Several of his senior officers were there, and the Governor used the meal as an informal council of war.

"Cniva seems to have brought the vast bulk of his army here," the Governor observed. "I'd say there are around fifty thousand Goths out there."

That was a terrifying estimate, but his aides agreed that it was accurate.

He went on, "I think we can assume that there will be other raiding parties and screening patrols elsewhere. He will want to spread panic as far as he can, and he'll also be on the watch for any Roman armies coming to relieve us."

Gnaeus Fabius Successianus, Prefect of *Legio I Italica*, was sitting beside the Governor. He told the room, "We have enough grain and other food stores to last twelve months, as required by regulations. The influx of civilians will make a difference, but they did bring in their livestock, so we have no concerns about running out of food. We have three wells for water, and can also fetch water from the river if necessary, although that would need to be done at night to safeguard us from the archers across the river. All in all, we have no worries about supplies."

"And our walls are strong," Gallus nodded. "The Goths have no siege equipment, so they will need to rely on ladders and sheer weight of numbers. That will be difficult for them. Our ditches will restrict them severely."

Successianus agreed, "I think we can afford to take men from the south wall. To reach that, the Goths will need to climb the hill just to get to our ditches"

"Agreed," Gallus nodded. "And our central reserve force?"

"Two Cohorts will be kept back so that they can reinforce any part of the perimeter where there is any danger."

"What about our Auxiliaries?" Gallus asked. "Can we trust them? How many of them were recruited from Gothic tribes?"

"Very few," Successianus assured him. "Most come from Gaul, Hispania or Britannia."

"That is something to be grateful for," Gallus said. "We've already lost too many of them who deserted and went over to join the Goths during the last war. No doubt some of those deserters are among that rabble now camped around our walls."

There was more talk about logistics, but then the Governor turned his attention to me.

"I plan a little surprise for Cniva," he told me after we had finished the main course of boiled beef and cabbage. It was not the sort of meal a Senator would provide to guests at his home, but this was an army fort, and Gallus was making a point of eating the same rations as his troops.

"A surprise, Sir?" I responded cautiously. I noticed a faint smile on Successianus' face, so he was obviously aware of the Governor's plan.

"Yes," Gallus grinned. "We're going to open the gates tonight."

"You're going to do what?" I gaped, almost choking on my last mouthful.

Gallus explained, "We are going to let them think that you really are betraying us. When they see the gate being opened, they will come running."

"And then what?" I asked.

He said, "And then we will slam the gates shut just before they reach the entrance. We'll throw down blazing faggots to illuminate the road, and we'll hammer them with arrows and spears."

One Tribune suggested, "We could let some of them inside. If we draw up a couple of Cohorts inside the gate, we could slaughter them."

Gallus shook his head.

"I don't want to risk them getting inside, but I think we can still slaughter them."

Successianus put in, "Why not have a couple of Cohorts ready to charge out? We could hit them really hard, then pull back before their main force arrives."

Gallus considered this for a moment, then agreed, "Very well. Provided they send forwards only a small force, we could probably do that. Make the arrangements. But I want a reserve force kept inside the gates just in case."

Successianus nodded, "As you command, Governor."

Gallus took a sip of wine, then asked me, "Do you want to watch?"

It was the sort of invitation which was really an order, so I agreed to accompany him. Needless to say, Aoric insisted on coming with me, and I noticed he had strapped on his sword.

"You've chosen your side, then?" I asked him.

He gave a grim nod.

"I think it's been chosen for me. Everyone inside the fort will be killed if Cniva succeeds in taking the place."

I wondered what it must feel like for Aoric, being compelled to fight alongside his tribe's traditional enemies against the very people he had grown up with. He seemed to be handling the situation well enough, but I silently promised myself that I would try to keep him out of any direct confrontation.

"We're not going to get involved in any fighting," I told him.

In response, he merely nodded.

It was a dark night, the moon and stars obscured by heavy clouds. Rain drizzled down in erratic showers, but Gallus was still in a confident mood as he climbed the steps to the ramparts above the western gate. I followed close behind and Aoric, uninvited, accompanied me.

"Remain as silent as possible," Gallus whispered in warning. "And keep your head down. I don't want them seeing anyone except our regular sentries."

The three of us crouched behind the outer rampart, and I could see a couple of dozen other men doing the same, each of them armed with a bow and a quiver of arrows.

"We need our bowstrings to be dry," the Governor explained. "So we'll need to time this between rain showers."

There were braziers set up at intervals on the inner edge of the wide walkway at the top of the walls. By their guttering light, I could see that Fabius Successianus had gathered around a thousand legionaries down below us. They were ready and armed, formed up behind the gates, and doing their best to remain quiet.

I could also see some bulky shapes lying on the walkway, each with a couple of soldiers sitting or kneeling beside them.

Gallus informed me, "We've bundled lots of sticks together and soaked them in oil. They are covered by fleeces just now, but we'll light them when the Goths draw near."

"If they come," I replied, half hoping this would all prove to be a waste of time.

"They'll come," he assured me confidently.

Every so often, he would poke his head up above the outer rampart and peer into the darkness. He also insisted on asking every passing sentry to report on whether they could see anything out beyond the walls. For a long time, long enough for me to begin to shiver in the cold night air, nothing happened.

And then Gallus looked out again, his eyes fixed on the approach to the gates.

"I'm sure I saw movement near the roadway!" he hissed in delight. "I think they have taken the bait."

He signalled down to Successianus, warning him to be ready, then returned to peering out over the wall.

I strained my ears, trying to detect any sound that might indicate the arrival of the Goths, but I could hear nothing.

"They are staying back," Gallus reported in a whisper. "Let's let them sit there a bit longer. They'll be all the more eager to rush in if they have been kept waiting."

He waited for what seemed an eternity, although I suppose it was only around half an hour, then he sent another signal down to Successianus.

"Open one gate a little way."

Down below, I heard the sound of soldiers heaving the locking bar aside, then there was a slow creak of hinges as they pulled one of the heavy, iron-studded gates inwards.

There was an expectant pause, a silence during which everyone seemed to hold their breath, and then Gallus hissed, "Here they come!"

He stared out into the night, waiting for the enemy to draw near, then called softly for the next part of his plan to be put into action.

"Light the bundles!"

The soldiers tasked with this job immediately hauled back the fleeces, picked up the bundles of sticks and held them to the nearest torches. The oil-soaked wood ignited, and the men rushed to the rampart, heaving the flaming faggots over the wall.

"Archers!" Gallus yelled, and the bowmen stood up, arrows already nocked on their strings, and began loosing volley after volley of death.

The result was instantaneous. From the road beyond the wall, shouts and screams of pain, alarm and fear now filled the air, and I heard Successianus echo the Governor's next order.

"Open the gates!"

Both of the massive gates were dragged fully back, and then the Roman legionaries charged through the short tunnel of the gatehouse and burst outside.

I risked looking over the wall to see what was happening. The legionaries were already charging in amongst the Goths, hurling javelins and slashing with their swords. There was room for them to move six abreast, and they ran as if their lives depended on it, yet they retained a ragged formation, the years of drill and training helping them keep together.

They struck like a hammer blow, causing panic among the Goths who were already reeling from the deluge of arrows.

It was impossible to see much detail in the dark. The burning bundles revealed little more than a seething mass of dark shapes, but the clash of weapons, the screams of battle cries and terrified men echoed up to us.

The archers were still loosing arrows, their aim now further out, beyond the immediate fighting.

Gallus was very calm, keeping half an eye on the combat below us, but always watching for the rest of the Gothic army which was expecting to charge into the open gateway once their advance party had seized control of the entrance.

Without turning round, Gallus called, "Trumpeter!"

A young man, his eyes wide with excitement, had clearly been waiting for this summons. He scurried up the steps and ran to stand beside the Governor, a long, brass horn clutched in both hands.

"Wait for my signal," Gallus told him.

Below us, I heard Successianus shouting orders.

"Hold the gates!" he told a Centurion who led the second Cohort. "Be ready to let the first Cohort return!"

A Cohort numbered around five hundred men, but only a fraction of that number could remain under the wide archway of the gates. Successianus was keeping most of his reserve close, but leaving enough room for the first Cohort, the men who had charged outside, to return. That would be a dangerous time. It would only need one man to stumble and fall for the entrance tunnel to be blocked. And if the gates could not be closed due to the press of bodies, the Goths would have a chance to batter their way into the fort. Successianus faced a delicate problem, and would need to judge things perfectly.

Gallus, still staring out into the night, said, "It will be soon."

Turning to the trumpeter, he said, "Be ready."

The lad lifted his long horn to his lips, nodding to confirm he was prepared.

I kept my eyes on Gallus, not wishing to see the slaughter taking place outside the fort. Not that it required eyes to know what was happening. The sounds of fighting were loud and dreadful, the clash of metal on metal, the grunts, shouts and screams all painting a vivid picture of the carnage being enacted on the roadway beneath us.

Then Gallus signalled to the trumpeter and snapped, "Now! Recall!"

The young man put the long horn to his lips and blew out a series of notes which blared out across the wall, signalling the retreat. He blew again and again, summoning the fighting men back.

As the call of the horn cut through the night air, the sounds of fighting diminished, to be replaced by the steady and rapid tramp of many hobnailed sandals and the calm, authoritative shouts of the Centurions as they brought their men back towards the gates.

"Hold your line!"

"Steady! Keep moving!"

"Now run!"

Soldiers pounded back beneath the archway of the gates, hurrying through the gap left for them by the second Cohort who stood ready to block any pursuit.

"Close the gates!" Gallus shouted, and we heard the creak and slam, then the sound of the huge locking bar being dropped into place.

"Archers!" Gallus called. "See them off!"

The archers loosed several more volleys, and I risked a peek over the ramparts to see more men falling to the ground as the few Goths who had been brave or foolish enough to follow the Roman retreat were cut down. Eventually, though, there were no more targets, and the archers ceased shooting. The blazing faggots had burned down, and now gave off little more than a faint glow, so it was too dark to see what might be happening, but our ears told us that only the dead and wounded occupied the approach to the fort, while the bulk of the Gothic army stood further back in helpless rage at being thwarted.

A ragged cheer went up from the legionaries, and Gallus trotted down the stairs to congratulate them.

"Well done, lads!" I heard him call. "You taught them a lesson."

Aoric was less enthusiastic.

"I doubt they suffered more than a hundred or so casualties," he confided to me. "That's not much more than a pinprick to an army that size."

"It's not about numbers," I told him. "It's about morale. Being under siege is as much about attitude as anything else. Every victory improves confidence among the defenders, while denting the morale of the enemy."

"Have you ever been in a siege, then?" he asked me.

"Once. It was about ten or twelve years ago. Maybe a bit more, come to think of it. I was in Aquileia when Maximinis Thrax was trying to capture the city."

"What happened?" he asked me.

I sighed, "It was brutal, but the defence held. And then Thrax's own men turned against him. They were hungry, tired, and disillusioned because they were Romans who were suffering casualties attacking a Roman city. They had no stomach for that fight, so they killed Thrax, and that ended the civil war."

Aoric nodded, "I remember you telling me how a lot of Emperors have died at the hands of their own troops. He was one of them, then?"

"He was, and you are right. It happens rather a lot these days. It makes me wonder why anyone would want to become Emperor, but I suppose the lure of power is too strong for some men to resist."

He muttered, "Let's hope the same doesn't happen to Messius Decius. We need him to bring his army here if we are to have any chance of getting out alive."

"Not necessarily," I told him. "Gallus is confident we can hold Novae. Cniva might give up and go in search of easier pickings if he can't breach our walls."

"He'll throw everything at us before he gives up," Aoric said. "All tonight's work will have done is provoke him."

Chapter 5
Besieged

The drums began beating an hour before dawn. Everyone in Novae heard them, and they struck fear into the hearts of the civilians, but Gallus called his troops to arms, putting on a proud display of calm confidence. Aoric and I joined him as he and Successianus made a circuit of the walls. They spoke to soldiers as they went, exuding an air of self-assurance, and telling the men that the defences were too strong for the Goths to break in.

"Stand firm, fight well, and they'll soon give up," Gallus repeatedly told the soldiers.

As the sky began to lighten, the ranks of Goths became visible. Spurred on by the booming drums, they chanted as they held their weapons high for us to see, stamping their feet in time to the beat of the drums.

"They will need to attack us on foot," Gallus reminded us. "Their cavalry are useless here, so we'll be up against men who are poorly armoured. That gives us a huge advantage."

While the Goths continued to chant their war cries, Gallus made sure that his men were provided with a breakfast of gruel and bread, the supplies being brought up to the walls.

"Let the Goths fight on empty stomachs if they wish," he grinned.

I expected the assault to begin once the sun had risen, but the drums continued to pound, their rolling thunder echoing all around the fort, and the Goths chanted their war songs as if they believed the walls might crumble at the sound of their fury.

"They are trying to frighten us," Gallus decided. "But we are safe in here, and they are the ones who should be afraid."

The catapults were ready, piles of limestone balls, and even simple rocks providing a stockpile of ammunition. The *ballista* bolts were ready, the crews eager to use their weapons at long last, and the archers were well supplied with feathered shafts.

"Every legionary has ten javelins at the ready," Successianus reported. "And more can be brought from the armoury if need be."

"It will depend on how willing the Goths are to die," Gallus replied with a cheerful smile.

After completing the circuit of the walls, the Governor took up position near the western gate, while Successianus commanded the eastern side. Senior officers were placed in command of the northern and southern walls, but Gallus did not expect any serious attacks from those directions.

"The river is a major obstacle to the north," he explained. "They may fire arrows at us, and they might even try to cross in small boats, but they won't be able to get many men across without suffering heavy casualties. On the southern side, the fort is protected by the height of the hill they will need to climb just to reach us. I'm guessing Cniva will focus on the east and west gates."

When the attack did come, it was heralded by a massive, reverberating roar as the Goths surged forwards, all three landward sides of the fort facing a wave of barbarians.

"Catapults!" Gallus yelled, releasing the crews to action. The huge wooden arms swung, hurling their boulders in high arcs, the range judged to perfection. Long hours of practice told the crews precisely where their rocks would strike. The boulders came down, crushing unwary attackers, and even if they missed because men had dodged aside, this created confusion in the massed charge as warriors stumbled into one another.

The catapult crews worked feverishly to wind back the long throwing arms, place another boulder in the leather sling, then release the missile at the onrushing horde. They had practised this so often that they were able to hurl rock after rock at the Goths.

"*Ballistas*!" Gallus yelled, and the iron-tipped bolts joined the barrage. These weapons had a shorter range than the catapults, but they were more accurate, and able to send a succession of bolts one after the other with astonishing rapidity. I saw men falling as they were struck, some of them knocked backwards by the power of the blow.

"Archers!" Gallus yelled, and the arrows flew, adding to the carnage.

But the charge came on. There were so many Goths that they could not be stopped. Catapults, *ballistas* and bows all fired their deadly volleys, but the Goths, eager for plunder and violence, came on. Some of the men in the front ranks wore armour, but while their shields and chainmail provided protection from the arrows, the *ballista* bolts could punch through the iron links of their armour, and I saw many of them fall. And the unarmoured Goths who made up the majority of the attack fell in droves.

But still they charged across the open ground, yelling and screaming defiance in the face of the horror they were enduring.

Until they reached the ditches. Here they faced an almost impassable barrier. Three deep ditches, each lined with sharp stakes, and each one of them too wide to leap over. Some Goths tried, but all of them tumbled into the filth-strewn ditches, fortunate if they managed to avoid impaling themselves on the sharpened stakes.

But the Goths had brought ladders, some of them traditional in design, others far more crude, consisting of long lengths of tree trunks with protruding branches. They had intended to use these to scale the walls, but now they flung them across the ditches and tried to run across them. They soon discovered that this only made them easy targets for the archers.

More Goths crowded the road, aiming for the gates. The gateways were always the most vulnerable part of any fort's defences, so Gallus had concentrated his best archers here. They were flanked by *ballistas* which flung bolt after bolt into the mass of men trying to reach the gate.

"They have a battering ram," Gallus remarked, apparently unconcerned. "Archers! Aim for the men carrying it!"

The Goths were shooting back now, their own archers sending shafts flashing up towards us, but we were largely protected by the high stone rampart, and the Gothic arrows found few targets.

The battering ram did not reach the gates. Warriors held shields over their heads, trying to protect the men who carried the great baton of wood they had created, but they were met by a hail of rocks which smashed limbs and crashed onto shields, knocking the men down. As soon as they fell, the arrows struck again.

In battle, things can turn in an instant. One moment the Goths were yelling fiercely as they strove to reach our gates; the next moment they were fleeing, running and staggering in panic, an uncoordinated mass of terrified men.

"Save your arrows!" Gallus called as he watched the retreat.

"They've dropped their ram," he said as he leaned out to take a look. "Centurion! Send some men out there to haul it inside.

If they want to break our gates down, they'll need to make another one. And collect as many arrows as you can."

His orders were quickly obeyed, a squad of men risking exposure to Gothic arrows as they ran outside, kicked and shoved dead and wounded men aside, and hauled the heavy ram in through the gates.

"It's very crude," Gallus said with an air of disappointment in his foes. "They haven't even given it an iron tip. That wouldn't have broken our gates even if they had reached them."

I glanced over the wall, horrified at the carnage left by the failed attack. Men were sprawled everywhere, many of them moving feebly, the sound of their piteous groans awful to hear. It was a sickening sight, but I knew there would be worse to follow.

The sound of fighting continued from the east, so Gallus set off, walking briskly around the wall, congratulating his men as he went, and commiserating with any who had been wounded by arrows. Only one defender had died, struck in the eye by an arrow, but there were a few injured men, and the medical teams were busy tending to their wounds. The mood among most of the men was, though, almost jubilant at their success.

"We showed them, Sir!" was a frequent comment shouted at Gallus.

"You certainly did!" Gallus replied.

At the south, he confirmed that his surmise had been correct. The Goths who had attacked there had been tired by the climb up the hill, under fire all the way. Few of them had reached as far as the ditches. Then they had retired without doing any damage.

The situation on the eastern wall was more serious, especially at the lower end near the river, where it seemed that Cniva had sent in a far more dangerous attack on this side. Even so, Successianus met us with a satisfied expression on his normally stern face.

"They got to the gates, and it was in the balance for a while," he reported. "But we hit them with everything we could, and there were so many dead that the others couldn't get close to the gateway. They gave up once they realised they could not get in."

The Goths had suffered hundreds of casualties, many of them dead, many more wounded. Some of these tried to crawl or drag themselves away, while others simply cried out for help. It was pitiable, but Gallus had little sympathy for the enemy.

"Cniva will ask for a truce," he guessed. "We'll let him take his dead and wounded away. That will take time, and the longer we keep him here, the more chance there is of the Emperor bringing his army."

Once again, the Governor was correct. Cniva did not come himself, but he sent an emissary to arrange a truce. Gallus conducted this negotiation himself, shouting down to the man from the high wall above the western gates. A truce was arranged, and the Goths sent men to carry away their wounded, then to drag away the dead.

Chewing on a chunk of dark sausage while he watched, Gallus mused, "The big question now is whether they will try again. And if so, when?"

He glanced at me, perhaps expecting some valuable insight, but I had little to offer.

"He might try one more time," I suggested. "But he must know he has little chance of breaching the walls unless he builds his own catapults. That takes time and expertise."

Gallus stood down most of his cohorts, sending the men to rest, eat and even sleep.

"If I was him," he said, "I'd try a night attack. Our artillery and archers are less effective at night."

This prediction was also correct, because the western gate came under heavy attack shortly after midnight. The Goths did not try using a ram to break down the doors, but brought several ladders. By staying on the road, they could place these up against the walls of the tall gatehouse and try to climb over the ramparts.

Gallus, though, was ready for them. Many soldiers were armed with long poles, each with a forked end which they used to tip the ladders sideways while men were climbing. Archers shot into the darkness, but the greatest damage was done by the simple expedient of dropping rocks onto the climbing men.

"Pour down some oil!" Gallus shouted.

Great vats of olive oil had been heated, and now these were tipped, sending torrents of boiling oil down onto the helpless attackers. The screams from this were appalling, and I recalled hearing a similar sound when I had been besieged in Aquileia all those years before.

"That's a horrible way to die," I told Aoric. "And if it doesn't kill you, it leaves terrible burns. Some men lose their eyes if it hits them in the face."

Faced by this dreadful barrage, the Goths gave up this attack as well. Only one man had reached the top of the wall, and he had been stabbed by no fewer than three defenders who sent him toppling back over the rampart before tipping the ladder and sending four more Goths into the ditches at the side of the road.

Gallus seemed indefatigable, snatching only a few hours of sleep during the lulls in the fighting. I tried to copy him, but I felt exhausted by the time the sun rose on another scene of devastation outside the fort. More dead and injured men lay in horrible poses on the ground, some of them dreadfully burned by the oil, others with several arrows protruding from their unprotected bodies.

Gallus was pleased at the way his men had defended the fort, but he clucked his tongue and frowned when he looked out at the enemy's vast camp.

"Nothing is happening," he said. "They must be holding a council of war. Cniva will be under pressure now."

I nodded, "Unless they've brought a lot of supplies, they'll run out of food before long."

"They brought wagons and livestock on the hoof," Gallus replied, still staring intently at the Gothic camp. "I expect fodder for their horses will be their main problem."

"So what will they do next?" I wondered.

Gallus grinned, "I think they are probably arguing over whether to try another attack or whether to move on and find some easier targets."

After a moment's reflection, he added, "I suspect they'll leave us in peace and go in search of less well defended places."

His understanding of the situation was once again accurate. By late morning, we could see our enemy begin to break camp. Horsemen rode off to the south, then the supply wagons were hauled away, and the ordinary warriors soon trudged after them. Within a couple of hours, all we could see of the vast Gothic army were a few hundred cavalry who formed a protective screen between us and their marching comrades. Then these men, too, rode away southwards.

"It could be a feint," Gallus decided. "Let's give them time to get well away, then we'll send some cavalry to track them."

I asked, "I suppose it's still too dangerous to try to pursue them?"

"Absolutely!" Gallus agreed. "That is precisely what Cniva wants me to do. We can match him easily enough if we stay behind our walls, but out in the field, he would have all the advantages. He'd simply surround us and slaughter us. No, we need to remain here."

I was uncomfortable about this plan of action, or plan of inaction as Aoric described it.

"There are other towns and cities with few defenders," I said to Aoric when we took a short break to eat a light snack of cheese and sausage. "If we don't try to stop them, they could ravage the whole province."

"That's what Cniva wants," Aoric nodded. He chewed on his sausage, then added, "He knows where Gallus' army is, so now he can move on. The Governor is caught between two impossible choices. If he stays, Cniva will have free rein to do as he pleases, but if he does go after him, the Goths will surround him and destroy his army."

This was the sort of dilemma which made me glad I was not a Governor. Whatever Gallus did, he could be criticised, and I heard some soldiers grumbling about the decision to remain inside the fort. Gallus, though, was adamant that he would not risk the army in open battle. His only concession was to send out a strong force of cavalry who soon scattered the few scouts Cniva had left behind to watch our movements.

Aoric said, "They won't get far. Cniva will have left a strong rearguard to protect his march. A few hundred horsemen won't break through."

I shrugged, "I don't think their task is to break through. The Governor just wants to know where the Goths are going."

"They are going to find easier targets," Aoric stated. "And they will be brutal after this defeat."

I sighed, "I know. But, like you said, if Gallus goes after them, he'll be destroyed, and then the Goths can plunder all they like."

"So he's going to let them run wild?" Aoric frowned.

"Unless the Emperor arrives soon, I don't see that he can do anything else. He's delayed Cniva for three days, but he can't do any more than that."

"Then let us hope the Emperor gets here soon," Aoric said. "Then maybe you and I can head back to Rome."

"Jupiter grant us that," I nodded. "But all I want to do now is sleep."

Chapter 6
Refusal

Gallus' cavalry scouts sent back regular reports, but they were not always helpful.

"They are scared of getting too close to the Goths and finding themselves cut off," the Governor confided to his aides. "I can understand that, but it means their reports are a little vague. However, it does seem that the bulk of Cniva's army is heading towards Nicopolis."

"Is there a garrison there?" I asked him.

He gave a shrug.

"Not much of one, I'm afraid. A couple of Auxiliary Cohorts. That's all."

With a rueful smile, he added, "And the Gothic army is so huge, we have no way of knowing whether they have sent large raiding parties elsewhere. Nicopolis may not be their only target."

This was always the problem. Distances were great, and messages could be out of date by the time they arrived. Except that, for five days, we received no messages apart from those brought back by gallopers from the cavalry scouts who were shadowing the Goths. That must have been a difficult and dangerous task. Gallus had over seven hundred riders at his disposal, but even if they stayed together in one mass, they were still hugely outnumbered by Cniva's raiders. And Gallus could not afford to keep his cavalry as a combined group because he needed to send patrols in all directions.

We had also discovered that not all of the Goths had left. The barbarians who were camped across the river remained in place, shooting arrows at anyone who ventured up onto the ramparts or out to the dock where two ships of the river fleet were berthed. Those ships were now targeted, with the Goths sending flaming arrows into them in an effort to set them on fire. However, several sailors remained on board, and they managed to extinguish any flames.

"Those barbarians are a nuisance," the Governor frowned. "But I have an idea about how we can deal with them."

He put that idea into practice that night. Under cover of dark, he filled the two river ships with soldiers, then sent them across the river to assault the camp. The barbarians' sentries saw them coming, but the ships' catapults, aided by the fort's artillery, sent a covering barrage against the northern bank of the river, and the marines were soon able to swarm onto the far side of the Danubius. It was, as instructed by Gallus, a short, sharp attack designed to create confusion and kill a few Goths who had assumed they were safe from attack. The marines hit them hard, charging into their camp among men who were still groggy from sleep, then they hurried back, the ships bringing them safely back to Novae.

"We lost five men," Gallus told us once he had spoken to the commanders of the raiding party. "But we set fire to parts of their camp, and a good few of them were killed."

It may have been a victory, but it was a small one, and the Goths were soon back in place. The next morning, they retaliated by loosing volleys of arrows at the wharfs on the northern side of the fort. They used even more flaming arrows, and this time they managed to set fire to one of the ships moored there. The sailors on that vessel were forced to abandon the ship and run for the fort, but most of them were cut down by a hail of Gothic arrows despite the fort's archers and artillery providing covering volleys. Only two of them made it back alive, and all they could do was join the rest of us as we watched the ship burn down to the waterline.

It was a dispiriting loss for the garrison, but Gallus seemed to regard this as little more than a nuisance, and he concentrated on other matters. He kept the garrison busy by ordering that supplies of ammunition should be replenished in case the main Gothic army returned. Arrows and javelins were collected from the ground outside the fort, Fresh weapons were forged in the armoury's workshop, rocks and stones for the catapults were hauled in, and new *ballista* bolts were fashioned.

Other men had the gruesome task of disposing of the dead bodies. The easiest option was to dump them in the river, but the Goths who still lurked on the far bank shot at anyone who ventured too close to the water, so the soldiers dug a pit which they lined with a layer of timber, then dumped the hundreds of bodies into the hole before setting fire to the makeshift pyre. It burned for a whole day, and then the soldiers covered the ash and bones with earth before replacing the turf.

It was on the sixth day after the Gothic army had moved on that another group of horsemen appeared on the ridge far off to the west. Sentries sent an urgent message to the *Principia*, and

Gallus hurried to the ramparts, with his usual band of aides scurrying after him.

When we reached the top of the wall, a Centurion informed us, "They look like Romans, sir. And there are a lot of them."

He was right. The men rode in an ordered column, four abreast, with several outriders moving ahead and to either side, and the long column continued to stream over the crest of the ridge, coming straight down the road towards us. Banners were held high, and Gallus gave a soft smile as the leading riders drew near.

"We are honoured," he announced. "If I am not mistaken, those banners proclaim our visitor as none other than our co-Emperor and Consul, Herennius Etruscus."

That created quite a stir, but Gallus refused to be ruffled by the arrival of the Emperor's son and heir, a man who had been named Augustus, making him a co-Emperor, although most definitely the junior partner in the ruling pair. Even so, Etruscus held a great deal of power, and had been appointed as Consul for the current year.

"Let us see what he has to say," Gallus remarked.

There must have been around five thousand horsemen in Etruscus' small army. The bulk of them reined in and dismounted some distance from the fort, seeking out what little grazing was left after the Goths had trampled the ground, but a small group of riders came on towards the gates.

They entered Novae in a clatter of hooves, the sound echoing from the tunnel of the gateway as Gallus and his aides gathered to meet them. Crowds of curious soldiers also congregated near the gate, their expressions displaying relief that the Emperor had clearly sent the help we had called for.

I loitered near the back of the crowd, aware that most of the men around me were wearing armour while I was still in my plain tunic and cloak.

Aoric sidled up beside me.

"Is it true?" he asked in a low voice. "Is it Herennius Etruscus?"

I nodded, "So Gallus says."

"You know him," Aoric said.

"Hardly," I replied. "I've met him once. He's a decent enough sort, but very young to be an Augustus."

Aoric persisted, "If his men are the advance guard of the Emperor's army, it means you and I can go back to Rome."

"I hope so," I said cautiously. "But let's wait until we know what is happening."

"I'll go and pack our bags," Aoric said confidently.

He swaggered off, leaving me watching the arrival of the Emperor's son.

The assembled troops gave a cheer when Etruscus entered the camp. I was not close enough to hear what was said between him and the Governor, but I saw the Emperor's son dismount from his horse when Gallus gave a bow of welcome.

The Augustus removed his iron helmet, wiping a hand through his close-cropped hair. As I'd told Aoric, he was a young man, barely out of his teens, but he had a very confident manner which I knew many people felt bordered on arrogance. When he spoke, his voice was loud and clear enough to be heard by most of the watching men.

"I am glad to find you safe," he said. "I hear you have driven off Cniva's rabble."

"The men fought valiantly," Gallus replied expansively. "And we are equally glad to see you, Augustus."

Etruscus gave a distracted nod, then said, "I must speak to you, Trebonianus Gallus. I bring word from my father, the Emperor."

"Of course!" Gallus beamed. "Please do me the honour of taking some refreshments with me."

He and Etruscus led the way up to the topmost level of the fort where they entered the *Principia*. I tagged along at the back of the aides and senior officers. Etruscus had brought half a dozen men who looked very tough and competent, and they stayed close to the young Augustus.

Gallus sent word to the kitchens, and a large chamber was prepared, extra seats being brought in to accommodate the two men and their entourages. Fabius Successianus was there, and I managed to find myself a seat near one end of the long table.

Wine and food were delivered, but Etruscus was keen to talk while he ate.

"My father received your report that the Goths had been driven off," he declared. "Your rider was fortunate enough to find us on the road."

Gallus nodded, refraining from pointing out that the road was the fastest approach to Novae, so it had made sense to send his most recent message by that route.

Etruscus went on, "We encountered another large force of Goths on the way. We drove them off, and they have fled in the direction of Nicopolis. My father has taken the bulk of the army in pursuit, but he asked me to come here to deliver his message."

"And we are delighted to see you, Augustus," Gallus said. "What word does Messius Decius Caesar Augustus send?"

With a hint of challenge in his voice, Etruscus said, "Nicopolis is not well defended. My father is hurrying to get there before the Goths take the city, and he intends to challenge Cniva to a battle."

Gallus nodded but said nothing.

"And we need all the forces we can muster if we are to ensure the Goths are defeated," Etruscus went on insistently.

It was plain what he wanted, but Gallus still refused to commit to anything, so Etruscus blurted, "You are ordered to bring your legion and all your cavalry to join the fight."

Every eye in the room was on Gallus, but he gave no indication that he felt at all self-conscious as he replied, "Sadly, Augustus, that will not be possible."

Etruscus blinked in surprise, and most of the others sat very still, waiting for an eruption of anger.

Etruscus, though, managed to restrain his temper, simply rasping, "You are refusing a direct order from your Emperor?"

"With regret," Gallus shrugged, "I wish I could comply, but the situation here remains highly dangerous. Only the other night we had to send men across the river in an attempt to drive off another force of Goths."

Etruscus had clearly not expected this, and he hesitated for a moment before asking, "And were you successful?"

"Sadly not," Gallus told him. "They sank one of our ships, and there is still a large force of Goths camped in the woods on the northern bank. They keep us under constant pressure."

This was true, although I felt Gallus was exaggerating the danger those Goths presented.

He went on, "And I need my cavalry to maintain patrols along the river to prevent yet more raiding parties coming to join Cniva."

"You do not need hundreds of horsemen for that!" Etruscus snapped, his young face flushing.

"Not to locate them," Gallus agreed. "But to stop them crossing, a force of seven hundred is barely adequate."

"The danger is to the south!" Etruscus almost shouted, waving an angry arm as if to indicate the direction.

"The danger is everywhere," Gallus countered. "If I march my men out of here, I leave a strong fort vulnerable to attack. A small garrison could not possibly man the entire length of the walls. Novae could fall to the enemy, and taking it back would be a major undertaking. It also leaves our entire army open to being attacked from the rear as we march south. By remaining here, I am pinning down thousands of Goths who might otherwise join the battle."

I shot a glance at Fabius Successianus, but his face was as much a mask as Gallus'. The Prefect must have known that the Governor was creating a menace where there was little more than a nuisance, but he said nothing. I wondered what was going on here. Neither Gallus nor Successianus were cowards, yet they seemed determined to remain in Novae while the Goths rampaged across Moesia. Was it out of genuine concern for the lives of their soldiers, or the risk to the empire, or was there more to it? I could not tell.

In the face of an increasingly agitated Etruscus, Gallus continued to explain his motives as if to a young boy. Etruscus, of course, was only a few years out of his childhood, and an experienced operator like Gallus knew how to make a good argument. Rhetoric and public speaking were an essential part of the education of any wealthy Roman, and Gallus was as good as any I'd seen.

"I understand the Emperor's concern," he said soothingly. "But there are strategic complications which he cannot possibly be expected to be aware of. My cavalry would barely make a difference to the numbers the Emperor has available, while the legion would take a long time to reach Nicopolis. The Gothic army is mostly mounted, so catching them on foot would be virtually impossible."

Again I waited for someone to contradict him, because there were plenty of Goths on foot, and they had slow-moving supply wagons and camp followers as well, but nobody said a word.

Etruscus had the appearance of a sulky child as he turned to ask his senior men what they thought. These men were veteran soldiers, no doubt assigned to help their inexperienced commander.

"What Trebonianus Gallus says makes sense," one of them conceded with little grace. "Provided the threat is real."

"Oh, it is real," Gallus nodded. "Feel free to take a stroll along our south wall. You'll find yourself a tempting target for the Goths."

Etruscus was clearly at a loss. His father had been Emperor for only a couple of years, and the young man's elevation to imperial rank must have come as something of a shock. He was out of his depth, although he did his best to rescue some pride from the discussion.

"My father will not be pleased," he growled at Gallus.

"I will be more than happy to explain it to him face to face once he has defeated Cniva," Gallus replied smoothly. "I am sure he will understand. Losing Novae would be a calamity."

Then, before Etruscus could make another point, Gallus conceded, "However, around half of my cavalry is shadowing the Gothic army. I would be happy to send them an order to join with you, provided it is understood that I can recall them if another large raiding party crosses the river."

It was not much of a concession, but Gallus managed to make it sound like a reasonable offer. Faced by the Governor's intransigence, Etruscus gave a surly nod, clearly having run out of arguments. But he was plainly unhappy, probably because he would now need to re-join his father and report his failure.

Gallus said, "You are more than welcome to stay here overnight. I'm sure we can supply enough tents for your men."

"We need to get to Nicopolis," Etruscus said scathingly, his tone intended to shame Gallus. The Governor, though, remained stolid and calm, refusing to rise to the bait.

The two men stared at one another for a long time, then Etruscus slowly turned his head, his eyes scanning every man at the table as if trying to gauge their loyalty. Gallus' officers remained silent, although one or two of them looked a little shame-faced. For my part, I was growing increasingly angry. I had little military experience, but I knew enough of our situation to realise that Gallus was exaggerating the risk to Novae. Yet all of his Tribunes sat silently, tacitly backing him up.

Perhaps my agitation was more evident than I had hoped, because when Etruscus' gaze reached me, I saw him give a slight start. He frowned, narrowing his eyes as he took in my civilian tunic which marked me out among the soldiers.

"Do I know you?" he asked uncertainly.

All eyes turned towards me, but I focused my attention on Etruscus, not willing to catch Gallus' eye.

"We have met briefly, Augustus," I nodded. "At the home of Publius Licinius Valerianus. I was there when you visited him once. My name is Sempronius Scipio."

A flash of recognition crossed his face. His father, the Emperor, was a close friend of Valerianus, and the two of them, along with a host of hangers-on, had arrived at Valerianus' home in Rome while I was paying my respects to my wealthy patron. I was surprised that Etruscus had remembered me, for we had barely exchanged half a dozen words before Valerianus had dismissed me.

"What are you doing here?" Etruscus asked, clearly seeking a distraction from his difficult situation.

"Licinius Valerianus asked me to come here," I said, conscious that everyone was still looking at me. "He had instructed me to cross the river to spy on the Goths. Sadly, by the time I arrived, the Goths had already begun their war. I was stuck here."

Etruscus may have been young, but he knew enough about Licinius Valerianus to understand that he would not have sent me here without good reason.

The young co-Emperor pursed his lips, frowned, then decided, "Then you will come with me. Valerianus remains in Rome, but I'm sure my father would like to talk to you."

"Of course, Augustus."

For the first time, I risked a glance at Gallus, and I could tell that he was less than pleased about this. I had a horrible feeling that I knew why. He had spun Etruscus a highly exaggerated story, and he feared I would tell the Emperor the truth of his current situation.

"We leave immediately!" Etruscus announced, rising to his feet.

Everyone scrambled from their chairs, offering salutes, and I hurried to follow the young Augustus and his retinue. Gallus, though, made a point of intercepting me before I could leave the room.

He held out a hand, a friendly smile on his face.

As I clasped his arm, he said softly, "It has been a pleasure knowing you, Scipio. You are a resourceful man. And, I believe, a clever one."

"It has been an honour to meet you, Governor," I replied, aware that he was still gripping my forearm very tightly.

Leaning closer and lowering his voice even further, he added, "I'm sure I can rely on you to provide Licinius Valerianus with a favourable report on my actions."

There was a huge amount behind that simple statement. Gallus knew I was working for Valerianus under duress, and he was reminding me that he could prove to be an ally, provided I did not badmouth him.

I said, "Of course, Sir."

"And anyone else who might ask, naturally."

Anyone else like the Emperor, he meant.

"Naturally, Sir."

He released my hand, reaching up to clap me on the shoulder.

"Good man! I do like you Scipio. I hope we have a chance to meet again."

I nodded and smiled, but privately I was thinking that if young Etruscus was going to take me into a battle against the Goths, my chances of survival were not high.

Chapter 7
Motivation

"You're kidding!" Aoric gasped when I told him that I had been ordered to accompany Herennius Etruscus.

"I'm afraid not. I think he regards it as some sort of face-saving action. Gallus basically told him to piss off, and he decided to demand my presence as a way of demonstrating his authority."

In a voice heavy with sarcasm, Aoric grunted, "I bet Gallus is terrified. I saw Etruscus leaving the *Principia*, and he didn't look at all happy."

"Then we'd best not keep him waiting," I suggested. "Let's go and get our horses."

In anticipation of leaving for Rome, Aoric had already gathered our few belongings in our small packs. I slung mine over my shoulder, then told him about the meeting as we hurried down to the stables.

"We could still ride away," he suggested.

I shook my head.

"That would only make Etruscus angry at us as well as Gallus."

"Gallus is angry?" Aoric frowned.

"Gallus is worried in case I reveal the truth about his excuses for not joining the Emperor's army. That's why we need to get out of here."

Aoric shot me an astonished look.

"You think Gallus would have you killed to keep you silent? I thought he liked you."

I shrugged, "That wouldn't stop him ordering my execution if he thought it would help his career."

We reached the stables, quickly locating our horses and heaving the heavy wooden-framed, leather saddles into place before fastening the bridles and reins. At a word from Aoric, the boys who tended the mounts brought us sacks of grain which we slung behind the saddles. Every cavalryman knew that it was essential to keep his mount well fed, and grain was an important part of keeping a horse healthy.

Aoric was still full of questions, talking while we worked.

"So what is Gallus up to?" he asked. "He's not afraid of fighting. We've seen that. So why did he refuse?"

"Politics and religion," I replied.

"Those are pretty much the same thing in Rome these days," Aoric muttered.

"That's right. I'm sure you remember that the late and unlamented Emperor Philippus treated the Christians very favourably."

"I remember," Aoric nodded.

"And a lot of Senators were unhappy about it. That's why Messius Decius issued his edict last year. Everyone had to visit a temple and swear loyalty to the Roman gods."

"I could hardly forget that," Aoric nodded. "I got a certificate to prove I'd sworn the oath."

"Keep that safe," I reminded him. "It looks as if we're going to join up with the Emperor's army, and without that proof, you could be executed for being a heretic."

"I am a heretic," Aoric chuckled. "I offered more prayers to my own gods after I gave that oath. I think they would understand that it was necessary for me to give my sworn word if it meant staying alive. Didn't one of the Christian leaders get executed for refusing to swear his loyalty to Rome's gods?"

"The Pope, the Christians call him. Yes, he refused, and he was executed. His successor fled the city and is in hiding somewhere."

By this time we had led our horses out of the stables, mounting quickly and setting off for the western gate. We discovered that Herennius Etruscus had already left the fort, but the gates were open, and we rode outside, the guards offering no challenge.

Beyond the fort, Etruscus' horsemen were preparing to leave, their short rest interrupted as the Emperor's son issued his commands to head south.

Aoric and I remained as spectators, staying well out of anyone's way.

Aoric was a sharp lad, and he did not take long to draw his own conclusion from our discussion.

"You think Gallus sympathises with the Christians?" he guessed.

"It's possible," I nodded. "Although it's equally possible that he simply wants to use Decius' edict as an excuse to set himself up as a rival. Christianity is spreading all across the empire, and a lot of people, even if they don't care for the new religion, didn't like the severity of the punishments dealt to those who refused to give their oath."

"Do you think Gallus wants to be Emperor?" Aoric asked.

I shrugged, "Who knows? He's certainly putting himself in a dangerous position by refusing to help. But he may well have Christian sympathies. Gallus has a wife back in Rome, and it's possible that she's secretly converted to Christianity. A lot of women seem to like the new religion. And remember, Licinius Valerianus wanted me to spy on Gallus. Perhaps he had his own suspicions about the Governor. Valerianus is vehemently against the Christians, and he's a close friend of the Emperor. Gallus, I'm guessing, isn't all that keen on their attitudes towards Christians."

Aoric sighed, "You Romans spend more time fighting each other than you do fighting your enemies."

I gave a rueful smile. I could not argue with his assessment. For almost all of my adult life, one Emperor after another had fallen victim to internal plots and intrigues.

"It looks as if we are ready," Aoric observed, nodding to the thousands of riders who were once again forming up in their various units. Scouts had already galloped southwards to check the planned route, and the Emperor's son was clearly impatient to leave. A bugle sounded the advance, and the huge column of cavalry set off at a brisk canter.

"Time to go," I said, nudging my own horse into motion. "Let's see if we can stay at the back."

That lasted only a short while. An officer in a plumed helmet had moved aside, letting the long column pass him while he waited for us. When he saw us, he kicked his mount into motion, wheeling around to ride alongside us. His helmet obscured much of his face, but I thought I recognised him as one of the aides who had accompanied Etruscus at the meeting.

"I'm Apurius Cimber," he introduced himself. "The Augustus would like to speak to you."

He shot a curious glance at Aoric, noting the young man's trousers. I had decided to stick with Roman clothing, but Aoric habitually wore trousers. Cimber also noticed his long sword.

I said, "This is Auricus, my grandson."

Cimber gave a gruff nod of acceptance, then urged his horse into a gallop as he called, "Come!"

We followed, riding swiftly along the length of the entire column. As we went, I counted the standards, then added up how many men were in this small army. I reckoned five thousand, a considerable number for any Roman army. But then, ever since the days of Maximinis Thrax, Rome had recruited more and more cavalry. When our enemies were almost invariably mounted on horses, Rome had to counter the threat by forming more and more cavalry units. It was all very well for a legion to sit safe behind walls as Trebonianus Gallus was doing at Novae, but men on foot could not prevent mounted raiders scouring the countryside.

Etruscus glanced round when he heard us coming, and we eased our mounts into a canter to match his pace.

"Sempronius Scipio," he nodded. "I do recall seeing you at Valerianus' home, and he often spoke of you."

That was a surprise. I had met Messius Decius only once, but I supposed he knew who I was because I had inadvertently stumbled into the plot he and Licinius Valerianus had initiated in their efforts to overthrow the previous Emperor, Julius Philippus. I knew that Valerianus had mentioned me to him, but I had no idea why they had discussed me more than once. Still, Valerianus must have spoken favourably, because young Etruscus seemed very friendly.

He told me, "I must admit it was a surprise to see you in Novae."

"I was only following orders, Augustus," I replied.

"Yes, you said that Licinius Valerianus sent you. If he trusts you, then I will trust you."

I refrained from saying anything. Valerianus only trusted me to do his bidding because of the threats he had made against my family. I decided Herennius Etruscus did not need to know that.

"Tell me about Trebonianus Gallus," he said, flicking me a glance as he spoke, then returning his attention to the way ahead.

"He led the defence of Novae with supreme skill," I said. "He had prepared it for a siege, and he drove off the Goths easily enough."

"And his reasons for refusing to join us?" Etruscus asked, his anger still evident in his voice and the downward turn of his mouth.

"I am not a military man, Augustus," I said. "But I do know that most of the garrison's cavalry are out on patrol, keeping an eye on the Goths and also scouting along the southern bank of the Danubius."

"What about the Goths he claims are still camped on the northern bank?"

"They are certainly there, Augustus," I told him. "And they did sink one of the ships."

"How many of them are there?"

That was the most important question, and my answer could condemn Gallus. Or condemn me.

"I honestly don't know, Augustus. More than a handful, but whether there are thousands or merely hundreds, I can't say. They remain out of sight most of the time, but I've seen smoke from their camp fires, and I know they have a lot of archers."

"So Gallus was speaking the truth?" Etruscus demanded. "It was more than a mere excuse?"

"That is impossible for me to say for certain, Augustus. But I do know that it would be very dangerous for the empire if Novae were to fall to the Goths."

The young Augustus snorted. It could have been an acknowledgement that I was right, or he could have been expressing doubt over both Gallus' motives and my vague answer.

"My father will deal with Trebonianus Gallus," he said after a while.

He did not ask me any more questions, something I was very glad about. I knew enough about imperial politics to know that I should avoid taking sides if at all possible. Choosing the wrong side often proved fatal.

Aoric and I fell back slightly, riding at the rear of the young Emperor's personal retinue. Apurius Cimber also dropped back to ride alongside us.

"Do you trust Trebonianus Gallus?" he asked me.

I judged that Cimber was in his mid-thirties, and he had a tough look about him. He was, I guessed, an experienced soldier, and he was clearly wary of any potential threat to Etruscus' safety.

I shrugged, "He fought well to drive off the Goths. I didn't get to know him well enough to judge how much I trust him as a person. But he is a Senator, and he was a Consul only a few years ago. That's not the sort of company I generally keep, so I'm not the best person to ask."

Cimber's expression suggested that holding the rank of Senator was not, in his eyes, a reason to trust a man. Privately, I agreed with him about that. I'd met several Senators over the years, and I knew they were as capable of deceit as the most common plebeian.

Cimber shot me an appraising look, but he let the matter drop. I suspected I had not yet earned his approval.

We rode in silence for a while, our route taking us over hills, along valleys and past dense patches of woodland. Normally, I'd have been wary of ambush, but the route we followed was already well churned by the passing of thousands of men and horses. The Goths had already passed this way, and the Emperor's army had followed.

I was concerned that our horses could not maintain the fast pace Etruscus was setting, but I soon discovered that Nicopolis was much closer to Novae than I had imagined. An infantry legion could have covered the distance in little more than a day, which made Gallus' refusal all the more difficult to justify. On horseback, we covered the bulk of the journey in less than three hours.

Our first intimation that we were approaching our destination was the presence of Roman troops ahead of us. Spread out in a long line facing a range of low hills, were thousands of soldiers, many of them on horseback.

"My father's army!" I heard Etruscus declare proudly.

It was an impressive sight. Most of the troops were mounted, but there were detachments of foot soldiers as well, some of them Auxiliaries, and some vexillations from various legions. The infantry numbered less than three thousand all told, but there were tens of thousands of cavalry. Each unit was well equipped, and each waited proudly under its own banner, the various colours and signs marking them out. The array of units stretched out a long way to left and right, and I knew the signs all too well. The Emperor intended to begin a battle.

Messius Decius himself came to meet us. He held a brief discussion with his son, both of them still on horseback, and both looking very grim. Then Etruscus turned in his saddle and called for me.

I nudged my horse closer, offering a solemn bow to Messius Decius, Emperor of Rome.

Decius was in his sixties, so I supposed he must have married late in life for his eldest son to be a teenager. I'd seen Decius from a distance several times in the past year, and had been close to him only on that one occasion at Valerianus' house where we had barely exchanged words. I was not nearly important enough to warrant his personal attention, although I knew he was aware of the small services I had done for him at the behest of Licinius Valerianus.

Decius always struck me as a man beset with worries. His lined, craggy face was noticeable for the permanent bags under his eyes. Still, he was always dignified and, most importantly, was held in high esteem by the soldiers of the imperial army. He had come to power with their backing, and nobody had yet challenged his right to rule.

He looked at me with a keen expression as he said, "Licinius Valerianus told me he had sent you to Novae. My son tells me that Trebonianus Gallus has refused my order to join us."

"He has, Augustus," I replied, giving him his honorific title. After he had seized the throne, the Senate had awarded him the title of Caesar Augustus, and also given him the name Trajanus as a way of improving his standing among the citizens of the empire. The long-dead Emperor Trajan was still revered by most Romans for his strong leadership and talent in war. By giving Decius Trajan's name, the Senate clearly meant to show their faith in him. Or possibly to flatter him in order to remain in his good books. With Senators, it's often hard to tell what motivates their sycophancy.

"But you don't know why he refused?" the Emperor asked me.

"No, Sir. I don't believe he is afraid of battle, but I do not know whether the threat to Novae is as great as he claimed. He may be right, but I cannot say for certain."

Decius scrutinised my face for any signs of falsehood, then he said, "Valerianus did warn me that you are not a man who tells people what he thinks they want to hear. You tell the truth as you see it, he told me."

"I always try to do that, Sir."

He gave a sigh, "Well, we shall deal with Gallus once we have seen off Cniva."

Turning back to his son, he added, "At least we found Gallus' cavalry who were following the Goths. I will attach them to your group. That's another four hundred or so men."

"I will ensure they fight well," Etruscus promised.

Decius then raised his voice to allow all of the nearby officers to hear him.

"Our scouts report that Nicopolis has already fallen. The Goths have ransacked the city, taking plunder and captives, and they are now preparing to move even deeper into Roman lands. But we are going to destroy them!"

This brought a loud cheer from the men, a cheer which spread through the whole of Etruscus' column.

Decius went on, "Cniva has around fifty thousand horsemen, but many of them will be drunk or tired. We have nearly thirty thousand, plus nearly three thousand infantry. And we are Romans! We have nothing to fear. We have defeated the Goths before, and we shall do so again! Follow me now, and let us ride to victory!"

Chapter 8
Nicopolis

"They'll need to get a move on," Aoric observed as Decius and his aides rode along the length of the army's front to allow the Emperor to deliver his speech to every soldier.

When he saw my puzzled look, he jerked his head, indicating the western horizon.

"There are only a couple of hours of daylight left," he pointed out.

Cimber, who seemed to have been appointed to keep an eye on us, growled, "That will be long enough."

Aoric's expression suggested he doubted the officer's claim, but he refrained from arguing with our escort.

At last, the trumpets blared, the banners and standards were held high, and the army advanced, the cavalry leading the way. They rode in two groups, moving out on either flank and climbing the hills which barred our route. The infantry set off after them, again splitting into two main groups to avoid marching through a dense woodland which lay immediately ahead of them. Only one group of around five hundred soldiers marched directly towards the forest.

"We are to stay with the reserve," Cimber informed us as he set off after this smaller detachment.

As our horses walked slowly behind the infantry, I took the chance to watch what the bulk of the army was doing. Etruscus' wing was on the left, while a larger group of horsemen, led by the Emperor himself, circled to the right. They all looked very formidable and confident as they surged up the slopes towards Decius' promised victory. Soon, though, they were out of sight because we had reached the edges of the woodland. The branches hung so low that we found it easier to dismount and lead our horses through the trees, plodding along behind the armoured soldiers who ploughed a path ahead of us to the accompaniment of muttered cursing.

The hill was not very steep, but the going was uneven and difficult, and it was a relief when we finally emerged from the woodland half way down the further side of the hills.

We mounted again, allowing us to see over the heads of the army's reserve Cohort which was being shoved back into a semblance of order by the barking shouts of the Centurions.

"Nicopolis is burning," Cimber said grimly.

He was right. Looking down into the valley ahead of us, we could see that the town, which lay at a confluence of two rivers, looked desolate and forlorn, wisps of smoke still rising to show where buildings still burned. Many of the roofs had caved in, and the gates in the city walls had been smashed open, left lying on the ground. Broken ladders lay scattered around the perimeter, showing where the Goths had swarmed over the walls.

"The place looks empty," I remarked, feeling the horror of what had happened grip my stomach.

Aoric nodded, "They'll have taken younger women and children as slaves, but most of the rest will have been killed."

"But where are the Goths?" I wondered.

Cimber pointed off to the right, towards a wide plain of fields and meadows. The crops had been trampled, and any livestock which might have grazed there had been led away by the victorious Goths. The remnants of hundreds of camp fires marked out where the besieging army had camped, the small dots of dark ash giving the surrounding land the appearance that it was suffering from plague. A larger mound of ash and burnt wood marked the site of a large funeral pyre where I guessed the Goths had cremated their fallen.

"There!" Cimber said, pointing off to the south-west.

The sun was low in the sky now, the light beginning to turn, but its fading brightness shone on the hills beyond the devastated city. We could make out the Emperor leading his huge cavalry force into a charge. The riders were arranged in three groups, the leading men ready to engage, the others acting as a second and third wave who could quickly add their support.

The Roman infantry had no chance of catching up with the horsemen, but most of them were now hurrying down the slope towards the city, but Cimber, Aoric and I remained high on the slope to watch the fighting. The distance was too great for us to make out much detail, but it seemed that Decius had spotted the rearguard of Cniva's army which was marching south-west into a range of high, steep mountains.

"The rest of Cniva's army is already well on its way," Aoric told me. "That lot will turn and run before long. And most of them will get away because it will soon be too dark to pursue them."

Despite Cimber's earlier confidence, Aoric was soon proved right. We could hear the distant sounds of conflict, but the dust thrown up by so many horses created a swirling cloud over the struggle, making it impossible to discern any details. The only clue to what was happening were the strident calls of the trumpets, but even those faint sounds meant nothing to me, and if Cimber could follow the action, he kept the knowledge to himself.

The entire battle was opening out before us now. More Roman cavalry galloped across the plain, riding to the Emperor's aid, while the foot soldiers formed into a defensive line between the smouldering city and the distant battle, ready to provide a place of safety should things go wrong.

Aoric said to Cimber, "You should send some troops into the city as well. Cniva might have left some of his army there in hiding, just waiting for you to follow the main column."

Cimber frowned, his brown eyes darting from the broken city gate to the ranks of the foot soldiers who were facing the cavalry battle, leaving their backs to Nicopolis. If the Goths had left part of their army in the ruined city, they could easily stream out and attack the infantry from the rear.

After a moment's reflection, Cimber said, "Wait here."

He set his horse into a canter, riding up to the commander of the reserve Cohort. They exchanged a few words, with Cimber pointing back towards the city. Moments later, orders were shouted, the soldiers about-faced, and they hurried towards the open gates of Nicopolis.

Cimber returned to us, his face grim.

"Do you want to go into the city?" he asked.

I shook my head.

"I've seen death and destruction before," I told him. "I have no wish to see any more. And if Cniva has left a strong force there, I'd rather we had a head start to get away."

Cimber gave me a disparaging look, clearly not approving of my apparent cowardice, but I did not care. I had not wanted to be here, and I had no wish to find myself in the middle of a desperate battle. Watching from a distance was as close as I wished to be.

So we waited. There were no sounds of fighting from within the city, and the cavalry soon returned from the far side of the valley, riding slowly to spare their mounts. Orders soon came to establish a camp for the night. Sentries were posted, the soldiers grabbed their entrenching tools, and the cavalry took their horses towards the river to find water and forage.

Herennius Etruscus led his five thousand riders, but he swerved aside to greet us as he passed. His young face was flushed with excitement, and he was still breathing in rapid gasps. He reined in, clapping a hand to his horse's neck as he grinned at us.

"We chased them off!" he declared proudly. "They didn't dare stand against us. My father has sent some scouts to keep track of them, but it looks as if Cniva has decided to hide in the mountains rather than face us."

Turning to Cimber, he said, "I hear you ordered the reserve into the city?"

Cimber nodded, "I wanted to be sure that the Goths had not left an ambushing force behind."

Etruscus nodded approvingly, asking, "And had they?"

"Apparently not, Augustus. But I deemed it right to check."

"Quite right!" Etruscus said. "Now, let us join my father for our evening meal."

He dismounted, passing the reins of his horse to an aide who led it away to be tended. More aides offered us the same, so we left our horses in their care and followed Etruscus to where a large fire had been lit in the centre of the sprawling camp.

"No tents for us tonight!" Etruscus announced cheerfully. "We travel light and fast. There's no baggage train to slow us down."

He was obviously proud of this military innovation, but one of the consequences was that there was little food to eat. The Emperor could normally rely on finding food and shelter at any Roman town or city, but Nicopolis had been sacked, the Goths having taken away every scrap of food worth carrying.

The Emperor himself relayed this information when we joined him and a host of his officers beside the blazing bonfire.

"I'm told there are bodies everywhere," he informed us. "The Goths were merciless. Most buildings were set on fire, and any people who were spared have apparently been taken as captives."

I glanced at Aoric who gave me a "I told you so" look in response. I had thought he might be annoyed that Cimber had claimed my friend's idea as his own, but Aoric kept any such thoughts to himself. Cimber, for his part, seemed to have forgotten the incident entirely.

"You defeated Cniva's rearguard, Augustus?" he asked Decius.

"We did," the Emperor nodded. "But we were too late to catch his main force. They must already be high in the mountain passes."

"So he is heading deeper into our territory?" Cimber frowned.

"He can reach Philippopolis once he crosses the mountains," Decius confirmed. "We received messages some days ago that another force of Goths was already heading towards that city. Now Cniva will join them."

Etruscus declared, "Good! That means they will be together, and we can destroy their entire army."

His confidence was infectious, although I noticed that some of the older officers did not seem to share his optimism. Even so, none of them spoke up to disagree.

The Emperor went on, "Titus Julius Priscus, Governor of Thrace, is in Philippopolis. I have sent a rider to warn him of Cniva's approach, and to tell him that we are on the way to relieve him. He has a decent enough garrison in Philippopolis, so I have instructed him to hold out until we reach him. That way, if we time it right, we can catch Cniva between our army and the city."

I was not so sure about that. Any messenger heading for Philippopolis would need to travel by a long and circuitous route to avoid stumbling into Cniva's army, and would then need to get past the other force of Goths who were already on their way to the city.

There was, though, another part of what the Emperor had said which caused me to frown.

I nudged Cimber, leaning in to whisper a question.

"Julius Priscus is Governor of Thrace?" I asked. "The brother of the last Emperor?"

Cimber smiled at my confusion. Our late and unlamented Emperor, Julius Philippus, had appointed his brother, Julius Priscus, to rule the eastern empire. Normally, any such relative would be executed as soon as a new Emperor had taken power.

Cimber told me, "You are thinking of Gaius Julius Priscus. The Governor of Thrace is Titus Julius Priscus. They may share a name, but they are not related at all."

"And what happened to Gaius Julius Priscus?" I asked.

Cimber merely shrugged, "What do you think?"

Which was answer enough.

There was no wine, so we drank water which had been fetched from the river. A few scraps of food were distributed, but it fell far short of a banquet. Cold sausage and hard cheese, supplemented by a few chopped olives formed our evening meal.

"We share the soldiers' rations," the Emperor told us as he tucked in. "The legionaries have some mule trains, but they cannot carry enough to feed the entire army as I would wish."

Then, giving a wry grin, he added, "I suspect our horses will be more satisfied with their grazing than we are with this, but that cannot be helped. Tomorrow, we will ride into the mountains where rations will be even more scarce. But we must reach Philippopolis before Cniva is able to capture it."

He and his officers discussed their plans, deciding to send the infantry ahead of the cavalry. The going would be tough on the horses, and the infantry could more easily defend themselves in the high, narrow passes of the mountains.

"We will follow the Goths, and we will destroy them!" Decius assured us. "Now, gentlemen, I suggest we catch as much sleep as we can. We set off at dawn."

So, like the rest of the army, Aoric and I lay down on the hard earth, wrapped in our cloaks, beside a camp fire.

Before trying to sleep, I asked the young Goth, "What do you think? Is Decius right about Cniva's intentions?"

Aoric thought for a moment before saying, "He's right about Cniva wanting to sack another city. He came for plunder, and Philippopolis is supposed to be a major city, isn't it?"

"So I believe. I've never been there."

"If it's home to a provincial Governor, it's an important place," Aoric pointed out.

"So it's a question of whether we can get there in time to stop him," I remarked.

Aoric scoffed, "No, it's a question of what traps he will lay to prevent us catching him."

"You think he'll try to ambush us?" I asked.

"Probably. I would if I was him. I told you, he's a cunning devil."

"We should warn the Emperor," I decided.

Aoric shrugged, "Go ahead. But my last warning turned out to be wrong, so he may not believe you."

"Maybe I should warn him anyway," I said.

"Suit yourself," Aoric replied disinterestedly. "But don't be surprised if he takes offence. You Romans are supposed to be professional soldiers. If the Emperor has any talent as a commander, he'll send out scouts ahead of his march to locate any traps. Then it's simply a matter of avoiding or overcoming them."

"Simply?" I replied.

"No," Aoric admitted. "Nothing is simple where Cniva is concerned."

I recalled my meeting with the King of the Goths, and I feared that Aoric was right. But there was nothing for it. One Roman city had already been destroyed, and another was under threat. Whatever traps Cniva had in mind, Emperor Decius had no option but to follow him into the mountains.

Chapter 9
Refugees

We rose before dawn, hurriedly ate a sparse breakfast, then prepared to leave. My whole body ached from the uncomfortable night's sleep, and I felt a little guilty when I saw the Emperor acting as if he'd slept in a comfortable bed. He was about the same age as me, yet he appeared to be immune to the aches and pains which plagued me that morning.

Or perhaps it was that my desire to leave the army was making me focus on every negative aspect of our trials.

Our horses were brought to us, and we mounted up. The legionaries were already on the march as the first hints of dawn crept over the eastern horizon, casting dim light on the ramparts of the mountain range we needed to cross.

"Our scouts are already climbing the hills," Cimber informed us. "Early indications are that the Goths have hurried on. They are obviously desperate to reach Philippopolis before we can catch them."

I said, "From what little I know of Cniva, I think we should be wary of ambush in the mountains."

The Tribune gave me yet another sour look, clearly resenting any intervention from a civilian.

"We know our job," he told me. "Now, let's get moving."

It was a tough morning under a hot sun. We climbed the foothills, then rose higher and higher into the mountains. Some were rounded and relatively gentle if steep, but others were rocky crags, and all had patches of forest or scrub scattered indiscriminately across their slopes. Patches of snow glistened on the highest peaks, and tiny streams of water trickled their way down to join the rivers in the valley behind us.

In places, we were forced to dismount because the path was so steep, but I was grateful that I was able to ride for most of the way. The path ahead was easy enough to follow because tens of thousands of Goths had already passed this way, and we could see from some of the ruts in the ground where their heavily-laden wagons had been hauled over the rough terrain.

"Their transport wagons will slow them down," Cimber declared confidently.

Not that we were travelling all that quickly. Roman legionaries could march at a fast pace on level ground or on one of our famous roads, but climbing steep slopes over uneven terrain while wearing full armour and carrying weapons was hard going. Hour after hour, they climbed, and hour after hour, the mounted contingent followed.

The foot soldiers did not stop for rest or food. Cold sausages, the staple of a march, were eaten on the go. Even those of us on horseback ate in the saddle whenever we made an occasional halt to allow our mounts to crop the sparse grass which had already been grazed by the Goths' horses.

On and on we pressed, climbing ever higher. It would have been an exhilarating journey with spectacular scenery had it not been for the urgency and purpose of our march. For everyone in the army, it was a hard slog.

As nightfall approached, word filtered back down the long column that the army would make camp in a high pass where there was room to accommodate all of our men and horses. Since Aoric and I, with Cimber constantly beside us, were near the rear of the long column, it was growing dark by the time we reached the camp site.

Fires had been lit, and there were even a few tents which had been carried on the backs of the legions' mules. Unlike most Roman marching camps, though, there was no defensive ditch, nor was there enough space to lay out the camp in the normal way. Men and horses simply crowded in wherever they could. Some sort of perimeter was established through the use of small boulders or a couple of tiny streams which would provide water for both men and horses, and there was plenty of firewood available from the forested slopes on either side of the pass.

"It's going to be a cold night," Cimber informed us as he led us towards the Emperor's fire after our horses had been led away for the night. "At least there is plenty of wood we can burn to keep ourselves warm."

Aoric eyed the forests suspiciously.

"There could be more than firewood up there," he muttered.

"What?" I frowned.

He said, "Over fifty thousand Goths came this way. It's a good site for a camp, but they don't seem to have stopped here. I'm wondering why."

"They are in a hurry," I replied. "Maybe they didn't take the time to stop here because they knew we would catch up with them."

"Maybe," Aoric nodded, his face tight and pensive.

Once again, our evening meal was sparse, but at least the gruel had been heated over fires, providing some warmth for our bodies.

Under a sparkling carapace of stars, with a gibbous moon adding a spectral light to the scene, we lay down and shivered in our cloaks. If anything, the ground here was even more uncomfortable than it had been the previous night, and I found sleep difficult. I could hear the snores of some companions, and Cimber was definitely one of the sleeping men. Aoric, though, was also awake. I heard him moving, then saw his silhouette sit up.

He leaned over to me, saying softly, "I think we should find another spot."

"Why?" I grunted. "The whole place is likely to be as hard and uneven as it is here."

"But maybe a bit safer," he replied softly. "Come on."

He rose to his feet, reaching out a hand to help me up. Groggy from lack of sleep, I slung my satchel over my shoulder and, uncertain of my bearings in the dark, I followed him as he picked a meandering route away from the centre of the camp.

"Where are we going?" I asked him. "Knowing my luck, I'm likely to trip over something and break my ankle."

"Better that than being dead," Aoric replied.

"What's going on?" I asked him. "Have you seen or heard something?"

"No, I just have a bad feeling about this place. I told you, Cniva will set traps. This is as good a place as any for him to strike."

"You want to leave the camp?" I asked in astonishment.

"I'd like nothing more, but I think that would be an unwise move. The sentries aren't likely to let us pass. But I do want to be a bit further away from the Emperor. If Cniva attacks, the imperial standards will draw his men like moths to a flame."

We ended up a bit further up the high valley, finding a spot between a legion's mules and a large contingent of sleeping cavalrymen. It wasn't any more comfortable than our earlier spot, and the stink of the mules made it even less savoury.

"This will do," Aoric insisted.

I was too tired to argue, so I lay down and tried to make myself comfortable.

I stayed awake for a long time, part of my mind unable to rest in case Aoric's fears came true, but sheer exhaustion eventually allowed me to drift off into a dreamless sleep.

And then I was woken by the sound of wild screaming and bellowed war cries.

I think every man in the camp must have jerked awake, rolling hurriedly to his feet. I certainly did, blinking in confusion in the darkness.

"The Goths!" someone yelled. It may have been one of the sentries, but his shout was cut off, fading into a gargling cry of pain, and the Goths were already streaming into the camp, spears, axes and swords swinging to hack down anyone in their path.

I scrambled to gather up my satchel, then Aoric grabbed my arm. I noticed he had already drawn his sword, but he crouched low, dragging me towards the line of panicking mules.

"In amongst them!" he hissed at me as he used the flat of his blade to smack a couple of the braying beasts aside.

The mules were tethered to a long line which was pegged into the ground, and all of them were bucking and kicking, but Aoric leaned across one, speaking to reassure it, and created a narrow space where we could crouch in relative safety.

I peered out, seeing thousands upon thousands of warriors streaming into the camp. They must have been hiding high on the slopes, too far into the trees to be seen, and now they swarmed into the valley like a tidal wave of death.

The Roman defenders were confused and disorganised, caught totally unawares. The sentries who had patrolled the perimeter must have been swamped by the charging Goths, and most of the rest of the army had removed their armour for the night. Still, they grabbed swords, spears and shields, and battled frantically against the attack, but the entire camp was in chaos.

Aoric told me, "Stay down."

That was easier said than done, because the animals around us were lashing out with their hooves in their fear. Aoric, though, remained impressively calm. Gripping his sword tightly, he swept the blade down, cutting through the long rope to which the mules were tethered. The animals were snorting and bucking in panic, and now some of them were able to break free, while others remained tangled, their halter ropes still attached to the now severed line. The ones who managed to break free ran into the night, adding to the confusion, and scattering men as they stampeded into the camp.

I could not fathom what Aoric was planning, but the panicking animals created a buffer around us where few men dared venture. The Goths were interested in killing and plunder, so they dodged aside, swerving around the milling mules, and plunging deeper into the camp.

The fighting moved on as the Romans either died or retreated, and the press of Goths swarmed after them. Most of the fighting seemed to be behind us. The legionaries and Auxiliary foot soldiers were superbly disciplined, and they managed to form a block of shields and swords which deterred all but the fiercest of the Goths. Further back, though, the cavalry were unaccustomed to fighting on foot, and with thousands of Goths streaming in amongst them, all discipline had vanished. We could hear shouts, screams and the harsh clash of weapons ringing all along the high valley, and I was completely confused, not knowing which way to turn.

"Time to go!" Aoric told me.

"Where?"

Pointing vaguely to the west, he said, "That way is safest. The legionaries are falling back towards the Emperor's standard. Cniva's men will follow them, so that means we can go the other way. Come on."

I had no idea how he could tell which direction was safest because the entire valley was full of fighting men, but we slowly edged away from the closest combat, cutting more mules free as we moved among them.

"Wait a moment!" Aoric told me.

I saw him run his left palm down the blade of his sword, drawing blood. He grinned at me, then reached up to wipe his hand across my forehead.

"You don't look much like a Goth," he said. "So play the part of a wounded captive. Try not to say anything."

He grabbed me, then shoved me ahead of him, holding his sword in a threatening manner and cursing at me in Gothic to move my Roman arse. Stumbling, I hurried out of the camp, guided by Aoric's bloody hand pushing me in the back.

I could scarcely believe what we were doing, but it seemed to be working. Men were still running past on all sides, but nobody seemed to be paying much attention to us.

Then, as I staggered across a hummock in the ground, four dark shapes appeared ahead of us, warriors hurrying to join the fight.

I stopped in fright, but Aoric called out in Gothic, "This one's mine, lads. There are plenty more for you down there, though."

The shadowy Goths moved on, paying me scant attention, and Aoric gave me another shove.

"Keep moving, Roman scum."

After only a few more steps, we were among the trees, but Aoric pushed me up the slope a little further before we stopped and turned to look back.

The sounds of desperate combat still echoed from the eastern end of the valley, and the pale moonlight illuminated a scene of frantic, chaotic battle, but we seemed to be alone. Cautiously, Aoric edged back towards the fringes of the woodland. He returned a moment later, looking grim.

"The sun is starting to rise," he informed me. "From the looks of things, the Romans are trying to get back down the pass to the east. The legions are battling their way back to the Emperor, and the cavalry are trying to get their horses organised, but I think escape is the only thing on their minds."

"So what do we do?" I asked.

"Trying to go east would mean passing through the bulk of both armies," he frowned. "We'd never make it."

He thought for a moment before continuing, "I suppose we could climb higher up the slope and wait it out, but we have no food or water, and I don't like our chances of surviving if we do that. Any passing Goth will wonder what we are doing there."

"Which leaves us with only one choice?" I guessed.

"We go west," he nodded.

We set off, with Aoric insisting on binding my wrists together with a scrap of cloth torn from my cloak. The bonds were loose enough for me to free myself quickly if need be, but he wanted me to keep playing the part of a prisoner. Then he led the way along the wooded slope, moving stealthily with his sword held at the ready.

Daylight gradually began to filter down through the interlocking branches of the fir trees. This made the going easier, but it also revealed where the Gothic warriors had passed, leaving a trail of trampled earth and broken twigs in their wake, along with scraps of cloth which had snagged on branches.

We moved in silence, Aoric concentrating on the way ahead, me listening to the muffled and fading sounds of fighting from behind us.

After what seemed an age but was probably only a few minutes, we reached the edge of the forest where we stopped to look out to where the land fell away to the west. There were more clumps of trees some way ahead of us, potential hiding places on either side of the wide pass which led to the far side of the mountains.

And there were more Goths.

We crouched low to watch several thousand mounted men canter up the pass towards the scene of the battle.

"That looks like Cniva himself," Aoric murmured. "He must have been waiting here to block any attempt to break out of the pass, but he'll know by now that the Romans are fleeing back the way they came."

I tried to make out the King of the Goths, but all of the riders looked much like one another to me. We waited until they had passed us, then we ventured out into open terrain, feeling horribly exposed.

Aoric, though, remained calm and self-assured despite our precarious situation.

"Let's go down onto the main path," he decided. "We don't want to be seen skulking along the ridge."

"You're going to keep trying to bluff our way out?" I asked.

"It's worked so far," he nodded. "And most of the Goths are behind us now."

We tramped on for more than a mile. My face was caked in dried blood, and Aoric's left hand was also smeared. He'd wiped it on his tunic, so we both looked as if we had been in a fight, but the going was relatively easy until Aoric suddenly slowed down.

"More of them!" he hissed in warning.

There were three of them, sitting by the side of the path, with three horses tied to a patch of thorny bushes. As soon as they saw us, they rose to their feet, doing their best to appear alert.

"What are they doing here?" I asked Aoric from the side of my mouth.

"Possibly acting as picquets," he replied. "Or, more likely, avoiding the fighting and waiting to join in when it's time to plunder the dead."

When I shot him a quizzical look, he shrugged, "There are cowards and shirkers in every army."

The men stood close together, one holding a spear, the tip glinting in the early morning sunlight as he held the weapon upright. The other two had swords, but they kept them in their scabbards. I did not like the look of any of them. They may have had horses, but they were not dressed in chainmail armour, nor did they wear much in the way of jewellery. Leather tunics and thick leggings covered their bodies, and their long hair was unkempt and tangled.

"Scouts, or more likely hangers-on," Aoric murmured softly.

The men stepped down to block the path, confident that their greater number would overawe us. The man with the spear stood to the right, now lowering the point of the weapon to aim it at us.

Aoric kept moving, but indicated that I should remain a step or two behind him.

"Greetings, brothers!" he called in Gothic. "You're missing out on a lot of good plunder up there."

"You don't look as if you've got much to show for it," the man in the centre replied. He was brawnier than his two companions, and had a deep scar on his right cheek, a memento of a previous fight.

Aoric grinned cheerfully as he kept walking towards them. He had his sword in his right hand, but held it casually as he walked, the blade pointing downwards.

"I've got a rich prisoner!" he announced proudly. "I'm going to ransom him."

"He doesn't look rich to me," the leader of the three scowled, his eyes scanning me up and down.

"He's got a load of gold coins in his bag," Aoric informed them.

At this, their interest picked up.

"Then you won't mind paying a toll to pass," the leader grinned wickedly.

Aoric slowed down as if in thought, turning his head back to me. The look he gave me was a warning of some sort.

"Bring me your satchel," he ordered.

I knew he was bluffing. My coins were either in my purse or hidden away in secret compartments on the inner side of my thick, leather belt. The satchel contained nothing but spare clothing.

"Hurry up, Roman!" Aoric snarled convincingly.

With my bound hands, I fumbled to get my bag off, trying to lift the strap over my head while I stepped tentatively towards them. The three Goths inched closer, and then Aoric swung on them with astonishing speed. Pivoting on one foot, he whirled around, his sword taking the leader in the neck, gouging deep and releasing a fountain of blood. The Goth's eyes were wide in mute horror, but Aoric had reversed his blow before either of the others could react. He smashed his long blade into the left arm of the spearman who let out a cry of agony as Aoric wrenched the blade free. Then Aoric lashed out with one foot, kicking the spear out of the wounded man's faltering grip before spinning to face the third man.

The last Goth had a sword, but instead of fighting, he turned and tried to run for his horse. Aoric darted after him, stabbing forwards to take him in the small of the back before he had covered half a dozen paces. The Goth let out a cry of agony as he arched his back before collapsing onto the ground. Without compunction, Aoric slashed down, almost severing the man's head.

The spearman was kneeling on the ground, his right hand clamped over his wounded upper arm, but the blood was pouring out between his fingers. His face was deathly pale, and he was muttering some sort of prayer. As Aoric stepped up to him, he looked up, appeal in his eyes, but Aoric had no mercy. He slashed down, driving the edge of his blade into the man's skull, burying it deep into bone and brain. He had to use both hands to wrench it free, then he went to make sure that his first victim was dead. Satisfied, he wiped his sword clean on the fallen leader's cloak, sheathed it, and then quickly searched the men's belt pouches.

"Not much here," he said as he shoved a handful of copper and silver coins into his own purse. "But the horses have bags which hopefully contain some food. Let's take a couple of them and get out of here."

I stumbled over to the horses, casting horrified looks at the three dead men as I went.

"Are we just going to leave them?" I asked.

"I'm not taking the time to bury them," Aoric said. "But maybe we should drag them into the bushes."

So we hauled the dead men out of sight, threw the spear after them, then took all three horses and rode away.

Sweating with exertion and fear, I asked Aoric, "Where are we going? Cniva's baggage camp will be somewhere up ahead."

"We'll need to go round it," he agreed. "I'd prefer to go north, then head back to Novae, but maybe Trebonianus Gallus wouldn't be too pleased to see us again."

"I'd prefer to avoid him if possible," I agreed. "If the Emperor escapes from that trap, he'll be looking for someone to blame, and Gallus will be top of the list."

"We could try to head back towards Italia," Aoric suggested, "but the route to our north looks difficult. I don't know these mountains, but circling to the south might be easier. That looks like another pass going that way."

"That will take us deeper into Thrace," I said.

"Let's worry about our destination once we get clear of Cniva's army," Aoric asserted.

"All right," I nodded. "But the safest place we can be is inside a fortified town. Cniva's raiders are looting everywhere else."

"Do you know any fortified towns in Thrace?" he asked me.

"Only one. Philippopolis. But the Emperor said there is already a Gothic army besieging it."

Aoric frowned, "We'd still be safer inside a city with walls. Let's head south and see if we can find one."

Chapter 10
Seeking Sanctuary

From the far side of the main pass, Philippopolis was only around eighty Roman miles, but the route we were forced to take made it a much longer journey. We had no wish to run into Cniva's main camp, nor did we have any desire to encounter any of his roving patrols. Our bluff of pretending to be a Gothic warrior and his captive would not work while we were both riding stolen horses. As it turned out, the route Aoric had decided to follow was a difficult path, climbing high into the mountains and giving very little cover. It took us almost the entire day to cross the pass and then begin the descent to the far side, often needing to dismount and lead the horses in single file along narrow, treacherous and uneven paths.

We were fortunate that the horses held small sacks of provisions, although these turned out to be mostly mouldy cheese and stale bread. This was enough to stave off the worst pangs of hunger, but there was little for the horses to eat when we reached the highest sections of the rocky pass. The only saving grace was that there was plenty of water flowing down the hillsides in rivulets from the snow-capped peaks, although those same streams had eroded some sections of the track we were following, making the going even more difficult.

"At least there's not much chance of any of the Goths following us over this route," Aoric said with grim humour.

Despite the problems, by the time dusk arrived we were on a downward path, and the going became much easier. We stopped for the night on a patch of grass where the horses could graze, and we even risked a small fire to ward off the chill of the night air. It was another uncomfortable stop, but when morning came we realised that we had been lucky when we had chosen to cross the mountains by this difficult route. As we descended the last slopes, we discovered that our longer path had brought us out into the Thracian plain many miles to the east of where the main pass descended from the mountains.

Aoric spent some time staring westwards, but he could see no sign of Cniva's army.

"They're probably still looting the Emperor's camp," he decided.

"What about the other Gothic army that's supposed to be heading this way?" I asked anxiously.

"I don't see any signs of them so far," he shrugged. "Do you still want to make for Philippopolis? We could try heading for somewhere further away."

I had to overcome a moment of reluctance to force myself to say, "We need to warn Governor Julius Priscus that Cniva is coming. The messenger sent by Emperor Decius may not have got through."

"It's your choice," Aoric shrugged. "But it's a risk. The plain doesn't offer much in the way of hiding places."

"There's no help for that," I said. "But we must have covered nearly half the distance to Philippopolis. It surely won't take us long to get there."

Aoric advised, "It will be safer to stay off the direct route. We'll keep going south, then circle back once we are sure we have passed beyond Philippopolis."

Neither of us were confident that we would know when we would have ridden far enough, but we set off at as fast a pace as our tired horses could manage.

Out of the mountains, we encountered green and fertile land, and we soon found small villages and farmsteads dotted amongst orchards, vineyards, wheatfields and meadows. There was no sign of Gothic raiders, but nor was there any sign of the local inhabitants. Word of the approaching barbarians had, it seemed, forced them to abandon their homes.

We rode on, and eventually encountered a group of villagers who were hurrying along an ancient trackway. They had several carts, flocks of sheep and goats, and were carrying all their belongings in crude wagons or on their backs.

When they saw us, they looked terrified, but I called out to them in Greek, reassuring them that we meant them no harm.

They still regarded us warily, but we rode alongside them, and managed to engage one old man in conversation.

"The Goths are coming," he told us. "The Governor sent soldiers out to warn us. They said we needed to leave our homes."

He spat on the ground as he walked alongside one of the creaking, overloaded wagons from where two children peered nervously out at us while a young woman sat on the driving board, determinedly avoiding looking at us.

The old man informed us, "Most of us don't have much that the Goths can steal. But we decided to go south. If they take all our animals, we will starve."

"Are you going to Philippopolis?" I asked him.

Shaking his head, he snorted, "No! That's where the Goths will go, I'll wager. We're going as far south as we can. With luck, the Emperor will chase the barbarians away before too long. Then we can return home."

Aoric shot me an inquisitive look as he said, "Heading south might be a good idea."

I thought about it for a moment, then sighed, "But someone needs to warn the Governor about what happened."

At this, the old man also shot me a keen look.

"What has happened?" he asked. "You have news?"

Trying to appear unconcerned, I told him, "There was a battle in the mountains. The Goths attacked the Emperor's army."

He studied me intently for a moment, then asked, "And who won?"

"I honestly don't know," I replied. "We were cut off and had to flee."

The look he gave me suggested he thought we were deserters, so I added, "We are not soldiers."

"Of course you're not," he said in a tone which clearly indicated he did not believe me.

Changing the subject, I asked him, "How do we get to Philippopolis from here?"

"Keep heading south until you find the Hebrus river. Philippopolis is on the far side. Just head upstream and you'll find it."

"And how do we cross the river?" I asked him.

He gave a shrug.

"There's a bridge at Philippopolis. You might get there before the Goths do. But we're heading for a ferry downstream of the city. It's a lot further away, but I reckon it will be safer."

"Are there any other crossing places?" I asked him.

In response, he gave a shrug.

"Maybe," he said, unwilling to admit his ignorance.

I took a couple of *denarii* from my purse, passing them down to the old man.

"For your help," I told him. "I wish you luck."

His eyes held a more amiable look when he accepted the gift, and he said, "And to you."

Then we kicked our horses into a canter and rode on.

We found the river that afternoon. It was wide and deep, with no obvious fords or bridges, but we decided to attempt the crossing.

"Let's put it between us and the Goths," I resolved.

We had no rope to tether the horses together, so Aoric offered to lead two of the beasts rather than let one go. The animals were in poor shape, and we had frequently changed mounts, rotating between them so that one was always free of the burden of carrying us.

We stripped off our clothes, bundling them onto the horses' backs, then gingerly led the beasts into the water. The current was not too strong, but the water was bitterly cold, sending a shock of icy chill through our bodies. Before long, the water was so deep that I needed to swim rather than wade. I clung to the saddle of my mount, kicking my legs and encouraging it on. It battled across, soon wading out onto the far bank.

Aoric had a more difficult crossing, but he managed to keep a hold of both sets of reins, and soon we were hastily drying ourselves with our cloaks.

Aoric said, "There's still time to change your mind. If Philippopolis is Cniva's target, we'd be a lot safer heading south."

"But if he sends out raiding patrols, we could be caught in open ground," I argued. "Philippopolis has strong walls and a garrison. We've already seen that Cniva doesn't have siege weapons. I think we'd be safe enough in the city."

"The Goths stormed Nicopolis quickly enough," Aoric reminded me.

"But there was no garrison, and the walls were not strong," I countered.

Aoric regarded me with a frown, then sighed, "Upriver it is, then."

The city came into view a little later. Its walls surrounded a series of low hills which sat beside the river. Outside the walls was an amphitheatre and a circus, showing that the citizens here were able to enjoy the almost ubiquitous Roman pastimes of gladiatorial shows and chariot racing.

Before we reached the walls, though, we were met by a group of around twenty horsemen, all of them decked out in chainmail armour. They came straight for us, so we stopped our horses and waited as they spread out to encircle us.

"You don't look like Goths," one of them said with a friendly grin.

He was right. Aoric may have been raised as a Goth, but his hair was dark thanks to his Roman mother, while I had a complexion which denoted my Syrian ancestry.

"We've come from the Emperor," I replied. "We have news for the Governor, Titus Julius Priscus."

The rider continued to smile, but his appraising look did not miss anything.

"You don't look much like imperial messengers either," he said.

"We're not," I admitted. "But we were part of Herennius Etruscus' retinue."

"And you say you have a message for the Governor?" the cavalryman frowned.

"That's right," I nodded, affirming that I was not about to give him the news.

"Then we'll escort you back to the city," he said.

He raised his arm, moving it in a wheeling motion, and soon we were on our way again, this time surrounded by armed men.

"We heard there was a Gothic army coming this way," I said to the commander of the horsemen who had introduced himself simply as Camillus.

"There is," he nodded. "They are coming down from the north. The Governor took a force out to try to chase them off, but we were severely outnumbered, so we retreated into the city. Their scouts are all over the northern plain, and their main force isn't far away. If you'd arrived tomorrow, you might have had more trouble getting to us."

"You expect a siege, then?"

"Almost certainly," he confirmed. "But we've brought in provisions from the surrounding countryside, and we have enough men to man the walls, so we should be able to hold out until the Emperor gets here."

I merely nodded in response. Glancing at Aoric, I could tell that he was less than happy at us riding into yet another city which was about to be besieged, but we could not turn back now.

We rode into Philippopolis to find it very much on alert, with soldiers patrolling the walls, and the streets crammed with refugees from the surrounding area. Dismounting, we handed our horses over to the cavalrymen.

"Where can we leave them?" I asked Camillus.

"Our stables are just inside the south gate," he told me. "I'll have them taken there while you are conducting your business with the Governor."

He seemed a little put out by my refusal to reveal my message to him, but he sent one of his men to guide us up to the Governor's residence.

This was a fine building near the top of one of the hills, commanding a view over the eastern plain and the river as it flowed through the flat land. We faced the usual bureaucracy, but my insistence that I had an urgent message from the Emperor forced the various junior officers and aides into action. Aoric was obliged to surrender his sword, but before too long we were led into a large office to meet the Governor.

Titus Julius Priscus was a tired-looking man in his fifties, with speckles of grey scattered through his brown hair. My first impression of him was that he was nothing like the confident, intelligent Trebonianus Gallus. Priscus may have been a Roman Senator, but he looked anxious and a little flustered. Several of his aides and secretaries remained in the room when we were introduced to him.

"You bring a message from the Emperor?" he asked. "We have heard nothing for nearly a month. What is happening? The Goths are almost at our gates."

Not wishing to lie, I told him, "We were with the Emperor's army. He did send a rider with a message for you, but it seems the man did not get through."

"But you did!" he snapped irritably. "What word do you bring?"

"Bad news, I'm afraid," I said carefully. "The Goths you fought the other day are only a small part of the barbarian army. Cniva, King of the Goths, leads another force of around fifty thousand men. They have sacked Nicopolis and were crossing the mountains to come here. We believe Cniva plans to join up with the barbarians who are already here."

Priscus began chewing his lower lip, his eyes blinking nervously, and I could feel the tension among his assistants, many of whom were shuffling their feet or fidgeting nervously.

I went on, "The Emperor drove Cniva away from Nicopolis, and was pursuing him over the mountains, but the Goths sprang an ambush two nights ago. They attacked the Emperor's camp. My grandson and I managed to get away, but we were cut off from the rest of the army, so we came to warn you."

A horrified silence filled the room. I could tell that every man was full of questions, but they deferred to the Governor. Unfortunately, my news seemed to have struck Priscus dumb. It took a while for him to ask, "And what of the Emperor?"

"I do not know, Sir," I sighed. "He was still fighting the last we saw, and the army was attempting to retreat back down the pass towards Nicopolis."

"So you do not know the outcome of the battle?" he asked, seeming to take some hope from this.

"No, Sir. But I would guess that, at best, the Emperor has been driven back. We saw no sign of the Goths fleeing from the site of the battle. My guess is that they have spent time plundering the Emperor's camp or pursuing him back towards Nicopolis."

While Priscus frowned in indecision, one of the military men standing close to him snapped, "And why should we believe you? You are certainly not an imperial messenger. Who are you, and why were you with the Emperor's army?"

The man who fired this question at me was middle-aged, with a haughty demeanour and piercing blue eyes over a beak of a nose. He wore a red, military tunic, but bore no insignia to denote his rank. I guessed from his manner that he was probably a military Tribune, and the other soldiers certainly deferred to him. All of them were watching this confrontation with avid expectation.

Deciding it was time for some name-dropping, I said, "My name is Sextus Sempronius Scipio. I was sent to Novae by my patron, Publius Licinius Valerianus. There, I assisted the Governor, Trebonianus Gallus, and we later joined the retinue of Caesar Augustus Herennius Etruscus."

I fixed my eyes on Governor Priscus, and he, at least, seemed impressed by my prestigious contacts. The Tribune, though, was not at all overawed.

He said, "So you say. Do you have any proof?"

With a shrug, I delved into my satchel, pulling out the crumpled parchment which confirmed that I had taken the oath to worship the gods of Rome. The soldier took it, examined it for a moment, then handed it back.

"You could have stolen that," he sneered.

Aoric was growing impatient with this hostile reception, but I said to the officer, "Then either let us go or keep us under arrest until Cniva arrives. You'll see then that we are telling the truth."

"If you are spies," he growled, "I'll have you crucified."

I returned my attention to the Governor, saying, "Sir, I can assure you that Cniva will be here in a few days. Then you will see that I'm telling the truth."

Priscus was clearly caught in a welter of indecision, but one of his civilian aides leaned in to whisper in his ear, and he gave a reluctant nod.

"If you are who you claim to be, then we should thank you for this warning. But these are dangerous times, and I cannot take too many risks. You will be kept under guard until we learn the truth of your report."

He flicked a finger towards his guards.

"Take them away!"

Chapter 11
Philippopolis

The room we were taken to was clearly a guest bedroom. There was only one bed, but it was big enough for two, and the mattress was soft and comfortable. The furnishings were of high quality although not extravagant, and we even had a window which looked out onto a central garden which had an elegant fountain at its centre.

Aoric said, "We can easily climb out the window and drop down to the roof of the colonnade which runs around the garden. From there, we can get down to the ground. And then it shouldn't be too hard to find our way out of the house."

"Why bother?" I said. "I don't want any trouble, and it would be nice to sleep in a proper bed for a change. I ache all over."

He sighed, "And they've still got my sword."

"You'll get it back once they see we are telling the truth."

"That Governor fellow doesn't fill me with confidence," he said. "He almost makes me miss Trebonianus Gallus."

I lay on the bed, stretching out and relaxing for the first time in several days, but Aoric had not finished complaining.

"We should have kept going south," he grumbled. "It's not as if they are going to do anything now that you've warned them."

"You're probably right," I conceded. "I'm sorry. But I didn't want to run away completely. Coming here and telling them what happened was the right thing to do."

"That depends on your point of view," Aoric muttered. "Getting killed for the sake of people who don't believe you doesn't seem very right to me."

"It's done now," I yawned. "And if the worst comes to the worst, we can use that bluff of me being your prisoner again."

He subsided into silence, still gazing out of the window as if wishing we could grow wings and fly away.

After a while, the door to our room was opened. We knew there was a guard outside, but he moved aside to allow a slave girl to enter. She was carrying a tray of food and drink which she set on the small table at the side of the room. Then she bustled out without a word, while another man stepped in through the door. He wore a long robe of pale blue and cream, the folds pleated in a rather old-fashioned Greek style. He was around thirty years old, with mousey hair and a short beard.

Closing the door, he indicated the tray of food.

"I thought you would like some refreshments. And I also felt I ought to talk to you."

Aoric walked over to the tray, studying the food and then pouring two cups of dark wine. He handed one to the newcomer.

"You drink first," he said brusquely.

The robed man gave a resigned smile as he accepted the cup. Without hesitation, he took a large swallow of the wine.

"The Governor's hospitality ought not to be questioned," he said reprovingly as he handed the goblet back to Aoric.

I offered, "I'm sorry. But we've had a very difficult time recently, and it is difficult to know who to trust."

The man gave a nod of understanding, then continued speaking while Aoric did his best to appear disinterested in what he had to say.

"My name is Cleitus," the robed man informed us. "I'm one of the Governor's freedmen. The Governor wants you to know that he's sorry about the need to keep you under guard."

I took a cup from Aoric, sniffed the wine, then drank. It was not bad at all.

Turning my attention to Cleitus, I asked, "But he's scared of his military advisers, so he needs to appear strong? Is that it?"

A crooked smile lit up the freedman's face as he grinned, "Yes, Quirinius Abundus, the senior Tribune, is quite a formidable character. He does not like you at all, but please don't take it too personally. He doesn't really like anyone very much, and he certainly doesn't like being in Philippopolis."

"Why not?" I asked.

"Because he's an unpleasant and rather odious man," Cleitus chuckled. "Do you know much about the history of this city?"

The sudden change of topic surprised me, but I admitted, "Nothing at all."

Still smiling, Cleitus pulled out a three-legged stool from beneath the table, then sat down before beginning his account.

He explained, "It is said that the city was founded many centuries ago by King Philip the Second of Macedonia."

"The father of Alexander the Great?"

"That is correct. Philip was, of course, a mighty king and a military genius in his own right. He has been rather overshadowed by his more famous son, but Alexander could never have succeeded without learning from his father."

I smiled, "Would I be correct in assuming that you are a Macedonian yourself?"

Cleitus gave a proud nod as he said, "Yes, I have that honour. That is partly why Governor Priscus brought me with him when he was appointed Governor of Thrace."

I picked some olives from the plate, waving a hand to invite him to continue his story.

He informed us, "It is said that, when Philip founded this city, he gave it his own name, but he populated it by sending all the thieves, beggars, cripples, prostitutes, fraudsters and other undesirables he could find."

I grinned, "That's an odd thing to do in a city you've just named after yourself. I suspect it's more legend than fact."

Cleitus laughed, "Oh, the locals take quite a pride in the story. I doubt that it's true, although you never know. But Quirinius Abundus, our esteemed garrison commander, believes it implicitly, and holds the opinion that the current population are little better than their legendary ancestors."

I asked him, "But the city has a strong garrison, doesn't it? The Emperor seemed confident you could withstand a siege."

At this, Cleitus looked less cheerful as he said, "There are three Cohorts from *Legio V Macedonica*, and another from *Legio I Adiutrix*. And there are also around two hundred cavalry. In addition, there are a couple of thousand Auxiliary troops, but Quirinius Abundus does not trust them since many of the men are themselves Goths who were recruited a few years ago. Abundus does not believe he can rely on them, and I fear he may be right."

I caught Aoric giving me a dark look, but he had the good grace not to say aloud that he had warned me that coming here was a bad idea.

Feeling dismayed, I asked Cleitus, "So there are barely two thousand reliable troops to defend the entire city?"

"I'm afraid so," Cleitus nodded. "Of course, many of the citizens have volunteered to fight as well, although they are untrained and poorly equipped."

Attempting to sound confident, he said, "But were the Goths not driven off from Novae? The garrison there was greatly outnumbered, but they resisted."

"That's true enough," I nodded.

"And the river will hamper the enemy," Cleitus went on. "They will need to cross it in great numbers if they wish to attack our walls. Do they have siege engines?"

"Not that we know of," I admitted.

"Then there is no reason why we should not hold them off until help arrives."

That, of course, was the big problem. Would any help arrive? Perhaps Emperor Messius Decius was already dead, and his army destroyed. If that were true, then only the garrison of Novae under the command of Trebonianus Gallus could send any aid, and Gallus had made it plain that he was not prepared to risk facing Cniva in open battle.

Philippopolis, it seemed to me, was on its own.

Cleitus returned that evening, bringing more food and more news.

"The Goths have encamped on the northern bank of the river," he told us. "So far, they have made no attempt to attack."

"How many of them?" I asked him.

"Quirinius Abundus says there are around eighteen thousand of them."

"So that's the smaller army the Governor faced a few days ago."

Aoric muttered, "And lost."

Cleitus shrugged, "They are staying well out of range of our artillery. Not that we have many catapults, but Abundus has archers ready to shoot at anyone who gets too close."

He left us with a promise to return in the morning, and also to ask the Governor if we could be permitted to visit a bath house.

"I'll see what I can do for you," he smiled.

The following morning, after I had enjoyed my best sleep in days, he returned with our breakfast and an invitation to accompany him on a visit to a bath house. We accepted without hesitation, although our excursion was rather spoiled by the presence of four armed guards who escorted us through the busy streets but, in fairness, soldiers were very much in evidence everywhere we looked. Quirinius Abundus, it seemed, wanted his men out on patrol to help maintain public order. Philippopolis may have been much like any other city, with the usual mix of people, but it was currently suffering from the influx of many refugees from the countryside, and feelings were running high. Our guards may have been there to keep an eye on us, but their presence did mean we were able to traverse the city without incident.

It was, though, a slow walk because of the crowds. Not only were the citizens of Philippopolis trying to go about their daily lives, the huge influx of refugees from the countryside meant that every street was crammed with people. Some had obviously slept outdoors, their crude blankets and sparse belongings bundled on the pavements. There was also the usual sprinkling of paupers and cripples who were begging for money, mostly without success because fear of the Goths had made everyone wary.

Even when we reached a small square, we were delayed because a couple of entertainers were putting on a show for the locals. A middle-aged man was juggling several brightly coloured balls, talking and joking while he tossed them high in the air. Beside him, a girl who appeared to be in her early teens, was dressed in a two-piece outfit which showed off her bare arms, legs, belly and back. With her long, dark hair tied in a ponytail, she was performing somersaults and handstands, attracting some applause and more than a few lewd remarks from the audience. She ignored them, moving to pick up a small sack which she held open, allowing the juggler to throw the coloured balls in high arcs, each of them falling into the open neck of the sack. It was quite an impressive feat, but the pair were not done yet.

Chatting amiably to the crowd, the man now delved in another sack, drawing out three long, double-edged knives and three apples.

"I'd like to share these," he told his audience, "but there are so many of you, I'll need to chop them into smaller pieces."

As he spoke, he began juggling again, alternately throwing knives and apples until they all spun in the air in front of him. This was impressive enough, but he then threw one of the knives to the girl who caught it deftly by the handle, bringing gasps of admiration from the spectators. The second and third knives followed, and she caught each one, holding two in her left hand, the other gripped by the blade in her right fist.

The man continued to juggle the pieces of fruit, but then he threw one of the apples high in the air, arcing towards the girl, and she flung the knife, splitting the apple in mid-air, then repeating the exercise with astonishing speed as the man threw the other apples towards her.

This was a dangerous stunt for the audience, but the man moved quickly to catch the daggers as they tumbled towards the cobbles. Immediately, he began juggling again, while the girl produced a small clay pot which she held out as she walked around the watching crowd. Some dropped coppers into the pot, while others simply turned away. When she came towards us, I dropped a couple of silver *denarii* into the offered pot.

"That was very impressive," I told her.

She smiled, but it was a wary expression, and her eyes showed no friendliness. Given some of the comments made by a few members of the audience, I supposed she was not inclined to engage in friendly conversation with anyone. She moved on, and the crowd began to disperse, allowing us to pass.

Cleitus murmured, "She probably earns more by offering herself to customers at night."

I said nothing. In Roman society, street entertainers, like actors, were considered to occupy the same social class as thieves and prostitutes. It was often an unfair comparison, but I knew it was also accurate in some cases.

Moving on through the busy streets, Cleitus led us to the city's most prestigious bath house, and I was grateful for the chance to have the ingrained dirt of several days scraped away by the slave attendants. I scrubbed my hair, luxuriated in the warm water, and I felt greatly refreshed after our wash, a shave and a change of clothes.

The trip also allowed me to engage Cleitus in more conversation, and he revealed that he had been sold into slavery by his mother who, after the death of his father, could not afford to feed all of her children.

"I ended up in Rome," he told us. "I was twelve years old at the time, and amazed by the sights of that great city. I was bought by Julius Priscus' *major domo*, and I worked in the kitchens for a few years. But I was also taught to read and write because Julius Priscus wanted his slaves to be educated. I displayed some talent, and soon I became one of his personal scribes. After a few years, he was gracious enough to grant me my freedom."

With a grin, he added, "And now I am back in Thrace, not far from my original homeland, although I will admit that the circumstances could have been better."

Cleitus was a friendly, cheerful companion although Aoric did not appear to appreciate his company.

"Compared to some, he's had a comfortable life," the young Goth grumbled when we were back in our room. "But I don't understand his way of thinking. He's grateful to Rome for giving him freedom when it was Rome who enslaved him in the first place."

"He seems a decent enough chap, though," I said.

"He's soft," Aoric stated, delivering the worst judgement a Goth could give.

We spent another dull day in that room, with nothing to do except eat, drink and rest, but Cleitus returned the following morning with an air of excitement.

"I expect you will be set free before long," he told us. "More Goths have been sighted. Some have crossed the river and are approaching from the east. Others are joining the ones who are already camped to the north."

"Cniva," I murmured. "So he did drive the Emperor away."

By evening, it was clear that a massive Gothic army was moving to surround the city, and Cleitus brought word that Governor Julius Priscus had agreed that we had been telling the truth.

"You are free to do as you wish," Cleitus told us.

"But we can't leave," Aoric said sullenly.

"I'm afraid not," Cleitus sighed. "Not unless you want to fight your way through the Goths. Besides, Quirinius Abundus has barred all the gates and set his men on the walls."

Aoric asked, "Can I get my sword back?"

"Of course!" Cleitus agreed. "Any man who can wield a sword is valuable now."

I said, "I'm too old to fight. But I'd be happy to help in any other way I can."

"I'm sure the Governor will appreciate your offer," Cleitus nodded cheerfully. "I shall inform him."

Once we were alone again, Aoric hissed, "I'm not going to fight my own people!"

"I know," I told him. "You can just stay with me. You're supposed to be my grandson, after all. But we may as well stay close to the Governor. If nothing else, it will mean we'll be fed and have a roof over our heads. If we go out into the city, who knows where we might end up."

Aoric was less than pleased with this suggestion, but he went along with it for my sake. The Governor, clearly remembering my claims to acquaintance with powerful people, invited me to his next council of war, and Aoric accompanied me, now wearing his long sword at his hip.

The red-cloaked Tribune, Quirinius Abundus, scowled when he saw us, and he pointedly looked at Aoric's sword.

"Do you know how to use that?" he asked, his voice acerbic.

"Yes," Aoric nodded.

Before the Tribune could find an excuse to have Aoric posted to one of his Auxiliary units, I hurriedly put in, "Auricus is my grandson. He was appointed by Licinius Valerianus to act as my personal guard while I was on this mission."

It was a safe enough lie since none of them could contact Valerianus to check, and Abundus let the matter drop. He had, after all, plenty of other things to worry about.

One thing he did not do was acknowledge that we had been telling the truth about the imminent arrival of a large army of Goths. He accepted their presence as a fact, but he was not prepared to publicly admit to his earlier error.

Addressing the assembly of officers and aides, he said briskly, "I estimate that there are now over eighty thousand Goths outside our walls. It is hard to tell, but I believe most of them will be warriors."

"Can we hold against such numbers?" the Governor asked anxiously. His face was pale, and he looked as if he had barely slept, lines of weary strain visible around his eyes.

"We must!" Abundus responded sharply, offering no deference to the Governor's rank.

"But if the Emperor has been defeated …" Priscus went on lamely, his voice trailing away.

"Then our task is to hold on long enough for him to gather his forces again," Abundus stated in true Roman fashion.

The Tribune went on, "We have enough food to last six months, even with the number of peasants who have come here. I doubt that the Goths will find enough food to last them that long. As for the refugees who have fled here, I intend to enrol as many of them as possible into the garrison. They may not be able to fight, but they can stand on the walls and keep watch."

Giving the Governor a pointed look, he added, "It would do the garrison, and the civilian population, some encouragement if you could tour the defences, Sir."

The way he spoke made it plain that he was giving an order rather than the suggestion it was framed as.

Priscus looked more than a little flustered by the Tribune's bluntness, but he nodded, "Yes. Yes, of course. Let us do that as soon as we are finished here."

So, after some discussion about stores of arrows, food and water, we all trooped out after the Governor who dressed himself in a tunic of chainmail, with a gleaming helmet on his head, a short sword at his hip, and a red cloak draped around his shoulders. He looked very martial, although the effect was rather spoiled by his lacklustre enthusiasm for the task Abundus had set him.

Aoric and I tagged along at the rear of the small procession of officers and aides, accompanied by Cleitus who seemed excited by the whole episode.

"Abundus may be an abrasive fellow, but he's very determined to do his duty," he said as we climbed a set of stone steps to reach the top of the city wall.

"Julius Priscus isn't too happy about it," I remarked.

Loyally, Cleitus asserted, "The Governor will do his duty. He is a Roman Senator."

I made no comment. Priscus may have been a Senator by virtue of his personal wealth, but he seemed out of his depth as a provincial Governor. No doubt he had believed Thrace would be a relatively peaceful province, protected from the incursions of the barbarians by the border provinces. Now he was in the middle of the greatest invasion in years, and he was clearly struggling to cope. Still, to his credit, he carried out the tour of inspection diligently, stopping frequently to talk to the soldiers who manned the walls. As a result, it took a few hours to complete the circuit of the ramparts, but this did give us plenty of time to look out and study the Goths.

It was much the same as at Novae. Cniva had left a significant portion of his army on the northern side of the river, but the majority had ploughed their way across the Hebrus and were encamped all around on the east, south and west.

"They've got some Roman tents now," Aoric observed. "They must have plundered them from the legions."

"And their wagons look as if they are full of loot," I said, pointing to what appeared to be a baggage camp on the northern side of the river.

"Full of plunder from Nicopolis, I expect," Aoric agreed. "And it seems to me that they have several thousand captives as well. They've placed their wagons in a large circle, and they're keeping some people inside the ring."

"Poor souls," I sighed. "Let's hope we don't join them."

The Goths seemed quite content to make camp, lighting fires for cooking and heating water, and thousands of their horsemen led their mounts to the river to drink.

"The fighting won't start until tomorrow," Aoric said. "But I imagine Cniva will send a delegation to demand our surrender before he attacks."

He shot me a quick glance, and I knew what he was thinking. I had spoken to Cniva outside Novae, so I knew it would be safer to stay out of the Gothic King's sight now. If he saw me again, I was unlikely to be as lucky as I had been the last time.

And yet, as I looked out over the vast array of men and horses surrounding Philippopolis, I could not help feeling that the city's main weakness was its leader. Titus Julius Priscus seemed a decent enough man as a Senator, but as a military leader, I was not at all convinced by him. He tried hard, but I don't think he was ever able to inspire the soldiers the way Trebonianus Gallus had done at Novae. The Tribune, Quirinius Abundus, was a problem in another way. It did not take great insight to see that he was disliked by the men under his command for his stern approach to discipline. Roman troops had always been controlled harshly, but Abundus seemed to hold his men in contempt. They, in turn, obeyed his orders with little enthusiasm, and I noticed a few of them mouthing silent curses behind his back. It did not augur well for the defence of the city.

"They need encouragement from somewhere," Aoric said to me as we made our way back to the Governor's palatial home. "I don't think that little tour made much difference."

The next day, we discovered that Aoric's gloomy remark was well founded. When we arrived at the Governor's office for the morning's meeting, we found Abundus in a furious mood. He was ranting and raving, his arms waving in rage as he stamped around the room.

"Three hundred deserters!" he shouted. "They let down ropes and simply climbed over the walls. We're bloody lucky they didn't invite the Goths inside the city, but it seems all they wanted was to get away."

"We must prevent any more of them deserting," the Governor said feebly.

"I'll lock the bastards in their barracks at night!" Abundus boomed. "And I'll have last night's Watch Commander flogged for letting those cowards desert us!"

His face was flushed with anger, his eyes blazing wildly, and I think every man in the room was hoping they would avoid attracting his attention in case he launched a tirade against them.

But then a messenger knocked on the door and hurried in, addressing the Governor in an excited rush.

"The Goths want to parley, Sir," he said. "Their King has sent an envoy."

Abundus snorted, "It will be the usual demand for our surrender. Tell him to piss off!"

The messenger flushed, but said, "He insists on speaking to the Governor, Sir."

"Where is he?" Priscus asked.

"Waiting outside the south gate, Sir. He's got four guards with him, but that's all."

Priscus glanced nervously at Abundus as if fearing being contradicted as he said, "I'd better go and talk to him, I suppose. The longer we can keep them talking, the longer it will be before any fighting begins."

Abundus gave a curt nod. The feral gleam in his eye suggested that he was contemplating what might happen if the Goths captured or killed the Governor when he went to talk to them.

Once again, we filed out of the room, left the Governor's headquarters, and walked through the streets, this time heading for the south gate. And once again I followed, with Aoric and Cleitus beside me.

"We'd better stay inside the city," Aoric advised.

Cleitus frowned, "Why? I'd like to hear what they have to say."

"It would be a lot safer to stay here," I told him. "I spoke to the Goths at Novae, and I was lucky to get back alive. Cniva can't be trusted."

When we reached the gates, Abundus and his officers went into the great towers of the gatehouse, climbing to the top from where they could watch the proceedings.

"I must go with the Governor!" Cleitus protested when Aoric and I made to follow the Tribune.

Aoric grunted, "Go if you like, but we're staying here."

Cleitus, clearly conflicted, screwed up his face, then turned and hurried away to join Julius Priscus who was standing at the gates with four aides. Horses were being brought for them, and men stood ready to unbar the thick gates.

"Poor fool!" Aoric hissed under his breath as Cleitus ran to join them.

"He's loyal to the Governor," I said. "You can't blame him for that."

We went into the cool gloom of the tower, climbing the stone steps to the summit from where we looked out over the southern plain. The vast Gothic camp was laid out before us, but a small group of riders was closer to the walls, waiting patiently just as they had done outside Novae.

The Governor and his retinue, including Cleitus, were riding slowly towards the waiting Goths, their nervousness plain to see.

I shaded my eyes as I stared out at the Goths. A short distance away, Quirinius Abundus was doing the same. But it was Aoric who recognised the leader of the barbarian delegation.

"That's Cniva," he said in a harsh, clipped tone. "He's here in person."

This was not a surprise, but I still felt a pang of dismay because Cniva's presence confirmed my worst fears. Any hopes that the Emperor had turned the tide of battle were now nothing more than fanciful dreams. The Goths had defeated the Roman army in that mountain ambush, and now Philippopolis was cut off from all aid.

Chapter 12
Offers

The parley went on for a long time, with Cniva doing most of the talking. We could clearly see him leaning forwards in his saddle, occasionally gesturing expansively with one hand, or jabbing a finger at Julius Priscus as he relayed his message. The Governor's plumed helmet bobbed once or twice, although whether that signified agreement or determination was impossible to tell.

Glancing to my right, I could see Abundus gazing out at the meeting with a hard stare. He was perhaps wishing he had gone with Priscus so that he could hear what was being said, or perhaps he was silently hoping that Cniva would seize the Governor, thus leaving the bellicose Tribune in absolute command of the city's defence.

The sun was growing hot now, warming the stone of the ramparts under our hands, and sweat was beginning to form on my face and back, although I knew that tension played as great a part in that reaction as the heat.

And then the meeting broke up. Both sides turned their horses and slowly rode back to their respective camps. I found that I had been holding my breath, and I now let out a long sigh of relief.

We hurried down through the tower to meet the Governor as he rode back into the city. He dismounted, and I could see that his brow was lined with concern. Then he drew all of his companions into a tight huddle and began issuing whispered commands. Normally, other men would have waited until the Governor had finished his impromptu conference, but Abundus was not prepared to wait.

Treating the Governor as if he were no more important than the lowliest soldier, the Tribune marched up to him and demanded, "Well? What did he say?"

The Governor turned, his face displaying an unusual hint of anger as he looked up at the Tribune who towered over him.

Stiffly, Priscus replied, "He has given us a day to consider his offer. He promises there will be no attack today."

Abundus snorted, "I suppose it was the usual demand for total surrender?"

"Yes."

Priscus appeared to be more than a little distracted, and the nod he gave was less than authoritative, but Abundus seemed to accept the reply without question.

The Tribune rasped, "Then he can stick his demands up his arse! They can't breach our walls."

He spoke with a bravado which was denied by the Governor.

Looking more worried than ever, Priscus said softly, "They are making ladders. Lots of them. And battering rams as well."

Abundus dismissed this with a wave of his hand.

"That does not matter. The fool has given us an extra day to prepare our defences. I shall see to it that we are ready."

With that, he spun on his heel, marching away, beckoning for his officers to follow him.

The Governor stared after him for a long moment, then turned back to his aides and resumed talking to them. I saw them nod, then the Governor turned and began the long walk back up the hill to his home. He looked like a man who was wrestling with his conscience, and he barely glanced at me as he trudged past.

Cleitus gave me a wan smile, but at least he beckoned the two of us to walk alongside him. Like the Governor, he seemed to be in a very grim mood.

"Did you learn anything?" I asked him, keeping my tone as light as possible.

He shot me a worried look, then hissed, "I'll tell you when we get back."

His unusual reticence made me wonder what had happened out there, but he maintained a stony silence all the way back up the hill to the Governor's headquarters. It was not until we had returned to our room that he revealed what had been said.

With an air of defeat, he slumped down onto a chair as he informed us, "It was Cniva himself. He said that the Emperor is dead, and his army has been destroyed. Nobody is coming to help us."

On the face of it, this news was dreadful, and Cleitus looked bereft, but I asked him, "Did he show you the Emperor's head? Or any of his imperial insignia?"

Cleitus frowned, then shook his head.

"No, he did not."

"Then the Emperor is probably still alive," I told him with rather more confidence in my voice than I felt inside. "Cniva would have shown off some proof if he had any."

"He said the proof is that he is here while the Emperor is not," Cleitus replied uncertainly.

"That only proves that the Emperor has been unable to cross the mountains," I assured him. "I can't dispute that Cniva defeated him, but perhaps the Emperor escaped. He may be rebuilding his army even now."

Cleitus shook his head as he said, "Even if you are right, that could take months."

Aoric put in, "You should not believe what Cniva says. He uses words like weapons."

Cleitus took a deep breath, then sighed, "There is more."

"More?" I frowned.

Cleitus gave a glum nod, then spoke in a voice that was barely above a whisper.

"The Governor told me not to say anything, but if you are right, he may be about to make a terrible decision."

Cleitus looked dreadful, his face pale, his short hair stuck to his skull by damp sweat, and his hands moving in helpless circles.

I asked him, "What do you mean?"

With a deep sigh, he admitted, "Cniva offered the imperial throne to Julius Priscus."

It took a moment for me to realise that he was serious. When I did, I gasped, "He did what?"

Wringing his hands, Cleitus said, "He told the Governor that he should declare himself as Emperor. If he does this, Cniva will back him. He says there is no Roman army, and he could march all the way to Rome to place Priscus on the throne."

A wave of shock ran through me, leaving an empty pit in my stomach. Was I wrong? Was the Emperor dead? Did Cniva really intend to march all the way to Rome?

Dreading what I might hear, I could scarcely bring myself to ask the next question, but I forced the words out.

"What did the Governor say to that?"

Looking totally forlorn, Cleitus said, "He said he would consider the offer. He must make up his mind by tomorrow morning."

He paused. Then, unable to meet my gaze, he added, "But he has already made up his mind. He told me to keep you out of the way until Quirinius Abundus has been dealt with."

That could only mean one thing, and the thought added yet another chill to my heart.

"He's going to have Abundus murdered?"

Cleitus' only reply was a reluctant nod. Then he sat with his eyes downcast, looking utterly forlorn.

I stood up, signalling to Aoric.

"We need to talk to the Governor," I told him.

Cleitus held up an imploring hand.

"You cannot do that. He has posted guards outside his door. Nobody will be allowed in."

"Bugger that!" I growled.

With Aoric close on my heels, and with Cleitus trailing behind us like a lost puppy, I marched out of the room, along a corridor and up a flight of stairs towards the Governor's private chambers. But I quickly learned that Cleitus was right. A squad of soldiers, commanded by a tough-looking Centurion, barred the way.

"I need to speak to the Governor!" I barked imperiously, adopting my best Roman nobleman attitude. "It is vitally important."

The Centurion was unmoved. He stood directly in front of me, daring me to try to push past him.

"It will need to wait," he replied implacably. "Nobody gets in under any circumstances. Those are the Governor's orders."

His soldiers stood behind him, forming a solid line between us and the door, and their expressions were as hard as that of their officer.

In desperation, I shouted towards the closed door, "Julius Priscus! Governor! You must not believe what Cniva told you!"

The only response was silence. Then the Centurion placed the palm of his hand on my chest and gave me a not so gentle shove.

"Get lost before I have you locked up," he hissed.

I glared at him for a moment, but I knew any further argument would be futile. Defeated, we trudged back down the stairs.

"Now what?" Aoric asked.

"Now we find Quirinius Abundus and warn him."

I shot a look at Cleitus, but he avoided eye contact again, lowering his head.

"I cannot betray the Governor," he mumbled.

"He's going to betray all of us," I snapped.

Turning our backs on the distressed freedman, Aoric and I hurried to the main door. Another of the Governor's aides was there, standing beside the open doorway. I strode past him, stepping out into the bright light of the day, then came to a sudden stop.

I had found Quirinius Abundus. Or, at least, I had found his head.

A group of soldiers was hurrying across the courtyard towards the doors, their leader holding his ghastly trophy in one hand. Abundus' eyes were still open, but although the expression on his dead face was as angry as it had been in life, the eyes stared blankly and unseeing.

"Oh, Jupiter!" I breathed.

The aide who had been waiting at the doorway hurried off to deliver the news, and Cleitus sidled up to me, saying softly, "Those men were recruited from among the Goths. The Governor sent word to them to do this."

All I could do was step aside as the soldiers tramped into the building, taking the proof of their loyalty to the Governor.

Aoric said, "This is bad."

I could not disagree. Helplessly, we shuffled aside as messengers ran out of the headquarters. Slowly, coming at first in small groups, then in greater numbers, units of soldiers began to arrive, forming up in the courtyard in formal ranks. Soon, the small yard was full, and then Governor Titus Julius Priscus appeared in the open doorway. He still wore his chainmail, his plumed helmet and his red cloak, but the soldiers immediately began the refrain I had heard all too often in my lifetime.

"Imperator! Julius Priscus! Imperator!"

I leaned close to Aoric, whispering in his ear, "We need to get away. He's going to open the gates to Cniva. Jupiter only knows what will happen then. But whatever it is, we need to avoid being caught up in it."

Aoric's response was a grim nod of agreement.

Priscus began making a rehearsed speech, accepting the role of Emperor, then declaring that he was going to bring the Goths under his direct command. With their aid, his army would march on Rome. Once there, he would use the imperial treasury to pay a large bounty to every soldier who supported him.

This was greeted with loud cheers, and the soldiers appeared to believe that they had won a great victory. The sound of their acclaim made me feel sick.

Surrounded by his aides, Cleitus among them, Priscus set off for the gates, his soldiers forming into ranks and marching behind him, still chanting his name to let everyone know that a new Emperor had been proclaimed. I tried to catch Cleitus' eye, but the Macedonian ignored me. His loyalty to Priscus was absolute, and he was prepared to follow wherever his patron led.

Aoric asked, "How do you propose to get out of the city?"

"We need to find our horses. That cavalry officer, Camillus, took them. He said the stables were near the south gate."

"I suppose he might help us," Aoric grunted. "Or he might hand us over to Priscus as traitors. But even if he does let us have our horses, then what? Once we get outside, there's a whole army of Goths to get past."

"We could try that trick again," I suggested. "I'll be your prisoner."

"Not on horseback," Aoric pointed out. Prisoners don't ride horses. And it won't work at all if Cniva carries on this pretence. If there's no fighting, there will be no captives."

"All right," I decided. "Let's find Camillus. We need to risk that. If we can get a couple of horses, we can wait until nightfall. In the dark, we can pretend to be messengers or something."

Aoric gave me a dubious look, but he had no better suggestions to offer, and this was the best plan I could come up with on the spur of the moment. Lacking any other ideas, we hurried through the busy streets towards the stables near the south wall. All around us, the mood was one of mixed relief and dread. A new Emperor who had made peace with the Goths was a good thing in the eyes of many, but fear of the barbarians was ingrained, and nobody knew whether they could really be trusted.

We found Camillus outside the stables. He had drawn his *turma* of thirty men up in ranks and was addressing them formally, telling them about their new Emperor. He stood with his back to us, so we could not see his expression, nor could we tell from his tone whether or not he approved of Priscus' sudden elevation, but the faces of his squad revealed a mixture of confusion, relief and dismay as they struggled to come to terms with the sudden change in the Governor's status.

We waited until Camillus dismissed his men with a command to ensure their horses were fed and watered, and that their equipment was in good order.

"We don't know what will happen next," he declared. "So be ready."

When the troopers filed back into the stables, Aoric and I went up to Camillus.

He frowned, asking, "What do you want?"

His tone was impassive, betraying nothing.

"Our horses," I replied. "And passage out of the city tonight."

He met my gaze sternly, then nodded, "I presume you will be carrying messages on behalf of our new Emperor?"

"Absolutely," I asserted confidently.

He clearly knew I was lying, but we both understood that he was covering himself by creating an excuse to help us, and I felt a wave of gratitude for his acceptance of our unspoken plea for help.

"The gates are already open," he pointed out. "You could leave now."

"We'd prefer not to ride out when there's an entire army of Goths around the city," I told him. "We thought it would be easier to pass them at night."

Camillus gave a weary smile.

"Your horses are in there," he said, jerking a thumb towards the stables.

Then he added, "But the Emperor is out there, greeting our new allies. I'm going up to the walls to take a look. Would you care to join me?"

I accepted the offer, and he led us up a flight of steps at the side of the stables. These led up to the ramparts which were already crowded as citizens and soldiers gathered to watch the proceedings.

The Gothic army had moved close to the city, most of the nearest men mounted on horseback and armed as if for a fight.

Facing them, Priscus had several hundred soldiers on foot. It was a paltry number when compared to the horde of barbarians, but Camillus informed us, "Those are not legionaries. He's taken a guard made up of Auxiliaries. A great many of them are Goths themselves."

We knew the truth of that only too well. I wondered whether Camillus had heard about Abundus' murder, but I decided not to broach that subject. Things were tense enough as it was.

Instead, I asked him, "Where are the legionaries?"

Camillus shrugged, "Scattered around the city at their watch posts, I expect. I received orders to keep my men in their barracks."

Having seen him address his troop, I knew he had interpreted that order loosely, but it seemed that Priscus was doing everything he could to keep the legionaries at a distance. Perhaps he feared they would not be in favour of his sudden rise to power and his alliance with the Goths.

We squeezed our way to the ramparts, looking out over the plain where the two commanders faced one another.

Horns blew a fanfare as the two parties met, then I saw Cniva raise his right hand high in the air. He swept it down, and his signal brought chaos.

There was no warning at all. Priscus had probably not even uttered a formal greeting before Cniva unleashed his army. As soon as he gave his signal, thousands of horsemen kicked their mounts into motion, aiming for the city's open gates. The Roman Auxiliaries made no move to block them, and the riders covered the ground in moments.

Camillus swore, "The bloody Auxiliaries are keeping the gates open!"

Out on the field, the chaos continued. Scores of Goths had surrounded Priscus and his small entourage, and they were hacking with swords and spears, cutting men down without mercy while the Roman Auxiliaries looked on, making no attempt to intervene.

"Cleitus is out there!" I cried, but my shout was drowned out by the screams of panic from within the city. People were running desperately to get down from the walls, although there would be no sanctuary now. The gates were open, and the Goths were already streaming into the city. Only the fact that there were so many thousands of them attempting to ride in through one set of gates slowed their progress, but there was no opposition.

Camillus drew his sword, his face grim.

"What are you going to do?" I asked him.

Grimly, he answered, "I'm going to try to close those gates. And if that fails, I'll die beside my men."

With that, he shoved his way to the steps and ran down, calling for his troop to assemble.

"To the gates!" we heard him bellow.

There was a lump in my throat as I watched him go, a man who knew he had very little chance of surviving the day.

The stairs leading from the ramparts were so congested that there was no possibility of leaving by that route, so Aoric and I decided to wait until we had a clear path, but the screams were echoing all around, and more Goths were entering the city by the moment. Out on the plain, Priscus' head was being paraded to the victorious army, and I knew that Philippopolis was doomed.

"You can't trust Cniva," Aoric repeated hoarsely.

The sound of frantic fighting reached us from below, a clear sign that Camillus and his troopers were putting up some resistance. Thirty men against thousands had no hope, but they were Romans, and they had decided to go down fighting. In other parts of the city, the legionaries might be doing the same, although some would no doubt surrender rather than face such odds.

"We can't go down that way," Aoric told me. "Come on!"

We ran along the ramparts, seeking another way down. The first staircase was blocked by dozens of bodies, some of the people still groaning and moaning where they lay piled on top of each other. Someone had obviously fallen, and this had resulted in disaster as others tripped and fell, all of them tumbling down the stone steps.

"Keep moving!" Aoric urged.

We found our way down at the next set of steps, emerging beside the base of a stone watch tower. Hurriedly, we ran into a side alley, then slowed our pace, seeking safety. I was already gasping for breath, bent over with my hands on my knees, shaking from both exertion and horror.

The people of Philippopolis had shuttered their windows and barred their doors, but the streets were full of rampaging Goths, some on foot, some charging along the cobbled streets on horseback, blood-stained swords held at the ready.

We stood uncertainly in the gloom of the alleyway, but then someone else careered in from the street, a lithe, long-legged teenage girl who ran with desperation as she sought to evade the Goths.

Moving from bright sunlight to relative darkness momentarily hid us from her eyes, but she saw us just before she ran into us, executing a nimble side-step to dodge past me. Aoric, though, was faster, reaching out to grab her as she tried to run past him.

She let out a stifled scream, but instead of wailing, she began fighting, lashing out with hands and feet. Aoric was forced to draw her close, squeezing her to his chest to prevent her hitting him.

"Quiet, girl!" he hissed in her ear. "We are not Goths."

That was not technically true on his part, but the girl calmed, and then her body slumped, and I heard her trying to hold back sobs.

"I'm going to put you down," Aoric told her. "Then we'll figure out how to get away from here. All right?"

She gave a miserable nod, and I saw him relax as he released his hold on her. Free of his grasp, she aimed a kick at his groin, but Aoric managed to move swiftly enough to deflect the kick onto his thigh.

He spat a curse, grabbed for her again, but I had managed to move in behind her, and I seized her by the shoulders.

"Stop! Both of you!" I snarled.

The girl whirled, hands raised like claws, but I managed to slap her attack aside. It was then that I recognised her.

"You are the acrobat!" I breathed. "The girl who threw those knives."

She hesitated, giving me time to signal to Aoric to leave her alone.

I asked her, "Where were you going?"

"Just away," she whispered, her voice choking with emotion. "They killed my father."

"I am sorry," I told her. "We're going to try to get out of the city. We have a plan. You can come with us if you like. It will be dangerous, but not as bad as it will be if you stay here."

With a visible effort of will, she lifted her chin to look me in the eyes.

"If you touch me, I'll kill you," she promised.

"You don't need to worry about us," I assured her. "Will you come with us?"

She looked around, taking in Aoric with his sword, and my plain appearance.

Giving a curt nod, she hissed, "All right."

I felt sorry for her, but she was doing her best to appear proud and strong. Her father may have been murdered by the Goths, but she was refusing to cry.

"I'm Sextus Sempronius Scipio," I told her. "This is Aoric. He's my grandson."

She batted away a rebellious tear with the back of one grimy hand, sniffed, then said, "I am Julia."

That was probably the most common name any woman could have in the empire. Ever since old Julius Caesar had expanded Rome's territory, barbarians who had agreed to become civilised had taken his family name. This meant that any daughter of such a man would be called Julia. There must have been thousands of girls named Julia.

She was dressed in a short tunic, an immodest garment for a young girl, and her long hair was still tied back in its ponytail. Up close, I could see her blue eyes were moist with tears which she was fighting to hold back, and she held her lithe body erect and challenging.

"So what is your plan?" she asked.

In answer, Aoric drew his sword.

"I'm going to become a Goth, and you two will be my prisoners. We'll just walk out."

"That won't work!" Julia protested. "You're mad!"

"It's worked before," I assured her. "Aoric is dressed like a Goth, and he speaks the language fluently. It will work."

"It will need to work quickly," Aoric put in, jerking a head to the clamour from around the corner of the watchtower. "Let's bind your hands."

Julia glared suspiciously at him, but he bent down to cut a strip of wool from my cloak, then cut it in two, placing one piece around my wrists, keeping the bonds loose enough for me to wriggle free in an emergency.

"See?" I said to Julia.

Frowning, she allowed Aoric to wrap the second strip of cloth around her thin wrists.

"Remember," he told us, "You are terrified captives. Keep your heads down and don't look anyone in the eye."

Julia snorted, "Didn't we put up a fight at all? We're not even bruised."

Aoric considered this, then nodded. As he had done once before, he ran the palm of his left hand across the blade of his sword, drawing blood.

"You're right," he agreed as he ran his hand over my face, smearing my forehead with his blood.

He stepped back, appraising the effect.

"Not bad," he grinned. "You won't look much of a threat, and you don't look rich enough for anyone to bother arguing with me."

Casting a look over Julia, he added, "And you look poor enough. But try to appear frightened and beaten."

"I can do that," she muttered. "Just you do your part."

We had been skulking in the dimly lit, smelly alleyway for a long time, but there were so many Goths rampaging into the city that even though thousands must have passed us, many more were still surging through the streets.

"We'll need to risk it," Aoric said. "Sooner or later, some of them are going to come down here."

So we edged around the corner of the watchtower, then crept along the alley towards the main street. As we reached the corner, Aoric gave me a shove which made me stumble. I stepped out into a maelstrom of blood and chaos, almost colliding with a young warrior who was waving a spear in one hand, and holding a jug of wine in the other. The red liquid was sloshing around, much of it already staining his tunic.

He blinked at us, frowned, then raised his spear.

"Hold, brother!" Aoric yelled in Gothic. "These ones are mine! I saw them first!"

He shoved me again, his sword held behind my back. Twisting my head, I glanced over my shoulder to see that his left hand, still oozing blood, was holding Julia's wrist as she feigned being dragged along against her will. She was acting the part perfectly, her time as a street performer paying dividends. Doing my part, I staggered slightly, weaving past the drunken Goth who took another gulp of wine as we passed him.

We were far from safe, though. In the street, a horde of barbarians flooded all around us, some of them smashing down doors, others hurrying on in search of prey. Their war cries mingled with the sound of iron weapons clashing and the screams of the defenceless civilians who cowered in their homes.

"Move, you poxy Roman bastard!" Aoric commanded as he shoved me along the road, heading against the flood of raiders.

Once again, the ruse seemed to work. Aoric maintained a stream of Gothic swear words, and the other barbarians simply parted around us. I could hear Julia crying, and it sounded genuine. Perhaps she had, at last, let her grief loose.

"Get to the gates," Aoric told me.

I was certain that being outside the city would be safer than remaining within the walls, but we would still have the problem of how to escape from the vast army Cniva had brought. But all we could do was take one step at a time.

As we neared the gates, the crush became even greater. More barbarians were coming into Philippopolis, but now most were on foot, presumably having left their horses outside. Undeterred, Aoric held his sword high, demanding to be let past.

Amazingly, the ruse continued to work. We shoved and stumbled our way through the dark tunnel beneath the gatehouse, bumping against the stone wall and being jostled by the men who were eager to plunder the city. Aoric held Julia close, wrapping an arm around her shoulders, and the three of us edged our way to the outside world.

"Prisoners coming through!" Aoric yelled, his voice echoing along the tunnel.

I could smell sweat and stale alcohol from the men pushing past us, but none of them offered any opposition. Our slow exodus was due solely to the sheer number of men trying to come the other way.

And then we burst out into the daylight again. I was pushed to the left, away from the main crush, and I gasped, taking huge lungfuls of air in relief. Aoric pushed me again, and I staggered on, moving away from the gates, heading to one side to escape the press of bodies still barging their way into the city. By now, I expected that other gates had been opened by the first wave of Goths, but still thousands were shouting and pushing their way through the south gate.

But we were free of them, and I began to think that we would escape after all. There were thousands of untended horses out on the plain, all tethered to await the return of their riders.

"Can you ride a horse?" I asked Julia in a low, urgent whisper.

She glanced up, red-eyed and with tear-stained cheeks. She may have been acting at the outset of our escape, but the walk through the city had truly terrified her. Tearfully, she managed to shake her head.

"You can ride with me," I told her. "Let's steal some horses."

There was so much confusion all around us that I was hopeful of being able to simply ride away, but then I realised that another group of horsemen was sitting patiently just ahead of us, the dozen or so men doing nothing more than watch the Goths surge into the city.

I stumbled to a halt, blinking against the afternoon sun, and I sensed Aoric stiffen as he stood close behind me, one arm still held around Julia's shoulders.

"Shit!" he swore.

I looked up at the riders who were no more than ten paces ahead of us, and I recognised the man who sat slightly in front of the others. The hawk nose and penetrating eyes were unmistakable.

It was Cniva, King of the Goths, the man I had spoken to outside the walls of Novae.

All of the riders were staring at us, and I wondered how we could possibly talk our way out of this desperate situation. But then I realised that it was Aoric who commanded their attention. Cniva barely glanced at me or Julia as he focused his gaze on Aoric.

Smiling grimly, he said, "Well, I never expected to see you again. And certainly not here. I suppose you have a long story to tell?"

Aoric was silent for a moment, then I heard him say, "Hello, Father."

Chapter 13
Tests of Loyalty

Cniva looked around, taking in the scene of devastation before returning his gaze to Aoric, then he gave a slight shrug.

"Well," he said, "the city is ours. Let the warriors have their fun. I think I can return to my camp fire."

Looking at Aoric, he said coldly, "You will come with us. I wish to learn why you have been living with our enemies."

Aoric's stance radiated helpless anger, but he gave a curt nod.

Then Cniva asked, "Do you require a horse?"

"Two horses," Aoric replied, gesturing towards me and Julia.

Cniva frowned, "They are Romans, aren't they? I'll have them put with the other captives."

Perhaps it was the dried blood plastered over my forehead, but Cniva didn't appear to have recognised me. That was the only positive aspect of our situation I could think of. He barely looked at me, and his tone was utterly contemptuous and dismissive.

Aoric refused to be cowed. Defiantly, he said, "They are not captives. This man is my friend."

At this, some of the other mounted men laughed derisively, but Cniva merely cocked his head to one side, his eyebrows slightly raised in question.

"You have made friends among the Romans, then?" he asked, managing to convey the impression that this was almost beneath contempt.

Aoric still stood his ground, telling him, "When I was captured, the Romans made me a slave. This man freed me. For that, I owe him my friendship at the very least. It is just one of the debts I owe him."

"Debts should always be honoured," Cniva nodded solemnly. "What about the girl? Is she yours?"

Hurriedly, I blurted, "She's my granddaughter."

Now Cniva peered more closely at me.

"You speak our language?" he asked, a deep frown furrowing his tanned brow.

"Aoric taught me," I explained.

He gave another nod, and I wondered whether I had said too much. If he recognised me as the man he had spoken to outside Novae, he would soon realise that Aoric must have been inside the fortress. For a long moment, the Gothic King held my gaze, then he shrugged and told one of his younger companions to fetch two more horses. While we waited, I shook off the loose cords around my wrist. Cniva saw this, and his keen eyes asked a silent question.

Turning to tug the cord from Julia's wrists, I told him, "It was a ruse to keep us safe from your warriors."

Cniva gave a disinterested nod, returning his attention to studying Aoric as if trying to divine the young man's reasons for being in Philippopolis. For my part, I was still coming to terms with the fact that my young friend was the son of the Gothic king. That was something he had not revealed, and I could not fathom what it might mean for us.

Before long, the three of us were mounted, Julia sitting in front of me, her head bowed. She had not spoken a word since we had escaped from the city, but I could feel the fear and tension in her body.

"Don't panic," I told her. "We'll get out of this."

If she gave any answer, I could not hear her.

Cniva led his entire group away from the city, heading towards the sprawling camp.

As we neared the spot where Julius Priscus and Cleitus had been struck down, I whispered to Julia, "Close your eyes. Don't look."

I could hardly dare look at the pile of mutilated bodies myself. It was a dreadful scene, and just the latest horrible event in what had proved to be a miserable sequence. Cleitus was dead, and I was sure Camillus would not have survived no matter how well he fought. Before that, Abundus had been murdered, and before that we had lost touch with the Emperor and his son, both of whom might be dead. I even felt a pang of loss at the thought of the Tribune, Apurius Cimber, who had been our nominal guard during the march from Novae. When I added in all the dead and enslaved citizens of Nicopolis and the ongoing sack of Philippopolis, I knew that Cniva represented the greatest threat the empire had seen in years. I tried not to think about what he could do to us with a single word of command. Aoric may have been his son, but my companion had said enough about Cniva in the past to tell me that their relationship was far from amicable. Aoric was certainly attracting less than friendly glances from the other riders who accompanied the King. He, in turn, sat in the saddle, staring stonily straight ahead, refusing to make eye contact with any of Cniva's retinue.

It did not take long to reach the camp, and I saw that it was far from empty. Some injured or more elderly Goths remained, and there were even a few women among them. There were also men who had been set as guards over the hundreds of captives who were still herded into a makeshift prison which was formed by dozens of wagons. Near the centre of the camp was the site of a fire which had more space around it than most of the others. Apart from that, there was nothing to distinguish it from the other blackened fire sites. Bundles of baggage lay around, and some young boys hurried to meet the King and his followers. They took charge of the horses when we dismounted, then one of them rekindled the fire. Spreading his cloak on the ground, Cniva sat down cross-legged, his men forming a ring around the circle of stones which contained the flickering flames. Aoric sat opposite Cniva, with me beside him, my arm held protectively around Julia's shoulders. She sat stonily silent, her head lowered, doing her best to appear invisible.

"Bring wine!" Cniva commanded, sending a couple of the boys hurrying off to the wagons.

There was a long, tense silence during which Cniva studied the three of us, while his companions scowled. It was clear that none dared speak until Cniva broke the silence, but the King was content to let the silence continue. I guessed he was hoping this would encourage Aoric to speak more openly once he was invited to tell his tale.

The wine came, served in elegant silver goblets which Cniva informed us had come from Nicopolis.

"I'll get more trinkets tomorrow," he grinned. "My men will bring tribute from whatever they plunder. I expect they'll keep the best stuff for themselves, but they deserve it. Plunder is what they came for."

Julia had not been offered a cup, and I dared not draw attention to her by handing her my goblet, so I took a sip of the wine. It wasn't at all bad. No doubt it, too, had been looted from Nicopolis along with the goblets.

I did my best to remain calm, but this situation was as bizarre as any I had ever encountered. Here I was, sitting on the ground, drinking wine while an entire city was being sacked less than one mile away. The sounds of that dreadful event were like a faint, distant crowd roaring inside an amphitheatre. To add to the sense of the absurd, I could see plumes of smoke rising in the distance, marking where farmsteads had been burned and looted. Small groups of Goths were riding into camp, some leading captured wagons, others prodding yet more captives who staggered and stumbled into the makeshift prison of the wagon circle.

After a moment, Cniva commanded food to be brought as well, but he at last fixed his eyes on Aoric and said, "So tell me what happened to you. All I know is that you were with Achila's war band. They told me your horse fell, and then the Roman cavalry charged, driving the rest of the band back."

Aoric nodded, his expression rueful.

"That's right. I was unconscious after the fall. When I came round, the Romans were still there, but my comrades had been driven off. The Romans took me captive."

Another voice cut in, "And turned you into a slave?"

This question came from a young man, a fair-haired warrior with a snub nose and mean eyes. He placed some emphasis on the word, "slave", revealing that he thought this was a dire insult to the honour of any Goth. It was a provocative statement, and I saw many of the other men focus their attention on Aoric to see how he would respond.

Speaking evenly, he said, "That is their custom. There was little I could do about it."

"You could have tried to escape," the belligerent young man argued.

Aoric dismissed this with a curt shake of his head.

"You clearly don't have a clue about what the Romans do to anyone who tries to escape slavery. It is not a pleasant fate."

The young man seemed on the point of continuing, but Cniva cut in, "But this man set you free?"

He directed a quick nod at me, but his eyes remained fixed on Aoric. This conversation, I realised, was a test of some sort, and Cniva would deliver his judgement after he had heard Aoric speak.

My young friend said, "The man who owned me wanted to get rid of me. He said I caused too much trouble no matter how often his overseers beat me. But he was a soft, decadent man, and he could not bring himself to have me beaten to death, so he sold me to his friend, Sempronius Scipio."

He turned to look at me, smiled, then returned his attention to his stern father.

He continued, "And Scipio set me free. He taught me a lot, and he even gave me the chance to kill the last Roman Emperor."

That claim caused considerable astonishment among the Goths. Even Julia must have realised that something out of the ordinary had been said, for she risked glancing up and scanning the faces of the warriors. Even Cniva looked surprised. Only the hostile young man gave a snort of disbelief.

I put in, "It is true. We were in Verona when Julius Philippus fought Messius Decius for control of the empire. Philippus was wounded and brought to a temple where we had been hiding from some of my enemies. Philippus was badly hurt, but he might have survived. Aoric made sure that he did not."

I kept my expression as blank as possible. At the time, I had been appalled by Aoric's action even though I had hated Julius Philippus more than I have ever hated anyone. Now, though, I needed to back Aoric's claims, so I stated the fact as if I approved.

Before Cniva could ask another question, I went on, "You should know that your son stood beside me when I faced a gang of thugs who wanted to do me harm. He refused to abandon me even when we were severely outnumbered, and I count him as my friend."

Cniva considered this for a moment, then demanded, "And why were you in Philippopolis?"

This was a dangerous question. I wanted to lie; to tell him that Aoric wanted to return to his homeland, and that we were travelling northwards. But if Cniva ever recognised me as the man who had spoken to him outside the fortress of Novae, he would know that was a lie.

I said, "My patron sent me to spy on some local Governors. Aoric offered to accompany me."

"Your patron?" Cniva frowned.

I mentally sighed. The Roman system of patronage was sometimes difficult to explain in simple terms.

I told him, "In Rome, wealthy men act as patrons to their clients. They offer help, money and protection in exchange for political support. My patron is a suspicious bastard, and he wanted me to spy on men he views as untrustworthy."

"And that fool Priscus was one of those Governors?"

"That's right."

"Well, he got that right!" Cniva laughed, the other warriors chuckling along with his joke. "Priscus was an idiot."

While the Goths cackled with delight, I kept my gaze on Cniva, and I saw that he was no longer laughing. Instead, he was staring at me with eyes as sharp and hard as flint.

He asked me, "And the Governor at Novae as well?"

So the devious bastard had recognised me after all. But now was not the time to hesitate. I needed to sound convincing.

I nodded, "Yes, him as well. We had just arrived in Novae when you crossed the river and put the fortress under siege."

Cniva stroked his beard in thought, then asked, "And I suppose you came to Philippopolis as soon as we left Novae?"

"Yes. I thought Novae was still too dangerous, and I had no idea you would come this far. I thought Philippopolis would be safe."

That elicited a round of amusement among the others, but Cniva had not done with me yet.

He demanded, "By which route?"

He was probing, either to discover whether we had been with the Emperor's army, or to catch me in a lie.

I said, "By a very long and difficult route. We wanted to avoid any fighting."

That was true as far as it went, but now Cniva returned his attention to Aoric.

"What about you?" he snapped. "Did you not think to come back to your people?"

The young man with the snub nose muttered, "He is half Roman. They are his people now."

The glare Cniva gave him forced the younger man into silence, but the point had been made, and a few of the others nodded in silent agreement.

Aoric said, "I promised to see my friend safe before doing that. Once he and his granddaughter were on their way back to Rome, then we had agreed that my debt to him was paid. That would have allowed me to return. I did not know you were planning this invasion."

"He's lying!" the antagonistic young warrior declared.

The atmosphere grew even more tense. A direct challenge had been made, and I knew enough about Gothic culture to realise that Aoric had no choice except to answer it.

"Take that back, Egica," he said in a low, hard voice, confirming my suspicion that the two young men knew one another.

The man named Egica glared at him, defiantly saying, "No. You are a liar and a coward. That is plain for everyone to see."

Aoric retorted, "I did not run from a small group of Roman cavalry, abandoning the King's son in the process. If you and your father had not fled, I might never have been captured in the first place."

Egica surged to his feet, his hand reaching for the hilt of his sword, but Cniva barked a command for everyone to remain still.

"Both of you have made accusations," he declared. "Now you must either acknowledge that this has gone far enough, or there must be blood. Which is it to be?"

Egica sneered, "I am willing to fight. I am no coward."

In response, Aoric gave a nod of his head.

He said, "I do not wish to fight anyone, but I will not back away from a challenge like that."

Cniva nodded, "Then take up your sword."

Aoric pushed himself to his feet. Everyone else around the fire also stood up, eager to watch the combat. Other men, along with the young boys who acted as attendants, were also gathering in expectation of a spectacle.

I helped Julia to her feet, and she shot me a worried look.

"What is going on?" she asked in a frightened whisper. "Are they going to fight?"

I tried to give her a reassuring smile. It must have been terrifying for her, sitting among that group, not understanding what was being said.

"A challenge has been made," I told her. "Aoric needs to fight or we'll all be in trouble."

"Can he win?" she asked fearfully.

"He's a talented warrior," I said.

What I did not know was how good a fighter Egica was.

Cniva pointed to a spot beyond his own fire where there was a patch of open ground.

"That will do," he said.

Aoric and Egica both stalked warily away from the camp fire, keeping a safe distance from one another. The spectators formed a group around me, and I found myself standing beside Cniva.

When he glanced at me, I said, "Aoric has no armour. Egica has a tunic of chainmail."

Cniva merely shrugged, "The gods will decide their fates."

After a slight pause, he added, "Egica's father, Achila, died at Novae."

Feeling my anger rising, I hissed, "Aoric is your son!"

Cniva shrugged, "I have other sons. And Aoric was always a rebellious lad. We rarely saw eye to eye. I suspect his Roman mother put a lot of silly ideas in his head."

"He's a good man, and a true friend," I shot back.

"Perhaps he is," Cniva conceded. "But a confrontation with Egica was inevitable. They may as well get it over with now."

"You knew this would happen?" I challenged.

In response, Cniva's lips curled in the ghost of a smile.

He admitted, "I thought it likely. And you had better hope that Aoric wins. If he dies, you and your granddaughter will be put with the rest of our slaves."

I knew that he was deadly serious, but I did not translate his words for Julia's benefit. If the worst happened, she would learn the truth soon enough.

A murmur of anticipation now ran through the small group of men around us. In the distance, the ruin of Philippopolis was still taking place. Dark smudges of smoke were slowly climbing into the air above the city's walls, and I could only imagine the horrors taking place within.

But the most important fight was taking place only a few paces from where I stood. Both men held long, heavy cavalry blades. Egica gripped his in his right hand, his left arm slightly extended from his body to act as a counterbalance, while Aoric adopted a two-handed grip, holding the sword in front of his body, the blade pointing slightly upwards. As I had said to Cniva, his only protection was a leather tunic, while Egica's body was protected by the iron links of his chainmail tunic. Below the waist, this tunic was split at front and back to allow Egica to mount a horse, but it still covered most of his body, and I could not see how Aoric could hope to win, especially as his left palm still bore a cut from where he had spilled his own blood to make my crude disguise. That cut would inevitably affect his grip on his sword.

Egica gave Aoric no time. As soon as Cniva signalled his assent, the young Goth charged towards Aoric, his sword slashing in a vicious, back-handed arc.

Aoric reacted with astonishing speed. Instead of attempting to block the blow, he leaped backwards, then dodged aside and darted in to Egica's left. The armoured warrior had put all his effort into his first attack, and his momentum carried him on another step as he struggled to swing his heavy sword back. In that instant, Aoric swung his own sword, aiming to smash the edge of the blade into Egica's side.

Egica dodged, frantically swinging his own sword back to block the blow, but the end of Aoric's blade did catch him a fairly solid hit before Aoric was forced to dance away again.

Egica's second attack was more cautious. He was obviously in some discomfort because, although his armour had prevented a serious injury, he had certainly felt the strength of Aoric's strike, and he became more cautious in his next attack.

The sound of the two blades connecting rang out again and again as Egica drove Aoric slowly backwards. Aoric maintained his two-handed grip, his sword always ready, and he parried Egica's slashes with relative ease, but he made no attack of his own.

Egica delivered another furious succession of blows, and Aoric needed to react with incredible speed to block the attacks. Then, when he deflected one of Egica's strikes to one side, the two men stood almost chest to chest. They were so close that there was no room to wield their weapons. It was only for a moment, because both of them knew that they must disengage in order to use their swords, but their obvious hatred of one another resulted in them pushing each other in a test of strength while they snarled curses at each other, their faces barely a hand's breadth apart.

In that moment, Aoric showed that he had learned from my brief lessons in *pankration*, the Greek art of unarmed combat. The main thing he had learned was that he could use any part of his body in a fight, and that the aim was to put his opponent down by any means possible, and then to ensure that he stayed down.

While Egica rasped a curse at him, Aoric flung his head forwards, his forehead catching Egica on the bridge of his nose.

Blood sprayed, And Egica staggered backwards, his sword dangling loosely in his hand.

Aoric did not hesitate. He jabbed forwards, the tip of his blade striking Egica in the chest, shattering iron links and driving into the thick woollen padding beneath the armoured coat. Then he closed the distance between them, flung out his right foot, hooking it behind Egica's left ankle, and he heaved again, sending the dazed warrior crashing to the ground.

Egica lay on his back, and Aoric hacked at his body with two vicious blows. The first brought a cry of pain as it smashed into the side of Egica's chest powerfully enough to break his ribs. The second cracked into his right arm just below his elbow, and I thought I could hear the bones splinter from where I stood.

Aoric stepped back, breathing heavily, but looking at his opponent with something like satisfaction etched onto his face.

"You are not worth killing," he said, speaking loudly enough for the spectators to hear. "And you are a warrior. My father may have need of you in the future. But if you dare challenge me again, I will kill you."

Then he turned his back on Egica, walking to confront his father, his sword still clasped in both hands.

Breathing heavily after his exertion, he asked, "Is that sufficient, Father?"

Cniva gave a nod. His expression was unreadable, but he said, "It is enough. I see that living among the Romans has not softened you too much."

Aoric said, "Then I will join your army. And Scipio will be permitted to go free."

At this, Cniva shook his head.

"I will set no Romans free," he asserted. "Not even one who aided you. He stays."

Aoric frowned, "Then he and his granddaughter will stay with me as my friends, not as slaves."

Cniva shot me and Julia another glance, then said, "Call them what you like, but you are responsible for them. I'll provide you with a horse and some armour. Then we shall see what happens next."

Which meant, I knew, that we were now fated to become part of the Gothic army. Where, I wondered, would that take us?

Chapter 14
On The March

The sack of Philippopolis continued for another day and a night. After that, Cniva sent heralds into the wreckage to call his men back. They came in small groups, some with captives, most carrying plunder of some sort. Cniva then ordered that stolen wagons should be loaded with food and wine to replenish the army's stores, and he also received gifts from the leaders of the various small tribes who formed his great army. The Goths had little time for statues unless they were made of a metal which could be melted down, but they did bring away gold and silver ornaments, jewellery and coins, as well as several wealthy Romans of senatorial or equestrian rank. Whether these men would be ransomed or simply enslaved was not clear, but what I did recognise was that the Goths considered the attack on Philippopolis to be a great success. The mood in their camp was boisterous and triumphant, and there was a great deal of drinking and celebrating while Cniva tried to reimpose some level of order.

Julia stayed close beside me, probably regarding me as the only friendly face in the seething mob of violent men. I had told her a few facts about myself in order to strengthen our story. Unfortunately, she had never been to Rome, but since she spoke no Gothic and few of the barbarians spoke Latin, I hoped she would not need to answer many questions.

My main concern was to keep her safe. I managed to buy a longer, more modest tunic for her, and I encouraged her to keep her hair and face dirty and untidy to avoid attracting attention. She had already seen what was being done to many of the women captured by the Goths, so she did not argue with my advice.

For her part, she told me she had passed her fourteenth birthday in February. She claimed that she could read and write reasonably well, but her main talents had been performing in her entertainment act with her father.

"My mother died when I was eight," she told me. "I was already part of their act, so I just carried on."

She did her best to appear strong, but I heard her crying at night, and she did ask whether it would be possible to find her father's body to allow him to be buried.

"I'm sorry," I told her. "It would be best not to. But when we get to Rome, we can put up a memorial to him."

She cried again, but only when she thought I was sleeping.

There was another person who was not celebrating the sack of the city. Egica had a broken arm and several cracked ribs, although I never heard him cry out when he was tended by some of the women who were assigned to the task of healing. Their care was probably rudimentary, and most wounded men received little more than a few stitches and a bandage of wrapped cloth, but when I did catch a glimpse of Egica, his arm was held in wooden splints and wrapped in a sling. When he saw me, he glared with a venomous expression which promised vengeance.

Aoric assured me, "He won't do anything. He lost the fight, and everyone saw it. Honour is satisfied."

I sighed, "He doesn't look the sort who believes in honour."

"No," Aoric grinned. "But my father does. Egica can't afford to anger him."

Aoric may have been right, because Egica did his best to avoid us, using his injuries as an excuse to stay away from Cniva's makeshift court.

There were some other injured men, but the Goths had suffered few casualties. The city's defenders had been caught completely off guard thanks to Cniva's treacherous ruse, and those few Roman troops who had survived were now shoved in among the slaves.

Our own situation was ambiguous to say the least. Cniva had provided Aoric with a horse, a tunic of chainmail, gauntlets and a helmet, but he had made no provision for me and Julia at all. As a consequence, we were forced to walk when the army broke camp and headed back towards the mountains. Aoric eventually managed to persuade one of the wagon drivers to allow us to sit among his cargo of looted food supplies, and Aoric often rode alongside, giving us time to talk.

"Egica was always an objectionable sod," he confided. "He hated me because my father had more status and power than his."

"So why were you riding with Achila's war band when you were captured?" I asked.

"My father thought it would help to toughen me up," he sighed. "Also, I think he still resents having a son by a Roman woman, and he didn't want to show me any favour."

Glumly, he added, "He's still doing that."

"So what do we do?" I asked him, switching to Latin in case the wagon driver managed to hear us over the rumble of his cart's wheels.

"We go along with things for the time being," Aoric decided.

"Do you plan on staying?" I asked him.

He gave me a wry smile as he said, "I don't know. But I do want to find a chance for you to get away."

"Your father doesn't seem keen on that," I pointed out.

"That's because he's being his usual, dictatorial self," Aoric said. "Give it time. We'll figure something out. You're usually better at that than I am."

"Maybe so, but we're among your people now. You know their customs and habits."

"So let's wait and see," Aoric suggested.

Later, Julia asked me, "Are we slaves, then?"

"I'm not sure," I admitted. "It might be best to act as if we are. If we claim to be under Aoric's protection, that should keep us safe. He's back in his father's favour now. At least, he is in part."

"I'm scared," she confessed.

"So am I," I admitted.

Slowly, the army retraced its steps, once again climbing into the mountains and returning by the same pass where they had ambushed Messius Decius and his overconfident army. It was a long, slow passage because of the sheer amount of booty and the number of captives who now trudged along behind the wagons. And the sight of the battlefield was filled with yet more horrors. Bodies lay scattered all around, most of them partially eaten by birds and animals. Men, horses and mules lay there, and the stink of decay was dreadful.

Once through the pass and back down the other side of the mountains, we passed the wreckage of Nicopolis, then continued towards the north-east. Our pace was slow, covering barely more than ten miles each day, but Cniva sent out huge raiding parties in all directions, leaving a wide swathe of pillaged countryside as we slowly headed towards the lower reaches of the Danubius.

"My father wants to avoid Novae," Aoric informed me. "But it will take at least twelve days to reach the river at this rate. So you still have time to come up with a plan."

The trouble was, I could not think of anything which might have the remotest chance of success. I could perhaps steal a horse at night, but Julia did not ride, so the horse would need to carry us both. And there were so many Goths, with their patrols ranging so widely, I knew we would have little chance of outriding them as most of them were excellent horsemen. For the time being, we were stuck.

We did our best to help Aoric, fetching food from the cooking fires, helping to tend his horse, and setting a small fire at night, but I felt more than a little useless as the horde slowly edged north and east.

One evening, while Aoric was watering his horse at a nearby stream, Julia was chopping vegetables into a small pot, and I was feeding twigs to a nascent fire when I became aware of someone watching us.

I looked up to see Egica standing some twenty paces away. He wore no armour, but he did have a sword and a dagger hanging from his belt. Quite how he could use them with his right arm in a sling I did not know, but a sword is a sign of status, so I presumed that was his reason for wearing it.

He was glaring at me like some malevolent devil, his eyes narrowed, and his face marred by bruising. When he was sure I had seen him, he slowly raised his left hand, then drew one finger across his throat in an unmistakable gesture threatening my death. I made no move, forcing myself to remain still, and then he turned and stalked off into the gathering gloom of twilight.

"He's just trying to frighten you," Aoric insisted when I told him what had happened.

"It's working," I muttered.

"Perhaps I should have killed him," Aoric sighed. "But then I'd have his whole war band after me."

"I thought you said your father would protect you?"

Aoric shrugged, "He'd take revenge on Egica if anything happens to me, but that's not quite the same thing. Still, I don't think Egica would risk that."

I murmured, "I hope you are right."

I took some comfort from the fact that Egica was unlikely to make an attempt on my life while he was hampered by a broken arm, but I could not rule out the possibility that he might send some of his henchmen to do his dirty work, so I was forced to remain alert, and I found this quite draining. My nerves were always on edge, and I found myself jumping at shadows, always wondering when Egica would strike.

Julia picked up on my anxiety, but she adopted a different approach to dealing with the threat. The evening after Egica's unspoken promise, the two of us were again preparing an evening meal when she slipped a dagger out from beneath her long tunic, letting me see the sharp blade.

"Where did you get that?" I asked her.

"I stole it," she replied, showing no remorse. "I thought it might be more useful than that small eating knife you've got."

She offered it to me, but I waved it away, more concerned with the fact that she had stolen the dagger.

"When did you steal it?" I asked. "And who from?"

She shrugged, "Most people are asleep at night. Some of the warriors sleep soundly because of the wine they've drunk."

"You still took a risk," I warned.

She snorted, "I've been able to pick purses since I was five years old. Taking a knife from a sleeping drunk wasn't difficult."

"As long as he doesn't see you with it."

"It's for you," she said, offering the wicked-looking blade to me once again. "Don't you want it?"

She seemed more than a little put out by my refusal, but I shook my head again.

"No," I said. "I've never been much good with weapons. Besides, it won't be much use against a man with a sword."

"It's better than nothing," she retorted. "But if you won't take it, I'll keep it."

Having seen her performance in the square in Philippopolis, I knew she was probably more capable of using the damned thing than I was.

I told her, "Fine. But keep it out of sight."

She tucked the dagger beneath the folds of her tunic, giving me a defiant stare.

Softly, I told her, "If anyone does ask where you got it, make sure you tell them you found it lying on the ground one morning."

Julia rolled her eyes, but gave a nod.

"I had thought of that," she informed me in a tone which made me feel as if she was an old, experienced person admonishing a foolish child.

"Just keep it well hidden," I said lamely.

As for Aoric, he may have joined his father's personal retinue, but he was still unsettled.

"The trouble is," he complained, "he won't give me anything to do. He won't even let me carry a simple message to another tribal chieftain. So I'm just following him around like a sheep."

The trek continued, but after several days, Aoric returned at dusk with some important news.

"The Roman army is following us," he told me. "It seems the Emperor has managed to put another force together. My father reckons the Romans scattered after the battle in the pass, but now they are back together, and our scouts say they have even more troops than before."

"Does that mean there will be a battle?" I wondered.

"Probably," Aoric nodded. "We can't outrun them unless we abandon all our wagons and prisoners. That would not go down well with the tribes, so we'll be forced to fight sooner or later. I doubt we can get across the Danubius before they catch us."

I gave him a serious look as I said, "A battle brings confusion. We might get a chance to escape."

"It will probably be your best hope," he nodded.

"But what about you? Will you come with us?"

He lowered his eyes, unable to meet my gaze as he sighed, "I don't know. Despite everything, I feel more at home here. And I feel I want to impress my father. Does that sound ridiculous?"

"Not at all," I replied. "It is your decision. But I need to return to the empire if I can. I hope you understand that."

He nodded gravely, "I understand. But I've realised that I'm not really a Roman. Speaking Latin and having spent four years among Romans doesn't outweigh my entire upbringing."

"I appreciate that," I assured him. "It is your life. You can make more of it than trailing around after an old man like me. But I fear for you with Egica looking to kill you."

"I can handle Egica," Aoric declared, although I suspected there was some doubt behind his boast.

"Well," I said. "Let us see what the battle brings. If we can steal a horse, I think we ought to take the risk while the fighting is taking place. We really don't want to find ourselves on the northern bank of the Danubius. That would make escape even more difficult."

"I'll help you," Aoric promised.

"Not if you want to impress your father," I reminded him. "The very fact of my escape will count against you."

He grinned, "I could tell him you are dead, and your body lost."

"Do you think he'd believe that?" I asked.

"Probably not," Aoric admitted. "But don't worry about me. If you get a chance to flee, take it."

I turned to look at Julia. She had been listening intently, her eyes moving to watch each of us as we spoke.

"What about you?" I asked her. "I've been assuming you would want to escape with me, but you can stay here if you like."

She replied without hesitation.

"I want to leave."

So now, I knew, all we had to do was wait for another battle. And with the Roman army closing on our heels, that was not going to be far off.

Chapter 15
The Marshes

The slow trek continued for several more days. If anything, the long, wide column of people and animals seemed to be travelling more slowly by the day. Despite the threat of a pursuing Roman army, there was little sense of urgency coming from Cniva or his tribal leaders. Many of the ordinary warriors who were marching on foot did betray some nervousness, and a few of the captives seemed to hold hopes of being rescued, but Cniva himself seemed completely unconcerned.

I saw little of Aoric during the day. He spent his time pestering his father to be allowed to do something useful, and Cniva eventually permitted him to accompany one of the scouting bands who rode back to keep an eye on the Roman progress. When he returned late that day, Aoric was in a good mood as he told me, "We only saw their scouts, but the main force can't be all that far behind. One of our patrols claims they have legions marching behind the cavalry, and that they seem to be staying close together. Their horsemen could catch us easily enough, but the Emperor must want his entire force here before he attacks."

"And what is your father planning to do?" I asked.

"He hasn't told anyone yet," Aoric replied. "But I know he has something in mind. I told you, he's very cunning."

"He's going to need to be if he wants to escape with all his booty," I said, indicating the hundreds of laden wagons.

Aoric shrugged, and I could tell that his own situation was playing on his mind. He had not been welcomed back with open arms, but he was a Goth at heart. Even so, his friendship with me had been forged by shared danger, and I knew he felt conflicted.

"Don't worry about me," I told him. "Do what your heart tells you."

He gave a weak smile, then wrapped his cloak around his body and lay down to sleep. When Julia and I awoke in the morning, he had already left to join his new war band.

"Is he going to fight against Rome?" Julia asked me.

I frowned, "I don't know. I think he probably will. He grew up as a Goth. The fact that he speaks Latin and spent a few years within the empire doesn't change his upbringing."

"But will he still help us escape?" she pressed, clearly concerned.

"Yes," I assured her. "He may be a Goth, but he's my friend. He'll help if he can."

Julia's blue-grey eyes held a solemn look as she told me, "My father always said that *if* was the biggest word in the world."

Nodding, I agreed, "Your father was a wise man, then. But Aoric will help us. I am sure of that."

"Even if it displeases his father?"

That was my own private fear, but I tried to reassure her.

"The Goths place great store in friendship and honour. I trust Aoric."

The expression on her young face told me that she did not trust anyone.

I said, "When the battle begins, there will be a lot of confusion. We'll find a way to escape whatever happens."

She gave an uncertain nod, clearly not convinced, but then she asked a question I had not expected.

"And what happens then?" she asked. "Where do we go once we've got away?"

That caught me off guard, but once I had gathered my thoughts, I asked her, "Do you have any other family? Any uncles or aunts anywhere?"

She shook her head, lowering her eyes and sniffing back a tear. She looked utterly miserable, and I felt a pang of sympathy for her. She was alone, young and female, and that made her very vulnerable.

"In that case," I told her, "you should come with me. I need to return to Rome."

"And what would I do in Rome?" she challenged, showing a spark of her ingrained determination.

"Whatever you like," I said. "We'll find a home for you. To begin with, you can stay with my friends, Fronto and Faustia."

She swallowed anxiously, then demanded, "Are you going to keep me as a slave?"

"No," I assured her. "You're a free citizen, aren't you?"

"Yes!" she snapped, perhaps a little too forcefully. "My father was a free man. He swore the oath to worship the gods of Rome."

"Then you are free as well," I told her. "I'll get you to Rome. After that, we'll work out what to do next. For the moment, remember that you are supposed to be my granddaughter."

"Do you have any children of your own?" she asked, displaying a teenager's ability to alter a subject at a moment's notice.

"Yes," I said. "And grandchildren, although I've never seen any of them."

"Why not?" Julia probed, suddenly interested.

"It's a long story," I shrugged.

"We have plenty of time," she pointed out. "It's not as if this army is moving very fast."

She was right, so I gave her a short, edited version of my family, explaining that I had lost contact with all of them for fear of what my patron, Publius Licinius Valerianus, might do to them if I did not obey his commands.

"My oldest son has nothing to do with me," I explained. "But that wouldn't stop Valerianus using him against me. My younger son is safe enough because Valerianus doesn't know where he lives. But my daughter and her family are most at risk."

Julia regarded me with something close to astonishment, then said, "It sounds as if you are that man's slave."

I sighed, "Sometimes it certainly feels like it."

"But you still want to go back to Rome?" she frowned. "You could go somewhere else. He'd think you were killed by the Goths."

"That had occurred to me," I admitted. "But let's think about that after we've got away from the Goths. If we stay here, we're likely to become genuine slaves."

The column moved on, passing farms, villages and small towns, every one of which was plundered, then set ablaze. Most of the occupants had fled at the rumour of the Goths' approach, but any who were too frail or too foolhardy to flee were either killed or enslaved. And the march went on like a slow, lumbering juggernaut, always heading north and east. The summer sun was hot, the occasional shower of light rain doing little to ease the sweat and discomfort, but on we went, creeping across the ravaged countryside with dogged determination.

A couple of days later, Aoric informed me that his father had ridden well ahead, scouting out the land for himself, and had returned looking very pleased with himself. He had sent several thousand riders ahead of the march to scour the land, while another huge force of cavalry formed a screen behind the army.

"He's up to something," Aoric told me.

And the next day, the route altered. The head of the column swung away from the easy route and entered a wide, low valley which instantly began to bog us down. Streams and rivulets criss-crossed the wide lowland between wooded hills, and the ground became increasingly muddy and marshy. Horses sank up to their fetlocks, men squelched ankle-deep, and wagons needed to be manually shoved when they became bogged down.

"This is madness!" I gasped as I put my shoulder to the back of my allotted wagon and heaved. Several warriors had joined me, and they were all cursing and grumbling. We spent an exhausting day shoving the heavily laden wagons through a terrain of mud and water. Long grass was trampled flat by our progress, but the small hummocks and dips made travel a desperately slow business. I estimated that we barely covered four miles that day.

"The Romans will catch us easily now," I said to Aoric when he joined me and Julia for an evening meal of gruel which Julia had prepared.

"But they can't attack us easily on this sort of ground," he pointed out. "Horses can't charge properly in this stuff."

"That doesn't mean they can't fight at all," I pointed out. "Why are we travelling this way?"

"He's planning a trap," Aoric told me. "He explained it to his senior leaders. Once the baggage is through the marsh, he's going to leave a strong force to face the Romans. When they attack, this force will put up a bit of a fight, then turn and feign a panicked flight. When the Romans pursue, he'll spring an ambush with the rest of his army."

With a shrug, he added, "Or perhaps they won't follow us into the marshes at all. In that case, we'll reach the river, then we'll be ferried across by boats."

"Boats?" I frowned. "Where will you get them from? You'll need a fleet of ships to get everyone across."

Aoric gave a wry smile as he explained, "Apparently, there's an entire Gothic fleet. It's been based out on the Black Sea, but my father sent word weeks ago that they are to sail up the Danubius to meet us, then ferry the army across."

"He's been planning this raid for a long time, then," I sighed. "He came this way on purpose."

"I think so," Aoric nodded.

I looked at him across the flickering light of our small camp fire.

"I need to escape," I told him. "I need to warn the Emperor."

Aoric gave a resigned nod. He was clearly torn between his friendship for me and his desire to be one of his father's principal aides. He was a Goth, born to a Roman woman, and he had confessed in the past that he felt he did not fit in either world. Now he would need to make a choice.

Ruefully, he sighed, "I don't mind fighting, but I think there has been enough death. If we can cross the river without a battle, nobody else needs to die."

"So you'll help me reach the Emperor?" I asked, conscious that Julia was listening to every word.

"If I can," Aoric nodded.

"What about your father? What will you do if he finds out?"

He gave that familiar grin as he told me, "Then maybe I'll need to follow you and become a Roman after all."

The next day brought a change. The baggage train still ploughed an exhausting path through the swamps, but eventually we reached firmer ground. And all the while, Gothic horsemen were heading back along the line of our march. Others were gathering in wooded valleys which led off to either side of the wide stretch of the marshes, and every clump of trees or bushes was used to conceal a few warriors. Horses could not be hidden easily, but men on foot could find dips in the terrain where they could lie, wet and miserable but unseen. Aoric, it seemed, was right about Cniva's intentions.

When a halt was at last called, I set about my usual task of trying to light a fire. I piled kindling and small twigs, begged a burning brand from another camp fire nearby where several women were busy cooking a meal, then once the fire was burning well, Julia and I set off with a small leather bucket to fetch water from one of the many streams. When we returned, Aoric was still not back, but I noticed something small and bright lying on the ground beside my satchel. I put down the bucket, then bent to pick up this unexpected object. It was a brooch, apparently made of gold, and the workmanship was very fine. Intricate patterns crisscrossed the central space inside an elaborate oval of gold.

"Where did this come from?" I wondered, shooting Julia a look.

"I've never seen it before," she replied. "Maybe it came loose from someone's cloak."

"The clasp is still fastened," I showed her. "It can't have fallen by accident."

She held up a hand as she insisted, "Don't look at me like that! I didn't steal it!"

I frowned, "Well, it doesn't belong to Aoric. I know that for a fact. But whoever owns it, he's a wealthy man. This is valuable."

"It could be stolen plunder," Julia remarked.

I nodded, "Yes, you are right. That seems more likely. But how did it get here?"

We both stood there, staring at the gleaming gold of the brooch, but a loud, authoritative shout suddenly interrupted us.

"There it is!"

The voice bellowed the cry from behind us. I spun around to see Egica and two of his warriors, all three of them wearing chainmail and carrying swords, marching towards me. Egica still had one arm in a sling, but he looked more than ready for a fight, and his left hand was pointing at the brooch in my hands.

"You stole it!" he shouted, his voice loud enough to attract attention from all the nearby fires.

Edging protectively in front of Julia, I held out the brooch towards him.

"I found it," I told him. "If it's yours, take it."

"I'll take more than that!" he snarled.

He used his left hand to slap mine aside, sending the golden brooch spinning away to the ground.

There was an evil glint in his eyes, and I knew that he, or one of his lackeys, had planted the brooch at our fire in order to provide him with this excuse. I was in real trouble, but I had dealt with enough bullies in my lifetime to know that showing fear would only make things worse.

"I didn't steal anything," I told him, speaking in a firm voice. "And how did you manage to see it in my hands when I had my back to you?"

"Show some respect, Slave!" he shouted. "You're a thief and a liar, and your owner is no better. I'll deal with him later, but you must die for your crime and your insolence."

He was putting on a show, justifying his actions in front of an audience, and I knew now what he intended. He would have me killed, and that would force Aoric to challenge him again. In his present condition, Egica could not fight, but the two men he had brought with him were both tall and hugely powerful. Both of them were much bigger and stronger than Aoric.

"I didn't steal anything!" I repeated, much louder this time.

My protest was in vain. Grinning, Egica used his left hand to draw a dagger from his belt.

"Seize him!" he commanded his men.

I had been expecting something like this, and I had been contemplating trying to run away. Men in armour are weighed down, but they were all younger and fitter than me. Besides, I had nowhere to run to, and I needed to keep Julia out of danger if at all possible.

On the other hand, fighting three armed men seemed a good way to commit suicide.

In the end, I reacted instinctively, not giving a thought to what might happen next. As Egica drew his dagger, I darted forwards, grabbing his left wrist with my right hand, and delivering a smack to his face with the heel of my left palm. I struck his battered nose, and when I felt him reeling, I used my grip on his arm to swing his body around. Then I jumped past him, twisting his wrist violently to force him to drop the dagger.

In normal circumstances, I would never have been able to overpower him, but he was injured and overconfident, and he did not expect an old man to put up any sort of fight. He staggered, twisted and dropped to his hands and knees while I snatched up his dagger and whirled to face the two other men.

"Stay back or I'll kill him!" I warned.

It was still a bluff. I doubt that I'd ever be able to kill Egica even though he was unarmed. In any case, he made up their minds for them

"Leave him!" he gasped. "He's mine!"

Hampered by his useless arm, he lurched awkwardly to his feet, tugging at the hilt of his sword with his clumsy left hand.

Blood was streaming from his nose, and his eyes revealed his pain, but his desire for revenge overrode all other concerns.

I knew I must prevent him drawing his sword. Even left-handed, it would give him too much of an advantage over the dagger I held. So I attacked again, thanking the gods that he was unable to use his right arm to fend me off. While he clumsily tried to haul his sword from its leather scabbard, I slashed at the back of his hand, drawing great splashes of dark, red blood.

Egica yelled in pain and anger, swiping at me with his bloody hand. His sword slipped back into its sheath, and I took a step back.

With both hands now almost useless, Egica resorted to a more basic tactic. He charged at me, lowering his head and roaring like a bull. I tried to jump aside, but he was too close, and he caught me with his shoulder, sending me sprawling on my back. The back of my head hit the ground hard, and I felt the dagger fall from my grasp. Egica, too, had stumbled after our collision, but he had managed to stay on his feet. Now he lurched towards me, delivering a vicious kick to my side, forcing all the air out of my lungs. Through pain-clouded eyes, I saw him bend down. When he stood up again, he held the dagger clumsily in his left fist. Blood still streamed from his wound, but he ignored the pain as he moved towards me.

My eyes were filled with tears of pain, and from somewhere far away I could hear the sound of thunder thudding in my ears. All my senses seemed paralysed, and I knew I could not escape. My side was throbbing, my head ached, and I had no breath to provide me with enough energy to stand or even roll aside.

Several things seemed to happen in quick succession. My eyes cleared just enough to let me see Egica's smirking, bloody face leering down at me, when a thrown dagger slammed into his chest. It did not have enough power to cut through his armour, but the blade lodged there, and Egica took a couple of staggering steps backwards.

At the same time, I realised that the sound of thunder was not in the roaring sensation in my ears. It was a horse, galloping fast, and I turned my head in time to see Egica's two warriors leaping aside to avoid being trampled. Egica himself was not so lucky. Startled by the dagger protruding from his chest, he stepped directly in front of the galloping horse. It crashed into him, spinning him wildly away to my right. The horse danced as it shot past, avoiding me, but catching Egica with one of its hind legs. I could hear the grinding of hoof against metal as it trod on him, and the explosive gasp from the fallen man which was suddenly cut off by the sound of a sickening thump.

Slowly, groggily, I pushed myself to my feet.

The horse had almost fallen, but had somehow maintained its balance. It had been hauled around, coming to a halt, and Aoric leaped down from the saddle, his face contorted with fury.

"Are you all right?" he asked me.

"Only bruises so far," I gasped in reply.

I glanced over to where Julia stood, a horrified expression on her face. She, I knew, had thrown the dagger which had struck Egica's armour. All I could do was give her a nod to acknowledge that she had probably saved my life.

Then I looked down at Egica.

"You've killed him!" one of the warriors exclaimed, pointing an accusing finger at Aoric. "Your horse kicked him in the head."

A closer look at Egica confirmed that he was no longer breathing. His chest had been crushed by the weight of the horse, and its trailing leg had caught him full in the face, smashing his features to an unrecognisable pulp.

Aoric merely shrugged. His horse had done what he would have needed to do himself, but then came the sound of metal blades being drawn.

The two warriors were ready to avenge their leader, but another voice cut in before they could make a move.

"Hold! Put those swords away!"

We all turned to see Cniva striding towards us. He was on foot, with half a dozen of his usual bodyguards and aides marching in his wake.

"What happened here?" he demanded, his gaze moving from one person to the next.

I said, "Egica accused me of stealing a brooch. He planned to kill me in order to provoke Aoric into a fight. I'm guessing he was going to appoint one of these men to fight on his behalf."

"So how did he end up dead?" Cniva asked, his eyes boring into me.

"I fought back," I told him. "I didn't steal the brooch. He left it there for me to find, then came up and falsely accused me.

Aoric came riding up to help me, and his horse trampled over Egica."

Cniva looked at Egica's two companions.

"Well? Is this true? Did Egica plot to kill this man?"

"He's only a slave," one of them protested.

"So it is true?" Cniva pressed.

The silence from the two of them was all the confirmation he needed. Each of the men was bigger than Cniva, but the power of his personality overawed them.

He turned to Aoric, his face still angry.

"And you? Did you kill him deliberately?"

Aoric shrugged, "I was only trying to stop him. But I'm not sorry he's dead. I would have had to kill him sooner or later."

Cniva frowned, thinking things over. After a moment, he told the two warriors to carry Egica's body away.

"See that he is buried with due honour," he told them.

Then he turned to Aoric, saying, "But you will pay recompense. A helmet full of silver. Give it to Egica's widow when we return home. I know you don't have enough just now, so kill some Romans and take it from them."

Aoric accepted this judgement without protest, and the two warriors grudgingly heaved Egica's corpse off the ground, dragging it back to their own camp site, the dead man's heels ploughing furrows in the grass. As they went, Cniva told them, "This is an end to it. There will be no blood feud. Make sure everyone knows that."

Struggling under the weight of their dead leader, the warriors trudged away through the camp, ignoring the curious eyes of the many onlookers.

But the show was not yet over. Hands on his hips, Cniva turned to look me up and down, his expression unreadable.

"What am I going to do with you?" he said softly, clearly not expecting me to respond.

After a moment, he continued, "I don't think you will be safe if you remain here. Whatever I say, I expect some of Egica's followers will want some sort of revenge. They probably won't dare attack Aoric, but you are a different matter."

His eyes shifted to look beyond me, and he added, "And the girl will no doubt end up as someone's bed slave."

I wondered how much of the fight he had seen. Had he witnessed Julia throwing the dagger? Even if he hadn't, plenty of others must have seen it, and he'd learn of it soon enough.

Turning back to me, he rasped, "It would not concern me overly much if one of them decided to kill you, but I owe you a debt for freeing my son from Roman slavery, and for bringing him back to me."

I could not suppress a look of surprise. Up until now, Cniva had not shown much regard for Aoric at all. But, despite his hostile tone, it seemed he had undergone a change of heart.

Addressing Aoric, he said, "In the morning, take this man back to the Romans. Let him go free as a reward for the help he gave you. Then we will be rid of him."

Aoric nodded, "I will, Father. Thank you."

Staring Cniva in the eyes, I said, "My granddaughter comes with me."

He shot another look at Julia, then gave a nod, his mouth twisting in a faint smile.

"Yes, she goes too. I doubt any man would want a slave who can throw a knife like that."

So he had seen, and he had clearly been impressed.

Jabbing a finger at Aoric, he barked, "Just make sure they've gone. And then make sure you come back."

"I will, Father," Aoric promised.

So I knew that Julia and I were safe and free, but I also knew that my friendship with Aoric was coming to an end. After this night, we would be on opposite sides of the war. This saddened me, but I also knew that I must now take the chance to warn the Emperor of Cniva's plan to ambush him in the marshes. And yet, even while I knew that was the right thing to do, a part of me felt that I would be betraying my young friend.

War, I reflected, presents us with difficult choices. We can find ourselves fighting alongside men we hate, and facing men who would normally be our friends.

But I was a Roman, and Aoric was a Goth, and our sides had been chosen for us. Soon, there would be a battle, and one of us would be on the winning side, while the other would be among the losers. Whatever happened, though, I offered up a silent prayer that both of us would survive the day.

Chapter 16
A Single Death

None of us slept much that night. We were too keyed up to rest, so we sat and talked for a while.

I thanked Julia for her quick action in throwing the dagger at Egica, but she merely shrugged.

"I should have aimed for his eye," she said. "But I was worried he might dodge it, so I chose the larger target of his chest."

"You did the right thing," Aoric told her. "If you'd killed him, his men would have wanted revenge, and there would have been nothing my father could have done to stop them. It was better that he died under my horse."

Chewing her lip nervously, Julia asked, "Do you think they will come after us anyway?"

"I doubt it," Aoric said. "Not tonight, at any rate. And in the morning, I'll take you both away from here."

He spoke reassuringly, but he and I took turns to stay awake during the night while Julia slept beside the fire, stirring restlessly.

"What are you going to do with her?" Aoric asked me.

"I don't know yet," I replied. "She suggested we could disappear, change our names and hide somewhere far away."

"You've done that before," Aoric reminded me.

"Yes, but if I'm going to talk to the Emperor, it won't be possible to disappear and hope that Licinius Valerianus believes me to be dead. The Emperor will tell him I survived."

There was an awkward moment as I realised my blunder, but Aoric soon treated me to a grin as he asked, "So you're going to warn the Emperor that my father plans to ambush him in the marshes?"

"I'm sorry," I sighed. "I am a Roman. If I don't warn him, I'd be haunted by the memory for the rest of my life."

Aoric shrugged, "I understand. And, to be honest, it would not bother me overly much if there was no battle. If you warn the Emperor, perhaps there will be no fighting."

With a rueful smile, he added, "Of course, that leaves me with the problem of how to find enough silver to pay my promised bounty to Egica's family, but I'll worry about that later."

I gave him a grateful smile, but he waved away my thanks for his understanding.

"You should get some sleep," he told me. "You look exhausted."

Which was exactly how I felt. Wrapping myself in my cloak, I lay down and eventually fell asleep.

Aoric woke us before dawn, and we packed up our things in virtual silence, not even delaying to eat breakfast. Then Aoric took his horse by the reins and led it through the camp, with Julia and me walking silently alongside him.

There was a lot I wanted to say to Aoric, but I could not find the words. I wanted to hear him say that he would return to Rome with me; that our friendship would endure. Yet I knew that the lure of his Gothic heritage was drawing him away from me.

We walked on in silence as the first hints of sunrise appeared in the east, and the camp began to stir into life.

Then, as if the tension between us was too great for him to bear, Aoric suddenly blurted, "Just remember you can't trust my father."

His grim tone gave me the opening I wanted.

"I'll remember," I nodded. "But what about you? There is still time for you to come with me."

To my dismay, he shook his head.

"No. I know it will sound ridiculous, but after the past few years in your empire, I feel as if I've come home. I know I face a lot of problems, but I faced them when I was growing up. I'm not going to run away from them. And I want to prove to my father that I am worthy of his approval."

He paused for a moment, then sighed, "I suppose you think I am being foolish."

"Not at all," I assured him. "It is your life, and you must do what your heart tells you. I'm just sorry that this war has put us on opposite sides."

"So am I," he said. "For what it is worth, you will always be my friend. You have been more of a father to me than my real one."

After a short hesitation, I replied, "And yet you wish to remain with him?"

Aoric's mouth twisted in an expression that was half way between a grin and a grimace.

"It's hard to explain," he informed me. "A part of me does want to return to Rome with you, but what would I be in your empire? You have enemies in high places, and all I would ever amount to is being your bodyguard. Here, I am the son of the King. A minor son, right enough, but I could become an important man. After years of being regarded as nothing more than Cniva's bastard child, that would mean a lot to me."

"There is more to life than being rich and important," I remarked.

"Maybe," Aoric shrugged. "But those things help."

I could not make up my mind whether he was trying to justify his decision or whether he really did want to stay among the Goths, but I knew him well enough not to push him too hard.

I said to him, "For what it is worth, you have been like a son to me. I won't forget that."

Around us, people were packing up, preparing to move. I guessed that Cniva wanted to send his precious booty to an even safer distance from the pursuing Romans, but Aoric made no comment, and I did not want to put further pressure on our relationship, so I relapsed into silence.

We were heading towards the low line of hills which marked one side of the wide valley. Here, we encountered a group of around fifteen horsemen, all of them mounted and waiting expectantly.

"Those are my new companions," Aoric told me. "I've been riding with them these past days."

The men were a rough-looking lot, with fierce expressions and a ragged, unkempt appearance. None of them wore chainmail, but relied on jerkins of thick, toughened leather, some of them sporting iron studs for added protection. They had swords held in saddle scabbards, but their main weapons were lances and bows. Lightly armoured, they could outrun any heavier cavalry. Aoric's horse, I guessed, would have its work cut out to keep up with them while Aoric was wearing his chainmail.

Aoric called a greeting, and the men acknowledged him with nods and murmurs. One of them brought a fine horse, already saddled, and passed the reins to me. The horse was a black gelding, with wild eyes and a rather aggressive mood. It pranced and snorted, shaking its maned head as I took hold of the reins.

"His rider was killed in the battle up in the pass," Aoric informed me. "He is yours now."

It was a generous gift, even if the horse did appear to be more high-spirited than I would have liked. I thanked him, then warily moved round, grabbing hold of the saddle horns and heaving myself up into the saddle. The horse skittered, but although I was far from an expert horseman, I knew enough to treat him firmly. He settled down, then I asked Aoric to help Julia climb up in front of me.

The poor girl was doing her best to appear unafraid, but the curious glances of the Gothic horsemen were obviously making her feel uncomfortable. Even so, when Aoric offered to boost her up, she waved him away, then sprang lightly up, gripping the nearest saddle horn and twisting in mid-air before landing in front of me, facing sideways away from the mounted scouts. It was an impressive manoeuvre, especially for a girl, and I heard some of the men murmuring in admiration of her agility. As I'd expected, a couple of them made lewd remarks which Aoric silenced with a curt bark as he mounted his own horse.

I placed my arms around Julia to grip the reins, then our group set off along the valley at a walk.

Aoric and I led the way, with the rest of the scouts a short distance behind. In a low voice, Aoric said to me, "I'm not sure whether my father has given them orders to protect me or to make sure I go back. But you can see that, even if I did want to go with you, I can't."

We both lapsed into silence again, each of us consumed by the knowledge that we would be parting, possibly forever. The past weeks had seen other partings, mostly enforced by war, but men like Gallus, Cimber, Julius Priscus and Camillus had all been fleeting acquaintances, while Aoric had been my closest companion for the past two years. Since I had lost contact with my family, he had been a surrogate son to me, and I felt genuinely pained that we would need to go our separate ways. But he was a Goth, and I was a Roman, and the gods had decreed separate paths for us.

As I rode, I realised that I could see much more of the valley from horseback. Without the need to push a bogged-down wagon, the valley and its surroundings seemed much wider than I had imagined. There were low hills, most of them forested, on either side of the marshy plain which was, I guessed, roughly two Roman miles wide. There was a river, too, not hugely wide or deep, but a river nonetheless, and this was the heart of the wetland.

Dotted all across this wide bog were small groups of men. Wet and filthy, they were chewing on chunks of salted meat while they waited to play their part in the upcoming battle. They watched us incuriously as we passed, presumably taking us for a scouting party. We were riding near one side of the wetland, and I peered closely at the woodland to our right. There were no camp fires sending ribbons of smoke up between the trees, but I could detect movement in the shadowy gloom. Aoric noticed me looking that way, and he gave a thin smile as if to acknowledge that I was right to assume that Cniva had concealed a great part of his army in the trees.

Julia must have been very uncomfortable sitting wedged in front of me, but she was too tense to complain. The past few days must have been horrible for her, and despite her determination to appear strong, I knew she was afraid to hope that we would soon be free.

"It won't be long now," I whispered in her ear. "We'll soon be free."

She gave a slight nod, but kept her eyes downcast. I could see her lips moving slightly, and I guessed she was offering up prayers for our safety. I hoped the gods listened to her with more favour than they generally listened to me.

As we approached the far end of the marsh, we found a large group of Gothic cavalry. These were the men who would form Cniva's front line, the thousands of warriors whose task it was to lure the Roman army deeper into the marshes where the rest of Cniva's forces were hidden. I looked all along the lines of horsemen, seeking out the Gothic King, but I could see no sign of him.

Aoric took us around the right flank of the Gothic cavalry, his scouts still close behind us. We continued for perhaps another half mile, moving more easily on firmer ground now that we had left the river valley behind us. Aoric reined in, and I stopped beside him. We were in an open meadow, with stands of trees and rising ground ahead of us.

"This is as far as I can go," he said. "Beyond that rise, you'll find the Roman army."

I took a deep breath, then slowly exhaled.

"Take care of yourself," I told him. "If there is a battle, make sure you don't get yourself killed."

"I'll be careful," he promised.

Julia twisted around to look at him.

"Are you really letting us go?" she asked, clearly nervous of betrayal.

"Yes," he said. "It will be up to you to look after this old man now. Be careful. He gets himself into all sorts of trouble."

The two of them nodded to each other in a silent agreement, then Aoric leaned over, holding out his hand for me to grip in a final farewell.

We exchanged a long look, both of us regretful, yet also thankful that we had shared a genuine friendship.

When we broke off our long handshake, Aoric said, "Go!" as he slapped my horse's rump, setting it off into a gallop. The move was so sudden that Julia had to cling tightly to the saddle horn, while I leaned forwards, my chin resting on her shoulder as the two of us struggled for balance. I wanted to turn around, to wave farewell, but I realised that Aoric had jolted my mount into action so as not to prolong our goodbyes. All I could do was hold on and let the horse have its head.

And then I did tug back on the reins because I saw more riders cresting the low rise and coming towards us. There were over a hundred of them, and they were obviously Romans. Not only that, I saw the dark cloaks of the Praetorians, and as I drew closer, I recognised the young man who led them.

"Who are they?" Julia asked in a frightened voice as I hauled the horse to a halt.

I told her, "That is Herennius Etruscus, the Emperor's son."

She turned to look at me, her eyes wide with surprise.

"Really?"

"Really. Let me do the talking."

Etruscus' men spread out into a two-deep line, then slowed and came to a halt. Etruscus himself rode forwards, with another man wearing a plumed helmet riding beside him. I recognised him as Apurius Cimber, the Tribune who had been my escort on the ill-fated march over the mountains.

Both of them stopped and stared at me incredulously.

"Sempronius Scipio?" Etruscus gasped. "We thought you were dead. How did you get here? And who is that with you?"

I said, "This is Julia. She is a Roman citizen. She helped me when we were both captured by the Goths. And I have vital news for your father, the Emperor."

Etruscus kept his focus on Aoric and the Gothic scouts who were watching us from the foot of the gentle slope.

"Those Goths were chasing you?" he asked.

"No, They were escorting me through the Gothic army so that I could reach you."

"They set you free?" Etruscus frowned. "Why?"

"It's a complicated story, Augustus," I said, not wishing to go into details of my recent misadventures.

Etruscus did not seem overly interested in any case. His eyes remained fixed on the Goths, and a cruel smile flickered on his lips.

He smirked, "Well, more fool them. We'll soon chase them back."

"No!" I protested. "They did not come to fight."

Etruscus' young face was eager with anticipation as he said, "That's their problem. Let's strike the first blow. We came to see what they were up to, so we need to get past them anyway."

"Augustus!" I implored. "I must speak to your father. I have vital information. And the main Gothic force is only a little way behind those men."

"Then we'll take a look. Cimber, take Scipio to my father."

Then he drew his sword, holding it high, and bellowed a command.

"Charge!"

I had to wrestle my horse into submission as it tried to turn to follow the riders who streamed past on either side. Cimber, his face a mask of frowns, stayed with me, but the entire force of Praetorian cavalry galloped down the shallow slope towards Aoric's small group of fifteen.

Julia let out a gasp, and Cimber snorted, "Don't worry. Our young Emperor is eager for glory, but those Goths won't stand and fight. They'll turn tail any moment now."

He was right, but before they fled, Aoric's riders drew their bows and loosed a small volley of arrows at the charging Romans. It was little more than a gesture of defiance because the Praetorians carried shields and wore chainmail armour, but one arrow did find a target. As Aoric and his men hauled their mounts around and kicked them into a gallop, the Roman charge faltered, the men in the centre frantically drawing to a halt, disrupting the line which soon collapsed into confusion as the men on the flanks discovered that their leader was no longer with them.

"Oh, Jupiter!" Cimber exclaimed. "The Augustus has been hit!"

He abandoned us, riding quickly down the slope. I followed more sedately, and by the time we arrived, he had confirmed his worst fears.

"He's dead!" I heard Cimber declare as he stood up from where Etruscus' armoured body lay stretched on the ground. All around, Praetorians looked on with horrified faces, scarcely able to believe what had happened.

Cimber held an arrow in his hands, frowning deeply as he held it up to display the blood-stained tip.

"It struck him in the throat," he told me as Praetorians lifted Etruscus' body and slung it over the saddle of his horse.

Julia turned to bury her head in my shoulder, and I could feel her trembling. I placed a hand on her back, trying to reassure her, but I was more concerned by the reaction of the Praetorians. It was plain to see what they were thinking. This was a bad omen, not only for the day, but for the empire. For the Emperor to lose his eldest son was a blow which could seriously harm our cause. Emperor Decius did have another son, I knew, but he was still a boy, and far away in Rome. Etruscus had been heir to the imperial throne, and one moment of bad luck had ended his life.

We rode back slowly, nobody wanting to break the bad news to the rest of the army. Over the rise, through tree-bordered pastures, we reached the main Roman camp which was little more than three miles from where Etruscus had fallen.

The army was preparing to march, but everyone gaped at us in near disbelief as we took the corpse of the Augustus towards the centre of the camp where his father and co-Emperor waited. He had a tent now, a large marquee decked in purple, but he emerged when word reached him of our approach. I saw him walk out, head held high, with a gaggle of red-cloaked senior officers around him. Already, the sound of wailing could be heard from the ranks of the soldiers. Word of Etruscus' death was spreading rapidly, and causing dismay throughout the camp. Legionaries ran towards us, crowding around and calling out their grief as we rode steadfastly on.

When we drew near to the *Principia*, we came to a halt, and Cimber dismounted. I lifted Julia down to the ground, then followed, but I placed a hand on her shoulder, making sure we stood a little way back because I had no wish to intrude on the Emperor's grief.

Messius Decius was dressed in armour, with a plumed helmet and the purple cloak which marked him out as ruler of the empire. He stood tall and proud, his lined face impassive as he spoke quietly to Cimber. After a brief exchange of words, he strode deliberately over to where his son's body hung over the back of his horse. He took one look, bowed his head, then stood erect again, one fist clamped around the hilt of the sword which hung at his hip.

"See that he is cremated with due honour!" he said, speaking in a loud, clear voice. "And let nobody mourn. The death of one soldier is no great loss to the Republic!"

It was a display of cold-blooded Roman stoicism which both amazed and appalled me, but Decius was Emperor, and I supposed that men who reach that exalted position cannot afford the luxury of normal emotions. His reaction was designed to instil determination in his men rather than grief over the loss of his eldest son. I supposed he must have been hurting inside, but he concealed his grief behind an implacable mask of resolution. He had even retained enough control to use the term "Republic" when speaking of the empire. Officially, Rome was still a republic even though it had been ruled by emperors for over two hundred years. The Emperor was designated as the First Among Equals, and it never ceased to amaze me how men of senatorial rank could happily maintain the fiction.

Etruscus' horse was led away, and then Cimber pointed to me. I saw the Emperor's surprise, then he beckoned me over.

"Sempronius Scipio!" he said, managing to give me a wan smile. "You have returned from the dead with news for me?"

I could only admire his attitude of determination. I could not have behaved that way if my son had just been killed, but I decided that the least I could do was attempt to match him.

Nodding, I said, "Yes, Augustus, I do."

"Then come into my tent. My staff officers will need to hear it."

I gestured towards Julia as I said, "Augustus, this girl is a Roman citizen. She was captured by the Goths, but I tricked them into believing that she was my granddaughter, so they let her come with me. But she is tired and hungry."

The Emperor waved towards one of his Tribunes.

"Have the girl taken care of," he commanded.

Julia stiffened, but I leaned down to whisper, "It's all right. I'll be back as soon as I've spoken to the Emperor."

"I don't want to leave you!" she almost wailed, gripping my tunic in two fists.

I shot a look of apology to the Emperor, but he was already turning away, his aides making to follow him.

I looked at the young Tribune who had been commanded to care for her.

"Let her wait outside the tent," I told him. "Just make sure she gets some food."

The Tribune scowled. Taking care of orphan girls was not part of his regular duty, but he gave a nod, clicking his fingers as he said, "Come on, then, girl."

We walked towards the huge tent, following the Emperor's party, but I noticed another of the helmeted men waiting for us at the entrance. He gave me an amused look as I drew near. Things were happening so quickly that it took me a moment to place him, but I realised it was none other than Trebonianus Gallus, Governor of Moesia and commander of the defence of Novae. Beside him was Fabius Successianus, Prefect of *Legio I*. Their presence confirmed what I had heard from Aoric; the Emperor had brought all of his reserves. And somehow, he had convinced, or perhaps commanded, Gallus to leave the safety of Novae and march with the army.

"You must have a tale to tell," Gallus said as he fell in beside me. "Where is your young friend?"

"You'll hear that when the Emperor does," I replied.

I was not at all sure how to respond to Gallus' presence here. I had instinctively liked him when we had first met, but I was not at all sure of his motives or loyalty to the empire.

Julia was another concern, but she sat down outside the entrance to the tent, placing herself to one side and crossing her legs. There were several Praetorians standing guard close by, so I reckoned she would be safe enough. The young Tribune ordered one of the guards to fetch her something to eat, then he followed me inside the tent, his duty done.

In the main chamber of the high tent was a large, wooden table on which was spread out a map of the local area. The Emperor and all of his officers stood around the table, most of them waiting for me to tell my tale.

As I approached the table, I glanced at the map, noticing that most of it was blank. Some settlements and rivers were marked, but there was nothing to explain what the terrain was like.

At a signal from the Emperor, Cimber began the meeting by explaining, "Scipio was captured by the Goths. He claims that they let him go."

The Emperor regarded me with one eyebrow raised. If he was feeling any grief over the death of his son, he was hiding it well.

"I think it is time we heard your story," he said to me.

I nodded, "Of course, Augustus. I'm sure you will remember the young man I introduced as my grandson. I'm afraid I was less than truthful. He was, in fact, a Goth, a former slave I had freed and who agreed to accompany me as a bodyguard."

Decius barely reacted to this. The man was, I thought, less than human.

I went on, "We were captured when the Goths ambushed us in the mountain pass, and I was held prisoner. But it turned out that, unknown to me, my companion was actually one of Cniva's sons. As a result, Cniva set me free as a reward for helping his son when he had been a slave in Rome."

I could tell that the Emperor was less than enthralled by this selectively edited version of events, so I hurriedly went on, "While I was in Cniva's camp, I learned how he plans to fight you."

Now I had the attention of every man there.

"Go on," the Emperor invited.

I said, "A few miles ahead, your route is barred by a large area of marshland. There is firm ground leading to it, but then it stretches away to east and west, with low hills on either side. Cniva has placed a large force near the entrance to the valley. Their role is to put up a fight, then turn and flee, luring you westwards into a trap. He has hidden half of his army in the trees on either side of the valley."

Decius nodded, "I see. How certain are you of this?"

"I saw many Goths moving into the trees, and I've heard this report from listening to conversations."

"Ah, yes. You speak their language," the Emperor nodded. "But I am surprised that Cniva set you free to bring me this news."

I smiled, "I think that is because he is actually planning something else, Augustus."

"What do you mean?"

"I mean that Cniva is a cunning devil. I think he made sure I heard and saw his plan, then set me free to bring you this news."

"To what end?" the Emperor wanted to know.

"I don't know, Augustus. But I do know that he has chosen terrain which is little more than a marsh. It is difficult ground for cavalry. The Gothic baggage is camped on firmer ground at the far end of the valley, although I think he intends to move them north towards the Danubius while his army faces you."

The Emperor frowned, "Much of Cniva's army is mounted. Why would he choose such poor cavalry terrain?"

I had no answer to that, so all I could do was give a helpless shrug.

"I can only tell you what I have seen, Augustus."

"Is there any way of getting around their flanks?" he probed.

"I'm not a military man," I replied. "But I don't think so."

Gallus intervened, "Our scouts suggest that Cniva's flanks are protected by hills and woods. It seems he's chosen a site where we must face him head on."

"But what other trap does he have planned for us?" the Emperor wondered, looking directly at me.

"I'm afraid I cannot say, Augustus. But I have seen his front line, and I've seen the men he sent into the hills."

"Could they be trying to circle around us?" Gallus mused.

"I don't think so," I replied. "They were still there this morning. At least, some of them were. I couldn't count their numbers because they were well hidden among the trees."

"Or because most of them were no longer there," Gallus countered.

I gave a shrug. I had no idea what Cniva's plan really was. All I knew was that Aoric had told me I could not trust him.

The Emperor said, "There could be another reason why Scipio was set free."

Everyone waited, watching him expectantly, and he explained, "Cniva knows we are about to overtake him. He has taken a lot of plunder, and he cannot move his baggage train quickly enough to escape us. But he is using this terrain to slow us, setting up a screening force. By allowing Scipio to see his supposed trap, he is simply buying more time for his main force to get away. He thinks we will fear to attack him in case we are trapped."

Nobody argued, least of all me. It sounded entirely plausible. I would not have put it past Cniva to use me as a dupe in a plan like that.

The Emperor looked around at his aides.

"Well?" he asked. "How do we face the enemy? We must defeat him. He has plundered Roman towns and captured many Roman citizens, some of them of senatorial rank. That must not go unpunished. Trap or not, we must attack."

It was Trebonianus Gallus who answered, "If we must face him head on, and if there is a risk of being ambushed, or possibly encircled, then I suggest we divide our army into three divisions. The first division must be comprised of cavalry, and it should attack Cniva's leading ranks. If they flee, we will know that Scipio has told the truth. If the Goths attempt to ambush our first division, a second cavalry force will be following at a short distance and will be able to counter this threat."

"And the third division?" the Emperor asked.

"Should form a reserve," Gallus replied. "A couple of thousand cavalry, plus all the infantry, can move up to the entrance to the valley. From there, it can either provide support, or, if the Goths do attempt to circle out from those hills, this division will block their path, so protecting the cavalry's rear."

The Emperor nodded. He was an experienced commander himself, and he had fought the Goths before. He had, in fact, become Emperor thanks to his victory over Cniva's predecessor.

"I agree," he said. "And in view of the potential danger of a trap, I want you to command the third division, Gallus."

Trebonianus Gallus nodded his acceptance of this role.

"I will lead the second division, " Decius went on. "Paulinus, you will lead the first. Strike hard and follow if they flee, but keep your men together. If they break ranks, they will be more vulnerable."

Paulinus, I saw, was an experienced man, grim-faced and with iron-grey hair. He gave a confident nod, offering the Emperor a salute as acknowledgement of the honour he had been given.

There was a lot more discussion about which units should form which part of the army, but eventually the Emperor clapped his hands together and announced, "That is enough. When we offered sacrifice this morning, the omens were favourable, but the morning is almost gone. It is time to deal with Cniva once and for all. Call the men to arms! We march now!"

Chapter 17
Ambush

When the Emperor and his entourage hurried out of the tent, none of them paid much attention to me. Idly, I followed them, watching them hurry off to various parts of the camp, while a string of horses was brought for the Emperor and his closest staff.

A couple of Praetorians still stood guard at the entrance to the empty tent, and Julia pushed herself to her feet, offering me a small piece of cheese and two olives.

"You haven't had any breakfast," she reminded me, her face serious.

"Thanks," I nodded, taking the offered food and chewing hungrily.

"What is going to happen?" she asked me. "Are they going to fight the Goths?"

"Yes."

"What about us?"

"We'll stay here, I think," I told her between mouthfuls. "There will probably be a few soldiers left behind to guard the camp. And there are all the slaves who belong to the officers, so we won't be alone."

"And then what?" she pressed, her demeanour still nervous.

I sighed, "I suppose that will depend on who wins the battle."

She looked beyond me, nodding to indicate something or someone.

"That officer wants you," she said in a warning whisper.

I turned to see Trebonianus Gallus striding towards me.

"There you are!" he beamed. "I wondered where you had got to."

I gave a shrug, still distrusting his apparent friendliness. I had not forgotten the thinly veiled threat he had made when I had left Novae in the company of the Emperor's son.

He said, "I'd like you to come with me, Scipio. You know the Goths, and I'd value your advice."

A horrible suspicion churned in my guts. Gallus was smiling, but I feared he might have decided to have me done away with in the confusion of battle. What, I wondered, had passed between him and Messius Decius when they had met? Did Gallus blame me in some way for the Emperor's decision to command him out of his haven at Novae?

Still smiling, he asked, "What's wrong, man?"

I gestured towards Julia.

"This girl is in my care," I told him.

He turned his charm on Julia.

"You won't mind staying here while Scipio accompanies me, will you? I'll have my slaves look after you."

Julia turned worried eyes on me in silent appeal.

Gallus went on, "There are things I need to discuss with Scipio. You'll be perfectly safe here until we get back. On my honour as a Senator."

Julia was tongue-tied, and I was little better.

"I'd prefer to stay here," I told Gallus. "I'm too old for fighting, even if I was any good at it."

He said, "I don't want you to do any fighting. Come, the army is leaving, and I want to talk to you."

He reached out, taking hold of my forearm to lead me away.

I hurriedly told Julia, "I'll be back as soon as I can. I promise."

The look on her young face was as full of loss and despair as any I had ever seen.

"My slaves will look after her," Gallus repeated.

Even as he spoke, two slaves came up to us, each of them leading a saddled horse. One of the mounts was the black gelding Aoric had given me.

"Come on!" Gallus said, his tone and stance framing it as somewhere between an invitation and a command.

As Gallus climbed into his saddle, he told the slaves about Julia, pointing towards her.

"Keep her safe," he told them.

Knowing I could not go against a man as powerful as Gallus, I had no option except to follow him. One of the slaves cupped his hands, helping me climb into the saddle, and then I nudged the horse into motion as Gallus led the way to the northern section of the camp. As I went, I twisted in the saddle, giving Julia what I hoped she would see as a reassuring wave. She did not wave back.

Gallus, noticing my concern, remarked, "You do seem to have a habit of acquiring waifs and strays, Scipio."

"Her father was killed by the Goths in Philippopolis," I told him, my voice bitter.

Gallus shrugged, "That was a bad affair, right enough. I'm sure she'll be grateful to you."

Since he had not been at Philippopolis, I wasn't sure how he could know how awful it had been, but I did not argue. His manner suggested he had other things on his mind, and he soon confirmed this.

"Most of the cavalry has already gone," he informed me. "The legions are forming up outside the camp now. You can stay with me as part of my staff."

"I'm sure you don't need me," I said, still hoping he might agree to leave me behind.

Ignoring my comment, he went on, "I would value your presence. You've spoken to Cniva, and you've sheltered his son."

"I didn't know he was Cniva's son," I reminded him.

"I believe you," he nodded in a tone which suggested he did not believe me at all. "But it's as well that I did not know we had Cniva's own son in our midst when the Goths were attacking Novae."

I told him, "It wouldn't have made a difference. They don't exactly see eye to eye."

Gallus pointed out, "And yet Cniva freed you because you helped his son when he was a slave of the empire."

I said, "I told you. He used that as an excuse to send me here with news of his alleged plan. He couldn't be seen to be freeing me unless he had a valid reason."

"Ah, yes. You think he let you go so that you could warn us about an alleged ambush. But if that is a trick, then he must be up to something else."

"That would be my guess," I agreed. "And I think the Emperor is probably right. Cniva is trying to delay us to give his baggage train more time to reach the river."

"Yes, that seems plausible," Gallus agreed. "But we must take precautions to ensure that we are not trapped by any other snare Cniva has laid for us. As I warned the Emperor, those hills and forests may make attacking his flanks almost impossible, but that doesn't mean he couldn't send his men through onto open ground. Once out of the trees, they might circle around behind us."

"Is that what you would do?" I asked him.

"Assuredly," he nodded. "Swamps are not conducive to cavalry battles. I'd put my horses where they can be of use. If he can get a sizeable force through the hills and forests, they could cause us a real problem."

With a confident smile, he added, "If they do that, it will be my task to stop them."

We moved outside the camp. Beyond the open gateway, rank upon rank of soldiers were arrayed in battle formation. The senior officers were mounted, but the Centurions with their plumed helmets stood in the ranks, and each unit held its identifying banners high. I counted three legionary eagle standards, along with dozens of flags denoting smaller units, probably vexillations from other legions or groups of Auxiliaries.

Gallus' own staff officers were waiting, but they fell in behind us at a discreet distance, leaving me alone with him as he trotted his horse to the head of the army.

"Advance!" he called, waving his right arm high, and the march began.

I saw that there were units of cavalry riding far out on the flanks as protection, and another group of a few hundred scouting the way ahead. Gallus had a fairly formidable force under his command, but it was slow-moving when compared to the swift-riding Goths and the larger contingent of the Roman army which was led by the Emperor himself.

As soon as we were under way, the horses moving at a walk so as not to outdistance the foot soldiers, Gallus picked up our conversation as if there had been no interruption.

"You were captured during the battle in the high pass?" he asked.

"That's right."

"Then what happened to you? Cniva must have taken you along with him when he went to Philippopolis."

I managed not to show any outward reaction. Gallus was too sharp to be fooled by a direct lie, so I decided to modify the truth.

"Yes, I was at Philippopolis. Cniva managed to persuade Julius Priscus to declare himself Emperor. Cniva promised to back him, and to help him get to Rome. Priscus believed the Emperor was already dead, you see."

"The man was a fool!" Gallus snorted. "Philippopolis had strong walls. He could have held out for weeks."

"He believed there was no chance of any help arriving," I explained.

"That shouldn't have mattered," Gallus insisted. "If the place was well provisioned, the Goths would have given up sooner or later for lack of food and fodder for their horses."

"I think Priscus was simply out of his depth," I replied. "But, for whatever reason, he believed Cniva's promises. He opened the city gates, and he was then set upon and murdered while the Goths sacked the city."

Gallus shook his head.

"Some men, even Senators, should not be given a governorship simply because they are wealthy. I'm sorry for Priscus, but it's as well Cniva killed him. The Emperor would never have let him live."

"Only provided the Emperor was able to beat the Goths," I observed. "If Cniva really had backed Priscus, it would have been difficult to defeat him."

At this, Gallus gave a pensive nod before saying, "Well, we shall soon learn who is the stronger. Cniva is going to face a genuine fight this time."

It was late morning by the time our army had gathered. The Emperor and his cavalry, divided into two strong divisions, waited atop the gentle rise where Herennius Etruscus had made his last, fatal charge. Down below, at the edge of the swampy valley, the Goths sat and waited. If the Emperor was correct, waiting suited them because it meant that their vast haul of plunder was being taken ever further towards safety with every passing hour.

When the legions arrived, Gallus promptly directed them into position, then sent a rider to inform the Emperor that he was ready. Decius did not wait a moment longer. Horns sounded the attack, and the leading cavalry broke into a slow advance, gradually increasing pace from a walk to a trot, then to a canter as they approached the Gothic lines. Arrows flew to meet them, and some men and horses went down, but then the leading Roman horsemen broke into a full gallop, thundering towards their enemy. In turn, the Goths kicked their own mounts into a gallop, knowing that to meet a cavalry charge standing still was to lose the fight.

Ahead of us, the Emperor had advanced his own division, and Gallus ordered the legions forwards. He also sent word to the flanking cavalry units to spread well out and to watch our sides in case Cniva had sent another force to encircle us.

With the advantage of being on horseback, and being near the top of the low rise, I had a good view of the battle. The clash as the two lines of cavalry met was awful, a cacophony of sound as weapons and armour crashed against each other, mixed with the screams of men and horses. It was a horrible, confusing mass of human and animal bodies seething together in a storm of ferocity.

Gallus watched the furious battle imperturbably.

"Most cavalry fights don't last long," he informed me casually. "One side will break off once they realise they are being beaten."

I looked on in horrified fascination as the battle raged, and then the Goths began to fall back. The initial Roman attack had been made by around ten thousand riders, but although the Goths outnumbered them, many of the barbarians were more lightly armoured, and the pressure of the Roman charge pushed them backwards. It began as a trickle, then a stream, and finally a torrent as the Goths turned tail and galloped wildly into the marshes, their mounts sending up splashes of mud and filthy water as they fled.

The horns sounded again, the calls ragged because the trumpeters were riding fast-moving horses, and the Romans chased their quarry. But Paulinus, the man appointed to command the leading division, remembered his orders and kept his men together as they ploughed into the morass in pursuit of the fleeing Goths.

"Now we shall see whether your information was correct," Gallus said to me, seeming almost amused. "That did seem remarkably easy."

We continued to advance, drawing up in formation around three hundred paces from where the initial clash had taken place. Ahead of us, the Emperor had led his own force of riders into the marsh, maintaining a distance between himself and Paulinus' triumphant horsemen. In their wake, they allowed us to see the detritus left behind by the fight. Men and horses lay in scattered confusion, some still moving feebly. A few men, their horses lost or dead, staggered back, some of them nursing horrible wounds. Slashed faces, broken limbs and bleeding bodies limped back towards us. Gallus sent out some of his medical orderlies to meet them.

"Take them behind our lines!" he called. "The ones who can walk should be sent back to the camp."

I was aware of all this, but most of my attention was on the receding battle. It was difficult to make out details as the armies moved further into the swamp, but the blare of horns alerted me to something important.

"Enemy on the flanks!" Gallus said, interpreting the military call. "It seems you were right, Scipio."

Then he added, "And there goes the Emperor to teach Cniva we won't be caught in a trap so easily."

The Emperor's second division of cavalry was now moving quickly, the horses struggling through the swampy ground to join the fight. Cniva's hidden men must have poured out of the woods to attack Paulinus' force, but now Decius was going to catch them in a trap of his own.

"It will be touch and go," Gallus declared. "The numbers will probably be fairly equal."

All the time, his head was turning, watching our flanks for any sign of an encircling attack, but the horizons to either side were empty of troops.

"Old Decius must have been right," he said softly. "Cniva merely wants to delay us."

I could not shake off the chill running through my bones. So far, it seemed that things were progressing just as the Emperor had hoped. Perhaps he was right, and Cniva had only permitted me to see his ambush in the hopes that my report would prevent a Roman attack.

And yet I could not shake off the feeling that Cniva was too cunning to place reliance on that one gambit. But what else could he have planned? If he was going to try to launch a surprise attack at our rear as Gallus had feared, he had left it very late indeed, because there was no sign of any flanking attack.

It was almost impossible to see what was happening now. All across the valley, men and horses were struggling ferociously, but once again, the fight did not last long. The Goths had tried to trap the Romans, but by dividing his army into two strong divisions, Decius had countered Cniva's plan, and the Goths fled once again.

"That will teach them!" Gallus shouted. "They are on the run, lads. A nice, easy battle for us. Give it a little while, then we'll move in and mop up."

The nearest soldiers, the only ones who could hear him, gave a ragged cheer. What he meant was that they would be able to loot the bodies of the fallen without having to risk themselves in the fight.

The distant sound of battle wafted back to us in the still air. Horns continued to sound, but the fighting pressed further down the valley, almost out of sight.

Then Gallus sat up straight, his eyes and ears straining.

"What's that?" he asked. "Rally? Enemy on the flanks?"

We waited in tense silence, and I could tell that Gallus was debating whether to risk advancing his legions into the swamp. After a while, he sent a messenger to order half of the flanking cavalry to ride ahead and find out what was happening. Soon, several hundred horsemen were moving into the quagmire, picking a way between fallen bodies of men and horses.

Gallus began to drum his fingers on one horn of his saddle, his mouth a thin line of concentration as he stared along the valley in hope of making out some detail. The fighting continued, because we could still hear the sounds of battle, and soon there was a great cheer like the distant roar of a rampaging pride of lions.

"I don't like the sound of that," Gallus murmured.

Then we could see riders galloping back, although their horses were floundering as they ploughed along the valley.

"Sound the readiness!" he called to his own trumpeters. "Watch for the enemy!"

The horsemen who were plunging towards us were Romans. They came in a ragged bunch, with many more scattered in small groups coming after them as quickly as they could. Some of the leading men were from Gallus' own units, others were Praetorians or heavy cavalry from the Emperor's division. All of them rode back towards us, their horses foaming at the mouths, with wild eyes, sweating bodies, and mud-caked legs. It was obvious that they had taken part in a desperate fight.

A Praetorian Centurion led the way. He hauled his exhausted mount to a halt just in front of Gallus, and we could see that he, too, was tired to the point of collapse. His face was grimy with sweat and mud, his sword dented and stained with blood.

"There was a second ambush!" he reported in gasping breaths. "It was a double trap. We thought we had beaten them, but there were more of them hidden further along the valley."

Gallus frowned, knowing this news signalled a defeat.

"What of the Emperor?" he asked.

The Centurion shook his head.

"The Goths surrounded him in huge numbers. We tried to reach him, but there were too many of them. He was pulled from his horse and cut to pieces."

"You are sure of this?" Gallus asked in a shocked whisper.

The Centurion gave a grim nod, his voice thick with emotion as he said, "Yes. The Emperor is dead."

Chapter 18
Treaty

More and more Roman horsemen emerged from the valley, many of the men and horses wounded, but even their safe return could not dissipate the sense of loss and dread which hung over Gallus' command.

"They won't stand if the Goths attack us now," he mused darkly, his eyes scanning the ranks of the infantry. The soldiers still stood in line, but there was a loud murmur of discontented voices from them.

Fabius Successianus, Prefect of *Legio I*, had obviously reached the same conclusion. He rode hurriedly over to Gallus' command post, saluted and said, "We should return to the camp, Governor. If we stay out here, the Goths could surround us."

Gallus frowned, "Give the order. But I want an orderly march, not a panicked flight. Tell the cavalry to form a screen to cover the withdrawal."

Commands were shouted, horns blown, and signal flags waved, and the legions turned about, setting off at a brisk pace towards the camp they had left only a few hours earlier.

Gallus, to his credit, left Successianus to oversee the retreat while he and his command staff withdrew only as far as the top of the slope from where we looked down on the distant marsh from where Roman horsemen were still struggling homewards in small groups or even singly. As they reached the battered cavalry contingent, Centurions and Tribunes hustled them into the ranks, forming a defensive line against any Gothic pursuit.

"They'll turn tail if the Goths do come," Gallus muttered. "Let's hope the barbarians are too busy plundering the bodies of the fallen."

We sat there in shocked silence for another hour, constantly watching the marshy valley. A few Goths did appear, but they quickly retreated when they saw the Roman cavalry waiting near the end of the valley.

"What is Cniva planning?" Gallus mused pensively. "Will he try to destroy us, or will he be content with what he has achieved?"

He looked directly at me as he spoke, so I offered, "The Goths came for plunder. They've already achieved more than most raiders. I cannot be sure, but I expect he will prefer to cross the Danubius with the booty he has already stolen."

Gallus nodded, his face grim, but he waited another hour before, to everyone's relief, he at last gave the order to return to the camp. We rode back quickly, the cavalry screen following close behind, and returned in time to see that the legions were manning the ramparts of the camp as a precaution against a Gothic assault.

While the cavalry troopers rode to their allotted section of the camp to tend to their mounts, Trebonianus Gallus led his small group of aides to the *Principia* where I saw Julia waiting anxiously outside the main tent. She ran to meet me when I dismounted and handed the reins of my horse to one of Gallus' slaves.

"I thought you were dead!" she sobbed as she clasped her arms around my waist. "They said all the horsemen were killed."

"Not all," I assured her, holding her close. "I was never in any danger."

"But the Emperor is dead?" she asked as she at last eased her grip on me.

"So they say," I nodded.

"So what will happen?"

I had a feeling I knew the answer. Trebonianus Gallus stood close by, all of his senior officers in attendance, waiting for his decision.

I heard Fabius Successianus say, "I have issued rations of *posca* to every man."

Posca, I knew, was a drink given to soldiers to refresh their energy. It was made by taking poor quality wine, or even good wine that had gone off, and mixing it with water. The wine on its own would have tasted like vinegar, but diluting it made the drink a little more palatable, and the flavour was improved by adding various herbs and spices to the mix, then putting in a pinch of salt. I had tasted this foul-sounding concoction in the past and, while it would not have been my drink of choice, it had not tasted too bad. Its main purpose, though, was to refresh tired limbs and reinvigorate exhausted minds. There was no doubt that it was needed that day. Our legions may have been unscathed, but the Goths had won a huge victory, and we all knew it. Emperor Decius had led around forty thousand horsemen into those marshes, and barely half of them had returned alive.

"Some will be prisoners," one of Gallus' aides remarked, as if this would soften the blow of our defeat.

"They are still lost to us," Gallus growled.

Standing close enough to hear every word, I could sense the mood of growing expectation among the senior officers. They were exchanging looks of anticipation, and eventually I saw Gallus give a determined nod in answer to a questioning look from Successianus.

"Call the men to parade!" Successianus barked, and the Tribunes hurried off to relay the order. In moments, the legionaries dashed from the ramparts to form up in their units. It was a testament to their training and discipline that this took a surprisingly short time.

Julia nudged me with her elbow as she asked, "What is happening?"

"The Emperor is dead," I replied. "The empire needs a new ruler."

"Doesn't the Emperor have a son in Rome?"

"Yes, but he's still a young boy."

"Rome has had boy Emperors before," she pointed out, her large eyes still scanning the soldiers as they formed into ranks.

"That's true," I conceded. "But usually only when their guardians had the backing of a large part of the army."

"So who will be Emperor?" she asked.

"Watch and see," I replied vaguely. It was fairly evident to me, but my mind kept drifting to Messius Decius' young son who was living in comfort in the palace in Rome, unaware that his father and older brother were dead. If the new Emperor followed custom, that innocent young boy would soon join them.

I kept my eyes on Gallus, who stood in front of the assembling ranks, his face unreadable. As soon as the soldiers had fallen silent, Successianus strode up to face Gallus and raised a fist to his chest, then gave a formal salute.

"Hail Caesar! Hail Trebonianus Gallus! Imperator! Augustus Caesar!"

His voice boomed out over the camp, and the legions quickly took up the chant, Gallus' aides enthusiastically joining in. The shouting was loud enough to startle birds from the trees outside the camp as legionaries, Auxiliaries and even the slaves and camp followers acclaimed their new Emperor.

Standing in front of his greatly reduced army, Gallus' eyes sparkled even though he kept his expression severe. He was, I knew, the natural choice now that Messius Decius and his elder son were both dead. Gallus was the most senior army commander left alive, and he was a Senator and Governor. He was the army's clear choice, and that made him the empire's choice because it was the army who made emperors these days. The problem was that, although Gallus' troops made up the bulk of Rome's main force, there were other legions based all around the empire, and some of them might have different ideas about who they wanted as Emperor. Gallus would need to move quickly to consolidate power.

The first step was to have himself draped in a purple cloak. Some of his aides must have plundered Decius' quarters, because they soon had Gallus' red cloak removed and a purple one fastened around his shoulders.

Gallus now strode up and down in front of his soldiers, acknowledging their shouts of acclaim with great dignity, and assuring them that he would reward them with a donative as soon as he had access to the imperial Treasury. This pronouncement resulted in even louder cheers.

The mood in the camp had lifted, and the soldiers returned to their posts with renewed determination, but Gallus had no time for self-congratulation because word soon arrived that a delegation of Goths was approaching the camp.

"Let us see what they want," Gallus said. He marched off towards the northern rampart, his staff in close attendance as always. Julia and I tagged along at the back of the group.

The wall of the camp was made of earth dug from a protective perimeter ditch. On each side of the fort was an open entrance which was closed by placing heavy timber logs on trestles. This was guarded by experienced and battle-hardened legionaries, but they now moved aside to let Gallus approach the barrier. I eased my way forwards, keeping one hand on Julia's shoulder.

Looking out beyond the camp, we saw a small group of Gothic horsemen riding towards us, one of them holding up a branch of green leaves as a symbol that they came in peace.

Gallus signalled to one of his senior Tribunes.

"Go and see what they want."

What they wanted, we soon learned, was a full-blown peace treaty. It took a lot of back and forth, but by early evening, it was agreed that Gallus would meet with Cniva within sight of our camp.

"Scipio!" Gallus commanded. "You will come with me."

I felt Julia clasp my hand, giving it a squeeze, so I assured her, "The fighting is over. This will be nothing more than talking."

I hoped I was right. I would not have put it past Cniva to try to kill another Roman Emperor. At Philippopolis, he had lured Julius Priscus into a trap by promising peace, so there was little reason to trust him now. Gallus must have had similar thoughts, because he ordered Successianus to maintain a strong force of cavalry at the ready in case of treachery.

"Why don't we try to kill him?" Successianus suggested. "We could charge out and reach him before he can summon help."

Gallus was clearly tempted, but he shook his head.

"We are sorely outnumbered," he said. "Someone else would take command of the Gothic army, then we'd face being besieged in our camp. No, let's talk to him."

The Gothic delegation arrived at the appointed spot a short while later, and I joined Gallus as he, his aides and a score of Praetorians rode out to meet them. As we neared the Goths, I noticed one of them edging his horse slightly forwards to meet us. It was Aoric, and he was smiling broadly.

"You survived," I said, returning his smile.

He nodded, "And I have enough silver to pay the bounty to Egica's widow."

He turned his horse, falling in beside me, apparently quite unconcerned that he was surrounded by Praetorians. All around, I could feel the tension, but Aoric smiled cheerfully, and I think his obvious lack of concern helped ease our suspicions a little.

The only other man who appeared relatively relaxed was Gallus, who was impatient to begin negotiations.

Once we were within a few paces of the Goths, Cniva looked at me with a sparkle of delight in his eyes, but he made no comment about the way he had used me to lure the Emperor into his elaborate trap. In return, I simply stared at him.

Cniva gave a curt signal to Aoric who dutifully trotted his mount back to join his father's group once again.

Nobody dismounted. Distrust was evident on both sides, but the area around us provided no cover for Cniva to have concealed an ambush, and our camp was far enough away to provide the Goths with plenty of warning if Gallus ordered an attack.

After some brief preliminaries, the two leaders began their negotiations. To my surprise, these turned out to be relatively straightforward.

"What do you want?" Gallus asked, speaking Latin, with Aoric acting as an interpreter. I was fairly sure Cniva could understand Latin perfectly well, but he maintained the stance of a ruler who needed his subjects to undertake such menial tasks as translation.

"I want to go home," Cniva replied. "What is it that you want?"

"I want you gone from our lands," Gallus said.

"Then we both desire the same thing," Cniva said. "The only thing to discuss is the terms."

There was very little haggling. I was astonished at how much Gallus conceded in exchange for promises that Cniva would lead his army back over the Danubius and would not return for as long as Rome paid him sufficient annual tribute. Gallus not only agreed to this, but also allowed Cniva to keep all of the plunder his army had taken, including all of his prisoners.

"I will be happy to ransom the wealthy ones if their families pay me enough," he declared as if this was a concession.

Agreements were made and sworn to, with the terms being recorded on parchment, and as dusk approached, both leaders confirmed that they were content. Cniva ordered his men to return with him, but Aoric remained behind for a moment, moving his horse close to mine once again.

"May your gods watch over you, Scipio," he said.

"And yours over you," I replied.

Then we clasped hands for the final time, and Aoric, who had once been a surly, disobedient slave, and had then become my bodyguard and friend, rode away to his new life as a member of the Gothic royal family. I wondered whether I would ever see him again.

I watched him go with a feeling of deep loss, but Gallus interrupted my gloomy thoughts.

"One day, he might be King of the Goths," he pointed out. "Will your friendship survive that?"

Softly, I said, "If I live to see it, I would like to think so."

Gallus, now Emperor of Rome, shrugged, then set about making plans for the evening.

"I want patrols out tonight in case that devious bastard tries a sneak night attack. And in the morning, I want a thousand horsemen to shadow them. I need to be sure they are leaving our lands."

Then, to my surprise, he turned back to me and said, "And tomorrow, Scipio, we will return to Rome. I'm sure we both have urgent business there."

He was right. I would need to report to my patron, Licinius Valerianus, and provide an account of what had happened over the past months. More importantly, Trebonianus Gallus would need to ensure his hold on the empire, and the only way he could do that was to return to Rome and browbeat the Senate into accepting him as their new ruler.

I merely nodded. I had seen too many Emperors come and go. Once, there had been six of them in a single year, and this year was shaping up to match it. Already, three men had worn the Purple. How long, I wondered, would Gallus last?

Part 2

The Plague

Chapter 19
Making Plans

Trebonianus Gallus was keen to set off for Rome as soon as he could, but the role of Emperor demanded that he spend time making a host of arrangements before he could begin that long journey. For two days, he sat in his imperial tent, dictating letters, giving orders and making new appointments. And, for some reason I could not quite fathom, he insisted that I should be among the many witnesses to his long hours of dedication to his imperial duties.

Julia, being both young and female, was not allowed to be present, but I managed to find a job for her among the cooks. Most of these people were slaves, and I think they believed Julia shared that status, but helping prepare food kept her busy and, I hoped, safe enough from the lecherous gazes of the thousands of soldiers who remained in the camp.

So I sat while scribes penned letters which Gallus signed and which were sent by fast riders to all the principal cities of the empire, with the Senate in Rome being sent several messages.

One of the letters dictated by our new Emperor surprised everyone.

"I wish to send a letter to Herenia Etruscilla, wife of our former Emperor, Gaius Messius Quintus Traianus Decius," he announced.

His principal secretary sat with quill and parchment balanced on his writing slab, hastily noting down the draft letter which would then be copied out neatly and presented to the Emperor to attach his signature and seal.

The reason for everyone's surprise was that new Emperors tended to send death squads of Praetorians to execute the family of former Emperors; they did not write letters to them.

"Tell her," he said to the secretary, "about her husband's tragic death, as well as the death of her elder son. Use the same wording as in my letter to the Senate. Then assure her that I hold her in high esteem as the wife of our former Emperor, and that I intend to adopt her son, and make him co-Emperor alongside me. Put his full name in the letter. I can't recall all of his names, but he is known as Hostilianus."

The scribe jotted down notes, other secretaries scurrying off to check on the full name of Messius Decius' sole surviving son. The boy, I had heard, was barely into his teens, and because he was the younger son, he could never have expected to become Emperor himself. Yet Trebonianus Gallus, going against recent precedents, intended to make him co-Emperor. It was a startling declaration which caused a great deal of speculation, although nobody openly voiced any criticism.

Idly, I wondered what Gallus' own wife and son would think of this arrangement. My patron, Valerianus, had informed me that Gallus' son was even younger than Hostilianus, so this surprisingly magnanimous act by Gallus would effectively rule his own son out as the next Emperor.

That, though, was a problem for another day, especially since it assumed that Gallus would survive as Emperor for several years. The way things were going, that had to be in doubt. Not for the first time, I wondered what drove rich and influential Romans to desire to rule the empire. The past thirty years had amply demonstrated that this was a highly dangerous position to hold.

Our new Emperor, though, had plenty of other things to deal with. He appointed Fabius Successianus as temporary Governor of Moesia, ordering him to ensure the frontier was properly secure, then he charged other senior men with the difficult and unpleasant duty of re-establishing the ruined cities of Nicopolis and Philippopolis. Then he appointed a temporary Governor of Thrace to replace the murdered Julius Priscus.

He sent letters to the commanders of each frontier region, demanding their acceptance of his elevation to the Purple, and he did the same to every existing provincial Governor. I was sure he would be sending private letters in addition to these public ones, so it was no wonder he began to look tired by the burden of administrative detail his new role required.

Late on the second day after peace had been agreed with Cniva, reports arrived from our scouts confirming that the Goths were leaving as their King had promised.

Sitting back on his chair, Gallus let out a soft sigh, wiped sweat from his brow, then declared, "Then tomorrow I shall set off for Rome."

To my surprise, he looked directly at me for the first time in two days. I was sitting near the back of the assembled audience, feeling utterly bored by the day's events, but now he beckoned me forwards.

"I wish to speak to you in private," he told me. "Come."

He stood up, everyone else rising quickly to their feet and offering bows or salutes, then he strode towards the rear of the huge chamber, pushing through to a smaller area near the back of the tent. Feeling more than a little self-conscious, I followed him.

Beyond the heavy drapes which separated this compartment from the main chamber, I found a comfortable rest area, complete with a couch covered in purple velvet. The Emperor, though, remained standing, turning to face me.

He kept his voice low when he spoke. There were Praetorians on guard just outside this tiny room, and the walls were thin enough to allow them to hear a normal voice.

He told me, "I will take the entire Praetorian Guard with me tomorrow, and we'll be travelling fast. I'm sure you appreciate that I need to secure my position with the Senate."

"Yes, Augustus," I nodded, remembering to address him by his new title.

"You are welcome to accompany me," he added, "although the pace we will set will be fierce."

"I'm honoured, Augustus," I told him. "But I doubt I could manage to keep up. Besides, I now have a new ward to care for. I promised to take her to Rome, and I'll need to find some way of getting her there safely."

Gallus nodded as if he had expected this sort of response. He said, "I'll arrange a carriage for you, then. I'll let you have a squad of Praetorians as escort."

"That is very generous, Augustus," I said. "Thank you."

I waited. There was no reason for him to single me out for assistance, so I guessed he must have some ulterior motive for making this generous offer.

He went on, "Naturally, I shall go directly to the Senate when I reach Rome. I expect your patron, Licinius Valerianus, will be there."

So that was it. As I'd anticipated, Gallus wanted something from me in exchange for his help.

"I expect so," I agreed warily.

Gallus gave a slight grin as he went on, "I suppose he, and quite a few others, will not be entirely pleased that I am now their Emperor."

I made no comment. He already knew that Valerianus had distrusted him enough to send me to spy on him.

He continued, "But, as Emperor, I cannot afford to let personal dislikes create a split in the empire. So, as a gesture of my good intentions, I will assure Valerianus that you are safe and well, and also free to do as you please. I will ensure that he knows you have not altered your allegiance."

I resisted the temptation to smile. Gallus was smart enough to know that his hold on the empire was shaky at best, with only a handful of legions having acclaimed him. He needed to keep powerful Senators like Valerianus on his side, so he was going to treat me well as a gesture to my patron. It was politics, and although it suited me to accept his help, I understood perfectly well that I was being treated like a plaything. I was simply a gaming piece on a board, moving at the whim of the men who rolled the dice. I had not forgotten the unspoken threat Gallus had made when he had feared I might give Emperor Decius an unfavourable report on his behaviour. Now, though, Gallus was Emperor himself, and he was at pains to appear friendly. No doubt he believed that his generosity would place me in his debt as well, and for a moment, I wondered whether he was going to ask me to spy on Valerianus. Once again, though, he surprised me by saying, "I value your insights and honesty, Scipio. You are Valerianus' man, and I will respect that. But if I do wish to talk to you again once we are both back in Rome, where will I find you?"

I told him, "I will be at the home of my friend, Sestius Fronto. He lives on the Quirinal."

The Emperor nodded, "Then I wish you well, Scipio. I will ensure that a carriage is ready for you in the morning."

He held out his hand, but instead of it being offered for me to kiss, he held it in such a way that I was invited to clasp it. This was an unusual gesture for an Emperor, and I doubted it would ever be repeated in public, but as I shook his hand, I said, "May I ask a question, Augustus?"

Smiling, he nodded, "Of course, although I might not answer it."

I asked him, "What do you want me to say to Licinius Valerianus when I see him?"

"The truth, of course," Gallus insisted, spreading his hands in a gesture of openness. "Why else do you think I wanted you to see how I have begun my reign? Knowing Licinius Valerianus, I am sure he will want you to corroborate my own version of events. You have been a witness, Scipio, and I am counting on you to report it truthfully."

So he had made his throw of the dice, and now he was trusting me to move as he hoped. The next move would be up to Licinius Valerianus.

The Emperor was as good as his word. He and his Praetorian Guard set off at first light, thundering out of the camp on their way to Rome. Julia and I followed at a more sedate pace, sitting in a small carriage pulled by two horses. I had no idea how Gallus had managed to locate a vehicle like this, but it was comfortable enough, although not a particularly fast way to travel. Eight Praetorians trotted along behind us, and our driver made for the nearest road. Once on the highway, he turned towards Rome.

It was a long and uneventful journey, but it did allow me to spend a lot of time with Julia. She insisted on sleeping in the same room as me when we stopped at night in one of the many imperial waystations, which brought a few smirking grins from the Praetorians, but I knew Julia still felt nervous at being on her own. Some nights, she cried herself to sleep, memories of her father tormenting her, but she was more confident during the days when we sat together in the rumbling, jolting carriage, and she gaped in wonder when we began the long haul across an Alpine pass on the way to the north of Italia.

"It's beautiful here!" she gasped as she leaned out of the tiny window, taking in the majesty of the mountains.

That night, seeing as she was in a more relaxed state of mind, we spoke of Rome and what we would do when we got there.

"My friend, Fronto, is an Equestrian now," I informed her. "He grew quite wealthy in recent years, and he owns enough property to be classed in the social rank just beneath that of a Senator. He was officially elevated to Equestrian rank by Emperor Decius. That means he is now allowed to wear a thin stripe of purple on his tunic so that everyone knows he is an important man."

This did not seem to impress Julia overmuch, and she remained concerned about her future.

"That's good for him," she frowned. "But what will I do when we get there?"

"I don't know," I admitted. "But Fronto's wife, Faustia, will be delighted to see you. They've never had children."

"I'm not a child!" Julia protested. "I'm past my first bleeding."

I smiled, "Then I'm sure Faustia will enjoy having another woman to talk to."

Julia did not look convinced, so I spent a long time assuring her that Rome provided endless possibilities for people of ambition.

"If you're a man, maybe," she replied with a frown.

"There are plenty of women who run their own businesses," I assured her.

"Doing what?" she asked, her eyes narrowing.

"Selling fruit, making clothes, all sorts of things."

Julia let out a snort.

"That doesn't sound very exciting," she said, folding her arms in protest.

I said, "Well, if you want to continue as a street performer, I'm sure you have the talent. But you'd need someone to work with you."

She gave a stiff nod, and I could see what she was thinking. She would need a man to act as a protector, effectively replacing her father. She sniffed, fighting back tears as that memory returned.

"In Rome," I told her, "all things are possible. The main thing is that you will be safe in Fronto's house. Then you can take time to decide what you want to do."

She stared at me, gave a brisk nod, then announced that she was going to sleep. She lay down on her thin mattress, turned her back to me, pulled her blanket over her thin frame, and left me recalling how difficult it was to speak to teenage girls. My own daughter had presented the same problem when she was that age, but the experience of dealing with Sempronia offered little help in coping with Julia's fears.

The long journey continued, our route taking us through the city of Aquileia, but I insisted that we should not stop there. This puzzled the guards, and prompted more questions from Julia. Questions which I refused to answer.

"There are people here I do not want to risk running into," was all I felt able to tell her.

"What people?" she pressed.

"People from my past," I replied.

Eventually, we reached the bustling city of Rome. The carriage stopped just before the Milvian Bridge, I said farewell to the driver and the Praetorians, then I led Julia into the city on foot.

Rome was much as I remembered it. There was no sign that Trebonianus Gallus' arrival had triggered a civil war, and daily life seemed to be going on as usual for everyone. Men and women went about their business, talking, buying, selling, working and begging.

"We need to head up to the Quirinal," I told Julia. "It is the northernmost of the seven hills."

She was constantly turning her head, looking this way and that at all the sights of the empire's capital, and I tried to imagine what it must be like to see this famous city for the first time. It made me feel young again to see her amazement. And yet it was a walk which also brought back many personal memories, not all of them pleasant. The ongoing building work, and the multitude of newly built homes reminded me that much of the Quirinal had been destroyed during the riots when Maximinis Thrax had been overthrown. My wife had died in those riots, her body crushed when the roof of Fronto's burning house had collapsed.

Sestius Fronto had been my friend since childhood, and he was the man I trusted most in the world. I had broken off all links with my family because they believed I was dead, and I had hoped that estranging myself might protect them. That was hard to bear, and I knew it had been only partly successful, because Licinius Valerianus knew all about my daughter and her family who lived in Aquileia, and he had demonstrated his power to harm them if I did not obey his commands. Still, I had resolved to maintain my distance, but even though I had stuck to the decision to keep my family in ignorance about my survival, I still maintained contact with Fronto.

He had a new home, built on the site of his old house, but this was a larger, grander home, set around a peristyle garden with many rooms and a small army of slaves to take care of his every need. Fronto was a rich man now, although he never ceased to remind me that his good fortune was due to my own past generosity. As far as I was concerned, he had repaid that many times over, and I knew I would be warmly welcomed in his home. When Aoric and I had briefly stayed in Rome after Messius Decius had become Emperor, Fronto and his wife, Faustia, had provided a safe and welcoming haven for us. I was sure they would do the same for Julia.

When I knocked on the door, it was opened by a slave who recognised me, so he scurried off to deliver word of my arrival, showing us into an elegant reception room to wait.

Fronto himself hurried in a few moments later, his face eager. Like me, he was in his mid-sixties now, and his hair was almost entirely grey, but he looked fit and well. He was of small build, no taller than me, but good living was beginning to have an impact on his waistline. His tunic, now embroidered with the thin purple stripe of an equestrian, was stretched tightly across his belly. Even so, the smile on his face was like a ray of sunshine.

"Sextus! You are back! And who is this you have brought with you?"

"This is Julia," I told him. "I met her in Philippopolis. She is an orphan."

Fronto reached out to take Julia's hand.

"I am delighted to meet you," he told her, and I saw her shyly return his smile.

He explained, "Faustia is out just now. She is visiting a friend, but I expect you could do with something to eat. I'll take you to the dining room and have some food and drink brought for you. We'll be having dinner later, but I'm sure you could manage a snack before then."

Looking uncommonly shy, Julia mumbled her thanks. She may have been a streetwise girl, but Fronto seemed to have made more of an impact on her than any of the Senators we had encountered recently.

"Come!" Fronto beamed, leading us through the large house. He placed Julia on a couch in the dining room, then called for his slaves to bring refreshments for her.

"Scipio and I will be back soon," he told her with a broad smile. "But we need to talk. Ask for anything, and the slaves will bring it."

Julia looked too stunned to argue. She simply nodded her head as she looked around the plush interior of the dining room with its three couches, low table and elegant murals.

Still smiling, Fronto turned to me and suggested, "Shall we bathe?"

I grinned. Fronto had his own private bath house now, a small thing by Roman standards, but large enough to accommodate half a dozen people in relative comfort. It was an extravagance, but one he was inordinately proud of. It would be nice to wash away the grime of travel, but the main thing about the bath room was that we could speak in private.

On the way, he asked me, "Where is Aoric? Is he all right?"

"He has returned to his own people," I said. "It's a long story."

"Then tell me while we enjoy our bath," he said.

So we stripped off, lounged in the pool, drank wine and ate small snacks while we exchanged our news. I told him about Cniva's invasion, Gallus' defence of Novae, the arrival of the two joint Emperors, their defeat in the mountain pass, Cniva's treachery which had led to the death of Julius Priscus and the sack of Philippopolis, and then the dreadful events of the battle in the marshes where both Emperors had died.

Fronto listened in amazement, especially to the parts where I explained Aoric's background and how he had returned to fight alongside his famous father.

Fronto had heard the official reports of the main events, but he shook his head in wonder at my account.

"That is quite a story, my friend," he told me. "As usual, your life is one of constant excitement."

"Not through my choice," I grumbled good-naturedly.

Fronto chuckled, recalling the many times we had held the same conversation. Then he went on, "And now Trebonianus Gallus is our Emperor. I wonder what changes that will bring?"

"I can't say," I shrugged. "Gallus is a man of contradictions. He's clever and cunning, although he is outwardly affable. And if he keeps his word to promote young Hostilianus to the rank of co-Emperor, that will mark him out as quite exceptional for an Emperor."

"We could do with someone exceptional ruling the empire," Fronto nodded.

He was right about that. A few of the Emperors who had ruled during my lifetime had genuinely attempted to govern the empire properly, but many had been more interested in the wealth and status that the role brought.

Fronto asked, "And this girl, Julia? She was a street entertainer?"

"Yes, and a skilled acrobat. She helped me a great deal."

"So you brought her here to repay her?" Fronto grinned. "Some might say that bringing her to Rome might count as a punishment. What do you intend to do with her?"

"I have no idea," I admitted. "I was hoping you and Faustia might have some suggestions."

Fronto shrugged, "I'm sure Faustia will be pleased, but a lot will depend on how the girl settles."

"I just want her to be safe," I said. Then, deciding I had spoken about myself for far too long, I asked him, "What about you? What has happened here while I've been away? How is your business doing?"

"Very well indeed," he assured me. "There is still a lot of rebuilding to do, so Mallius Proximus and his lads are kept hard at work. Not that Proximus does much of the labouring these days. He leaves that to his son, but he still runs the place with his usual efficiency."

This was how Fronto had acquired his wealth. Years before, my wife, Circe, had bought a builder's business run by a young man named Proximus, and Fronto had been appointed to oversee it, to acquire new properties and have Proximus' workers renovate the buildings. Since half of the city had burned down during the riots, every builder in Rome had more work than they could handle. And because Fronto had spent his entire life in the city, he knew where to build and what to build. He also had connections with some of the people who worked in the imperial offices which dealt out contracts. In short, Fronto was the ideal man for that sort of work, and he had spent several years looking after our business affairs in Rome. I had no appetite for that sort of thing so, when Circe died, I had sold the entire business to him for a nominal fee, and he had continued to thrive.

"The main news, though," he told me, "is personal."

I cocked my head, waiting for his explanation.

He smiled, "You remember young Dextrus, of course?"

I nodded. After the destruction of the riots, Fronto had opened one of his few undamaged properties to provide shelter for many of Rome's homeless people. He still allowed several families to live in that same building for a very modest rent, and often did not bother collecting even that. Those families now acted as his clients, although I knew that Fronto was very far from the usual patron. Still, some of those people had remained loyal friends, and one of them had been a young lad named Dextrus. His entire family had been killed during the riots, but Fronto had taken him in, and the boy had been devoted to him ever since.

Fronto now beamed as he said, "Faustia and I decided to formally adopt him as our son."

"That is wonderful news!" I declared, and I meant it. Fronto and Faustia had never been blessed with children, and I knew that had been a source of frustration and regret for them.

Fronto could not conceal his delight as he added, "His name is now Quintus Sestius Dextrus Carelianus."

"And I'm sure he will be a credit to your family name," I said.

In the Roman way of things, Dextrus' full name told the world who he was. His *praenomen* of Quintus would only be used by close friends and family. His *nomen* of Sestius meant that he was now a member of the Sestius family, and the alteration of his final name from Carelius to Carelianus, signified that he had been adopted out of the Carelius family. Most people, of course, would continue to know him by his *cognomen* of Dextrus. He was, I knew, a bright lad, now in his late teens, with a rather quiet, serious demeanour but an undying love for Fronto and Faustia.

"You've made an excellent decision," I assured my friend.

"I know," Fronto grinned. "And I must admit that it is a relief to me that I will have someone to leave my estate to."

"You've got a good few years left in you yet," I said.

"As do you," he replied. "Although I expect you'd live even longer if you managed to stay out of trouble for a while."

"Trouble just seems to come looking for me," I grunted.

"And yet you survive," Fronto said with a friendly smile. "Emperors come and go, wars and rebellions rage around you, and still you remain unscathed."

He hesitated, then added, "I'm sorry, Sextus. I know you have suffered many losses. I should not have said that about you being unscathed. I know you carry many wounds in your soul."

I nodded gravely, then forced a smile.

"Not so many that I cannot enjoy life when it brings good things. And your friendship is one of the best of those things."

Fronto raised his goblet in salute.

"I'll drink to friendship," he said. Then, after a slight pause, he added, "But don't you think it is time to tell your children that you still live?"

I shook my head.

"It would be too dangerous for them. You know that. My son, Sextus, and my adopted son, Hama, have made new lives for themselves without me. If I contacted them, and if Valerianus found out, he would no doubt use them against me, just as he is using Sempronia. The bastard knows he can ruin my daughter's safety to force me to do what he wants. And if I did let her know I'm still alive, that would only make it worse for her when Valerianus sends me on another mission."

Fronto sighed, "I think you are wrong, my friend. Sempronia would rather have a few years or even months knowing you are alive. Emperor Philippus may have declared you a traitor, but Decius pardoned you after he came to power And, from what you say, Trebonianus Gallus seems to like you."

"I'll reserve judgement on that," I said. "He's a clever man, but you know how power goes to people's heads. If he wants something from me, he'll soon make sure I do as he says."

Fronto gave a rueful smile as he said, "You and I, Sextus, are not important in the great scheme of things. The best thing you could do is keep your head down. Or you could try disappearing again."

"No," I said. "Licinius Valerianus has made it quite plain that if I do try that, he'll make sure that Sempronia and her family suffer."

Fronto sighed, "He's a real bastard, isn't he?"

"That's too nice a thing to say about him," I muttered.

Fronto put down his goblet and rose from the hot bath, water dripping from his naked body.

"Well," he said as he reached for a towel, "that is more than enough discussion of unpleasant topics. Let us go and find your new companion. If Faustia is back, we shall be able to have dinner. That, at least, ought to cheer you up."

Refreshed after our lazy relaxation in the bath, I dried myself off, donned my one and only spare tunic, then accompanied Fronto through to the family section of his house where we discovered Faustia deep in conversation with Julia. Young Dextrus was also there, looking a little uncertain about Julia's unexpected appearance, but all five of us stretched out on the couches to enjoy a leisurely dinner.

I did most of the talking, once again relaying my account of my recent adventures. I ate well, drank rather too much wine, and slept for eight hours once I had been helped to a room which had been prepared for me. It was a happy, carefree evening, and I felt as good as I had done for months.

And then, in the morning, while Julia and I sat eating a light breakfast of fruit, bread and olives, one of the slaves came to inform me that a message had been delivered for me.

"Publius Licinius Valerianus wishes to talk to you," he informed me.

Chapter 20
Informant

I have met many people in the course of my life, and while I have disliked many of them, I have rarely hated any of them. I may have hated the things they did, but I had always tried not to let that result in personal animosity. Everyone should be able to live the life they want, provided it does not harm others. That, of course, has always been the problem, because powerful men, and women too, it must be said, often make decisions which seriously harm or even kill ordinary people.

Yet still I have rarely hated those people as individuals. I may have feared them, and wanted to stay well clear of them, but I could almost always understand their perspective, and sometimes I even respected them for their abilities.

There are, though, a few exceptions. I had detested Julius Philippus because of the way he had murdered anyone who blocked his path to the imperial throne, and because his actions had resulted in the deaths of some of my friends, and in my estrangement from my family. I had hated his lackey, Neratius Mauritius, who had tried to kill me several times. But both of those men were dead now. Philippus had been fatally wounded in battle while trying to defeat Messius Decius, our recently deceased Emperor, and Neratius Mauritius had been dumped into the river Euphrates to feed the fish.

But one man still remained alive whom I did hate because he watched over me like a hungry predator, his presence always lurking in the back of my mind.

I had first met Publius Licinius Valerianus in Africa some thirteen years ago. Back then, my wife and I had decided to leave our family estates and drop out of sight for a while because we wanted to avoid the attention of the new Emperor, Maximinis Thrax. That giant of a man, who had risen through the ranks of the army to become its most senior commander, had seized the throne after overthrowing Severus Alexander in a bloody coup. Circe and I had both been present on that dreadful day, and although we had survived, we had felt it best to remain out of sight should the giant Thrax decide he wanted me to spy for him.

So we had moved to the small town of Thysdrus which lay on the Mediterranean coast of Africa. There, our daughter had met a young man by the name of Carbo, and the two of them had fallen deeply in love. We had agreed to their marriage because neither of us would ever have prevented Sempronia marrying whoever she wanted, and also because Carbo was in Thysdrus as part of the retinue of a Senator named Licinius Valerianus, a wealthy and aristocratic man who had also moved to Africa in order to avoid the wrath of Maximinis Thrax. As Carbo's patron, Valerianus took an interest in the young man's marriage, and that was how we met.

But there was more to Licinius Valerianus than that, and even though some of our interests aligned, I soon learned that he approached things in a very different way. He was out of favour with the new Emperor, but he was not content to remain in hiding. Instead, he was plotting a revolt, using others to achieve his aims while he remained in the background. In this, he was personally successful, because Thrax was overthrown and killed. The cost, though, was extremely high because that awful year saw no fewer than six men become Emperor for a brief time, and five of them had died violent deaths. By the end of the year, only a teenage boy named Marcus Antonius Gordianus was left wearing the purple robes of Emperor, and Valerianus, elevated to be leader of the Senate, was the power behind the throne.

The momentous events of that year deeply affected me. Valerianus had no qualms about manipulating me and sending me on a mission which almost resulted in my death. I was lucky to escape, but I had often felt it would have been better if I had died because Circe, the love of my life, was killed during the riots in Rome which resulted from Valerianus' plot.

Two more Emperors had come and gone since then. Julius Philippus had killed young Gordianus, and Messius Decius had defeated Philippus. Now Decius, too, was dead, and Trebonianus Gallus sat on the imperial throne.

Valerianus, using the threat of my daughter's safety to force me into working for him, had sent me to spy on Gallus in Novae, and he had made no secret of the fact that he distrusted Gallus. Quite how he would react now that his rival sat on the imperial throne, I really did not want to find out. But I would learn soon enough because the bastard had summoned me to his opulent home on the Esquiline.

I knew Valerianus' home reasonably well. The property had once belonged to the Gordianus family, but had then become part of the imperial property owned by Julius Philippus. With

Philippus' death, Messius Decius had granted the home to Valerianus in recognition of the support Valerianus had given him in his rise to imperial power.

The large house had wide gardens, a place of apparent peacefulness, with trees and flowers arranged in elegant settings, with tasteful fountains trickling water into shallow pools in which golden fish swam slowly around in circles. The high walls which surrounded the garden were patrolled by men who carried heavy sticks, but the gate guards admitted me without question. They had no doubt been warned to watch for my arrival.

I trudged up the gravel path, and was admitted to the huge home by the door slave. He led me to an audience room off the wide *atrium*. Here, I found a tray of food and a jug of wine.

"The Master will join you soon, Sir," the slave assured me.

I sat down, ignoring the food and wine. Valerianus entered a short while later, wearing his purple-striped tunic with the comfortable ease of a man who was accustomed to wielding authority.

He was the same age as me, and his unfashionably long hair was mostly grey now. He also disdained the fashion of sporting a beard, having always gone clean-shaven. On first appearance, people often thought him harmless because of his chubby features, but that was misleading. His eyes, which bulged above a prominent nose, missed nothing and revealed very little of what went on behind them. And what went on inside his head was, I knew from bitter experience, dark and murky.

"Scipio!" he declared with a smile. "Thank you for coming."

"It wasn't as if I had much choice," I muttered, adopting the surly manner which always afflicted me when I met Valerianus.

He sat down in a padded armchair, still smiling at me.

"Are you not hungry?" he asked, glancing meaningfully at the untouched food on the tray.

"I ate before I came here," I told him.

"It's not poisoned, you know," he said, displaying his uncanny ability to read my thoughts.

"So you say," I shot back.

He reached out, picked up a small slice of melon and popped it into his mouth, chewing contentedly.

"I'm still not hungry," I told him.

He shrugged, then stated, "Your mission did not go quite as planned. And now we have a new Emperor."

I merely nodded.

"Tell me about him," he said.

"You know him better than I do," I replied. "He's a Senator. I only met him for the first time when I arrived in Novae."

"And what did you make of him?" Valerianus asked.

"He's a clever man," I told him. "A good commander who is respected by the troops. But you must have known that before you sent me."

Valerianus nodded, "What of his views towards Christians?"

I'd been expecting that question, but I was damned if I was going to give him the answer he craved.

"I saw no evidence either way," I told him. "He performed a sacrifice before the siege began, but he's the sort of man who would do that even if he did have Christian beliefs because he knows the troops expect it."

"So he is a pragmatist," Valerianus observed.

He sounded a little disappointed. Like his now dead friend, Decius, Valerianus loathed Christians. I was fairly sure that he had been behind Decius' proclamation demanding that every citizen swear loyalty to Roman gods on pain of execution. Decius had enforced that edict with bloody ruthlessness, but now Trebonianus Gallus ruled, and I knew that Valerianus was wondering whether he would revoke that law and its persecution.

"Well," Valerianus sighed, "we shall see what our new Emperor decides to do. Now tell me everything that happened."

So I told my story yet again, missing out very little, and I stressed Aoric's position as Cniva's son because I knew this would annoy the pompous Senator. Like Gallus, if Valerianus had known Aoric's true identity, he would have found some way to use that to his advantage. He certainly frowned when he heard that part of my tale, but he kept his thoughts to himself. Whatever else you could say about Valerianus, I knew that he, too, was a pragmatist. If Aoric was beyond his reach, he would not waste time complaining over what might have been.

When I had finished, he asked me, "So why did Gallus let you live? If he knew you were a spy, he ought to have had you killed."

"He likes me," I said. "Also, he wanted me to give you a full report on everything he has done. He knows he needs to have friends within the Senate."

"He thinks I am his friend?" Valerianus asked, his eyebrows arching.

"He does not want you as an enemy," I replied. "So he let me live rather than give you an excuse to set yourself against him."

Valerianus rubbed his chin thoughtfully, so I decided to give him something else to consider.

I said, "As well as all that, although he hasn't said it openly, I'm fairly sure he wants me to spy on you on his behalf."

Annoyingly, Valerianus displayed no emotion at this, merely nodding as if Gallus' intention was perfectly normal.

After a moment, he asked me, "So it is true that he allowed the barbarians to leave the empire unmolested, taking all their plunder and captives with them?"

I shrugged, "He did, but he didn't really have any choice in the matter. Much of the army died in the marshes with Emperor Decius, and those who survived were exhausted and in shock. The legions hadn't taken part, but there were only a few thousand of them, and they could not chase mounted Goths. Gallus was in no position to make demands."

Valerianus rubbed his chin again, then said, "He is indeed a clever man. More clever than I gave him credit for. Allowing barbarians to go free will not please the people, but he has ended the immediate danger, and he has also allied himself to the house of Messius Decius by proclaiming young Hostilianus as co-Emperor."

When Valerianus said that the people of Rome would not be pleased, I guessed that he would make it his business to ensure that this black mark against Gallus would become common knowledge. That, in turn, would inevitably increase the level of animosity between Valerianus and the new Emperor, a situation which could ultimately threaten the safety of the empire once again. These two powerful men held very different views on how society should be controlled, and I dreaded what might happen if the two of them openly fell out. For the moment, Gallus held the upper hand, and Valerianus seemed content to bide his time. But he had been a close ally of Decius, which meant he might find himself a marked man if Gallus decided he could not trust him.

It was all becoming too complicated for me. With a sigh, I eased myself up out of the chair.

"If that is all, I am going home. I've had a harrowing few months, and I think I deserve some rest."

Valerianus merely gave a slow nod of his head. But he allowed me to leave. I suspect he had more important things to worry about. A new Emperor always resulted in Senators jostling for position and favour. That, though, was no concern of mine. Let them squabble and gossip, curry favour or backstab. That was all far above me.

I spent several more days with Fronto, relaxing, and occasionally walking out, the two of us wandering the city streets just as we had done when we were young boys. We reminisced, pointing out buildings, statues or monuments which had survived the years, and also noting the new buildings, both private and public. Julia often accompanied us on these walks, although I think she was more impressed by the city than by our reminiscences.

The subject of what Julia would do remained an open question. Faustia had enjoyed buying new clothing for her which she deemed more suitable for a young lady, and she spent some time attempting to teach the girl the art of spinning wool which was still regarded as an acceptable pastime for a Roman matron. Julia, though, obviously hated this task, preferring to perform acrobatics in the garden, much to the astonishment of the slaves who gawped as she performed handstands, somersaults and tumbling rolls. She wore her two-piece outfit for these exercises, and I realised she must have been wearing it beneath her tunic all the time I had known her.

"She is a bit wild," Faustia admitted one evening after Julia had gone to bed. "I really don't know what to make of her."

"Dextrus seems quite taken with her," I remarked. "Give her a few years and I expect a lot of young men will be paying her compliments."

Faustia frowned, "The wrong type of young men unless she learns more respectable ways."

Julia herself, it soon became apparent, was not going to be content with Faustia's ideas of what a Roman girl of good upbringing should be. We learned that she had developed the habit of going out on her own, investigating the streets of the city. When Faustia heard about this, she tried to forbid such excursions, and stated that she would order the door slave not to let Julia leave unless accompanied.

Julia simply replied, "Then I shall go out by a window and climb down to the street. You cannot keep me locked up in here."

Faustia was perplexed by this attitude, but I had to struggle to contain my amusement.

I said, "She's a superb acrobat. I doubt you could keep her in."

"It is too dangerous for her to be out on her own," Faustia insisted.

To which Julia archly responded, "Then I'll take a knife with me."

Eventually, Faustia gave up, although she did draw a concession from Julia who agreed to wear a simple tunic and carry nothing of any value.

"Except a knife," Julia insisted. When Faustia argued about this, Julia took some sharp knives from the kitchen and proceeded to put on a display of throwing in the garden, hitting her targets every time.

Fronto and I found all of this highly amusing, but we did our best to conceal our amusement from Faustia who remained concerned every time Julia went out on one of her exploratory walks.

Despite the problem of what might become of Julia, those weeks were a happy, carefree time which ended when a messenger arrived from the palace, summoning me to see the Emperor.

The message was brought by a solitary freedman. There was no squad of Praetorians come to enforce my presence, but the messenger made it plain that I could not get out of this.

"The Emperor desires your presence as soon as possible," he told me.

So I accompanied him down the *Vicus Longua*, the main street which runs down from the Quirinal, passing the mean streets of the *Subura*, and eventually leads to the magnificent Flavian amphitheatre which was now repaired and functioning again after several years of disuse. Then we moved through the busy *forum* to the Palatine Hill which was now entirely occupied by the sprawling mass of inter-connected buildings which comprised the Emperor's palace.

My guide knew where he was going, and clearly had the authority to let us pass the many officials whose job it was to keep people away from the Emperor unless they had good reasons to be there. I still had to wait for around half an hour, sitting in an antechamber while freedmen and slaves bustled in and out of the imperial offices. Eventually, though, I was admitted, passed through yet another large office which was crammed with studious-looking scribes, and then I was ushered into a smaller room where I found Trebonianus Gallus sitting behind a wide desk. Scrolls and tablets abounded, but he looked remarkably cheerful, and gave me a friendly welcome.

"Sempronius Scipio! Thank you for coming."

He indicated a chair which faced his own across the desk, so I sat down while he shuffled papers around.

Amiably, he said, "I have hundreds of scribes and secretaries to take care of paperwork, and still they seem to find more and more things for me to read."

He shoved a few scrolls to one side, clearing a space on the desk in front of him, where he clasped his hands together as he leaned forwards, regarding me intently.

"I presume you spoke to Licinius Valerianus?" he asked.

"Yes, Augustus. A couple of weeks ago, just after I returned to Rome."

"And you told him everything?"

"Yes."

"Good. I have met him in the Senate House a few times now. He has been extremely polite and friendly. He does not seem to have taken the death of his friend, Decius, too badly."

I said nothing. In situations like this, I always felt that was the safest policy. We were alone in the room, but I was only too aware that a single word from an Emperor could seal my fate. Such situations generally required caution.

The Emperor, though, seemed perfectly relaxed as he went on, "But I must admit that I distrust his motives. What can you tell me about his plans?"

"Nothing, Augustus. I only spoke to him on that one occasion. And he does not confide in me in any case."

Gallus gave a faint smile as he said, "What you are not saying is almost as important as what you are saying, Scipio. I know you dislike Licinius Valerianus, and that you only do his bidding because he has some hold over you."

It was a statement rather than a question, but I gave a slight nod of my head.

"The question I need an answer to," he went on, "is whether I can trust him. He was apparently loyal to Julius Philippus until Decius raised his revolt. There are, though, rumours among the Senators that Valerianus may have had more to do with that affair than he lets on."

"He was in on it from the start," I said. "He and Messius Decius were the prime movers behind the plot to overthrow Julius Philippus. I know that for a fact."

Gallus sat back, his hands now clasped on his belly. He was twiddling his thumbs while he considered my revelation.

He asked, "That sort of thing makes trusting him difficult, wouldn't you say?"

"I wouldn't trust him at all," I said.

The Emperor nodded, "Ah, I thought as much. So what am I to do about him?"

"You could have him exiled," I suggested.

"This would not cause you some concern?" he asked. "He is, after all, your patron."

"It would not bother me in the slightest," I assured him. "Although I'm not sure he could be trusted even if he was exiled. He has a lot of influence in Rome, and you might find him stirring up a revolt wherever you send him."

Gallus nodded. He knew what I was suggesting even though I had not voiced the thought. Exile was a relatively lenient sentence for someone who had displeased an Emperor. A far more common solution to the problem of a troublesome Senator was to encourage them to slit their own wrists as an alternative to being executed.

Gallus said, "I appreciate your honesty, Scipio. It tallies with other reports I have received. And, as you know, I am familiar with Valerianus from our shared time as Senators."

He paused, rubbed his chin, then went on, "The problem is that he has a lot of support. I would need a very good reason to dispose of him, and he has always been careful not to be caught saying or doing anything which could be interpreted as treason. I fear that punishing him without evidence of malfeasance will only increase hostility towards me in the Senate."

"He planned the coup against Julius Philippus," I reminded him.

"So you say. Is there any proof of this?"

"No," I admitted grudgingly. "Just my word."

"Which would count for little in a court of law when put against the word of a very senior Senator."

The Emperor continued to twiddle his thumbs while he considered his options. At length, he asked me, "How do you think Valerianus would react if I revoked the Edict of Messius Decius, and ended the persecution of Christians?"

That was an easy question to answer.

I told him, "He would be very much against it. For whatever reason, Valerianus detests Christians."

Gallus frowned, "Yes, I was fairly sure of that."

I studied his face, seeking clues as to whether he really did intend to put an end to the persecutions, but he gave nothing away.

He said, "So I need to send him somewhere far from here, but to give him a suitable position which will not be seen as a demotion of any sort."

I waited. It was increasingly clear to me that Gallus had already made up his mind. My presence here was merely to provide further justification for his decision.

I ventured, "May I ask where you intend to send him?"

Gallus did not appear to be offended by my boldness. He simply smiled and said, "Gaul, I think. His son is there with the Rhine army. It would be better if I could keep the two of them in the one place. That gives them less opportunity to create trouble in two places at the same time. It also distances him from his support in Rome. And Gaul, while it has manpower, does not have the riches of the eastern provinces, so that will restrict his ability to buy local support."

"There is that," I nodded. "But it's a vital frontier, and he'll have a large army under his control."

"That is true," the Emperor agreed. "But it is a position worthy of a senior Senator, while still being some distance from the real danger. It is the Danubius frontier and the Black Sea where the main threat comes from these days. I'm sure the German tribes will provide sufficient nuisance to keep Valerianus occupied, but they do not present an existential threat to the empire."

I nodded. Gallus had clearly thought this through. I still believed that it would be better for him to have Valerianus executed, but that opinion was influenced by my hatred of the man. Sending him to Gaul was a calculated risk, but it did make some sort of sense.

"Be careful of him, Augustus," I warned.

"Fear not, Scipio," he grinned. "As Emperor, I command the *frumentarii*. If Valerianus steps out of line, he will be dealt with."

Which meant, I knew, poison or a dagger in the night would be used to get rid of him. In fact, I would not have put it past Gallus to have Valerianus killed once he reached Gaul. Senators in Rome might still be annoyed, but a story of accidental death or a sudden illness could cover the assassination.

The Emperor gave me a probing look as he said, "I expect Valerianus might wish you to accompany him."

I frowned, "He might. Or he might want me to remain here to send him reports about what is happening."

Gallus dismissed that notion with a flick of one hand.

"He has plenty of friends in the Senate who can do that for him. No, I believe he will ask you to go with him."

I felt a weight pressing down on my spirits. Gallus was probably correct.

"It might not be such a bad thing," he told me. "Valerianus will naturally suspect you of being a spy who will be sending reports to me. And if his attention is on you, he might not realise who my other agents are."

I shrugged, "He's not stupid, Augustus. He will know you will send *frumentarii* to watch him."

"Of course he will," Gallus agreed. "But your presence might still prove beneficial."

"He's likely to have me killed if he thinks I can cause him trouble," I pointed out glumly.

"That," the Emperor told me, "is a risk you will need to take. If he summons you, go with him. And be sure to watch for any signs of his disloyalty."

All I could do was nod and say, "Yes, Augustus."

I left the palace in a grim mood, wondering if it would be possible to disappear again without risking my daughter's life, but I had still not come up with any workable plan by the time I returned to Fronto's house.

"Do you think Valerianus will agree to go to Gaul?" Fronto wondered when I had recounted my conversation with the Emperor.

I said, "If he doesn't, he'll need to start a war. He can't disobey a direct order from the Emperor. I doubt he's ready for that."

"He's not ready yet, you mean?" Fronto sighed. "So you'll go with him?"

"I don't see that I'll have much choice," I muttered.

"Gaul isn't so bad," Fronto told me.

"How would you know?" I shot back. "You've never set foot outside of Rome."

He grinned, "True enough. But I hear it is very Romanised. You'll be a lot safer than you were up in Moesia."

Fronto's attempts to cheer me up did nothing to improve my mood, and I went to bed that night in a very solemn frame of mind. I still felt downhearted the next morning, but I was jolted out of feeling sorry for myself when another messenger arrived at the door with a summons for me.

"A woman wants to see you," the door slave informed me. "But the slave won't give her name. She just says you are to go with her."

Faustia and Julia, sitting together on a couch while they worked on an embroidery, both frowned, but Fronto's eyes arched as he gave me a suggestive grin.

"A woman?" he chuckled. "Maybe your luck is changing at last."

"I won't count on that," I murmured as I rose to my feet and followed the door slave to the front door.

Who, I wondered, was this mysterious woman, and what could she possibly want with me?

Chapter 21
Temptation

The slave had been kept waiting in the *atrium* where she stood to one side, paying very little heed to her surroundings. She was an older woman, perhaps in her fifties, with a broad, plump figure and a square, unsmiling face. The door slave nodded towards her before retreating to a discreet distance to let me talk to her.

"I'm Sempronius Scipio," I said as I walked up to the stocky woman. She was wearing a long tunic which was plain but of good quality, and she had a long cloak fastened with a bronze brooch. Her hair was tied and bunched on her head, small strands of grey slipping out from beneath the multitude of pins.

She regarded me with blank eyes as she said, "My Mistress wishes to speak to you. She sent me to fetch you."

"And who might your Mistress be?" I asked.

"Her name is Cornelia Gallonia," the woman said with an air which suggested I ought to know who she was referring to. The name did sound vaguely familiar, but I could not place it.

"And what does she want with me?" I asked.

"You will need to ask her that, Master," the slave replied in a tone which reminded me of an extremely strict household slave who had ruled over me when I was a very young boy. One bark from her had always been sufficient to make me stop whatever mischief I had been up to. Hearing that tone again made me shiver involuntarily.

Doing my best to conceal my reaction, I asked her, "And where will we find her?"

"In a villa on the Pincian," she replied, her tone almost begrudging the words.

However gruff this elderly slave woman might be, that information made a difference. The Pincian Hill was not counted as one of the traditional seven hills of Rome because it lay a little to the north of the heart of the ancient city, but it was where a great many very wealthy families had established villas and wide-ranging gardens. It was often referred to as "The Hill of Gardens", and it was still one of the better off suburbs. If this woman's Mistress lived there, she was almost certainly a member of a very wealthy family. Quite why anyone from there would have an interest in me, I could not fathom, but it was clear that there was only one way to find out.

"All right," I said. "I'll go with you."

The woman nodded as if she had expected nothing less, and made for the door. Fronto's slave had brought my cloak in anticipation of my departure, so I hurriedly slung it around my shoulders, then pinned it in place with a plain brooch before setting off after this strange messenger.

Outside, the old woman set a surprisingly fast pace. I fell in beside her as she headed up the hill towards the *Via Salaria*.

"What is your name?" I asked her.

"Apollonia, Master," she replied, her eyes fixed on the way ahead.

"And how long have you served Cornelia Gallonia?"

"Many years," she shrugged.

Being a slave, she could not refuse to answer my questions, but it soon became plain that I was not going to learn anything from her. When I asked about her Mistress, she simply repeated, "You will need to ask the Lady about that."

After I had listened to this refrain several times, I gave up, settling for allowing her to guide me in silence. In this uncomfortable way, we strode along until we reached the lower slopes of the Pincian Hill. We climbed only a little way before Apollonia led me to a high wall with a heavy gate which was opened by a huge man in a tight-fitting, sleeveless tunic which displayed his impressive physique for all to see. Dark-haired, his skin was deeply tanned and smooth. I could see no signs of scars which might have betrayed him as a former gladiator or soldier, although he looked far too young to have been either, being probably no older than in his mid-twenties. He was taller than me by a head, and his arms and legs were twice the thickness of my own, with every visible limb seeming to bulge with muscles.

He glanced at Apollonia who nodded, "This is him."

The big man inclined his head in a slight bow, his brown eyes studying me from head to toe.

"Welcome, Master," he said in a deep voice, his words conveying that he, too, was a slave. "Come in."

He closed and bolted the gate once we were inside, then he led the way along a gravel path between flowering shrubs and raised garden beds full of flowers. Bees buzzed around us, and the scent of the flowers hung in the still air like perfume. Had it not been for the bizarre circumstances, I might have appreciated the scene a little more.

Sitting at the centre of the garden, the villa was large and extravagant, with painted statues adorning every façade, and red tiles gleaming on the roof. We climbed a few steps, passed between marble Ionic columns which flanked the main doorway, then stepped into a cool, marble-floored *atrium*. It was no wonder Apollonia had seemed unimpressed by Fronto's home if she was accustomed to this level of luxury. Everything about this place screamed wealth and ostentation. The statuettes here were of gold rather than copper or bronze, and the wall paintings were exquisite, clearly created by a highly skilled artist. The floor of veined marble matched the *impluvium*, the indoor pool which caught rainwater for household use.

We walked through the *atrium*, our sandals sending echoing footsteps around the high-ceilinged room, then we were outside again, and I saw that the villa was built in the traditional style with four joined buildings creating a square around a peristyle garden. This, too, was a luxurious place, with a fountain in the centre, water cascading from the head of an effigy of Neptune who stared at his surroundings with sightless eyes, a trident held upright in one hand. Statues of nymphs and dryads were dotted around the garden, all of them partly concealed by flowering bushes and small trees. Beyond the fountain, I saw a man wearing a dark apron and holding a pair of shears which he was using to trim a hedge which had been fashioned into the shape of a peacock. A young boy, perhaps around eight years old, was picking up the trimmings and placing them in a wicker basket, keeping the garden pristine. Other hedges had been shaped to create green images of other beasts such as a lazing dog, a sphinx and a cat. It was yet another example of time and effort being spent to create a sense of luxury and wealth.

I would have liked to have spent more time examining these creations, but my large guide pressed on, heading across the garden to the rear wing of the house. That was interesting, and it made me wonder about the mysterious Cornelia Gallonia. Visitors would normally be met in one of the reception rooms off the *atrium*, but I was being taken to the private quarters in the rear wing. The buildings to left and right would contain stores, lavatories and probably a private bath house which would no doubt make Fronto's bathing chamber seem small and inadequate. As well as these functional rooms, the side wings might also contain slave quarters, although some Roman nobles still adopted the custom of making their slaves sleep in tiny cubicles in the basement of the main wing. Either way, this home was very impressive indeed if you like dwellings which display the owner's wealth.

We moved on in single file, with Apollonia walking behind me. Inside the building again, the muscle-bound slave turned right, led me down a short corridor, then knocked on a wooden door. I heard a woman's voice call out in response, and he pushed the door open, stepping aside to allow me to enter.

I gave him a nod as I passed him, but he did not react at all. His expression was stern, as if he were giving me a warning to behave. He stayed in the corridor, but to my surprise, Apollonia followed me in. She closed the door, then she scurried past me, keeping to one side, but circling around behind a pair of couches which faced one another across a low table.

"Here he is, Mistress," she said as she walked past the woman who sat in the middle of the furthest couch, looking at me with an expression of anticipation. Her seat was fit for a queen, a long, comfortable couch covered in pale blue velvet, with the gold-painted wooden arms at either end carved into the shape of snarling lions.

But the expensive couches were not what demanded my attention. For a moment, I stopped dead still, simply staring at the seated woman who had summoned me here. I have seen many beautiful women in my life, but I had rarely seen anyone quite like Cornelia Gallonia. She sat very still, her figure draped in folds of blue and white cloth which hung to a modest length just above her ankles but which nevertheless managed to convey an aura of sexuality the like of which I had rarely encountered. The dress seemed to shimmer and flutter even though it so obviously clung to every contour.

Above all, though, it was her face which drew my eyes and would not let them go. She was lightly tanned, her dark hair piled high on her head in the style of a married woman, but her long-lashed eyes flashed in the most seductive manner I had ever encountered. I guessed she might be around thirty years old. She was certainly no teenage temptress, but a mature woman who had grown into her full beauty. Moreover, it was clear that she knew it.

Even though she sat primly, with her hands clasped loosely in her lap, everything about her was alluring.

"Sextus Sempronius Scipio," she said in a light, pleasant voice. "Do come and sit down. Have some wine. Or there is fruit juice if you prefer."

Feeling like a captive entering an arena for the amusement of the crowd, I moved around the nearer couch, sitting down opposite her.

"Juice, I think," I replied, reckoning that wine might intoxicate me even more than the sight of her.

Apollonia quickly came over to pour from a jug into a goblet of coloured glass, one of the most expensive drinking vessels money could buy.

"I'm sorry, Lady," I said. "You have the advantage over me. I know we haven't met before. I would remember."

She smiled, her eyes sparkling, and she laughed, "You are a flatterer, Scipio."

I smiled, taking a sip of the cool juice, reminding myself that I was old enough to be her father.

She said, "I apologise for all the secrecy, but I have wanted to meet you for some time. However, I do not want my husband to find out that we have spoken."

I almost blushed as I nodded towards Apollonia who stood behind Gallonia's couch.

"You have a chaperone," I pointed out.

Gallonia laughed again, a light, happy sound which sent a thrill down my spine.

"It is one thing to flatter me," she said, "but you should not flatter yourself."

Then she placed a delicate finger against her chin, revealing that her nails were neatly manicured and painted a dark red. In that affected pose, she regarded me thoughtfully.

"Mind you," she teased, "you certainly don't look your age. Unlike my husband."

Clearing my throat, I enquired, "Can I ask who your husband is?"

Her smile lit up the room as she replied, "You don't know?"

"No, I'm afraid not."

She gave a mischievous grin as she said, "You know him very well. His name is Publius Licinius Valerianus."

She studied me for a reaction, and I think I gave her what she expected. I sat very still, the blood draining from my face, and a curdling sensation gripping my stomach. It took an effort of will not to drop the glass. Carefully, I set it down on the table, then faced her again as I gathered my composure and forced my brain to stop paying attention to her looks and to start thinking properly.

"This is not Valerianus' home," I told her. "He lives on the Esquiline."

"And so do I," she confirmed. "This is my father's home. I could not invite you to our own house without Publius finding out. So I told him I was coming to visit my mother who is unwell."

"I'm sorry to hear that," I said. "About your mother, I mean. I hope it is not too serious."

Cornelia Gallonia fluttered a hand as she said, "Oh, my mother has been unwell all her life. She spends most of her time in bed, believing she is about to die from some exotic illness or other. We have given up trying to persuade her that she is perfectly healthy."

Her offhand manner seemed more than a little uncaring, but I had no desire to spend time discussing her mother's wellbeing. There was a more important question which needed an answer.

I asked, "And who is your father?"

"Marcus Cornelius Siculus. He is a Senator. He is at the Senate House today, as is my husband."

So her father was a Senator. That explained the opulence of the house. I had never encountered Cornelius Siculus, but that did not mean a great deal. There were a great many Senators I had never met. For all my dealings with Emperors over the years, I tended to move in rather different social circles to the men who wore thick purple stripes on their tunics.

Like a child dipping his toes into water to test the temperature, I ventured, "So your husband does not know I am here?"

"Definitely not," she assured me. "And you can rely absolutely that Apollonia and Torquatus will never divulge anything about our meeting."

"Torquatus?" I frowned. "That would be the young giant who met me at the gate?"

"Impressive, isn't he?" she smiled flirtatiously. "So good looking. And so large. In every respect."

If she was trying to shock me, she failed. Gallonia was less than half Valerianus' age, and she probably sought pleasure wherever she could find it. If she wanted to invite slaves into her bed when her husband was away, that was none of my concern. The only surprise was that she was openly admitting her infidelity.

She went on, "My father insisted on buying a slave to act as my personal bodyguard. I chose Torquatus. I don't think Papa was very pleased, but he's always allowed me my own way."

"And your husband obviously doesn't mind," I put in.

Gallonia laughed again, re-awakening that shiver down my spine.

"Publius married me to make an alliance with my father," she explained. "His first wife died a long time ago. My first husband was killed fighting the Persians, so my father suggested the match. He's always had an eye on a chance to get closer to powerful men, and Publius decided it would help him as well."

It felt odd to hear my treacherous patron, Licinius Valerianus, being referred to by his *praenomen* of Publius. Somehow, it made him sound less threatening.

"I see," I said, struggling to gather my thoughts in the face of this highly attractive and distracting woman. "So why did you want to talk to me?"

Her smile was radiant as she explained, "Because my husband talks about you so much. When I heard you were back in Rome, I thought I must make the effort to speak to you this time."

She pulled a face as she added, "Publius never allows me to talk to interesting people. If he has visitors, I am banished to my rooms, and even when he hosts dinner parties, I am forced to sit in dutiful silence while his rich friends get drunk."

"I'm flattered that you think I might be interesting," I said, not at all sure where this was leading.

"Oh, you must be," she assured me. "There are very few men who Publius is afraid of, but you are one of them."

I blinked in astonishment at that.

"I doubt very much that he is afraid of me," I offered.

"Oh, but he is," she insisted, leaning forwards as if to speak more confidentially. It was a movement which caused the folds of her dress to move in very unsettling ways. I was sure she had caught the momentary flicker of my eyes to take in her shape, and she gave a slight smile of satisfaction.

Lowering her voice to a seductive whisper, she continued, "He says you are one of the cleverest and most capable men he knows. I once heard him say that he ought to have you killed, but that you are far too useful to him. But he seems constantly afraid that you will turn against him. That is why he threatens your family."

"So you know about that?" I challenged, keeping my eyes on her face now, although it was scarcely less distracting than the rest of her.

She said, "I listen, Scipio. There are some advantages to not being permitted to offer an opinion. It allows me to overhear things."

I shrugged, "All I know is that, if he is afraid of me, he hides it very well. I'm more scared of him, I think."

"Oh, he hides everything," Gallonia said, leaning back on the couch in yet another provocative pose. "And he uses people to accomplish his own ends."

"Many wealthy Romans do that," I pointed out.

"Yes, they do," she agreed, her tone adopting a slightly bitter tone. "And men without power, as well as women, need a great deal of luck if they wish to avoid being used."

I said nothing, simply waiting for whatever she was going to say next. I sensed that she was drawing near to explaining her real reason for wanting to see me.

She sat up straight again, folding her arms across her chest and fixing me with those lambent eyes.

"I think you and I could help one another," she told me. "Publius has both of us trapped, and we each need some help."

"What sort of help did you have in mind?" I asked warily. I knew I needed to be very careful here because this could be a test of some sort. I would not have put it past a devious sod like Licinius Valerianus to have his wife attempt to entrap me to either give him a further hold over me, or to provide an excuse to get rid of me permanently.

That was assuming Gallonia really was his wife. So far, I only had her word for that. Valerianus had always been very careful to keep his family separate in all our dealings. I'd met his son, but that was because he was very much his father's lieutenant. But Valerianus' first wife had been dead by the time I had first met him, and he had never so much as mentioned his second wife.

Gallonia said, "I'm not sure yet. We have only just met, after all. But I think we should stay in touch. We ought to see a lot more of each other."

She paused, then added, "Would you like to see a lot more of me?"

As she spoke, she sat back on the couch again, stretching out her arms on either side, placing them along the back of the seat as she regarded me with frank openness.

This was way beyond flirting, and I could hear all sorts of alarms trumpeting inside my head.

I said, "I wouldn't want to upset Torquatus."

She laughed again, clearly amused by my refusal of an offer most men would have leaped at.

She said, "I think I see why Publius is afraid of you, Scipio. But be careful around him. And I do think you and I need to be allies. Who knows how we might be able to help one another?"

I should have kept my mouth shut. Perhaps I could have ended this burgeoning relationship then and there, but I spoke almost without thinking.

I told her, "I'm afraid we probably won't have any opportunities to speak again. Not for a while, at any rate."

"Really?" she asked, her eyes widening. "Why is that?"

"I spoke to the Emperor yesterday," I informed her. "He is thinking of giving your husband an important appointment which will take him away from Rome, and I fully expect he will want me to go with him."

"You spoke to the Emperor?" she asked, clearly impressed. "Are you turning against Publius, then?"

"No, Lady. I am caught between two powerful men, and I tell each of them the full truth whenever they ask. I will not take sides. My only allegiance is to Rome."

"The Emperor is the embodiment of Rome," she reminded me.

"So was the last one. And the one before that."

She smiled at that but said nothing for a long moment. When she did speak, she surprised me again.

"Perhaps I will accompany Publius. Is he being sent somewhere nice?"

Thinking it better to conceal the truth, I said, "The Emperor had not yet made up his mind when we spoke."

"But why did he tell you this?" she wanted to know.

"Because he wants me to spy on your husband."

"And did you agree?"

"I always agree with Emperors, Lady. It is not wise to refuse a direct order."

She nodded, "As I recall, Publius sent you to spy on the Emperor when he was merely a provincial Governor."

"He did. And I told your husband everything I saw and heard. As I said, I will not take sides."

She smiled again, then said, "Well, I do hope you will be on my side, Scipio. You and I should be friends. But now I will have Apollonia show you to the gate. Thank you for coming. It has been very interesting to talk to you."

So I was dismissed. I stood up, gave a slight bow, then followed Apollonia to the door. Torquatus, the huge bodyguard, was standing outside in the corridor. He looked blankly at me as I passed, but then I heard Cornelia Gallonia calling out, "Torquatus! Come in here! I want you!"

I could not get out of that house quickly enough. It had, I reflected, been a narrow escape. A woman like Cornelia Gallonia was probably just as dangerous as her husband, and I wanted as little to do with her as possible. And yet I might not have any choice in the matter. If Valerianus did take her to Gaul with him, and if I was compelled to accompany him as well, Gallonia would inevitably have plenty of opportunities to summon me to talk to her again.

Apollonia, stone-faced, escorted me to the front gate where another slave had assumed duty. He let me out, then bolted the gate behind me, and I set off for Fronto's house with my mind consumed by one burning question. Was the woman I had just spoken to really Cornelia Gallonia, wife of Licinius Valerianus?

And if she was, could I afford to let myself get close to her?

My world was, I mused, becoming more complicated by the day, and I looked forward to putting my feet up and discussing the latest events with Fronto. When I reached his house on the Quirinal, though, I learned that he was away visiting Proximus' building yard, so I joined Faustia and Julia in the family room where they were still busy embroidering one of Fronto's cloaks. Julia looked impatient and bored, and she began asking me questions about where I had been and who the mysterious woman was. Faustia tried to shush her, but Julia was determined not to behave like a proper Roman girl.

"If I'm going to live here," she stated, "I think I ought to know what is going on."

She had a point, but before I could give her any answers, Fronto burst into the room with uncharacteristic urgency.

We all turned in surprise. Fronto's face was pale, and his eyes held a look of desperation and horror I had never seen before.

Faustia, abandoning her needlework, rose quickly to her feet as she asked, "What is wrong?"

Fronto stood there, trembling with emotion, and when he spoke, his voice was little more than a hoarse whisper.

"Plague," he said. "There is plague in the city."

Chapter 22
Plague

"There have been reports from Egypt," Fronto informed us between gulps of wine, his goblet held in trembling hands. "They say thousands have died in Alexandria."

"And now it is here?" I asked anxiously.

Fronto nodded, still shaken.

"Two of Proximus' workers fell ill the other day," he explained. "One of them is dead already, and the other looks unlikely to survive. And there are more reports among others who work down near the river. According to Proximus, several nearby businesses are reporting men falling sick."

"Boats transferring supplies up from the port at Ostia must have brought the plague," I said.

Faustia looked terrified, but Julia asked, "What happens? What does it do to people who catch it?"

Fronto tried to smile, but his lips refused to obey, twisting instead into a grimace. Through a visible effort of will, he did manage to sound calm as he replied, "I have not witnessed it myself, but Proximus tells me that it brings diarrhoea and vomiting. It leaves people helpless, and they can die within a few days of catching it."

"What can we do?" Faustia moaned.

I suggested, "Bring in as much food as we can. Preferably things that will last a while before going off."

Shooting a look at Julia, I added, "And we should go out as little as possible."

She frowned, but acknowledged the suggestion with a reluctant nod.

Fronto agreed, "Yes, and we should burn incense against noxious fumes."

"And pray to the gods," Faustia added.

Fronto did not look at me. He knew well enough that I despised the gods for their uncaring attitude, and that I often doubted their existence. Only some incredible escapes from danger during my various adventures had left a small residual grain of belief that some deity or other was looking after me.

Fronto said, "Yes, we should offer prayers and sacrifices."

I put in, "I'm sure all the main temples will be doing the same."

"Adding our own offerings can't hurt," Faustia insisted.

So we began to take precautions, although life in the city continued pretty much as normal for the next few days. Even so, Fronto insisted that he should be the one to go to the market to purchase food. I went with him, but he would not allow anyone else to accompany us, not even his adopted son, Dextrus.

"You must stay here," he told the young man.

"Why?" Dextrus argued. "If you bring the plague back here, I will probably catch it anyway. And I'm a lot younger and fitter than you, so I'll be able to fight it off more easily than you can. It's better for me to take the risk, not you."

His reasoning was sound, but Fronto put his foot down.

"I am the head of the family," he insisted. "This is my responsibility. You must stay here. That is my final word on this."

So Fronto and I undertook the unfamiliar task of purchasing provisions for the household. It seemed easy enough until we had to carry the sacks of grain and assorted foodstuffs back up the hill, but we persisted, visiting several markets over the course of the next few days, stocking the house as best we could. Fronto also warned the residents in each of the properties he owned throughout the city that they should stock up on food as much as they could. He even handed out coins to many of them to help them buy extra food.

"I wish we could do more," he sighed.

With all of this going on, it was a while before I turned my mind back to Cornelia Gallonia, but I did ask Fronto about her one evening while we were enjoying a jug of wine in his study. As briefly as I could, I outlined my visit to her, skipping over the more salacious aspects of our encounter.

"I remember Valerianus getting married," Fronto agreed. "It was while you were up in Verona, I think. It was a very private affair as I recall, but word does tend to leak out about people like Valerianus. And, of course, she is the daughter of Cornelius Siculus."

"I don't know him," I said.

"Oh, he's not one of the Senate's leading lights," Fronto informed me. "But he is extremely rich, so he does have a lot of so-called friends, and he can use his money to buy influence whenever there is an important vote."

"That will be why Valerianus wanted a marriage alliance," I said sourly. "He could get Siculus to bribe other Senators to vote the way he wants."

"More than likely," Fronto agreed. "But don't forget that other wealthy Senators could do the same to buy opposition. And some Senators are so rich that bribes won't work on them in any case."

I waved a hand impatiently, saying, "Never mind that. Have you ever seen Cornelia Gallonia?"

"I don't think so," he frowned.

"You would know," I told him. "She's not easy to miss."

"So you believe the woman you spoke to might be someone pretending to be her?"

"Anything is possible," I shrugged.

Fronto sighed, "Well, I have a lot of contacts in the city, so I might be able to find out a bit more about her."

He paused, then added, "Although it might be difficult considering the current situation."

"It can wait," I assured him. "We should stick to the plan of staying indoors as much as possible."

Naturally, being confined to the house did not sit well with others. Faustia was used to this, but both Dextrus and Julia were impatient to go out into the city, as were some of the slaves who normally ran errands or bought supplies. This was understandable, but Fronto stood his ground, and by the end of that week, things began to change.

Rome is the largest city in the world, with over a million inhabitants, many of them crammed together in small rooms overnight. Any disease is likely to spread rapidly in the poorer quarters, and we soon learned that this plague was no different.

Where it did differ from the usual bouts of malaria or other diseases which were common in Rome was in how fast and far it spread, and how deadly it was for anyone who fell ill. Hundreds of people were falling sick, some dying within a few days, and anyone who ventured outside did their best to maintain a distance from other passers-by.

Food soon became scarce, because farmers feared to bring their produce into the city, and the Emperor was forced to extend the grain dole, distributing even more grain which came from Egypt and Africa thanks to the massive cargo ships which traversed the sea in a never-ending series of back and forth journeys. He also announced that he would be taking part in rituals at the temple of Capitoline Jupiter to beseech the aid of the gods in warding off the spreading sickness.

It was a frightening time, with fear of illness and death an ever-present threat. Naturally, there were many different theories about how the disease spread. Many people insisted it was down to the will of the gods; others believed it was spread by coming into contact with someone who had caught the plague. Nobody knew for certain, so Faustia decided to take all sorts of precautions. As well as declining all visitors, she had the slaves busy cleaning the entire house from top to bottom on a daily basis, scrubbing floors, walls and doors, beating rugs and wiping furniture. Incense burned throughout the house, making it smell like some eastern temple, and everyone used the small bathing chamber as often as possible. Prayers to the *lares*, the household gods, as well as to major deities, were offered several times a day. When any of us did need to venture outdoors, we made sure to soak rags in wine or vinegar and hold these over our mouths.

Only one good thing came of this as far as I was concerned. I had primed the door slave in how to respond if Licinius Valerianus sent a summons for me. The slave reported to me early one morning, managing to smile at the deception he had fashioned on my behalf.

"A messenger came very early this morning, Sir," he told me. "He said Licinius Valerianus is going to Gaul, and that you are required to accompany him."

"And what did you tell him?" I asked.

The slave grinned, "As you instructed, Sir. I told him you were ill with the plague. He could not leave fast enough."

Fronto was less pleased with this outcome than I was.

"What if Valerianus sends men to examine you?" he asked me.

I shot back, "Would you enter a house where there is plague?"

"No," Fronto agreed. "But Valerianus is not the sort of man to concern himself over the safety of his lackeys. He might send them anyway."

"I doubt it," I assured him. "I'm not important enough for Valerianus to risk transmission of a fatal disease into his own household."

"He seems to think you are important," Fronto pointed out. "He's always sending for you."

"Only because it amuses him to order me around," I countered. "I'm sure he'll leave me this time. But if he does send anyone, you can scare them off with lurid tales of my illness."

I had not told Fronto about Gallonia's assertion that her husband was afraid of me. For one thing, I still wasn't entirely convinced that the woman I had spoken to really was Valerianus' wife, and for another I suspected that, even if she was, there was a good chance she had invented that tale in an attempt to flatter me. As far as I was concerned, Valerianus regarded me as little more than a useful idiot.

As it turned out, my prediction was correct. Licinius Valerianus and his household left for Gaul, and I remained behind.

"I wonder if his wife went with him?" I mused.

"Most wives remain at home when their husbands go on official business like that," Fronto said. Then, grinning, he asked, "Were you thinking of paying her a visit?"

"Absolutely not!" I insisted. "And if she sends her slave woman to fetch me, your slaves can give her the same message they gave to Valerianus."

Fronto laughed, but then said, "Perhaps it was a mistake to give him that message. It might be better for you if you had gone with him. You could have escaped the plague altogether."

"Valerianus is worse than the plague," I muttered. "Besides, who is to say that someone in his retinue hasn't already got it? He might be helping to spread the disease rather than escaping it."

"I suppose so," Fronto conceded. "But Rome is a dangerous place to be just now. Why don't you leave and find somewhere safer?"

"Because you are my friend," I told him. "I'll only leave if you do."

"I've never left Rome," Fronto reminded me. "I've survived riots and civil wars. I'm not going to flee now."

"Then we both stay," I asserted.

So I stayed, and endured some of the worst months of my life. Day after day, more people fell sick. Very few survived the illness which seemed to drain a victim's body, burning them with fever and evacuating their stomachs and bowels through severe vomiting and diarrhoea. We heard wailing from nearby houses, and saw bodies being carted away. Heralds came through the streets, proclaiming that the Emperor had banned private funerals, commanding that every death, no matter the cause, required the body to be buried in one of the many mass graves being dug outside the city, or burned in a huge, communal funeral pyre.

"It's not right," Fronto complained. "Burying bodies in pits, then covering them with lime. People deserve a proper funeral."

But there were so many deaths all across the city that individual funerals were no longer an option, and we all dreaded to hear the rumble of carts trundling down the street as the city's slaves collected the dead.

We locked ourselves in the house for several days until lack of food compelled us to venture out again, paying exorbitant prices for meagre amounts of basic foodstuffs. These expeditions also allowed us to hear the latest news. Unfortunately, rumour was rife, and it was always hard to tell the truth from exaggeration, but some people claimed that thousands were dying every day.

"How long can this go on?" Faustia asked plaintively, but none of us could provide an answer.

The plague showed no discrimination in who it afflicted. No matter what precautions people took, it could strike anyone. Not only did it spread rapidly within the crowded tenement buildings, it found its way into the homes of the wealthy. It even worked its way into the palace, and we learned that Decius Hostilianus, our young co-Emperor, had died from the sickness. Like everyone else, his body was consigned to one of the huge grave pits, an ignominious end for anyone, let alone a Roman Emperor.

Fronto and I, having ventured outside in search of more food for the house, heard this story which was relayed by men and women who all had anxious, haunted looks in their eyes.

"The Emperor has named his own son as co-Emperor now," one man told us sourly. "Hostilianus' death was very convenient if you ask me."

I tried to pay no attention to such rumours, but Fronto was always keen to hear the latest gossip.

"Do you think Gallus would have killed Hostilianus so he could promote his own son?" he asked me. "Was that his intention all along?"

I shrugged, "It's possible. I suppose you have to be ruthless if you become Emperor. But there is sickness everywhere, so who knows? Maybe young Hostilianus really did die of the plague."

Fronto frowned, "I suppose so. But, as that fellow said, it is very convenient for Trebonianus Gallus."

I shrugged, "My fear is that, if the plague has reached the palace, Gallus himself might succumb. If he dies, we could see a civil war break out. With the plague rampaging as it is, that would be disastrous."

"Then we should pray for Gallus' survival," Fronto suggested, giving me a mischievous look.

"I'm not going to go that far," I grinned back. "Gallus can take his chances like the rest of us."

We did our best to maintain our spirits through this sort of grim humour, but obtaining food became an increasing problem as the weeks turned into months. The plague, we learned, had spread beyond the city, killing many of the farmers who supplied fresh produce for Rome. And many other rural inhabitants fled their homes and came to the city in search of some sort of sanctuary. All they did, of course, was increase the number of people who were crammed into the city's slums, thus providing the plague with more victims.

Fronto and Faustia continued to lead the household in daily prayers to various deities, especially to Aesculapius, God of Healing. I took part in these rituals despite my own lack of faith because Fronto and Faustia were my friends, and because I reasoned that offering prayers could do no harm.

As it turned out, the prayers did not do much good either. I never did work out how the plague wormed its way into the household, but Faustia fell sick, as did two of the slaves. All of them lapsed into a fever, their eyes turning red with blood, and the stink of their bowels emptying filling their rooms with noxious air.

This was when Julia revealed her inner strength. With a vinegar-soaked cloth tied over her mouth and nose, she did what she could to keep Faustia clean, wiping her body with damp cloths and changing copious amounts of bed linen. Fronto and I did our best to help, trying to force water between Faustia's lips, but she spewed it back out again, and she became visibly weaker as the hours dragged by.

"Her skin is falling off!" Fronto wailed in despair when he saw patches of cracked skin appear on her arms and legs. In places, thin slivers of mottled skin sloughed off, like the discarded skin of a snake.

Julia worked desperately, but I could see tears of despair in her eyes as Faustia grew ever weaker. I felt helpless, and my friend was in torment, but he had one last attempt to make.

"We will take her to the Christians," he decided. "They have a church nearby, and I'm told they are accepting the sick."

Dextrus and Julia insisted on helping, so, with the aid of four slaves, we carried Faustia and the two sick slaves to the nearest Christian church where a constant stream of people were coming and going, most of them depositing loved ones into the care of the priest and his helpers.

"Put her over here," a middle-aged woman told us when we carried the unconscious Faustia into the tiny church. "And the others beside her."

By the light of dozens of candles, I could see that the entire floor was covered in thin mattresses, most of them occupied by people who were in the grip of the plague. The smell of incense battled with the stink of human waste, and many of the Christians, mostly women who wore a wooden cross as a symbol of their faith, were moving from one to the next, cleaning, praying and offering what hope they could.

"How long has she been ill?" the woman asked.

Fronto said, "Two days."

"Leave her in our care," the woman told us. "Go with God and offer up your prayers."

"Will your God listen to me?" Fronto frowned.

"Of course. He listens to us all if we open our hearts to him."

Fronto, looking lost and bewildered, looked around at the awful scenes of the dying, then asked her, "Is there any hope? Do any survive?"

The woman smiled, although her eyes were untouched by the expression.

"Some do," she assured us.

Fronto seized on this fragment of hope, nodding his thanks.

Then he asked her, "Are you not afraid that you will fall ill?"

"If God wills that it should be so, I will accept his judgement," she replied calmly. "But I do not fear death. We are promised ever-lasting life in the hereafter, so there is nothing to fear."

Gently, she waved a hand, ushering us away.

"Go now and offer your prayers. We will do our best for her."

Fronto was in a thoughtful mood as we trudged back home. His shoulders were slumped, his head down, and I knew he feared the worst.

Dextrus, too, was in a despondent mood, but Julia, although very worried, seemed to have found some hope from our visit to the Christian church.

She asked me, "Can their God really save her?"

"I don't know," I replied. "I hope so. They seem to take strength from their faith."

Fronto put in, "It's a strange religion. Some people say it is a death cult. They are rumoured to drink blood and eat flesh."

Julia gaped at him in shock, but I said, "I expect those are exaggerations."

He nodded dully, "Yes. I have spoken to some of them from time to time. They are fervent in their religion, but they claim it is a religion of love and peace."

"I'm surprised they survived Decius' persecutions," I remarked. Gallus, as he had hinted, had revoked Decius' edict, allowing Christians to openly worship their single God once again, and it seemed that many of them had somehow avoided being exiled or executed for not swearing loyalty to the Roman pantheon.

Fronto said, "I think many of them took the view that their God would want them to live, so he would forgive them for obeying the Edict."

"That's convenient," I murmured.

Fronto did not rise to my scepticism. He said, "They seem so unafraid. I heard that they face death in the arena without fear, singing songs even when the wild beasts are loosed upon them."

"That does take a lot of courage," I agreed. "But I suppose if you believe your spirit will go to a better place, then it may be worth the agony of that sort of death."

"You don't believe them?" Julia asked accusingly.

"I don't suppose we'll ever know until our own time comes," I replied. "But I do believe that they believe, which is why they are able to accept their own deaths, even if it does make them martyrs."

Julia lapsed into a contemplative silence, but Fronto spoke in a voice that was full of heartfelt anguish.

"I need her to live!" he wailed.

I don't know whether he prayed to the Christian God. I expect he did, for he was prepared to do anything for Faustia. But the next day, Dextrus was found in his bed by one of the slaves, and he, too, was ill with the plague. He was feverish, moaning and rambling incoherently, so we hurriedly carried him to the church as well.

The woman we had spoken to the previous day was not there, and neither was Faustia. The mattress where she had lain was now occupied by an elderly man, and one of our two slaves was also gone. The second slave lay there, his skin hot and tight, looking more like a skeleton than a living person.

Another woman directed us to place Dextrus on one of the few remaining mattresses, but Fronto demanded to know where Faustia was.

The woman looked exhausted, her eyes heavy and red-rimmed, but she mustered herself when Fronto persisted.

"Oh," she sighed. "I'm so sorry. She died last night. Her spirit is now with God in Heaven. Her body has been taken away."

Julia let out a wail of anguish, and Fronto's knees buckled, forcing me to catch him. Struggling against his weight, I asked the Christian woman to help Dextrus, then I hooked an arm under Fronto's armpit and eased him out of the church, both of us crying tears of grief.

Chapter 23
No Respite

Fronto was Roman to the core, and he did his best to adopt a stoic attitude towards his grievous loss, but his fortitude was severely tested when Julia brought news that Dextrus, too, had died from the plague.

"Are you sure?" I asked her as Fronto slumped in a chair, his hands clamped to his face, sobs wracking his body.

Julia gave a sad nod, her own eyes filling with tears.

"I went to the church to help them," she said. "I was with him when he died."

"You were in the church?" I asked.

She gave a defiant, tear-stained nod.

"They need help," she said.

"It's too dangerous," I told her. "Don't go back."

"Everywhere is dangerous," she sniffed. "I want to help."

I had already learned that arguing with her would achieve nothing, so she visited the Christians every day. And every day I watched her for signs that she, too, had caught the sickness, but she remained healthy in body if not in mind. I could see that she was haunted by the deaths she was witnessing every day, but she stuck to her resolution, and she kept offering her services to the church.

Fronto was a problem in another way. He managed to remain stoic in front of the slaves, but in private, I knew he spent the long hours of darkness letting his tears flow freely. I had suffered a similar loss years before when Circe had died, so I could empathise with my friend's grief, but that did not mean I knew how to comfort him except to be there when he wanted to talk. After three days, though, I took him into his private study, set him down in one of the comfortable chairs, and ordered the slaves to bring wine.

"And keep bringing it!" I told them.

So Fronto and I got drunk together, and as the wine flowed, so did our memories, and so did our stories of Circe, Faustia and Dextrus. With those tales came more tears, but it was a cathartic evening, lasting long into the night, and both of us fell asleep in the chairs, sodden with wine and sadness.

After that, Fronto managed to mostly remain composed. He also decided to throw himself into keeping busy, so I accompanied him as he insisted on visiting each and every one of the many properties he owned in the northern part of Rome. Here, we found that the plague had struck hard, but Fronto organised deliveries of food, and he insisted on joining Julia in helping to treat the sick.

"Be careful," I warned him. "I don't want you catching the sickness."

Giving me a sad smile, he said, "Do not concern yourself, Sextus. If I die, I will join Faustia in the Underworld. Or perhaps in the Christian Heaven if they are right after all."

With a shrug, he added, "And if I live, I will keep working to better the lives of my fellow Romans."

Neither he nor Julia fell ill, and neither did I, although I had a worrying day when my stomach gurgled and rumbled, forcing me to run to the lavatory. I feared it was the onset of the plague, but I had no fever, and all that happened was that I did not feel hungry for a couple of days.

However, while I escaped, one of Fronto's remaining slaves did fall ill. She was a young woman, scarcely more than a girl, who had been Faustia's body slave. When she collapsed and was carried to her bed, Julia and Fronto insisted on caring for her. With their faces protected by vinegar-soaked masks, they did what little they could for the poor girl. This time, Fronto refused to take her to the Christian church. Not that it would have made much difference. The poor girl lasted only two days before she died, her body wracked with fever and empty of all fluids.

"Poor child," Fronto sighed wearily. "She was afraid of death, but she was also afraid of life."

"What do you mean?" I asked him.

"She thought I was going to sell her because I have no need of her any more. Now that Faustia ..."

His voice trailed off, but I understood.

"I wouldn't have sold her," he continued after clearing his throat. "But I don't think she believed me."

We wrapped the dead girl in old linen, then carried her out to one of the many carts which were being pushed through the streets on a daily basis. The undertakers, their heads completely covered by makeshift hoods, leaving only slits for their eyes, looked weary and uncaring as they shoved their loaded cart away, heading for the mass graves beyond the city walls.

"Perhaps she will be placed near Faustia," Fronto whispered wistfully.

The house was solemn for a long time, but we were fortunate enough that nobody else fell ill. Across the city, however, the death toll was dreadful. Gradually, though, as autumn turned to winter, the grip of the plague lessened, but hunger was now almost as much a problem. Had it not been for the grain dole, many would have starved that winter. Food was increasingly difficult to obtain, much of that year's harvest having rotted in the fields because the plague had killed so many of the agricultural workers who helped to feed the city.

Rome was not entirely free of the sickness, and people continued to fall ill, but there were fewer cases, and the spread became less virulent. Slowly, life in Rome returned to something approaching normal.

Those months were the longest time I had spent with Fronto since our childhood, but I cannot say they were good times because of the awful losses he had suffered. Julia, though, seemed to have come through the ordeal stronger than ever. I had feared that I had brought her to Rome only to increase her danger, but she soon began to take on the running of the household. For someone so young, this was a test of character, but Julia possessed a great deal of common sense, and she had obviously been paying more attention to Faustia than I had suspected.

Fronto confided, "I think she looked up to Faustia even though she felt constrained. But she's never really had a mother, so perhaps she felt closer to Faustia than we imagined."

Julia certainly did her best, although she frequently asked Fronto's opinion on various domestic matters. She could never entirely replace Faustia, but she took much of the burden of running a household off Fronto's shoulders. She did, though, fling one surprise at us.

"I'm going to join the Christian Church," she announced one evening.

She sat there, watching me and Fronto for any signs of disapproval, but Fronto smiled and nodded, "They have done a great deal of good over the past few months. I'm sure you will be a credit to them."

Then, with a hint of his dry humour, he added, "Just don't try to convert Scipio. He already has the favour of the gods."

I snorted, "The gods haven't done me many favours!"

Fronto wagged a finger at me as he said, "I wouldn't be so sure about that. You've been in wars, riots, plagues and storms. You've been caught up in imperial politics, assassination plots and had all sorts of criminals after you, and yet you still survive. You will outlast us all, Sextus."

He hid his sadness behind a smile, and gave Julia words of encouragement about her decision to become a Christian. I wanted to warn her that many powerful men in Rome detested the new religion, but I understood that trying to persuade her not to join them would only result in a furious row, so I held my tongue. I did wonder whether Fronto might have been tempted to become a Christian as well, but although he admired their fortitude during the plague, I think that their failure to save Faustia and Dextrus gave him little confidence in their God.

Slowly, life resumed. Fronto's building business had suffered quite badly, but Proximus and his family had survived, and work began to pick up again. Fronto also maintained his habit of visiting all of his tenants, talking to them and handing out small donations of coin to help them through the difficult times they faced.

"Money's not much good when there's no food to buy," he grumbled, although I noticed that this did not prevent him distributing coins to those in need.

Spring arrived at last, banishing the cold, sleet and rain of winter, and still I stayed with my friend, but events beyond our immediate circle soon began to impinge on our outlook. Stories came from the Senate House where reports from all over the empire were delivered to the Senators, and then filtered out to the wider population. The plague, we heard, had spread to Greece and Asia Minor, as well as Syria. This was bad enough, but then we heard another alarming report.

"The Goths have broken the peace!" an excited citizen announced in the *forum*. He stood on a *rostrum*, delivering an impassioned speech to the crowd, waving his arms to reinforce his words.

"The Emperor failed to pay them the promised bounty, and they are now ravaging Roman lands again!"

"Can it be true?" Fronto asked me, his concern evident.

I shrugged, "I'd have said that the Emperor is a man of his word, but you never know. Perhaps Cniva took the money but decided to launch more raids in any case. I wouldn't put that past him."

Despite my belief in our new Emperor's fundamental honesty, it seemed that I was wrong. Over the next couple of days, we heard the same story from Senators who also addressed the crowd. They relayed tales of slaughter and burning, the Goths having devastated wide tracts of land all along the northern frontier and around the Black Sea provinces.

"Perhaps Gallus isn't as capable as you thought he was," Fronto remarked when I expressed my incredulity that the Emperor had not kept his part of the bargain. It had been a very one-sided bargain to be sure, but breaking it was always going to invite a violent response from the Goths. That, in turn, was turning many Romans against the Emperor because of his failure to protect the empire.

"I thought he was smart enough to realise that he can't break promises to the Goths," I grumbled. "I'm just grateful that I'm not in the middle of it this time around."

Naturally, even thinking that sort of thought was enough to drag me back into imperial politics. I had expected to remain unaffected by events in the wider world, but against all expectations, I received another summons to go to the imperial palace where Trebonianus Gallus, Emperor of Rome, wanted to speak to me personally.

"What does he want?" Fronto wondered when an imperial freedman delivered the summons.

"Nothing good," I guessed.

But I donned a fresh tunic and cloak, then set off for the Palatine, the Emperor's freedman ensuring that I was soon led to the same office where I had met Gallus the previous summer.

"Sempronius Scipio!" he beamed. "I was so glad to learn that you survived the pestilence."

"I was lucky, Augustus. Others close to me were not so fortunate."

"I am genuinely sorry for your friends, Scipio," he said, sounding sincere. "But I am glad you still live. It is also fortunate that you did not accompany Licinius Valerianus to Gaul."

I wondered how much he knew or had guessed about my excuse for not obeying Valerianus' summons, but I merely asked, "Why is that, Augustus?"

Looking me in the eye, he told me, "Because I have something I need you to do for me."

Those words sent a chill down my spine, and I fought to maintain a calm expression as I replied, "Me, Augustus?"

My attempt at inscrutability clearly failed because Gallus admonished, "Don't look so surprised. I've been asking questions about you, you know."

I said nothing, merely holding his intent gaze to let him know I would not be intimidated.

He went on, "Details seem scarce, but I have heard that you know the province of Syria quite well. You speak the language?"

I frowned. I had not expected my background in Syria to be the topic of our conversation. I had assumed that this meeting was related in some way to Licinius Valerianus, but it seemed the Emperor had something else in mind.

Reluctantly, I nodded, "I speak Aramaic."

"Fluently?"

"Yes, Augustus."

I could feel a dark chasm opening beneath my feet the more he probed at my knowledge. I was tempted to lie, but I knew the fate that awaited anyone who tried to deceive an Emperor, even one as apparently genial as Trebonianus Gallus.

He went on, "You were there during the reign of Severus Alexander, were you not?"

"I was," I nodded warily.

"There are rumours that you undertook a dangerous mission for the Emperor."

"I had no choice," I replied, letting him hear my annoyance. "And it went horribly wrong. I was lucky to escape with my life."

"Indeed? But you returned there some years later, when Emperor Gordianus waged war on Persia."

I sat very still. I had not realised that was common knowledge, although I perhaps should have guessed that someone in the palace would have heard the stories of my peripheral involvement in that ill-fated war. I had, after all, been sent on a spying mission by the former Emperor's father-in-law and Praetorian Prefect. He may have kept the details secret, but plenty of influential people would have been aware of my meetings with him. Gallus, I reminded myself, now had access to the imperial archives, and reports of all sorts reached this central hub of the empire. What bothered me was just how much he had learned about my past.

I told him, "Again, I had little choice. But all I did was deliver a message."

"You did more than that if my information is correct!" Gallus said with a sly grin. "You attempted to thwart Julius Philippus' seizure of the throne."

"I failed," I told him.

"And that failure resulted in you being condemned to work as a slave in the salt mines."

I cursed silently. He knew far more than I had hoped. Still, I was not about to divulge anything more if I could help it, so I remained silent.

After a short pause to see whether I would say anything, Gallus went on, "After that, things are a little unclear. Somehow, you avoided the fate Philippus had decreed, and you next appeared in Verona where Philippus himself died. And then my predecessor, Messius Decius, gave you a formal pardon and reinstated you as a fully free man."

All I could do was nod.

Gallus steepled his fingers as he regarded me thoughtfully.

He said, "It seems you are even more resourceful than I had thought. No wonder Licinius Valerianus keeps you at his beck and call. However, Valerianus is up in Gaul, and on this occasion your talents may be of help to me."

Again, I said nothing. What could I have said?

Gallus sat back, letting out a soft sigh.

Speaking softly, he told me, "The empire is too large to be ruled by a single person, you know. I have appointed more Governors than I can count, and I have relied on advice in many cases because I do not know whether I can depend on the loyalty of every Governor. And, as you may have heard, the Goths have begun raiding again."

I nodded, "Yes, Augustus. I had heard that. It seems Cniva cannot be trusted to keep his word."

At this, Gallus' brow furrowed, and he waved an impatient hand.

"It is my fault," he admitted gruffly. "I promised Cniva that we would pay tribute, but the plague has left our coffers almost empty, so I could not pay him. That is why he has sent his ships to attack in the east, and why his horsemen are plundering in Moesia and Pannonia again."

"So the reports circulating around the *forum* are true?" I asked, unable to conceal my dismay.

"They are," Gallus confirmed. "And there is very little I can do except hope that the local garrisons are strong enough to drive the barbarians off."

I frowned, "So you are not sending an army to assist the border legions?"

Gallus eyed me sternly for a long moment, and I knew I had over-stepped myself.

Speaking in a low but determined voice, he said, "I do not answer to you, Scipio."

I held his gaze as I said, "No, you don't. You answer to every Roman citizen."

It was the sort of remark which would have seen many Emperors call for his guards to drag me away and throw me to the lions, but Gallus actually gave a twisted smile after he had recovered from the initial surprise at my temerity.

He growled, "By Jupiter, you are an insolent devil, Scipio! But I suppose you are right. Many lives depend on the decisions I make."

He hesitated, then blew out a resigned breath.

"I cannot send an army to Pannonia," he told me. "The plague has devastated our reserves of manpower, and the few troops I have left are going to Syria."

He stared at me, waiting for me to respond. Clearly, his earlier references to my knowledge about the eastern province had not merely been to establish what he knew about me. Something serious had happened in Syria, and that was why I was here.

Cautiously, I said, "I have not heard of any trouble in Syria, Augustus. Have the Persians attacked again?"

"If only!" he sputtered. "No, it seems I have a rival as Emperor. Some upstart nobleman by the name of Mariades has raised a revolt in Antioch, and has proclaimed himself Emperor. I have sent orders to Egypt that the army there should march to put down this rebellion, and I am also sending what remains of our reserves to join them."

"You are not going yourself?" I asked.

With a flash of impatience, or possibly frustrated anger, he told me, "No. The Goths are a greater threat at the moment. I am going to try to raise more troops, a task at which even Hercules might take fright."

He lifted one hand, running it through his hair in exasperation, and for a moment he was no longer Emperor of Rome, but simply a man who faced a multitude of problems.

"It is one thing after another, Scipio," he sighed. "We face dangerous foes on several fronts, and I need things settled quickly. Above all, I'd prefer that the army I am sending to Syria could be diverted north, but I cannot permit a rival Emperor. I'm sure you understand that."

"I do, Augustus," I nodded.

Leaning forwards on his desk, he said, "Which is where you come in. I want you to go to Antioch. Find this traitor, Mariades, and kill him for me."

Part 3

Rebels & Rivals

Chapter 24
Return To Antioch

I swallowed nervously before saying, "Augustus, you should know that, although I have been a spy in the past, I have never been an assassin."

Gallus' reaction was to smile and raise his eyebrows.

"Really? Licinius Valerianus informed me that you were responsible for the death of our former Emperor, Maximinis Thrax."

"He told you that?" I gasped, astonished that Valerianus would reveal such a thing.

Wryly, Gallus explained, "I think he was trying to scare me into believing that your powers of persuasion could turn the army against me. That is what you did when Thrax was overthrown, was it not?"

I shook my head.

"The soldiers did that. They didn't need me to persuade them."

"Even so," he said, "I want you to go to Syria. I have very few *frumentarii* out there, and Mariades has executed every member of the former Governor's retinue, so I have nobody close to him at all. If any of my agents do attempt to approach him, they will be recognised."

Raising a hand and extending a finger to point directly at me, he added, "You will not be recognised."

Speaking as firmly as I dared, I said, "I am not an assassin, Augustus. Even if I was, the task you are setting me would be difficult for a younger man, let alone someone of my age."

He shrugged, "I must work with the tools I have, Scipio. You must know that."

I said, "I do understand, Augustus. But trying to turn me into an assassin is using completely the wrong tool for the task. You are right that I can easily fit in among the people of Syria, but that does not mean I am capable of getting close to a self-proclaimed Emperor."

"You are close to me," he pointed out with a flash of grim humour. "Talking yourself into difficult situations seems to be what you are good at."

I was more concerned with my ability to talk myself out of danger, but I kept that thought to myself. What really bothered me was that Gallus seemed to be hinting that I should be prepared to sacrifice my life in an attempt to murder a man I had never met.

The Emperor kept his raptor gaze on me for a long time, then let out an exasperated sigh as he sat back on his chair.

"I want Mariades dealt with, Scipio. Kill him if you can, or get rid of him some other way. At the very least, stir up trouble among the locals, and ensure they turn against him. That will make the task of my army much easier. If they gain a quick victory, I can use them to fight off the Goths instead of wasting time getting rid of malcontents."

His voice was suddenly stern, containing all the iron of a military commander, and I knew I would have little choice in the matter.

He told me, "Return to the palace by the second hour of the afternoon. I will have someone escort you to Ostia. There is a ship leaving on the midnight tide. You will be on it."

He stared at me, all trace of friendliness evaporated, and his eyes as hard as flint.

"The empire is in danger, Scipio," he asserted. "I need to use any methods I can to protect it. I need you to go to Syria and do whatever is necessary to overthrow Mariades. Do you understand me?"

There was a glint of ferocity in his gaze, and I knew I was trapped. All I could do was reluctantly nod my head to accept the mission.

Then, his expression softening a little, he said, "Do not let me down, Scipio. My troops will defeat Mariades eventually, but I cannot afford to wait. I need a quick resolution to the problem. Do whatever it takes. Do you hear me?"

With a leaden heart, I nodded, "I understand, Augustus."

"Good. Then go and prepare whatever you need to take. But travel light. Don't bother taking an army of slaves and a thousand trunks full of luggage."

"I always travel light, Augustus," I told him.

I left the palace in a grim mood, stalking my way back up to the Quirinal. When I told Fronto and Julia what the Emperor had demanded, they were horrified.

Fronto gasped, "He wants you to become an assassin? That is ridiculous! How does he expect you to get away even if you do manage to kill this false Emperor?"

"I don't think he's too bothered about me surviving the mission," I muttered darkly.

"He's given you some leeway at least," Fronto sighed. "If you can find some other way to get rid of the rebel leader, you might not need to attempt the assassination."

I grunted, "That's assuming I can find some other way to overthrow him."

Julia was equally appalled, but she had a different concern.

"You cannot leave us!" she protested, her voice tinged with anguish at the thought of another parting.

"I have no choice," I told her. "It is unwise to disobey a direct order from the Emperor. I need to be on that ship or he'll send a squad of Praetorians to hunt me down."

Anxiously, Fronto asked, "What do you plan to do when you reach Antioch?"

"I have no idea," I admitted. "Unless you can think of some way I can get out of this?"

Fronto shook his head.

"You can't claim to have the plague," he pointed out. "I suppose you could try to flee."

Sourly, I grunted, "Gallus would just arrest you and threaten to execute you unless I returned. He knows that's how Valerianus keeps his hold over me, and I'm sure he'd do the same thing."

"I thought you liked him?" Fronto frowned.

"Only comparatively speaking. He's got the makings of a decent Emperor, but he's obviously capable of ruthlessness when it suits him."

Grimly, Fronto sighed, "In that case, I'll give you plenty of money. And my prayers, of course."

"I suspect I'll need both," I nodded glumly. "But there is one other thing you could let me have."

"What is that?" he asked.

"Something to let me get past official barriers."

I reached Ostia in plenty of time, thanks to an escort of Praetorian Guards and a fast horse. I did not see Trebonianus Gallus again, but the commander of the Praetorian squad handed me a small bag of gold coins.

He told me, "I don't know what your mission is, but the Emperor says you are to use that to cover your expenses and to pay bribes."

Taking the bag and stuffing it inside my old satchel, I trudged up the gangplank onto the ship, and introduced myself to the Captain.

"I was warned to expect you," he said. "You can have one of the cabins below deck."

As I knew from experience, these cabins were dark, usually hot and stuffy, and very uncomfortable. The only difference this one enjoyed was that I did not need to share with anyone else. This suited me, and I stayed out of sight as much as I could, only venturing up on deck for some exercise twice each day. Food was brought to my cabin, and the Captain pointedly ignored me for the entire three weeks of the voyage. Most of the crew followed his lead, acting as if I was not there. Knowing how sailors loved to gossip once they reached harbour, I stuck to my cabin and tried to work out what in Jupiter's name I was going to do once I reached Antioch.

Fortunately, the voyage was uneventful, and since the ship was a merchant vessel, we had little trouble docking at Seleucia Pieria, the closest seaport to Antioch. There were, though, warships being gathered in anticipation of an attack from Rome, and I quickly discovered that the town was full of soldiers, all of them apparently loyal to their new Emperor, Mariades.

I spent a short time wandering the streets of this port city, checking out the defences and counting the number of warships in the harbour. I suppose this could have been classed as spying, but it was more out of habit than anything else. Information, I knew from long experience, was valuable, and you never knew when having a bit of knowledge might come in useful.

I briefly contemplated staying here in Seleucia Pieria. It would have been easy to stay out of sight, wait for events to transpire, then tell Gallus that I had been unable to achieve what he wanted. But I had wrestled with my conscience during the voyage here, and I knew that, much as I would have preferred to let matters run their course without the need for me to become involved, I could not do that. The safety of the empire was at risk. While this may sound idealistic, I had family living in various places within Rome's borders, and their safety concerned me. No less a person than the Emperor had asked for my help. More correctly, he had demanded my help, but my conscience would not let me take the easy option when there was so much at stake. Much as I wanted a quiet life, I knew I would do as the Emperor had commanded. Not that I wanted to physically kill anyone, but I had devised a plan of sorts during the long voyage from Ostia, and it was an idea which offered a slight chance of success. On the other hand, I reminded myself, it was a plan which could easily get me killed.

One thing did become clear very quickly. Whatever Gallus believed about my powers of persuasion, they would not work on the sailors and soldiers who made up Mariades' fleet and army. I was old enough to be the grandfather of most of the troops, and even many of the Centurions, men of long service and experience, were considerably younger than me. No soldier was going to sit and listen to an old man like me spread false rumours even if I did offer to buy drinks for an entire Cohort. That in itself would have been a careless tactic, since anyone throwing cash around while spreading false rumours was soon going to come to the attention of people in high places, and not in a good way.

This left me with only one, very risky, course of action, so I visited a bath house where I had a barber shave me and trim my hair into a neat, Roman-style fashion. Then I stripped off, leaving my belongings in the care of one of the house slaves. That was always risky, but I had little choice. I'd not had an opportunity to wash properly throughout the three week voyage, so a bath was essential.

My transformation from a shabby, ordinary citizen to a refined, wealthy equestrian was completed when I had dried myself after my bath. I retrieved my belongings, and dug out one of Fronto's purple-striped tunics which he had let me borrow. This, I hoped, would open doors and overawe any officious bureaucrats who might prevent me reaching Mariades.

"You could be executed for wearing that when you are not entitled to the rank," Fronto had warned me when he handed it to me.

I had replied, "Assuming I'm not executed by Mariades just for turning up in Antioch, I can always appeal to the Emperor. He'll forgive me."

"You hope," Fronto had sighed, shaking his head.

But this was a risk I needed to take. Wearing my new tunic with its insignia of rank denoted by the thin stripe of purple, I paid for passage up to Antioch on one of the small river boats which plied up and down the fast-flowing Orontes river, taking passengers and goods from the seaport to the city.

I had spent a few years in Antioch when I was much younger, and I had made a few brief visits in the time since, but I was still not sure what to expect this time. Our boat docked on the southern bank of the river, beside one of the great stone wharfs, and here I found yet more soldiers. They were stopping every passenger, asking questions and creating long delays for everyone who wanted to leave the docks and enter the city.

It was, I decided, time for me to act like an upper class Roman, so I barged my way to the front of the crowd which clustered around the gate leading away from the river docks, and presented myself to the guards with what I hoped was a suitably haughty expression on my newly-shaved face.

"I am here on important business!" I announced in a loud voice. "I must see Emperor Mariades immediately. I have come from Rome with important news."

As I had hoped, the soldiers looked uncertain. Army discipline meant that they were conditioned to obey orders from a superior, and I was acting in as superior a manner as I could, with the purple stripe on my tunic acting as a symbol of my importance.

This did not escape the attention of a junior officer, an Optio who hurried over, abandoning whatever restful occupation he had been engaged in. Clearly, he knew that dealing with an Equestrian from Rome was not something that could be left to ordinary rankers.

"Your name, Sir?" he asked, his voice adopting a tone which was somewhere between officious and deferential.

"Sempronius Scipio. I have urgent news for the Emperor. I require an escort to take me to the palace."

I could see the palace out of the corner of my eye. The large building complex was situated on a large island in the middle of the river. Tall buildings rose behind high walls of stone, with banners flying from the tops of several towers. That building complex was the home of whoever ruled in Antioch, so I was fairly certain Mariades would be there. The palace and its surrounding buildings were joined to the north and south banks by bridges, and it was only a short walk to the southern bridge from where I now stood.

The Optio was so flustered that he did not even question the fact that I had turned up with no slaves or baggage. He simply ordered one of his men to escort me to the palace. The victim of this order was a young recruit who looked barely old enough to bear arms. He led me to the palace and I, in true equestrian style, ignored him completely.

What little I could see of Antioch was both familiar and strange. Much of the city had suffered during the great earthquake which had devastated wide areas of the eastern empire during the reign of young Gordianus, but that had been years ago, and rebuilding had obviously taken place. Even so, many buildings sparked memories, and I felt that old love of the city returning. It was, though, odd that the places I recognised seemed somehow smaller and less imposing than my memory had told me.

But there was no time to dwell on memories. My guard took me to the palace where I repeated my demand for an audience several times, each time being passed further up the chain of command as I was permitted ever deeper into the palace complex. I did my best to maintain my act, but it was late in the afternoon, and I was growing tired and hungry by the time I was confronted by a middle-aged man who gave the impression of being very senior in Mariades' household.

The room we were in had once been part of a suite occupied by Julia Domna, mother of Emperor Caracalla. I had been a secretary to that formidable woman for a couple of years, and it felt strange to be standing in the same room where I had once worked.

The current occupant was a lean, middle-aged man with a serious face and a grave manner. He sat behind his desk like a sentinel. A curtain hung on the wall behind him, but I knew that it concealed a door which led into the main quarters which Emperor Mariades had obviously taken over as his personal chambers.

"The Emperor does not grant an audience to just anyone who turns up," the man behind the desk told me.

"He had better see me," I shot back. "Time is of the essence."

"Then tell me your story first," he insisted.

"And who might you be?" I demanded. "I was charged with delivering my message to the Emperor in person."

I had refused a seat, hoping that the extra height I gained by standing might intimidate him a little, but I was sadly disappointed. He wore his official position like a suit of armour.

The man preened, "I am Hertius Menander, principal secretary to the Emperor. You can give me your message."

He held out his hand, waiting for me to pass him a sealed document.

"The message is verbal," I told him, adding a touch of condescension to my tone. "It was considered too important to be written down."

This was a gamble on my part. Roman society thrives on paperwork, and every order is written down. A messenger with no written missive was highly unusual, but I was counting on my feigned urgency to overcome any officious objections.

Menander's hand withdrew, and we engaged in a staring competition for a long moment.

Frowning, and becoming increasingly irritated with me, for which I could not blame him since I was behaving like a real boor, he snapped, "Then tell me what it is you have to say."

I tapped my sandalled foot on the stone floor, planted my fists on my hips and let out an exasperated sigh. Then, knowing I would get no further unless I divulged something, I said, "My patron is Publius Licinius Valerianus. He has sent me here with information on how Trebonianus Gallus plans to react to Emperor Mariades' declaration of supremacy."

This was all nonsense, of course, but Licinius Valerianus was a very famous man, and even here in Antioch they would know his name. I detested the devious bastard, but if I could use his name to help me, then I had no qualms about it.

As I'd hoped, Menander clearly knew the name. His eyebrows twitched, and his lips pursed when he heard this.

After a moment's thought, he asked me, "Why would Licinius Valerianus send word of Gallus' plans?"

Leaning slightly towards him, I adopted a conspiratorial tone as I answered, "Because Licinius Valerianus is not pleased that Trebonianus Gallus has claimed the imperial throne. He has no love for him at all."

Menander considered this, then asked, "And how does Valerianus come by news of Gallus' intentions?"

I said, "Licinius Valerianus, as you probably know, is in Gaul. But I have been his eyes and ears in Rome. I know what

Gallus is planning, and when Valerianus received my report, he sent a fast messenger to me, urging me to come here."

Menander studied me for a long time, uncertainty clouding his expression, then he said, "Wait here."

He rose from his chair, then pushed aside the curtain and opened the door behind it. He went through, leaving me alone in his spacious office. I listened hard, but the walls were made of solid stone, and the door was thick oak. After an interminable wait, Menander opened the door again, beckoning me to go through.

"The Emperor will see you," he told me drily.

I walked through into a large, opulently furnished chamber. Memories of Julia Domna returned, although the room had been completely redecorated with mural paintings, and the furniture was all very new. Even so, I almost smiled at the memories evoked by simply being here. I had liked old Domna, and when I saw Mariades, I knew she would have eaten him for breakfast. He sat on a couch which had a frame of gold and was covered in purple cloth. His own tunic was purple, and his fingers bore many jewelled rings. His hair was short in the Roman style, his beard thin and wispy. He was of very average build, not much taller or broader than me, and he looked to be in his fifties, about the same age as Menander.

What struck me most, though, was his petulant expression. He struck me as being someone who had been dreadfully spoiled as a child, as a youth and as a man. He had probably grown up believing that he was destined for great things by virtue of his noble birth.

I stood in front of him, receiving no invitation to sit. Menander took up position slightly to my right and in front of me, ready to intercept should I make any attempt to attack his Emperor. There were, I could not help noticing, four very pretty slave girls standing some distance behind Mariades' couch, and two armoured soldiers standing against the walls, one to either side. Their presence was, I decided, more ceremonial than practical since the chamber was so large they could not have reached me in time to stop me if I did harbour violent intentions.

I wondered what Trebonianus Gallus would have thought if he could have seen me. He would have probably expected me to draw a dagger from beneath my tunic, leap at Mariades and stab him to death, then willingly allow myself to be cut to pieces by the vengeful guards.

I had other ideas, so I simply stood there, proud and haughty as any Roman Senator.

Mariades' voice was languid and bored, and his eyes refused to meet mine as he said, "Menander tells me you have word of Gallus' plans. Is that right?"

"It is, Augustus. My patron, Licinius Valerianus, sends you greetings and a pledge of his loyalty."

That was safe enough to say, I thought. Valerianus' loyalty meant very little since he was far away in Gaul, with practically the whole extent of the empire between him and Antioch. Nobody here would have any way of confirming or contradicting my assertion.

"Does he plan to send military aid?" Mariades asked me.

"Sadly, Augustus, he is engaged in difficult warfare against the Allemanni, a particularly fierce Germanic tribe. He has no troops available to send you since Gallus has stripped the border provinces of as many soldiers as he could."

I was quite enjoying myself now, fabricating stories which I hoped would unsettle this rather unprepossessing Emperor. At the very least, rumours would soon spread throughout the palace thanks to the watching slaves and guards.

"So why did he send you?" Mariades demanded. "What is it you have to tell me?"

I launched into my prepared speech, a tale I had invented during the sea crossing.

"Gallus is sending a very large army against you," I said. "His fleet is transporting twenty thousand men to Egypt, where they will join with the legions already based there. That will add another ten thousand men. He has also detached troops from the northern border provinces as I mentioned, and he has raised an additional force to join them. They are marching south now, and will come across the Bosporus, down through Bithynia and Lydia to attack you from the north. I believe this force numbers another twenty thousand."

Mariades blinked, then cast a nervous look in Menander's direction, clearly seeking guidance.

Menander frowned, "Gallus can spare fifty thousand men to oppose us? What about the Goths? They are attacking the northern frontier."

With a dismissive wave of one hand, I replied, "The Goths are raiding because Gallus did not pay them their promised bounty.

He is making arrangements to settle that debt. The Goths will return home once they have been paid a sufficient bribe. That has freed up troops for the army which is marching against you."

Putting on my most earnest expression, I added, "Gallus knows there can only be one Emperor, so he is putting all his resources into this war against you."

"Gallus is with the army?" Mariades gasped.

Menander said, "That is not what our own spies in Rome tell us."

So they had spies in Rome? Well, that was only to be expected.

I told them, "Your spies have been deceived. I spoke to the Emperor myself."

With a sly grin, I added, "He believed that he could trust me."

Menander scowled, "And why should we trust you? How do we know that you are who you say you are?"

I gave him the sort of disparaging look that true Romans usually reserve for provincial officials as I said, "Anyone who knows anything in Rome can tell you that Sempronius Scipio is Valerianus' man, and everyone knows that Valerianus hates Trebonianus Gallus."

There was a long silence before Mariades asked again, "And Gallus has fifty thousand troops?"

"At least that," I nodded. "He is determined to attack you here. And, while I know that Antioch's defences are strong, even if all the legions who guard the Persian border come to your aid, you will be severely outnumbered."

Mariades' face had gone quite pale, and he looked to be at a loss as to what to say. Once again, Menander came to his aid.

He asked, "What does Licinius Valerianus advise?"

I shrugged, "He sends a warning, not advice."

"That is not particularly helpful," Menander snorted.

I said, "I am sorry. What would you have me say? Your only chances are to go out in force to confront one or other of Gallus' armies in the hope of defeating it quickly. Then you will need to race to confront the second army before they join forces. Unless you are lucky enough to kill Gallus in battle, he will besiege Antioch."

I gave another shrug as I added, "Or you can stay behind the city walls and hope that you can withstand Gallus' attack."

Mariades' eyes betrayed his fear, and I knew that he realised that neither of these was a viable option. Personally, I had little sympathy for him. He should have known before he raised his rebellion and murdered the former Governor along with all his aides that Gallus would respond with violence. As I had told him, there could only be one Emperor. All I had done was exaggerate the extent of Gallus' forces.

Mariades continued to blink nervously, but Menander announced, "We thank you for bringing this warning. We will think on it. In the meantime, you will be our guest here."

"I really ought to return to Rome," I said.

Menander's gaze was as hard as iron as he repeated, "You will be our guest."

He ordered one of the guards to take me to a room in an adjoining building, and he gave orders to one of the slaves to ensure that the room was prepared for me.

Dismissed from Mariades' presence, I was taken to an upper floor, to a room which overlooked the river and the city to the south. It was a small chamber, comfortable enough, with a large bed, a sumptuous couch and thick rugs of Persian design on the floor.

"I will have food brought," the slave girl assured me after she had made the bed.

She and my guard left the room, but I heard the very distinct sound of a lock being turned as soon as the door was shut. It was evident that I was not a guest. I was a prisoner.

Chapter 25
The Priest

I had spent time in far less comfortable prisons, but it was a prison nonetheless, and having nothing to do except sit and think was tiresome to say the least. I ran through various schemes for making an escape, but none of them seemed likely to have much chance of success. Whenever the door to my room was unlocked to admit a slave bearing a tray of food, I could see two armed soldiers standing guard in the corridor outside. Menander was obviously taking no chances of me escaping.

I frequently demanded to be allowed to see Mariades or his Principal Secretary, but the guards simply shrugged and told me that their Emperor had given orders that I should be kept locked in the room. So I rested, planned, and imagined several very unpleasant endings for both Mariades and Menander. I also spent a lot of time gazing out of my window, looking out over the rooftops of Antioch and listening to the distant sounds of a bustling city going about its business. I longed to go out and wander the streets, but all I could do was spectate while the world passed me by.

On the third day, though, after a slave had cleared away the tray which had held my evening meal, one of the soldiers hesitated before closing the door. He looked around anxiously, then stepped back into the room and asked in a low voice, "Is it true, Sir? Is the Emperor really bringing eighty thousand men against us?"

I had to conceal a self-satisfied smile. It seemed that my lie had not only spread, it had grown in the telling.

I told him, "I don't know the precise number, but he was intent on bringing as many troops as he could. It may well be around that number by now."

The soldier regarded me grimly, then gave a slight nod and moved out of the room, pulling the door shut behind him. No doubt the rumour would now spread even further, and the number of imperial troops would soon expand to an even greater number. It was a small victory, but if nothing else, I had obeyed Gallus' injunction to damage the morale of the rebels.

The following morning, I asked to be permitted to bathe. The guards promised to relay this, and I was pleasantly surprised when a visitor arrived in my room a few hours later. My door was opened to admit a tall, slim man in his fifties who carried himself with an air of authority. Dark hair, a beak of a nose, and olive skin suggested he was a native of Syria, and he wore long robes which were fashionable among some in the east. His brown eyes sparkled with amusement, and a smile played around his lips as he introduced himself.

"My name is Julius Aurelius Sulpicius Uranius Antoninus," he told me. "Which is quite enough names for any single person to bear. I, too, am a guest here, and I have been asked to accompany you to the palace bath house."

"You are a guest?" I asked, rising to my feet and warily clasping his offered hand. His grip was firm and confident, and he continued to smile warmly as he carried on with his introduction.

"Yes," he grinned, "but a genuine guest. I'm not in the same category as you at all. Come, let us go before that prig Menander changes his mind. I'm afraid we will have an escort of soldiers, but I have given my word that you will not attempt to escape. I do hope you do not intend to make a liar of me."

His manner was bright and engaging, and he bustled me out of the room before I had time to object.

As I'd expected, the two soldiers who were guarding my room fell into step behind us, but another group of soldiers, these ones wearing leather cuirasses and carrying short, curved swords, also trailed in our wake.

"Those are my men," Uranius informed me. "They are intent on keeping me safe, that is all."

I regarded him with a questioning look. He was clearly a man of some importance if he had his own soldiers to protect him, but he merely laughed when he saw my curiosity.

"All in good time," he told me.

He led the way through the maze of passages and stairs which eventually brought us to a courtyard which lay near the perimeter wall surrounding the palace island. Crossing this space, we reached the bath house where another pair of Uranius' guards stood as sentries outside the entrance.

Uranius told the soldiers to wait outside, then he led me into the baths. It had been many years since I had been in this building, but not much had altered. It was luxuriously appointed, with marble pillars rising to the high ceiling, and painted tiles decorating the walls and floors. It was bright and airy, the large rooms creating echoes of our voices and footsteps.

"We will have the place more or less to ourselves at this time of the morning," he informed me as we took off our tunics and sandals, grabbed towels and donned the heavy wooden clogs designed to protect our feet from the heat of the floor tiles.

When we went through to the hot pool, I saw that he was right. The place was deserted, which was unusual no matter the time of day. Even the slave attendants had made themselves scarce. Uranius, though, acted as if this were perfectly normal.

Despite the almost eerie absence of other bathers, I slipped into the steaming water with a sigh. I reached for a small lump of tallow soap which had been conveniently left by the poolside, and began scrubbing at my hair and body, working away the days of sweat. Beside me, Uranius did likewise, speaking to me as we washed.

He told me, "I am in Antioch on official business. My role is as High Priest of Emesa, a city some way to the south-east. Do you know it at all?"

"I know of it," I replied. "I've never been there."

Now I began to understand. Emesa was an ancient city, with its own traditions. One of those customs was that it was ruled by a man who held the rank of both High Priest and King. If Uranius was the current ruler of the city, his wish to bathe in private would have been enforced by his soldiers who would have cleared the place before we arrived.

He went on, "Emesa was the home of our late Emperor, Elagabalus. In fact, I now hold the same role he did when he resided there before he became Emperor."

I said nothing. Elagabalus had been elevated to the imperial throne when he was a young teenager, placed there by the machinations of his grandmother. His rule had been a disastrous one, and he had met a brutal end. An end which I had been unfortunate enough to witness. I had no wish to recall that particular memory, although a vision of it flashed through my mind, making me grimace slightly.

Uranius must have seen my expression, because he gave a soft laugh.

"Do not worry, my friend. My family and his are only very distantly related. I believe we descend from cousins some five generations back. But I have no ambition to rule the empire. I am content to be the leader of my own city."

"Is that why you are here?" I guessed. "Are you paying your respects to your new Emperor?"

"Exactly!" Uranius nodded.

By this time, we had both relaxed, sitting on the step which lay just beneath the surface of the hot water, and leaning our backs against the side of the pool. It still felt odd to be in a deserted bath house, but I could not deny that I was enjoying the warmth of the water. Even so, I remained wary of my companion, and I resolved to be careful of what I said to him.

Uranius, though, appeared to have no such qualms. After a moment, he said, "The man is an idiot, you know."

I blinked in surprise, asking, "Who is?"

"Mariades, our new Emperor. He only raised his rebellion because the Governor, now deceased, was going to have him arrested on charges of corruption and incompetence in public office. He used to organise theatre shows, chariot races and such spectacles, but he bungled things quite badly, upsetting the citizens, which is never a good idea."

"And yet they support him as Emperor?"

"Oh, he managed to blame everything on the Governor. After he'd had him executed, that is. And he granted a tax holiday, so everyone loves him."

"That's certainly unusual," I remarked cautiously.

Uranius obviously felt no need to be careful in what he said. He told me, "It was reckless and stupid. He's soon going to find he needs money to pay for the extra troops he has recruited, and for the warships he is having built. His lickspittle, Menander, is the brains of the pair, if you ask me, although that's not saying much."

"But he's going along with Mariades' policies?"

Uranius grinned, "I don't pretend to understand his motives. Perhaps I have misjudged him, and he really is as stupid as his master. Or perhaps he intends to overthrow Mariades when things begin to go wrong."

"I'd say they will start to go wrong before much longer," I said.

Uranius chuckled, "Ah, yes. This massive army which is on the way to crush the rebellion. That story came from you, didn't it?"

I nodded, keeping my face as impassive as I could.

"A grand tale!" Uranius laughed. "I expect it is mostly horseshit, isn't it?"

I pretended puzzlement. For all I knew, Uranius was in league with Mariades and was merely pretending to befriend me in order to trick me into revealing the truth.

I said, "No, that is the information I learned when I was in Rome."

He eyed me speculatively.

"Really? Ah, well, we shall learn the truth before much longer, I expect. Personally, I do not intend to wait around to find out. I am returning to Emesa tomorrow."

When I said nothing, he continued, "Mariades insisted that I pledge to raise a force of troops to support him."

I looked at him, still saying nothing.

He grinned, "Oh, I gave the promise easily enough, but it will take me a while to raise such a force as he has demanded. Probably two or three months, I expect. Perhaps longer. A year or two maybe."

He was openly laughing as he added, "You see, I plan to arrive just a little too late to take part in whatever battle takes place. And then I shall, naturally, pledge my undying loyalty to whoever has won it."

He seemed to think this was a great joke, but I could detect the seriousness behind it. What he was outlining was a fairly standard practice among local leaders who were not convinced that joining either side was in their best interests. What was different was Uranius' openness about his intentions. Or, I reminded myself, his apparent openness, and only to me.

We moved through to the warm pool, spending a short time there before advancing to the cold pool. The water here gave me a shock after the heat of the other pools, but we both engaged in short bouts of swimming, crossing the pool in a few strokes, then turning and swimming back.

When we stopped to regain our breath, Uranius told me, "I think you ought to know that Menander has sent a messenger to Rome to check on your credentials. That is why he wants you kept locked up. He is trying to verify your warning."

"That could take months!" I protested.

"Of course," Uranius agreed. "And it will be far too late by then in any case. As I said, Mariades is an idiot, and I am increasingly coming to the opinion that Menander is not much better. He is a born bureaucrat, and while he may have more intelligence than his master, he does not have the wit or insight to be a proper diplomat."

When I said nothing in response, Uranius asked me, "Does it bother you that he is trying to learn the truth about you?"

I shook my head.

"Not at all. I am who I say I am. If his messenger does manage to return before the imperial army arrives, he'll learn nothing about me that I haven't already told him."

Uranius considered this, then grinned, "My friend, you are either a very good liar, or you are telling the truth."

I smiled back, "Both of those could be true."

At which he burst out in happy laughter, splashing his hands on the surface of the water.

"I like you, Scipio," he told me. "It would be a pleasure to speak to you again, but I will be leaving in the morning."

"After you've told Mariades and Menander what we've discussed?" I probed.

He inclined his head in a slight bow as he admitted, "I am sure they will ask me. I won't mention any of my own statements, of course, but since you are adamant that you have told the truth, then I see no harm in telling them."

I suggested, "You could tell them that they may as well release me, then."

"I could do that," he said. "I doubt it will make much difference."

There was not much more for either of us to say, so Uranius clapped his hands loudly, calling out to summon a pair of slaves who came in from a side room. They quickly moved to stand beside a couple of tables which stood at one end of the large chamber, their surfaces draped by thick towels. Uranius and I emerged from the pool, then lay down on the tables, allowing the slaves to massage our bodies, rubbing in oil which they then scraped away with a *strigil*, leaving us as clean as it was possible to be. As if by mutual agreement, neither of us spoke during this process. Uranius, I realised, was more discreet than his earlier behaviour had suggested. Whether his comments had been genuine, or merely designed to catch me out, he was not going to risk repeating them in the presence of slaves. Some Romans spoke quite freely in front of their slaves because they regarded them as little better than ignorant beasts, but I had long ago learned that slaves can chatter and gossip as well as anyone, which was how rumours spread.

As Mariades, I hoped, was finding out.

Uranius and I parted on good terms, with him clasping my hand and assuring me of his friendship. I thanked him and wished him well, and then my guards led me back to my room and locked me in.

I spent another uneventful day, mulling over my encounter with Uranius. How, I wondered, would Mariades and Menander react when they heard his report? All I could do was wait to find out, so I went to bed and tried to still my whirling thoughts.

I had not expected to see Uranius again, but I was woken from sleep early the following morning when my door was flung open and he strode into my room, arms waving, a broad smile on his face.

"Ah, Scipio! Rouse yourself, man! Great events are passing you by."

I sat up on my bed, pushing aside the blankets and wiping sleep from my eyes.

"What is it?" I asked.

He was in a fine humour, but full of energy, pacing restlessly backwards and forwards across the small room as he spoke.

"Your warning has had an effect," he told me. "Whether it is the effect you desired or not, it has caused something of a crisis in Antioch."

I was wrestling with my tunic as I struggled to pull it on while simultaneously trying to slip my feet into my sandals.

"What has happened?" I asked. "What crisis?"

"A crisis of leadership!" he chuckled. "Mariades, no doubt terrified after I told him that I believed your warning was true, has fled. Menander has gone with him, along with a handful of others."

"Gone?" I gaped. "Gone where?"

He grinned, "At a guess, I'd say they are heading for Persia. Nowhere within the empire will be safe for them. They left in the middle of the night, riding hard as soon as they left the city."

"So who is in charge?" I asked, finally managing to pull my tunic on.

"An excellent question," he said with a mischievous smile. "I have called for a meeting of the most senior officials, plus the military commanders and a handful of leading citizens, but there is really nobody in charge. Mariades made sure to execute all of the senior officials who had worked for the former Governor."

Fastening my sandals, I asked, "So what happens now? Am I free to go?"

"I don't think anyone will stop you," he replied. "But why not stay a while longer? I'm sure the new Council would like to hear the truth about the armies you say are coming here."

Uranius was smiling, but I still didn't feel able to trust him completely. For all I knew, this might be an elaborate plot to get me to contradict my warning to Mariades.

I told him, "I'd rather leave. If the Emperor's army finds me here, and learns that I warned of their coming, I might find myself charged with treason. I'd rather not take that risk."

I felt a little guilty lying to Uranius, but I was determined to maintain my role, and I wanted to call his bluff if that was what it was.

He gave a shrug, "Very well. I can appreciate that. Where will you go?"

"My patron, Licinius Valerianus, is in Gaul," I said. "I will find my way to him."

Uranius nodded, "And I intend to return to Emesa as soon as I've knocked some heads together here."

Holding out his hand once again, he added, "It has been a pleasure to meet you, Scipio. I wish you well wherever your fate takes you."

"May the gods watch over you," I replied as I shook his hand.

"I am the High Priest of Emesa," he reminded me with a grin. "The gods always watch over me."

Then he left, striding briskly out, calling for his guards to accompany him, and I was left alone. I peered out into the corridor, but there were no soldiers blocking the way, and nobody lying in wait for me, so I packed up my things, changing out of the equestrian tunic and pulling on my old, plain one.

I ventured out into the deserted corridor, descended some stairs, and kept walking purposefully. I passed a handful of slaves, and even some worried-looking soldiers, but nobody so much as spoke to me. Mariades' flight had left a vacuum of leadership, and nobody seemed to have any idea about what to do.

So I simply walked out of the palace and made my way to the docks. I felt only a sense of relief, glad that I had accomplished my mission so easily. It was just as well that I could not see into the future, because Mariades flight was destined to bring about events which would have dire consequences for the eastern provinces. Not that there was anything I could have done to alter things in any case, but perhaps I should have foreseen what was to come. At the time, though, I was tired and feeling put upon by Emperor Trebonianus Gallus, so all I could think about was returning to Rome and returning to a quiet life.

Chapter 26
Imperial Retainer

"You have done well, Scipio. Very well indeed. That was remarkably quick work."

I was sitting in the same private office deep in the bowels of the palace complex in Rome. The only difference this time was that another man was present, sitting as a silent witness to my conversation with the Emperor. This spectator was none other than Fabius Successianus, former Prefect of *Legio I*, who had aided Trebonianus Gallus in the defence of Novae, and who was now, according to the introduction Gallus had provided, one of the Emperor's closest confidants, having been called back from Moesia to act as an aide in the palace. Successianus now wore the thin purple stripe of an Equestrian, and the fact that he was permitted to attend a private meeting like this showed that Gallus trusted him implicitly. But then, Successianus had been the man who had instigated Gallus' acclamation as Emperor after the disastrous battle in the marshes, so it was no wonder he had been rewarded with a promotion to equestrian rank and a prime position within the imperial administration.

Successianus, looking a little out of place among the opulence of the palace, seemed content to sit in the background, and my attention was on the Emperor as he went on, "But word of Mariades' flight reached us two weeks ago. I had begun to believe that he had done away with you before he fled to Persia."

I gave a slight shrug. I was weary and badly in need of some rest, and even a personal interview with the Emperor could not banish the sense of tiredness which enveloped me.

I explained, "I found a ship to bring me back, but there was an outbreak of plague among the sailors. The Captain put in at Paphos on Cyprus, but we were confined to the ship for a couple of weeks until we were sure that nobody else had caught the disease."

"Well, you are here now," Gallus smiled. "And I thank you for your service. I must admit I did not think you would succeed so swiftly."

"Cheaply, too," I said as I reached down to pull the small bag of golden coins he had issued to me before I had left Rome. "I didn't need to spend much of this at all."

"Keep it," he said with a wave of his hand.

"That is very generous, Augustus."

"It's a small price to pay for the removal of a rebel," he assured me. "My army has been able to take control of Antioch without a fight."

"Thank you, Augustus," I said as I dropped the coins back into my satchel.

"You will be returning to the home of Sestius Fronto?" he asked me.

"Yes, Augustus."

"Then enjoy what is left of the summer. I may have need of you again."

I managed to keep the disappointment from my face as I offered my farewell.

Successianus also stood up, telling the Emperor he had some correspondence to read, and he accompanied me out of the room. To my surprise, he waved away the freedman who would normally have escorted me back to the palace entrance. Instead, Successianus fell into step beside me.

As always, his bulk and his air of confidence were quite intimidating, but I was more concerned with his reasons for acting as my escort. Such a duty was well below his new-found status as an equestrian.

As we walked, he asked me, "Did you really use Licinius Valerianus' name to establish your credentials when you met Mariades?"

"Yes. It seemed the best approach. They were hardly in a position to verify my claims seeing as Valerianus is up on the Rhenus frontier."

Successianus nodded, "I suppose so. But it was a risk. Valerianus has many contacts throughout the empire."

I shrugged, "It worked."

He gave a thin smile as he agreed, "Yes, it did. But I'm not sure how Licinius Valerianus will react if he finds out."

"I don't plan to tell him," I said, a comment which brought nothing except a slight nod from Successianus.

We walked through a wide chamber, then into another corridor which was lined with marble busts of famous Romans from the past. Then, as we drew near to the main entrance hall, Successianus asked, "So you survived the plague? That was very fortunate. Few live to tell the tale."

"I did not catch the plague," I replied. "I left the ship as soon as it docked at Paphos."

The look he gave me was very disconcerting as he said, "Then that is the second time you have escaped the contagion. I heard you had caught the plague a few months ago. Clearly, either my information is incorrect, or you recovered."

There was danger here, I sensed. The way he had spoken put all my nerves on alert. It took me a moment or two to realise what he was driving at. I had avoided accompanying Valerianus to Gaul by telling his messenger I had caught the plague. But how, I wondered, did Successianus know that?

Thinking quickly, I told him, "Oh, that. There was plague in the house. I was lucky enough to remain healthy, although several other members of the household were not so fortunate. My friend's wife and son both died, as did several of their slaves."

Successianus' expression was unreadable as he said, "I am sorry to hear that. The sickness has claimed many lives. But I am glad you remain fit and well. I'm sure the Emperor will have need of you before too long."

We had now reached the bustling entrance hall. Successianus indicated the way out with a wave of his hand, then said farewell and turned to walk down one of the many side corridors, leaving me wondering what that conversation had really been about.

Fronto was delighted to see me return safely, and declared that I must spend the entire evening going over every detail of my adventure.

Julia, though, was less enthusiastic. She greeted me with a sullen nod, mumbled something about being glad I was back, then hurried off to her room. I had the impression that she was close to tears.

"Is she all right?" I asked Fronto.

He gave a shrug, his expression serious as he told me, "I think she is angry that you went away."

"I had little choice," I frowned. "I could not disobey a direct order from the Emperor."

"I know that, Sextus," he said soothingly. "But Julia has suffered a great deal of loss in the past year. She does not know what became of her father, then the plague took away Faustia and

Dextrus just as she was beginning to know them. Your departure made her fear you might not come back."

We sat facing one another in the family room, each of us with a cup of wine. I took a sip, then asked, "What should I do?"

Fronto smiled, "You are the one who has had children, Sextus. I never had that fortune. I am the wrong person to ask."

I sighed. Fronto was right.

"She needs a home and a family," I said. "But I can't give her that."

Fronto nodded, "I told her much the same thing. I hope you don't mind, but I had to tell her a little about your background. I did not give her any details, but I did say you had become estranged from your family."

"That might make things worse," I sighed. "She might think she can be my new family."

"You should talk to her," Fronto advised.

"I will," I promised.

Fronto hesitated, then said, "I have decided to erect a memorial to Faustia and Dextrus. I have spoken to a stonemason who will carve something suitable in the necropolis."

"That is a good idea," I nodded.

"And," Fronto went on, "I have told Julia that the memorial will also be dedicated to her father."

"She should like that," I said.

"She seemed pleased," my friend confirmed.

"I'd better go and talk to her," I said, putting down my cup and rising to my feet. "Wish me luck."

Julia answered my knock at her door, eyeing me suspiciously. From the redness of her eyes, I guessed she had been crying.

"What do you want?" she demanded, her tone that of an angry teenager.

"Just to talk for a bit," I told her.

Resignedly, she allowed me into her neat, comfortable room. It was painted in shades of pink and yellow, with small statues of birds and animals sitting on top of a dresser. Unlike the bedrooms of some teenagers, the floor was clear, her bed neatly made, with the only obvious sign of her hobbies being a small sketch pad on which she had been drawing a face with a charcoal stick. She hastily put it away in a drawer when she noticed me looking at it.

She sat on the bed, and I placed myself on a wooden chair, turning it to face her.

"I'm going to tell you a story few people know," I said.

She gave a nod, and I explained my life to her, telling her about my early years as an imperial spy, my marriage to Circe, our children, and how I had too frequently been pulled back into imperial politics. I even admitted to her that I had been enslaved and sentenced to death by Emperor Philippus, only to have that rescinded by Messius Decius when he seized power.

"But my family believe me to be dead, and I dare not let them know I am alive."

"Why not?" she asked, her first words since I had begun my tale.

Taking a deep breath, I confessed, "Because Licinius Valerianus, a very powerful Senator, has threatened to harm them if I don't do his bidding. He knows where my daughter and her family live, so I need to keep him away from the others."

"But your daughter ought to know you are alive!" Julia exclaimed.

I shook my head.

"I can't afford anyone else to know. I can't risk Valerianus learning where my other family live."

Julia pondered this for a moment, then frowned, "Are you sure he would really hurt them?"

"Oh, yes, I am very sure. He's already demonstrated that."

Julia waited patiently for me to continue. In that instant, she looked far more mature than her years, perhaps grateful that I was treating her as an equal.

I told her, "Fronto keeps in touch with my daughter and my adopted son. He writes to them at least once a year. Last year, he received a reply from Sempronia saying that she and her daughter had been attacked and robbed while they were walking home late one evening. The thieves took their valuables, but also cut a lock of hair from young Gellia."

I shuddered at the thought of the terror my daughter and granddaughter had faced, but there was more to tell.

I said, "Some weeks after this happened, Licinius Valerianus gave me a lock of hair. He did not say where it came from, but I knew what he was telling me. It was a warning."

Julia looked as horrified as I felt. After a long pause, she said, "I still think you ought to let your daughter know you are alive."

"That's what Fronto tells me," I admitted. "But I have made my decision, and I will stick to it. I cannot risk Valerianus gaining any further hold over me or my family."

I sat back in the chair, feeling a weight lifted from my shoulders at having explained my situation. Julia rose from the bed, crossed the room and bent down to hug me.

"I am so sorry," she whispered.

Gently, I returned her embrace. When she stood up again, I told her, "So you see why I brought you here. I cannot provide you with a safe home, and if Valerianus learns you are close to me, he could use you against me as well."

"He could threaten to harm Fronto," she pointed out.

"Yes, he could. But Fronto understands the risks, and he is my oldest and best friend. Neither of us will abandon the other, no matter what."

Hesitantly, Julia asked, "What about me? What can I do?"

"You can do whatever you like," I told her. "But a young woman like you would find it difficult to earn a living on her own. There's usually only one profession they can take up."

"I'm not doing that!" Julia objected.

"No, which is why you should stay here a while longer. Help Fronto as best you can. He's a good man. But now you know that even here is not entirely safe for you. If there is anywhere else you would prefer to go, I'll take you there."

She gave a brisk headshake.

"I have nowhere else to go," she admitted in a sad voice.

"Neither do I," I said.

We exchanged smiles, then we both went down to the family room where Fronto had finished one jug of wine, and was well into a second.

He grinned when he saw us.

"All sorted?" he asked.

"I've told Julia my story," I confirmed.

"Then all three of us are in on the secret," Fronto said, raising his cup in a toast. "That is as it should be."

I poured myself a cup of wine, while Julia, still not accustomed to asking the slaves to bring her things, hurried off to fetch herself a fruit juice. When she returned, I gave them an account of my time in Antioch. Julia sat quietly, paying close attention, although I supposed she must feel a little awkward sitting with two old men discussing political events. But then, if she was to grow to adulthood in Rome, it would do her no harm to understand how Roman society operated.

When I had finished my account, Fronto said, "We were worried about you. We heard that Mariades had fled, and we expected you back here weeks ago. Still, at least you have earned the Emperor's favour."

"I'm never very sure whether that is a good thing or not," I muttered. "I feel as if I'm caught between two equal dangers."

"The Emperor and Licinius Valerianus?" he guessed.

"Exactly."

"So you are like Odysseus needing to choose whether to risk sailing past Scylla or Charybdis," Fronto said, referring to the old Greek legend.

"At least Odysseus found a way out for himself and most of his crew," I said. "He avoided the whirlpool and only lost a few men to the monster. That doesn't apply to me. I am trapped between two equally dangerous men. There is no lesser of two perils."

Fronto sighed, "I understand, my friend, but I hold you in higher regard than Odysseus. You have escaped more deadly situations than he ever did."

"If you are trying to cheer me up, Tiberius, it's not working," I said, using his *praenomen* as only close friends and family do.

I caught a brief glimpse of his old smile, a happy expression which lit up everyone's life when they saw it. I had seen far too little of it in the past year, and it soon vanished as his face grew more solemn.

He said, "You should know that relations between the two of them will only worsen in light of what is happening here in Rome now."

I cocked an eyebrow at him, so he went on, "You know that the Emperor rescinded the Edict of Decius? Persecution of Christians has stopped, and they are gaining a great many followers. The fact that they helped people during the worst of the plague has drawn many people to follow their religion."

We both looked at Julia. She sat there, her face full of resolve.

Fronto went on, "I understand that, but I fear it will cause trouble. There are many powerful Senators who detest Christianity."

"Why?" Julia asked. "It is a religion of peace and love."

Fronto smiled, "It is also a religion which demands that its followers obey the wishes of their God over the gods of Rome. Many Romans cannot abide that. For them, allegiance must be first and foremost to Rome and the Emperor."

I put in, "And foremost among the opponents of Christians is Licinius Valerianus. He won't be at all pleased that the Emperor has ended the persecutions."

Fronto added, "I fear that a confrontation between the two of them is inevitable."

I frowned, "I'm not sure Valerianus has his eyes on the Purple. He usually works behind the scenes, promoting the interests of one or other of his friends."

"Perhaps you are right," Fronto agreed. "He might try to promote his father-in-law, Cornelius Siculus. He would be little more than a puppet ruler, I expect."

"That would suit Valerianus, right enough," I nodded.

"Speaking of Siculus and Valerianus," Fronto said with a grin, "a message came from Cornelia Gallonia while you were away. She asked you to visit her. I sent her slave away with the news that you had left Rome and I did not know when, or if, you would be back."

"Thanks," I told him. "She's another one I want to stay away from."

"That should be easy enough," Fronto told me. "I heard she has gone to Gaul to join her husband."

"She has? That's a surprise. I wonder what lies behind it?"

"Perhaps he misses her," Fronto suggested sarcastically. "Or perhaps it is a prelude to Valerianus making a move against the Emperor."

I shook my head.

"I can't see that," I said. "Yes, Gallus might try to use Gallonia as a hostage, but Valerianus wouldn't bother about that."

"He would if it ruined his relationship with Cornelius Siculus," Fronto pointed out. "Gallonia's father might not take it well if Valerianus allowed her to be used as a hostage."

"Maybe you are right," I conceded. "Fortunately, it doesn't affect me. If she's gone to Gaul as well, they are safely far enough away."

I paused, frowned, then pulled a face.

"What is it?" Fronto asked.

"Just an odd conversation I had at the palace," I told him.

Briefly, I explained about my bizarre encounter with Fabius Successianus.

"Was it a warning, do you think?" he asked me.

"It sounded like it. But from who? And why?"

Fronto offered, "It sounds to me as if Successianus was relaying a message from Valerianus."

I held up my hands in frustration as I sighed, "You may be right. I thought Successianus was Gallus' man to the core, but perhaps he's decided to back someone else."

"Or perhaps he is playing both sides," Fronto suggested. "That's how things often go in Roman political life."

I recalled Sulpicius Uranius, the Priest-King of Emesa, confiding in me that he intended to stay out of Mariades' war until he knew who had won. Was Fabius Successianus also keeping his options open?

I said, "If Successianus has been in touch with Valerianus, it would explain how he knows I used the excuse of having the plague when Valerianus summoned me to accompany him to Gaul. Successianus has been up in Moesia until recently, so he couldn't have known that any other way, could he?"

"Perhaps," Fronto replied. "This is Rome. It is hard to keep secrets."

It was Julia who suggested, "Maybe it was that woman, Cornelia Gallonia, who told him."

"She would have known about me using the excuse, right enough," I reflected. "But why would she tell Successianus?"

Julia's cheeks flushed a little as she replied, "You said she was looking for allies against her husband. Maybe she spoke to this man you call Successianus."

"You might be right," I conceded. "But we're just speculating. I must say I don't like the thought of influential people talking about me, but what really bothers me is what Successianus is up to."

Fronto, looking pensive, suggested, "There is another possible explanation. You said Successianus is close to the Emperor, didn't you?"

"Yes, he's always seemed very loyal to Gallus."

Fronto said, "Then you ought to keep in mind that the Emperor controls the *frumentarii*. Perhaps they have been watching you. The Emperor does seem to have taken an interest in your career."

"I wish he hadn't," I muttered.

"I can understand that," Fronto said with a gentle smile. "But he has, and I suspect the reason is that he is trying to think of some way of using you against Valerianus."

I grunted, "You're still not doing a great job of cheering me up."

Fronto waved his wine cup airily as he said, "I would not panic, Sextus. As you said, we are merely speculating."

I was more confused than ever, but I was sure about one thing. If the *frumentarii* were watching me, I would need to be very careful in everything I did.

Chapter 27
Divine Displeasure

A part of me wanted to leave Rome, to go into hiding as I had done before, but the truth was that I did not want to leave Fronto. We had known each other all our lives, having grown up together living in the same street. Now we had both lost our families, although in different ways, and I knew I would feel guilty if I went off once again. And, truth to tell, I was tired of running and hiding. Every time I had done that in the past, someone in authority had managed to track me down. For the time being, I decided it would be easier to stay in Rome.

Julia was another consideration. She continued to help organise the household, but both Fronto and I noticed that she still liked to venture out on her own, often dressed in a very plain tunic so as to blend in with the ordinary citizens.

"I worry about her," Fronto admitted to me. "She could get into all sorts of trouble."

"Worrying about teenagers is normal," I told him. "She's still trying to discover herself."

"I hope she finds herself soon," Fronto sighed. "I'm not used to this at all."

"Maybe you should get her involved in your business affairs," I suggested. "You never know, she might have an aptitude for property investment."

Fronto looked at me sceptically, but eventually admitted he might invite her to accompany him the next time he visited any of his many properties.

"But what about you?" he asked. "What are you going to do?"

"I'm going to get back to my writing," I told him. "I've still got a lot I need to record. I'll need to buy some more ink and parchment."

"I thought you had a chest full of scrolls already," Fronto remarked.

"I do," I agreed. "But I've still got a lot to cover in telling the detailed story of my life."

"But you still won't let anyone read what you've written!" Fronto accused. "You've spent a long time scribbling away, but you're keeping it all secret."

"You can read them after I'm dead," I told him.

Fronto chuckled, "How morbid, Sextus. There is no guarantee I'll outlive you, you know. Besides, what is the point of writing your life's story if you aren't going to let anyone read it?"

"It could be dangerous knowledge," I said. "I've told everything."

"Everything? Now I am intrigued. Do I feature in this tale of your life?"

"Of course you do!" I assured him. "I could hardly miss you out, could I?"

He chuckled, "In that case, I don't want to read it. You may have said some unpleasant things about me."

"Don't be daft!" I told him.

"Then why not let me read the first few scrolls?"

I shifted uneasily on my couch.

"It's still very personal," I told him. "Once I'm dead, you can have them published. They might create some interest."

"That will depend on how cruel you have been towards your social betters," he said, still smiling. "Knowing you, I expect you have been very cruel indeed."

"I've only told the truth as I see it," I assured him.

"The truth can be dangerous, right enough," he nodded. "But I shall employ an army of scribes to copy the text, and I will charge people a fortune to read them. I expect I will become ludicrously wealthy. I might even earn enough to qualify as a Senator."

"Anything's possible," I said. "There's always a demand for accounts of the past. Julius Caesar wrote his own version of history, and so did Cornelius Tacitus. And do you remember that stuck up prig, Cassius Dio? Even he wrote a long and detailed history."

"And yours is the same as their accounts?" Fronto probed.

"Mine is my story," I said.

"Well, you've certainly had an eventful life," he nodded. "But I pray your story will remain unpublished for many years yet. If you are going to wait until after your death to have them distributed, there is a lot more that could happen."

I told him, "You're probably right. But, now that I think about it, it might be safer to wait until Licinius Valerianus is dead as well."

"Ah, you don't portray him in a favourable light, then?"

I knew that Fronto was teasing me, and that he was enjoying himself immensely.

I spat, "He's a devious, ruthless bastard, and I have said so in my writings."

"Then your story may never be published," Fronto warned. "Even if you wait until Valerianus is dead, he has a son who is almost as important. He wouldn't like you saying bad things about his father."

"I've said bad things about the son as well," I informed him.

Fronto shook his head in an exaggerated way, placing one hand theatrically on his forehead.

"Perhaps you should consider burning the manuscript," he advised, only half-joking. "Upsetting powerful people is not a good idea."

Then, with a smile, he added, "Mind you, you've been doing that for most of your life."

I did not rise to the bait.

I said, "I find that writing things down helps me order my thoughts and memories. I don't really care whether anyone else ever reads them. It's very personal."

"Then I shall respect your privacy," Fronto assured me. "Until you are dead, that is. Then I shall read them, after which I will burn them."

I simply shrugged. And the next day, I resumed my writing, searching my memory for the details of events and people long past.

At the end of summer, there was another outbreak of plague in the city. It was not as severe or virulent as before, but it was a reminder that the gods could still wreak havoc with human lives. The cooler weather of winter brought some respite, and we managed to enjoy the winter festivals. Fronto and I attended some theatre shows, mostly bawdy comedies, and once we took Julia to the Circus to watch some chariot racing. This was not a successful outing as I generally disliked the dangerous sport which put the lives of charioteers and horses at risk, but there are many avid supporters, and even the Emperor puts in an appearance among the spectators from time to time. For me, though, it reminded me of the last time I had been here, many years before, when Circe had been with me, and when our children had been young. Now, apart from memories, Fronto and I were all that remained from that distant day.

One evening, the two of us sat together after dinner, chatting inconsequentially, when Fronto asked for my advice on something.

"If I can help," I agreed, wondering what he might need my advice on.

He cleared his throat, seeming unusually hesitant, then said, "I was thinking of formally adopting Julia. Do you think she would object?"

I blinked in surprise, but rallied quickly.

"I honestly don't know," I said. "What has prompted this?"

Fronto waved a hand to take in our surroundings.

"I have all this," he said. "But I have nobody to leave it to now. If I have no heir, everything will be forfeit to the imperial Treasury."

"I see," I nodded. "But Julia is a woman. If she marries, it will all pass to her husband."

"Then I will pray that she chooses a good husband," Fronto said. "She is fifteen years old now. If she becomes my heir, she'll soon have suitors queuing at the door."

"Do you want me to mention it to her?" I guessed.

Fronto's relief was evident, so I spoke to Julia who was not as enthusiastic as I'd expected. She took a couple of days to think about the idea before she agreed.

"I don't know how to be a Roman lady," she told Fronto.

"Then be yourself," he replied.

So Fronto arranged the formalities, and Julia became his daughter. I was pleased for both of them, and it made the dedication of their joint memorial in the necropolis even more poignant, although Fronto had to pay the stonemason an additional fee to carve some extra letters on the impressive monument to reflect Julia's new status. He also had to hold his tongue when Julia insisted on having a Christian priest bless the adoption in the eyes of her God. Fronto, still agnostic on whether the Christian God was more powerful than the gods of Rome, went along with this suggestion without argument.

The change in Julia's status did not alter her behaviour in any way. She continued to perform acrobatic exercises in the garden, much to the amazement of the slaves, and she maintained the habit of walking out on her own until, a couple of months after her formal adoption, she came home looking very pale and frightened. She was visibly trembling as she entered my study where I was busy writing another chapter in my life's story.

"What's wrong?" I asked her, my heart beating faster.

She slumped into a chair, clasping her hands together to prevent them from shaking.

"A man spoke to me," she said in a soft voice.

"Did he hurt you?" I asked, speaking urgently as I sought to learn the cause of her obvious distress.

She shook her head, then cleared her throat as if to drive away the fear. Speaking in as normal a voice as she could manage, she said, "He told me I was to give you a message."

"A message?" I frowned. "Who was he?"

"He didn't say, and I didn't recognise him," she replied. "But he came up to me while I was walking home and he asked if I was your girl. When I said I knew you, he leaned in close and hissed a warning."

My heart was pounding now, driven by fear of what might have happened to her, and by fear of what warning the stranger had given.

"What did he say?" I asked.

Looking me in the eye, Julia told me, "He said I was to remind you of where your loyalties should lie. And to remember your granddaughter's lock of hair."

I closed my eyes as I cursed, "Valerianus! The bloody man must have heard about my trip to Syria."

The threat was clear. Both Julia and Fronto understood it implicitly. If Valerianus believed I was working against him, they were both at risk.

After that, Julia never went out on her own. Fronto insisted that at least one male slave should accompany her if she needed to go anywhere. For her part, Julia stayed in the house for several days before daring to go outside. I went with her that first time, strolling the streets and visiting the *forum*. We had no real purpose except to reassure Julia that she did not need to be terrified of leaving the house. She dealt with the pressure well, but all of us were shaken by this warning, and we made a point of never leaving the house without a companion.

There were no more threats, and our fears gradually settled as the weeks passed, but there were dark clouds gathering beyond the confines of our home. Over the course of a few weeks in summer, a succession of reports of bad news assailed Rome. Day by day, the news emanating from the Senate House grew worse.

It began with reports of Berber tribes raiding all across the province of Africa. This concerned me deeply because my elder son, named Sextus after me, had inherited the estates Circe and I had owned near Leptis Magna. His home was close to the desert where the Berbers lived, and I feared a rich estate like his would be a prime target for raiders. Sextus, though, had completely cut himself off from me several years before, and he had refused to reply to Fronto's letters. All I could do was imagine what might have happened, and worry the way a parent always does, no matter what their child has done.

Incredibly, there was even worse news to come, a report so dreadful that it sent a shock wave through the entire city.

"The Persians have destroyed our army in Syria!" we heard one afternoon.

We listened in stunned disbelief as Senators, dressed in formal togas over their purple-striped tunics, came out of the Senate House to relay the news to the assembled citizens. It seemed that Mariades, after fleeing from Antioch, had indeed travelled to Persia. There, rather than simply skulking in exile, he had persuaded the Persian King, Shappur, to invade Syria and re-install him as ruler. Shappur, who had spent his entire life attempting to seize control of Rome's eastern provinces, had needed little encouragement to begin a new campaign of conquest. He had gathered an army and invaded Rome's eastern provinces. The army which our Emperor had sent to throw Mariades out had advanced into Armenia to block Shappur's progress, but the Persians had cut them to pieces. Shappur's victorious army had rampaged all across the region, and Antioch had fallen to the Persians for the first time in centuries.

"What about Mariades?" I asked one elderly Senator who looked as shocked as we felt.

"We don't know," he grunted sourly. "He's certainly not King of Syria. I expect Shappur only used him as an excuse, and has done away with him now that he's served his purpose."

A feeling of guilt swept over me.

"This is my fault!" I hissed.

Fronto did his best to calm my worries.

"It's not your fault that Shappur invaded," he assured me. "You got rid of Mariades, but you are not to blame for what he did after he fled. Besides, Shappur would have found some other excuse once he realised how weak the empire is."

Fronto was right, but I could still not shake off the feeling that I was to blame. The loss of the east was a disaster for Rome, but Trebonianus Gallus had been correct when he had said to me that he was faced by one problem after another. Before long, we heard that the Goths had launched yet another major invasion of the north, and this time they had also sent a fleet of ships sailing down from the Black Sea. They had passed Byzantium, and had raided Ephesus, a far richer target, and one which was so far inside the empire's borders that nobody had ever considered it might be in such danger.

"The Temple of Artemis has been sacked!" a herald announced, a cry which was greeted by groans of dismay.

That news stung me to the core. Ephesus was a walled city, and we were assured that it had been spared ruin because the Goths had been unable to storm the walls, concentrating instead on the magnificent Temple which stood a little way outside the city and which held riches beyond the dreams of most men.

That was shocking enough, especially for me because I had once worked at the Temple before embarking on my life as an imperial spy. What was far worse, though, was the knowledge that my adopted son, Hama, lived on a farm near Ephesus.

I was almost paralysed by fear of what might have happened. Had Hama and his family escaped? Had they had time to flee into the city before the raiders arrived? Were they far enough to the south of the Temple to have avoided the raid?

Above all, the question that haunted me was whether they were alive at all.

Fronto tried to offer solace, but he knew as well as I did that we had no way of discovering Hama's fate.

"It's not as if you can go there now," he said. "The Goths have a huge fleet, and they are raiding all across the Aegean."

I knew he was right, but the news caused me many sleepless nights, and my food tasted like ashes. Every day brought more bad news, but no details of the fate of individuals. The Goths, we heard, had plundered several islands, and had also attacked the Greek mainland, ravaging Athens which was virtually undefended.

And all the time I listened to these reports, I wondered whether Aoric was involved. In my mind's eye, I saw him hacking down Hama as he led a band of Goths who plundered Hama's farmstead, killing everyone there.

"Aoric will be with Cniva," Fronto said when I confessed the fear that had caused me to awake in the middle of the night, shouting in alarm and soaked in sweat.

I began to dread walking down to the *forum*. How much more bad news could the empire withstand? And what was Trebonianus Gallus going to do about it?

"The Emperor is raising another army!" heralds declared, reciting official proclamations which assured us that the barbarians would be punished for their sacrilege.

"The Emperor didn't punish them last time," someone grumbled, remembering how Gallus had allowed Cniva to keep all of his plunder and captives after the sack of Philippopolis.

My worry was that the Emperor would be unable to do anything.

"Raising an army isn't easy," I told Fronto and Julia. "Raw recruits and half-hearted Auxiliaries can't do much. And which threat does he deal with first? The Goths are a major threat to our existence, but so are the Persians. We could lose half the empire if Shappur is not stopped."

The gods, it seemed, were displeased with us, and the empire was under threats the like of which it had not seen before. This knowledge hung like a cloud over everyone, and several angry mobs gathered to protest, only disbanding when the Urban Cohorts faced them down.

"It's a wonder there haven't been any full-scale riots," Fronto observed, adding an admonition to Julia not to venture out alone while the situation was so fraught with tension.

The mood in Rome continued to simmer, always close to boiling over, but then, seemingly miraculously, came some good news.

"The Persians have been pushed back!" was the cry, a phrase which brought both joy and satisfaction to the hearts of everyone who heard the words. "Syria has been re-taken!"

"Re-taken?" Fronto frowned. "How? And by whom?"

When we heard the answer to that question, I could not help smiling.

A herald called out, "Sulpicius Uranius Antoninus, King and High Priest of Emesa, raised an army and has defeated Shappur! The Persians have fled back to their own lands!"

"Uranius?" I laughed. "He's a remarkable man."

Soon, though, Roman admiration for the bravery and military skill of Uranius was completely soured. I heard it from Fronto who had gone to the *forum* while I had decided to spend a day catching up on my writing.

"Your friend Uranius has gone a step too far," Fronto informed me breathlessly, having hurried back to relay the latest news. "It seems he has declared himself Emperor."

I gaped at him in disbelief.

"What? That can't be right. He told me he had no ambitions to rule anything beyond his own city."

Fronto shrugged, "Success in war brings power and prestige. They, in turn, feed ambition. And he has driven off the Persians, which is no mean feat."

I was still puzzling over why Uranius, that clever, amicable and shrewd man, might have declared himself Emperor when Fronto's door slave announced that we had visitors.

"Soldiers, Sir," the slave told Fronto in a frightened voice. "They are looking for Sempronius Scipio. The Emperor has called for him."

I groaned, "I should have guessed. Gallus will want me to go back to Syria, this time to deal with Uranius."

"That's ridiculous!" Fronto exclaimed. "You were lucky with Mariades, but if what you've told me about Uranius is true, he won't be so easily fooled."

"I know," I nodded. "But Gallus can't spare an army to go to Syria. If the Persians have been defeated, he'll concentrate on driving back the Goths, so he needs to do something about Uranius. I expect that's why he's summoned me."

The Praetorians who waited for me in the *atrium* were a grim-looking bunch with their dark cloaks and chainmail armour.

"I'm Scipio," I told their leader, a Decurion with a scar on his left cheek.

"The Emperor wants to talk to you," he told me. "You are to pack a bag and accompany us to the palace."

Feigning ignorance, I replied, "Pack a bag? Am I going somewhere?"

I tried to sound light-hearted, but I could already feel the dread of returning to Syria weighing down on me.

The Praetorian shrugged, "All I know is that the Emperor wants you. He says it's urgent, and it's not a good idea to keep him waiting."

Out of habit, I always kept my satchel packed with spare clothing, so I was ready in a few minutes, fastening a plain cloak over my unadorned tunic and slinging the old leather satchel over my shoulder.

Julia hugged me with tear-filled eyes, promising to pray to her God to keep me safe, and Fronto, looking even more worried than I felt, insisted on clasping my forearm and embracing me.

"Take care, Sextus."

"I will," I promised him. "But if I don't come back, you can do what you like with my scrolls."

He nodded, then said, "You must do as you have done before. Make sure you survive."

He looked me in the eye as he said this, and I understood his hidden meaning.

"I will do whatever I must," I told him.

Then we parted once again, and I left his elegant home on the Quirinal, walking down to the Palatine with my escort of four armed soldiers. As I trudged down the street, I wondered whether I was making this walk for the last time.

Strangely, most of my fear and worries had left me by the time we approached the palace. The empire was crumbling all around us, my family may or may not be dead, and I had been summoned to meet with the Emperor once again, no doubt to be sent on yet another potentially fatal mission. But instead of fear, my main emotion was determination. Fronto had known what I must do, and that knowledge burned inside me. The Emperor was going to send me back to Syria, with orders to depose Uranius in any way I could. That was plain enough to see, but this time I would not play by the Emperor's rules. I would go to Syria if I must, but then I would do as I had done before, just as Fronto had advised.

I would need to fake my own death convincingly enough that Licinius Valerianus would not harm my family. To accomplish that, I would need to sever the few remaining ties I had. I would never be able to contact Fronto again. I would need to disappear so completely that nobody would ever hear the name of Sempronius Scipio again.

Chapter 28
Usurper

The imperial palace is always busy. There must be hundreds, probably thousands, of people employed to keep the central heart of the empire operating smoothly. Praetorian Guards are always in evidence, standing sentry at every door, and placed at strategic points throughout the vast complex of buildings. In addition, there are freedmen acting as scribes and secretaries, slaves who keep the place clean, cooks, launderers, keepers of the imperial stables, functionaries with obscure job titles and roles, and a host of hangers-on who follow the Emperor and his family members wherever they go. I was accustomed to this because I had visited the palace several times over the past decades, but this time I felt a difference in the atmosphere as soon as I was escorted into the main entrance. There was an air of nervous anticipation, and everyone seemed to be going about their business rather more quickly than usual, all of them looking very serious.

My guards were impervious to this, marching me stolidly through the maze of corridors in a direction which was now becoming familiar to me. Sure enough, I was led to that same office where Trebonianus Gallus had met me several times before. We were forced to wait in the busy antechamber for quite a while because the Emperor was busy with other people, and a succession of men entered and left the office, most of them hurrying out with a clear purpose in mind. The Emperor, I assumed, was issuing orders designed to counteract the current state of emergency.

Eventually, it was my turn. The Praetorians handed me to the care of a secretary who bustled me in to meet the Emperor. Nothing much had changed in the room, and I took my usual seat facing Gallus across the wide desk which was, as usual, cluttered with paperwork. Once again, though, Fabius Successianus sat to one side, regarding me with a solemn expression which gave nothing away.

"Ah, Scipio," Gallus began with a weary smile. "Thank you for coming. I need you to do something for me."

I nodded, saying carefully, "Of course, Augustus."

"You have heard about Aemilius Aemilianus?" he asked me.

Caught off guard, I frowned, "No, Augustus. I don't recognise the name. Who is he?"

The Emperor sighed, "He was, until very recently, Governor of Pannonia, up on the Danubius frontier. He was tasked with keeping the Goths at bay until I could raise an army to go and support him."

I was confused. I had come here expecting to be ordered to travel to Syria. I had anticipated being forced to listen to a diatribe aimed against Uranius Antoninus, but instead Gallus was talking about the Governor of Pannonia.

I managed to engage my brain enough to put in, "He was? But no longer, I presume?"

A grimace of irritation flickered across the Emperor's face as he informed me, "Aemilius Aemilianus has proved to be very effective at fighting the Goths. He recently won a great victory, killing thousands of them, and driving Cniva's forces back across the river."

"That is good news," I offered, although a part of me felt a flicker of fear for Aoric. He may have chosen to return to his native people, but he had been a true friend before that, and I hoped he had survived his father's defeat.

It quickly became apparent that I was not the only person in the room who felt conflicted by the news. My remark brought another frown of irritation to Gallus' tired face. He seemed to have aged ten years since he had assumed the Purple, but he managed to remain calm in spite of being clearly annoyed by something.

He let out a long breath, then sighed, "Aemilius Aemilianus has been so successful that his troops have proclaimed him as Emperor."

I sat very still, saying nothing. It was no wonder that the palace was swarming like a beehive. No sooner had my secret mission removed Mariades than Uranius and Aemilianus had been declared as Emperors. Gallus now had two rivals, and he must act quickly if he wanted to retain his position.

"It is a folly, of course," he went on. "The man comes from a very humble background. He is highly capable, which is why I promoted him to the rank of provincial Governor. But he is an equestrian, not a Senator. The empire has already had one low-born barbarian as Emperor, and it cannot repeat that disastrous episode."

He was referring to the short reign of Maximinis Thrax, the giant soldier who had murdered his way to power, and had then outraged Rome and his own soldiers so much that they had turned against him.

Gallus went on, "I am leaving for the north tomorrow, and will be marching with the forces I have gathered so far. I have called legions from Hispania to join me, and they will be crossing the sea even as we speak."

I nodded to let him know I was paying attention.

He continued, "But I need to crush this upstart before I move against Uranius in Syria, so I need as many men as I can. That is why I need you."

Again, I gave a silent nod, wondering what was coming next.

The Emperor picked up a scroll case, already sealed with wax and embossed with the imperial seal. He handed it across to me.

"I need you to take this to Licinius Valerianus in Gaul," he told me.

I was so stunned that I almost forgot to take the scroll from him as he held it out to me. When I did, he gave a curt nod.

"You will be provided with an escort of Praetorians to ensure you reach Gaul safely. Valerianus is, I believe, in Moguntiacum. Go there and deliver the message. Tell him I need troops quickly. He is to bring as many of his cavalry as he can to Pannonia. I have recruited enough infantry, but I am short of trained horsemen, so I need the Gaulish cavalry. Valerianus will join forces with me, and we will put down this rebellion."

I had so many questions, I did not know where to begin, but the Emperor gave me no time to ask anything.

He said, "Tell Valerianus I need his army, and I need them quickly. Do you understand?"

"Yes, Augustus. But why me?"

"Because he knows you," Gallus replied. "He seems to trust you as far as he trusts anyone. I am well aware that he dislikes me, but I am relying on your proven ingenuity to convince him to help me save the empire from another civil war. I need his army, and I need you to tell him anything that will persuade him to come. Create any tale you like, but convince him that the safety of the empire depends on him joining forces with me."

"I will do what I can, Augustus," I promised.

"Good. Now go. Successianus has arranged your escort. My secretaries will guide you out to the stables. Ride quickly, Scipio. Do you hear me?"

"I hear you, Augustus."

With that, I was dismissed, hustled out of the room and led along a winding route which took me to one side of the palace grounds where the stables were located. Already, a squad of eight Praetorians were waiting, each man with a horse. I expected they had been summoned down from the Horse Barracks on the Caelian Hill. They had even brought a spare horse for me. The sight of it dismayed me. Even while the Emperor had been giving me his orders, I had retained some faint hopes of being able to slip away into hiding, but there was no way I could evade eight Praetorians.

Their commander was a surprisingly young Decurion with a thin face and a pugnacious jaw. Casting a jaundiced eye over me, he introduced himself by the name of Livius Mento.

"We have a long way to go," he said as if I was not aware of the distance involved. "Are you ready?"

"As ready as I'll ever be," I muttered.

I stuffed the sealed scroll case into my satchel, accepted the reins of my allotted mount, and clambered stiffly up into the saddle with the aid of a slave who cupped his hands to help me mount.

The horse was a sturdy beast, built for stamina, and easy enough to ride. I fell into place beside Mento, and his seven troopers fell into line behind us, riding two abreast with one man bringing up the rear. To me, they all looked ridiculously young and inexperienced, and I reckoned they were fairly recent recruits, perhaps youngsters who had joined up as part of the Emperor's recent raising of reinforcements.

We clattered through the streets of Rome, crossing the Tiber by way of the Milvian Bridge, then broke into a swift canter once we were out on the *Via Flaminia*.

Mento was surprisingly friendly for a Praetorian, and he seemed keen to talk.

"You have a message for Licinius Valerianus?" he asked.

"That's right."

He nodded, "I expect the Emperor is demanding reinforcements from him."

I said, "The orders were sealed inside the scroll case when they were handed to me."

From the twisted smile Mento shot me, I knew that he had guessed I was well aware of the contents of the scroll case.

"It doesn't take much to work it out," he told me. "The Emperor has only one legion here in Italia. He'll need more than that to defeat the legions of Pannonia."

"I'm no soldier," I told him. "I leave military strategy to others."

"So you are just a messenger?" he asked good-naturedly.

"That's right."

He said, "If you don't mind me saying so, you're a fair bit older than most imperial messengers. Those lads ride hard and fast."

"My old bones won't manage that," I grumbled.

"They will need to," he countered. "My orders are to get you there as soon as possible. We'll up the pace to a gallop shortly."

When I said nothing in response, he went on, "So I'm guessing there is some special reason why you are being sent with this message. Would I be right?"

I gave another nod, then said, "And I expect you have orders to kill me if I don't follow your instructions?"

The grim smile he gave me in return confirmed that my guess had been accurate. So much for my dreams of disappearing from sight. Not only was I not going to Syria where I could easily blend in with the locals, I was travelling north with a bunch of Praetorians who were equal parts escort and captors.

Mento was as good as his word, increasing our pace to a gallop. The clattering thunder of hooves on the paved road made conversation impossible, which suited me because I was in a foul mood as I tried to work out what I was going to say to Licinius Valerianus. Had Emperor Gallus been foolish or very clever in choosing me as his envoy? Only time would tell, and that time would not be long because our horses were eating up the miles as we pounded northwards.

No horse can maintain a gallop for very long, so we frequently slowed to give them some rest before pushing on again. When we reached an imperial waystation, we changed mounts, pushing the replacement horses just as hard as the first ones. Using this system, Mento reckoned we would reach Moguntiacum within ten or twelve days.

"It will depend on the weather," he informed me during one of our rest periods. "But it's summer now, so we should have no problems."

That night, we were able to find food and beds in an imperial *mansio*, something for which I was grateful. I had a reasonably comfortable bed, with blankets to keep off the chill of the night. Several hours' rest would do my aching bones good. Except that I did not intend to have much rest at all.

I waited for an hour or so, enough time for everyone to fall asleep, then I picked up my satchel, donned my cloak, and moved silently to the door. I lifted the latch, then eased the door open. The hinges creaked, so I opened it just far enough to squeeze into the dark corridor.

"Can I help you, Sir?" came a voice full of amusement.

I froze, staring out into the darkness where I saw a human shape move towards me.

"The Decurion thought you might try to leave, Sir. My job is to make sure you stay in your room. I hope you won't give me any trouble."

He was a Praetorian, so I didn't believe him at all. He was probably dying for me to cause trouble so that he could dish out a beating.

There was no point in trying to invent an excuse. I closed the door again, took off my cloak and sandals, dumped my satchel beside the bed, then went to sleep.

In the morning, Mento gave me a studied look, but he made no mention of my attempted escape.

"Eat up, lads," he told his squad. "We have another day of hard riding ahead of us."

So our journey continued, making use of the excellent roads which make travel within the empire so fast. The only delays were for rest stops, change of horses, and the need to pass other road users, mostly travelling merchants or farmers transporting goods to their nearest market. Their wagons always eased aside to let us pass.

The journey was tiring but uneventful. I kept to myself, refusing to divulge any information to Mento no matter how often he asked probing questions. He did not seem at all put out by my surliness, but his apparent friendliness was contrasted by the care he took to ensure that I was never left alone except when in a room at night.

"I have my orders," he told me. "I don't need to understand them. But I was told to make sure you deliver your message, and that's what I'm going to do."

I found it hard to dislike Mento. He was a good soldier, and his men seemed to respect him. He was also less boastful and self-important than most Praetorians I had met. He went about his business in a quiet, confident and highly competent way.

Which meant I was unlikely to find any opportunity to slip away.

I did my best to resist his attempts to engage me in conversation, but he was a shrewd young man, and he paid close attention to the few grudging responses I did give him. Again, this was unusual in a Praetorian of any rank, for they generally carried out their duties with little interest in the lives of their prisoners. Naturally, I ascribed an ulterior motive to this behaviour. Mento, I suspected, had been charged with testing my loyalty, to see whether I could be relied upon to support the Emperor. Whether he had been assigned that task by the Emperor or by Fabius Successianus was the big question. I could understand the Emperor wanting to know whether he could trust me, but it was Successianus who had arranged my escort, and his motivations remained unclear.

So we continued northwards, travelling up the length of Italia, always following the fastest route. As I had known it would, this presented me with a slight problem.

"The next city is Verona," Mento remarked during one of our brief rest stops to change horses. "We can stay overnight there."

"I'd rather not," I told him.

He looked at me, his pugnacious jaw twisted to match the frown on his face.

"Why not?" he asked.

I shrugged, "I spent some time in Verona recently. There are some people there I'd rather not meet again. And some I'd love to meet but who would only delay us by insisting I spend time with them."

Mento considered this for a moment, then nodded, "All right. We can keep going a little longer and hold up at the next *mansio* beyond the city. But we'll need to go through Verona to reach the road to the west."

"I know," I agreed. "I'll keep my hood up, and I'll stay in the middle of the group. Just in case."

"So what were you doing in Verona that you need to hide from people?" he probed, a faint smile on his thick lips.

"Hiding," I told him.

He regarded me with obvious curiosity as he asked, "From who?"

"Several people," I replied vaguely.

Mento continued to stare at me, but I refused to divulge anything further.

"It's all in the past," I assured him. "And most of the people I was hiding from are dead. But I met a lot of ordinary citizens when I was in the city, and it would be best if I avoided them at the moment."

Mento gave a shrug.

"You're a mysterious fellow," he told me. "Very well, our mission is to get you to Gaul as quickly as we can, so we won't hang about in Verona. Now, here come our fresh mounts, so climb into the saddle and let's get moving again."

We turned west at Verona, then north again to skirt the foothills of the Alps. We continued to ride hard and fast, an exhausting experience for me, and we reached the fortress city of Moguntiacum ten days after leaving Rome. It was not as fast as a solitary relay messenger could have covered the distance, but it was still a very creditable time.

Moguntiacum is one of the main forts which line the great Rhenus river, the unofficial boundary between Romanised Gaul in the west and barbarian Germania in the east.

We slowed our tired horses as we approached the walled city. I, for one, was grateful for that. I had ridden long distances before, but rarely at such a pace, and I was feeling every mile in my tired bones.

Mento pointed ahead as we came up behind a couple of farmers' wagons which were heading for the city.

"I was told that Moguntiacum lies in a bend in the river," he informed me. "Apparently, we don't need to go through the city itself. We can cut across before we reach the gates. The legionary fortress is on a hill overlooking the settlement."

He grinned at me as he went on, "This is where Maximinis Thrax murdered Severus Alexander and was declared Emperor."

"Yes," I nodded. Then, unable to resist giving him something extra to think about, I added, "I was here that day."

That startled him, but he recovered quickly.

"You do get around, Scipio, I'll say that for you. But what were you doing in Moguntiacum?"

With the end of our journey in sight, and wanting to distract myself from the confrontation I knew would soon take place, I decided to tease him with some snippets of information. He had sounded very self-important when he had been telling me about Moguntiacum, and I rather pettily decided to deflate him.

I said, "I was attempting to foil a plot to kill Emperor Alexander."

Mento managed a grim laugh.

"Well, you failed in that."

"No, I succeeded. The plot I knew about was foiled. But what I didn't know at the time was that Thrax also had his eyes on the Purple."

I shivered slightly at the memory of that bloody day, and at the desperate risks I had taken. I had seen too many Emperors die, and returning to the scene of one of those deaths seemed to me to be an omen.

"Are you all right?" Mento asked me, a tinge of concern in his voice. "You've gone a bit pale."

"I'm just tired," I replied.

He jabbed his long chin at me as he warned, "Tired or not, you'd better be alert. With any luck, you'll be able to deliver your message to Licinius Valerianus before the day is out."

I nodded, then said, "Do you remember I told you I was hiding from several people when I lived in Verona?"

"I remember," he nodded, shooting me a puzzled look. "Why?"

"Because one of those people was Licinius Valerianus."

He thought about that for a moment, then said, "My orders are to bring you here safely, then to make sure you stay alive."

"Who gave you those orders?" I asked.

"Fabius Successianus," he informed me, confirming what Emperor Gallus had told me. "Why does that matter?"

"I don't suppose it does," I shrugged. "But you may have a fight on your hands, and Valerianus commands the entire army in this province. Eight of you won't stand much of a chance if he decides to do away with me."

"Is he likely to do that?" Mento asked with a frown, clearly disturbed by my revelation.

"I honestly don't know," I admitted. "My relationship with him is unusual to say the least."

Mento sighed, "Then all we can do is follow orders and see what happens."

"You and your men could ride away now," I suggested.

He shook his head.

"I have my orders," he insisted. "We'll face whatever is coming."

I smiled grimly to myself. It had not escaped my notice that Mento had not dismissed the prospect that Licinius Valerianus might order the deaths of an imperial messenger and his escort. The tensions between Valerianus and the Emperor were clearly not much of a secret.

We rode on in gloomy silence, the mood having spread to Mento's squad. I supposed they must have overheard our conversation, and they were no doubt wondering what faced them. I glanced around, noticing their nervous young faces, but Mento was also aware of their mood.

"Smarten up, lads! We are Praetorians! Don't let the Guard down."

The troopers straightened in their saddles, but I could see that they remained anxious, and we had no more time to reflect on what awaited us, because the fort was directly ahead of us now. Perched atop its hill, it had walls of stone, towers at each corner, and a strong garrison. The pass Mento had been given allowed us entrance without question, and after handing over our horses to the care of the fort's stables, Mento asked the Duty Centurion where his men could be billeted.

"There are some spare rooms in Block D," the Centurion replied. "I'll have someone show them."

There was an air of grudging hostility from the legionaries, but I did not think it was anything more than the usual resentment the ordinary soldiers felt towards Praetorians who were paid a lot more, and who generally faced less danger, their principal role being to guard the imperial family.

Mento, affecting not to notice the Centurion's antagonistic attitude, thanked him, told his men to find their quarters, then to requisition food and wine.

"Scipio and I are going to the *Principia*," he informed them. "We'll see you later."

The two of us walked through the camp, barely attracting anything more than the occasional curious glance from the many soldiers in the fort. When we reached the Headquarters building, we were informed that Licinius Valerianus was in the *Praetorium*, the personal residence of the fort's commander. Valerianus, as local Governor and commander of the Rhenus army, had appropriated this place for himself.

The *Praetorium* lay just behind the *Principia*. Since this was a fortress, the building was plain enough on the outside, although it had a walled courtyard and a small garden. Inside, though, it was very opulent, decorated with murals and many statues of bronze and marble, along with ornaments made of coloured glass and intricate strands of woven gold. These decorative pieces served as a reminder that Valerianus was a very wealthy man who could afford the finest things.

Mento did his best to appear calm and confident, but the ten days we had spent in close proximity allowed me to detect an undercurrent of nervousness. He was, I reminded myself, still a young man, and possibly not very experienced in warfare or diplomacy.

"Just let me do the talking," I whispered to him. "All you need to do is look warlike and arrogant. You've been sent here by the Emperor, remember."

"I'm not likely to forget," he muttered in a low growl.

Armed with our imperial pass and sealed scroll case, we were met by one of Valerianus' freedmen who, after keeping us waiting for some time, eventually led us into a large dining chamber where two men and a woman were reclining on couches as they ate an evening meal.

I recognised all of them. I knew Valerianus very well, and his greying hair and prominent eyes made him easily identifiable in any case. He had obviously been drinking for a while, for his cheeks were flushed, and his eyes seemed to bulge more than ever.

Beside him, stretched out on the couch but now half-propped up as she regarded me with a surprised expression, was Valerianus' wife, Cornelia Gallonia, whom I had last seen in her father's house when she had practically invited me to make love to her. She was dressed in a long, clinging robe of silk, and her own features suggested that she, too, had imbibed several goblets of wine.

For my part, I did my best to ignore her. It was not easy, since she was a very attractive woman, and the dress she wore only added to her allure.

I briefly glanced at the third person, the younger man who was lying on the couch facing Valerianus and Gallonia. I had not seen him for several years, but I still remembered his fresh face with its faint fuzz of a beard and his longer than usual hair. He had a stern, unforgiving expression, but he also appeared to be completely at home in the presence of Valerianus. That was only to be expected since the younger man, now in his forties, was Valerianus' son, Licinius Gallienus.

All three of them were now staring at me. They had been told that an imperial messenger had arrived, but they had not expected to see me.

Gallienus recovered first, eyeing me with deep suspicion.

"Sempronius Scipio," he drawled. "Have you come to accuse me of murder again?"

I sensed Mento growing tense, but I ignored Gallienus. This was not the time to rake over our previous encounter. Instead, I turned to his father.

"I am sorry to interrupt your dinner," I told him. "But I have a message from the Emperor."

I held up the scroll case, letting him see the imperial seal.

Valerianus took a slow sip of wine, letting me know that a message from Trebonianus Gallus was less important than his own comfort, then he placed his goblet on the low table between the couches, and held out a languid hand. He had still not spoken, and although the room was warm, I felt a chill of fear, wondering how he would react once he had read the message.

I stepped closer, placing the leather tube in his hand. When he took it, he looked me in the eyes with a cold, impassive stare.

"You told me you had the plague," he said, his voice hard.

I had a prepared answer for this, having already explained myself to Fabius Successianus.

"Your messenger was told there was plague in the house," I said. "I was fortunate enough not to catch it, but I dared not leave the house in case I spread the disease."

Valerianus held my gaze for a long moment, as if he were trying to see into my thoughts. Then he casually broke the seal on the tube and tipped out the scroll.

I took a step back, standing with Mento at my shoulder, and I now shifted my gaze to Gallonia and Gallienus. Neither of them was looking at me. Gallienus was studying his father for any hint as to what the message might contain, while Gallonia was looking down at the table, refusing to even glance in my direction. To my eyes, she appeared very guilty about something, and I offered a silent prayer to Jupiter that Valerianus would not notice her reaction.

For a while, he was intent on the letter. He read it slowly, his face registering barely a flicker of emotion, then passed it across the low table to his son, who read it with a slight frown.

When Gallienus returned the scroll to his father, he said, "It is as you expected."

"Indeed it is," Valerianus nodded.

Then he turned those bulbous eyes on me again.

"You went to Syria to overthrow the usurper, Mariades."

It was an accusation, not a question.

"I did," I nodded.

"And you used my name to help you gain access to him."

Again, it was a statement. He clearly knew all about my mission even though it had supposedly been a secret operation.

"I did," I said again.

A faint smile twitched his lips as he said, "How inventive of you. But then, you always were a clever devil, Scipio. Mariades clearly believed you."

"Apparently so," I nodded, at the same time thinking that, if Valerianus really was afraid of me as Gallonia had insisted, then the feeling was mutual, and he was probably concealing it a lot better than I was.

"Not that it turned out very well in the end," he said acerbically. "It gave Shappur an opportunity to invade Syria. And now we need to deal with yet another eastern usurper."

I held my tongue. If Valerianus learned that I had met Uranius Antoninus while I had been in Antioch, there was no telling what he might ask me to do.

I said, "The Emperor's first concern is the revolt in Pannonia. He asked me to impress upon you the urgency of his request. He needs your cavalry to hurry to join him before Aemilius Aemilianus can march on Rome."

Valerianus reached out to one of the silver dishes on the table, picked up a stuffed dormouse, popping it into his mouth and chewing contentedly. He took his time, then washed it down with another mouthful of wine. Only then did he respond.

"Yes," he said. "He wrote as much in his letter. The question is, why did he send you here? Is he attempting to trick me? Are you his man now?"

"I serve the empire," I replied, holding my ground against his antagonism.

"Really? I thought you served me. We have an understanding, do we not?"

"We do," I agreed, wanting nothing more than to avoid the topic of my daughter and the fact that Valerianus knew precisely where she lived. Nor did I want to give him the satisfaction of knowing that his more recent threat against Julia had terrified me.

"But you refused my summons when I was sent here," he reminded me.

"I did not think you would wish to risk catching the plague," I countered.

"And then you served Gallus," he said as if I had not spoken.

"He is the Emperor," I replied. "We all serve him."

Gallienus gave a soft snort, but Valerianus only stared at me before giving a slow, thoughtful nod.

"My men will find quarters for you in the fort," he said. "You may leave."

"What about the Emperor's message?" I asked. "He was adamant that you need to join him as soon as possible."

Valerianus gave me the sort of look he would use if he had trodden in something unpleasant which had stuck to his sandal.

"It is an order from the Emperor," he said, clearly choosing his words carefully. "As you say, we all serve him. I will obey his command as soon as I can."

Then he returned his attention to his meal, and his guards opened the door behind me, clearly signalling that our audience was over. As I turned to go, I caught a brief glimpse of Cornelia Gallonia shooting me a surreptitious look from behind the curtain of her dark hair. I hoped Valerianus had not noticed.

One of Valerianus' freedmen escorted Mento and me to the barracks room where his men had been housed. Neither of us spoke as we followed our guide. Mento at least had the sense to know that anything either of us said would be reported back to Valerianus. It was a stiff, uncomfortable walk, and both of us let out audible sighs of relief once we had entered the room and closed the door behind us.

It was a typically cramped barracks room, with four sets of bunk beds and a small, clay oven in one corner. Mento's seven men looked at him expectantly, and one of them asked, "What's happening?"

Mento looked to me for an answer, so I shrugged, "Nothing yet. All we can do now is wait."

It sounded ominous, even to me, and I could not shake off the feeling that we were like prisoners who were waiting for a magistrate to decide their fate.

Chapter 29
Friends and Enemies

Mento clearly wanted to talk to me privately, so he ordered his men to go out.

"Why don't you go down to the town," he told them. "Take a wander around. But make sure you don't get into any trouble. Stay together if you can, and stick in pairs if you do split up."

The young troopers looked mystified, but they filed out of the room, their hobnailed sandals clumping on the wooden floor. Once they had left, Mento turned to me.

"We need to talk," he said.

Nodding, I sat down on one of the lower bunks, gesturing to him to say his piece.

"What do you want to know?" I asked him.

"For a start, who were the woman and other man with Valerianus? I recognised the Senator, but I don't know the others."

"That was his wife and his son."

When Mento frowned, clearly confused by the discrepancy in their ages, I hastily put in, "His son from his first marriage. Cornelia Gallonia is his second wife."

"She's quite something," he observed.

"She certainly is," I agreed.

He had clearly noticed Gallonia's stunning looks, but he quickly switched to his main concerns.

"And the other man was Gallienus? What did he mean when he asked if you had come to accuse him of murder?"

I'd hoped Mento might have been so busy admiring Gallonia that he would have forgotten that particular comment by Gallienus, but he was obviously clear-headed enough to have picked up on it.

With a sigh, I explained, "I met him a few years back. I was helping the *vigiles* in Verona who were investigating the murder of a prostitute. She'd been at a party with Gallienus and some of his friends the night before. She overheard him saying something she shouldn't have heard, so he had her killed."

Mento did not appear to be shocked by this at all. He sat on the bunk, his legs slightly apart, his elbows resting on his knees and his hands clasped together as he leaned forwards, intent on our conversation.

"You can prove that?" he asked with an uncertain frown.

"I can't produce any witnesses," I said. "But I know it was him. In any case, he fled Verona before he could be arrested. Then the civil war started when Messius Decius declared himself Emperor. Valerianus and Gallienus were part of that plot. That's what the poor girl overheard."

Again, Mento barely reacted to this news. His jaw and lips moved as he mulled over my account, but there had been so many Emperors in recent years that learning about plots to overthrow a ruler was hardly a surprise.

After a moment, he asked me, "Valerianus said you and he have an understanding. What did he mean?"

I closed my eyes and took a deep breath before giving him the answer.

"He means that I must do as he demands or he will harm my family and friends."

Mento gave a nod. Again, he understood how that type of blackmail could be used.

He guessed, "So that's why he was annoyed when he was talking about you working for the Emperor?"

"That's right. I'm caught between the two of them, and each of them thinks I am spying on behalf of the other."

"And are you?"

It was a question which confirmed that Mento had a sharp mind behind his less than handsome appearance.

"I'm just trying to stay alive," I replied. "I always tell both of them the truth. It's a compromise of sorts."

Mento said, "Then I suppose all we can do is wait to hear what Valerianus intends to do. Will he let you go, do you think?"

"I don't know. It's hard to tell what's going on in his devious little mind."

He nodded ruefully, "So we might be here for a while?"

Mento was deep in thought for a long moment, clearly unsure what to say next. Thinking it would be wise to change the subject, I took the opportunity to ask a question I could have asked days earlier.

"Would I be right in thinking that your lads are new recruits?"

He blinked, then nodded, "That's right. I transferred to the Praetorians from *Legio II Parthica* a few months ago, but those lads joined up as part of the Emperor's recruitment earlier this year."

"They came straight into the Guard without joining a legion first?" I frowned.

"You can do that if your family has enough money," he told me. "Some parents think it is worth it to keep their sons out of serious fighting. The Praetorian Guard spends most of its time in Rome."

"And the imperial Treasury earns some income from the payments?" I guessed.

"That's how it works," Mento nodded. Then, pulling a face, he added, "I suppose we were sent on this mission because we are expendable."

I told him, "All soldiers are expendable when it comes to the whims of powerful men."

"I suppose you are right," he agreed glumly.

At that point, we heard footsteps outside as several men approached. The door opened to reveal Mento's squad returning.

"We couldn't leave," one of them informed us bitterly. "They said we are confined to the fort. Those are the Governor's orders, apparently."

Mento gave me a quizzical look, but all I could do was shrug in response.

"Then we shall stay here," he stated, allaying his men's fears with an air of relaxed calm.

Standing up, he began to issue brisk commands.

"There are only eight bunks," he said. "Scipio can have one of the top ones furthest from the door. The rest of us will take turns to stay on watch. That way, everyone will have a bed for part of the night."

The concept of needing to remain on watch inside a Roman fort was a serious one, but his young troopers seemed to accept it. They may have been new recruits, but they had clearly picked up on the aura of hostility surrounding us.

Mento then told them to begin preparing an evening meal from the supplies they had requisitioned from the fort's storehouses.

"There's no point in being hungry," he told them.

So we huddled in that cramped room, listening to the familiar sounds of a Roman camp, but knowing that we were effectively prisoners, with hundreds of soldiers surrounding us.

The night was a long one. My mattress was thin and uncomfortable, the small room filled with the smells and snores of the others, and the frequent changing of the guard created several interruptions to what sleep I did manage to get.

In the morning, Mento sent three men to find breakfast. They returned with freshly baked bread and some cold sausages which we chewed on while Mento opened the door and stood looking outwards like a sentinel.

The men began to play dice as a way of passing the time, but as it turned out, we did not have too long to wait. Before the third hour had passed, we received a visit from a Tribune, dressed in red cloak and plumed helmet, his young face partly concealed by his neatly trimmed beard. Mento called a soft warning to summon me, then waited for the Tribune to approach the doorway. Mento offered him a formal salute.

"Good morning, Sir!"

The young Tribune, probably just starting out on his military career, tried to portray an air of confidence, but all he achieved was to come across as haughty and condescending.

"You and your men are ordered to return to Rome," he told Mento.

Mento, his pugnacious jaw set in a determined scowl, said, "Yes, Sir. Thank you, Sir. Does that include Sempronius Scipio?"

The Tribune shot him a dark look as he said, "No. The orders are only for you and your fellow Praetorians."

Mento stood his ground as he said, "In that case, Sir, my orders from the Emperor still stand. I was specifically told to act as Scipio's guard until such time as he returned to report to the Emperor. I am not to leave him under any circumstances."

The Tribune seemed more than a little flustered by this. He attempted to bluster, saying that the orders he was relaying had come from the Governor, but Mento refused to back down.

"So you are refusing a direct order from a superior officer?" he barked, attracting the attention of several legionaries who were passing by. Some of them were grinning, and one made a crude gesture behind the Tribune's back. To Mento's credit, he did not so much as smile at the clear insult to the officer.

Speaking firmly, he stated, "I am obeying a direct order from the most senior authority in the empire, Sir."

The Tribune glared at him, almost spitting the words as he rasped, "You will answer for this!"

At that, he spun on his heel and stomped away, heading for the *Principia*. The legionaries who had been mocking him suddenly found other things to do, scattering at his approach.

"Superior officer, my arse!" Mento muttered. "Senior, maybe, but not superior."

"You could be in trouble now," I warned.

"I'm only obeying my orders," he shrugged.

"And I'm very grateful," I told him. "But you can't take on an entire legion."

"We have our orders," he said stiffly. "We will do our duty."

Then, turning back into the small room, he shouted at his men to sharpen their swords.

I felt more than a little anxious. Mento clearly meant what he said, and I did not want the deaths of these eight young men on my conscience. I silently prayed that Valerianus would be sensible enough not to take any direct action against them. If he did, it would signal the beginning of yet another civil war. Was he ready for that? I had almost persuaded myself that he would not risk that final gamble, but his attitude the previous evening had made me realise that he was capable of anything if he put his mind to it. How, I wondered, would he react to Mento's refusal to leave me unprotected?

The answer came a short time later when another visitor arrived. This time it was a freedman wearing civilian tunic and cloak. He gave Mento a slight bow, then asked me to accompany him.

"Publius Licinius Valerianus wishes to speak to you," he told me. He spoke politely, giving no hint of threat.

I glanced at Mento who nodded, "I'll come with you."

I turned back to the freedman, but he offered no objection.

"Lead the way," I told him.

Mento told his men to wait, then followed me. Without glancing back, the freedman led us along the wide avenue between buildings to the Headquarters. Inside, he guided us to a busy chamber where several secretaries and military aides were busy reading reports or scribbling away at wax tablets.

"Wait here," the freedman told us before offering a slight bow and leaving the room.

There was an office beyond this room, the heavy door firmly closed. Mento and I stood there, waiting patiently until the door opened and another Tribune stepped out, hurrying off with a clutch of scrolls in his hand.

The clerk who sat closest to the office now looked at us for the first time.

"You may go in now," he told us.

In the office, we found Valerianus seated behind a desk on which stood an inkpot and quills. He was alone. He looked up from a small wax tablet he had been reading, cast his eyes over Mento, then focused his attention on me.

"I thought you should know that I have set things in motion," he told me in a formal tone. "I have sent despatch riders out all along the frontier, and to various garrison towns and training camps. As instructed by the Emperor, I am gathering my cavalry forces and will bring them to his aid as soon as I can."

His stilted manner seemed a little out of place, and I wondered whether he was suffering from a hangover after the wine he had consumed the previous evening. Or perhaps it had been Mento's refusal to obey his order which had irritated him. As usual, though, the pompous bugger gave nothing away. Even his confirmation that he would obey the Emperor's command had been delivered without a trace of emotion.

Copying his stiff manner, I said, "Thank you. I shall return to Rome to inform the Emperor. May I ask how soon you expect to be able to ride?"

He gave the slightest of shrugs as he said, "A few days, I think. My forces are spread all along the Rhenus frontier. It will take time to bring them together."

I breathed an inward sigh of relief. He had not countermanded my statement that I would return to Rome.

"How many men do you think you can muster?" I asked him.

"Forty thousand horsemen," he replied evenly.

"That is good to hear," I said. "But will the frontier be secure enough during your absence?"

Valerianus said, "My son will retain all the foot soldiers and some Auxiliary cavalry to act as messengers and scouts. He will manage."

"Then the empire will be safe," I nodded.

There was an undercurrent of mistrust between us. We were speaking formally, saying all the right things, yet there was a great deal being left unsaid.

He held my gaze for a long moment, then said, "You may go, Scipio. Return to Rome and inform the Emperor of my answer. But remember our arrangement."

"I never forget it," I assured him truthfully.

As soon as we stepped out of the office, one of Valerianus' aides hurried in, bearing a small bundle of messages on wax tablets. The door closed with a loud bang, and we were free to go.

We found our own way outside, and then Mento breathed, "Forty thousand cavalry! He must have been recruiting hard to raise that number in only a few months."

"Or he might be lying," I murmured.

"Do you think so? Why would he do that?"

"I'm not sure, but I do know it usually doesn't hurt to exaggerate the size of your army. It causes dismay among your enemies. Believe me, it works."

Mento shot me another of his intensive stares.

"You're a bloody odd character, Scipio. You investigate murders, you act as an imperial spy, and you have Senators and Emperors as acquaintances. Who are you, exactly?"

"I wish I knew," I told him. "My life gets confusing sometimes."

"Well, at least we can get out of here now," he said as we strode towards our assigned barrack block. "I had a horrible feeling he was going to keep us here."

"I think that might have been his original intention," I replied. "But your orders from the Emperor complicated things for him. Now I think he wants rid of us as soon as possible, so let's get out of here before the bastard changes his mind again."

That was when I heard the sound of hurrying footsteps coming up behind us. When I turned around, I was surprised to see the hulking figure of Torquatus, Cornelia Gallonia's supposed bodyguard and possible lover. He looked as big and handsome as ever, although the tunic he wore covered more of his muscles than the revealing one he had been wearing when I had last seen him in Rome.

He stopped when he came close, giving me a cursory bob of his head.

"The Lady Cornelia Gallonia wishes to speak to you," he told me. "Now."

I had not expected that, but I could hardly refuse. Turning to Mento, I said, "You'd better let me do this on my own. I'm sure it won't take long."

He did not look too pleased about it, but he let me go with the giant Torquatus who led me to the *Praetorium* where I had interrupted the family dinner the previous evening. This time, he guided me to a small, private chamber near the rear of the building. He let me in, then remained outside after closing the door behind me.

The room was a comfortable living area, with padded chairs and couches, and with a window looking out onto the rear of the courtyard. Gallonia was standing near that window, but she turned and gave me a grateful smile when she heard me enter the room.

"Thank you for coming, Scipio."

"It is good to see you again, Lady," I replied cautiously, wondering what it was she wanted from me.

"You have spoken to my husband?" she asked.

"Just a few moments ago. I am returning to Rome immediately."

She nodded, "He was tempted to keep you here, you know. He still worries about your loyalty to him."

"I have no loyalty towards him," I told her. "I serve him only because of his threats against my family and friends."

She sighed, "I told you once before, Scipio, that you and I could help one another."

When I did not reply, she gave a slight shake of her head, then walked over to a writing desk which stood at one side of the room. She picked up a small scroll which was, I saw, sealed shut.

"I would like you to take this to my mother," she said. "I could entrust it to one of the military messengers, but since you are leaving now, you will be able to deliver it quickly."

"Is it urgent?" I asked her, thinking that I would need to report to Trebonianus Gallus before delivering any private messages.

"It is private," she said. "That is not quite the same thing, but I would like it delivered as soon as possible. And with discretion."

"Of course," I nodded, reaching out to accept the scroll from her.

As I did so, she stepped close and whispered, "Publius is up to something, Scipio. Do not trust him."

I almost looked around to check whether we were being listened to, but I resisted that urge. I was very aware of her closeness, and the faint hint of lavender from her perfume. I wasn't sure whether it was that or her words which had caused my heart to beat a little faster.

Keeping my own voice low, I asked her, "What, precisely, is he up to?"

She reached out with her left hand, gripping my right bicep as she hissed, "I don't know. But he and Gallienus have been holding private discussions for months now."

"That is understandable," I told her. "They have a big job guarding the frontier."

She looked almost distraught as she told me, "It is more than that! They hold regular meetings with their senior officers, and those are not secret. But they often lock themselves away, with nobody else invited. I have tried to listen in, but they are very secretive about whatever it is they are planning."

I frowned, "I don't think I can do much about it. I am going back to Rome now, with a message for the Emperor that your husband is gathering his army to help him."

She shook her head vigorously.

"He is planning something, Scipio."

If she was right, there could only be one thing her husband intended to do.

"He is going to make a bid for the Purple?" I guessed.

She chewed her lip for a moment, still gripping my arm tightly.

"I think so," she nodded eventually.

"And why are you telling me this?" I asked. "If he succeeded, you would be the Augusta."

Now she released my arm and clenched both fists as if in anger.

"Because he's an odious man. That's why. He treats me little better than a slave."

She paused, lowering her eyes, then added softly, "And he beats me."

There was not much I could say to that. A Roman husband was entitled by law to punish his family in whatever way he saw fit. I could well believe that Valerianus would behave that way, and her vehement accusation certainly sounded genuine.

I asked, "What is it you want me to do, Lady?"

"Warn the Emperor," she said, her tone urgent and demanding. "Tell him to have Valerianus killed. He must have some agents here in the fort."

I was sure she was right. Trebonianus Gallus had more or less admitted that members of the *frumentarii* would be watching Valerianus. The problem was that there was no way of telling who they were.

It was, though, another question which burned uppermost in my mind.

"You want your husband to be killed?" I asked.

She did not answer, but she stood there, staring into my eyes with a stance which gave me the answer.

Speaking softly, I said, "You must be aware that such executions usually extend to the entire family."

A faint smirk touched her lips as she whispered, "Not if I have helped the Emperor."

I gave a slight nod of acceptance. She might be right about that.

"And then what?" I asked. "What do you want in return?"

She let out a deep breath, then stepped even closer, pressing herself gently against me.

"The chance to marry again," she said, her tone suddenly sultry and inviting. "This time to a man of my choice."

I reached up to touch her shoulders and ease her away from me.

"I will deliver your message," I promised. "Both messages."

"Thank you!" she said, visibly relieved.

Then, before I knew what was happening, she pushed herself against me, flinging her arms around my neck and kissing me passionately on the lips. I felt her tongue probe my mouth as she held me close, too astonished, and perhaps too delighted, to resist. The pressure of her body against mine sent my pulse racing, but I managed not to respond too overtly, although some parts of me were reacting without any conscious prompting from me. I did place my hands on her waist, feeling the curve of her hips, but only so that I could ease her away from me once again.

She broke off the kiss, breathing heavily and giving me a burning look from those glorious eyes.

"I told you we could help one another, Scipio. This time, I hope you believe me."

All I could do was nod. She could take that as agreement, as farewell, or both. I wasn't entirely sure myself which it was.

"May the gods protect you," I said, my voice thick with the effort of keeping my emotions under control.

"And you, Scipio," she said, running her hands down the front of her dress to smooth out the folds, a gesture which could hardly have been more provocative if she had tried.

I hurried out of the room, her scroll still clutched in one hand. I was sure my face was burning, and I could not get back to Mento and his men soon enough. It was time to leave, and to deliver three messages. Whether any of them was from a friend or an enemy, I honestly did not know.

Chapter 30
Indecision

We rode out of the camp under the scornful eyes of the legionaries who manned the gate. Mento stared straight ahead, ignoring their hostility, leading us past the city of Moguntiacum and back down the road which led south.

"We can't afford to delay," Mento told his squad. "Scipio has important news which the Emperor needs to hear."

He was more right than he knew, for I had not told him what Cornelia Gallonia had told me about Valerianus' imperial ambitions. And, as we began our race towards Rome, I realised that I had a difficult decision to make.

Cornelia Gallonia had told me to warn the Emperor about Valerianus, but I knew that to do so would be risking the lives of Fronto, Julia, and my daughter's entire family. If I warned Gallus, Valerianus would inevitably hear about it. It was not the sort of news that could be kept secret in a place like Rome. And if Valerianus heard about it, he would know that it could only have come from one source.

I was in a terrible quandary. I hated Valerianus, but I dared not act against him openly because he could, and would, make my family and friends suffer.

I fretted over this every day as we galloped south, stopping at waystations each night, then riding on again at first light.

Mento must have noticed my distraction, because he asked me one evening, "Are you all right? You look concerned about something."

"I'm just tired," I replied, forcing a smile. "I'm too old for this sort of charging around."

"You'll survive until we get to Rome," he assured me.

The question that bothered me was what I would do when I got there. The more I thought about it, the more I knew I could not risk telling the Emperor what Gallonia had told me. I rationalised this by telling myself that she had not, in fact, provided anything more than her personal suspicion. She had no proof at all, and I still suspected her motives. I convinced myself that I could not pass on her claims. After all, she had openly admitted to me that she hated Valerianus. What if she had concocted this tale simply in order to turn Gallus against

Valerianus? They already mistrusted one another, so it would not take much to persuade Gallus to order Valerianus' execution.

The other problem was that Gallus desperately needed Valerianus' reinforcements. If he had Valerianus killed, would that army willingly follow another commander? Could Gallus trust anyone with an army of that size?

I wrestled with these dilemmas all the way south, sometimes deciding I would risk telling the Emperor, at other times resolving that to do so would be folly. I had no proof, only a scheming woman's suspicions. From my two meetings with Cornelia Gallonia, the only thing I was sure of was that I could not trust her in spite of her protestations that we should be allies. Any woman who offered herself to me the way she had done was, I told myself, capable of anything in order to get her own way.

All the while, we hurried on as quickly as we could. We reached the coastal road, heading east along the southern fringes of the Alps, then back through Verona with scarcely a pause, and rode south towards Rome. It was a seemingly endless slog, day after day of pounding along the roads, interspersed with brief, blessed, moments of rest.

We reached Rome on the eleventh day of travel, slightly slower than our outward journey, but even the young troopers were almost worn out by the pace we had set, so it was little wonder we had taken a little more time than on the first leg of our round trip. Bone-weary, we clattered along the *Via Lata*, skirted the *forum*, then arrived at the Palatine.

"Take the horses back to the barracks on the Caelian," Mento told his men. "I'll go with Scipio. I'll catch up with you later."

The seven troopers took our horses, then rode slowly back towards their main camp which lay within the city walls.

Mento and I walked into the Palace, presenting ourselves to the usual barrier of aides, but the urgency of our message meant that we were ushered through very quickly. The Emperor's private secretary even interrupted the Emperor during a meeting to alert him to our arrival, and Trebonianus Gallus immediately cut his discussion short, sending most of his visitors out. These men, every one of them a Senator, regarded us with unfeigned curiosity as they passed us, and then we were ushered into the meeting room.

This was a different chamber to the one I had become accustomed to visiting when I saw Gallus. This room was larger, containing a long table and enough chairs to seat twenty people. Daylight filtered in through horizontal slits high in one wall, giving the place an airy feel compared to his usual, stuffy office.

Gallus sat at one end of the table. Fabius Successianus sat close to his right, while his senior private secretary took up position on the left. Successianus and the secretary looked alert and keen to hear our report, but the Emperor's face was almost haggard. His complexion was grey, his eyes sunken and with dark bags beneath them. He looked like a man who had not slept in days.

Mento and I remained standing even when the Emperor beckoned us closer.

"What news?" he asked, maintaining a surprisingly calm manner in light of the seriousness of his situation.

For a moment, I could not speak. All the indecision of the past eleven days came flooding back to me, and it took a conscious effort to bring myself to speak. I hoped the small audience would put this down to my exhaustion.

In a croaking voice, I said, "Licinius Valerianus has promised to come as soon as he can, Augustus. He claims he will be able to bring forty thousand cavalry."

Gallus' relief was evident even though he did his best to conceal it. His posture relaxed, and he forced a thin smile.

"That is good news," he nodded. "Did he say how long it would take for him to join us?"

"He was unclear on that, Augustus," I said. "But he acknowledged the urgency of the situation, and he hoped it would be only a few days before he could set off."

"So he may be on his way already?" Gallus asked, unable to conceal his eagerness to hear his hopes validated.

I said, "I would certainly hope so by now, Augustus. It is eleven days since we left Moguntiacum."

"That is good to hear," he nodded, letting out a sigh of evident relief. "He cannot come soon enough."

"Is there any news of Aemilius Aemilianus?" I asked.

The Emperor almost flinched at that question, and he sat very still, but Successianus stepped in, saying, "Another messenger arrived only a short time ago with the news that Aemilianus reached the Alps six days ago. The bulk of his army is on foot, but he has probably crossed the mountains by now."

I blinked in astonishment. If that news had only just reached Rome, we could not have been very far ahead of Aemilianus' scouts when we had reached Verona.

"So he is marching on Rome?" I guessed.

Gallus seemed lost in thought, so again it was Successianus who said, "He is. And we should march out to meet him."

That remark was clearly aimed at the Emperor, and Gallus shifted in his seat, seeming to focus on our conversation once again.

"We have barely ten thousand men," he said. "Until we know the size of Aemilianus' army, we are safer in Rome. Let him advance. He will move only at walking pace, so that will allow Valerianus more time to come up behind him."

Successianus, clearly going over an old argument, countered, "But if we march north, we can block his path to Rome. Then we have a better chance of trapping him between our two armies."

The Emperor argued, "The legions from Hispania have not yet arrived. If we wait for them, they will almost double our numbers."

Successianus countered, "But Aemilianus may reach Rome before they arrive. We should march out and face him."

Gallus sat up, waving one hand at his advisor.

"I will think on it," he said brusquely. "Issue orders that the Praetorians and the Second Legion are to be ready to march at a moment's notice."

Then he turned his attention back to me.

"Thank you, Scipio," he said. "You have served me well."

That cut me more deeply than I would have hoped, for I could not help feeling that I might be betraying him.

Mustering my spy's false face, I smiled, "Thank you, Augustus. Can I commend Decurion Livius Mento for his help?"

"Of course. Thank you, Mento. I shall not forget this."

This brief exchange let me see a glimpse of the Trebonianus Gallus I had first met in Novae. His ability to inspire the ordinary soldiers had not deserted him, even though he remained in a dangerous predicament.

I asked permission to leave, and the Emperor nodded his assent, so Mento and I left, making our weary way back to the main entrance hall of the palace.

"What will you do now?" the Decurion asked me.

"I'm going to my friend's home on the Quirinal," I told him. "And then I'm going to sleep for a week."

"If we have a week," he answered. "If Aemilianus has crossed the Alps, there will be fighting before much longer."

That was not a pleasant thought, but I knew he was right.

"It is in the hands of the gods now," I told him. "Or, at least, in the hands of men who wield a lot more power than either of us."

To my surprise, he offered me his hand, and we parted on good terms, me heading for Fronto's home, he making his way to the Praetorian Horse Guards' barracks on the Caelian Hill.

That, I fervently hoped, would be my last involvement in the dance of diplomacy and battle which was about to erupt.

Both Fronto and Julia were full of questions when I returned to the house on the Quirinal, so despite my body feeling as if I needed to sleep for several days, I sat with them in the garden and told them all about my frantic ride to Moguntiacum and back again. It was strange to talk about such potentially momentous events in a peaceful garden, shaded by the branches of a lime tree, while birds hopped around our feet, and the muted sounds of the city filtered through to us from beyond the walls of the house. Here, it seemed, we were insulated from the problems which were gathering in the world outside.

When I had finished my account, Fronto mused, "So the war will be decided soon, then?"

"I think so," I replied. "If Valerianus was telling the truth about the number of men he can bring, then Aemilianus doesn't have much of a chance, although that still leaves the question of how far Valerianus is prepared to go."

Julia put in, "She told you he plans to become Emperor."

I smiled, "She did. The question is whether she can be trusted to tell the truth. Personally, I'm not at all sure about that."

"But if she is right," Julia frowned, "the Emperor ought to be told."

"Not by me, though," I said. "Valerianus would soon find out who had warned him."

Julia scowled, but Fronto said, "That is true enough. But Gallonia clearly doesn't know about the hold her husband has over you."

"He seems to keep her well away from his public life," I shrugged. "That's another reason I'm not sure her story is reliable. She has no proof at all."

"She seems to like you, though," Fronto teased.

I snorted, "I doubt that. I think she sees me as little more than a means to helping her escape a loveless marriage."

"If that's all she wants," Fronto said, "there are easier ways to achieve her aim."

Julia frowned, "What ways?"

With a sad smile, Fronto explained, "She could always persuade her pet slave to murder Valerianus in his sleep. Then she can have the slave executed and claim she knew nothing about his intentions."

Julia looked horrified by this suggestion, and I shook my head.

I said to Fronto, "You are becoming as cynical as me, my friend."

Fronto grinned, "You are obviously a bad influence on me, Sextus. However, if Valerianus really is planning to make a play for imperial rule, I suspect that a more likely scenario is that Gallus' *frumentarii* would have taken action to stop him. That they have not done so suggests there is no evidence at all that he is plotting against the Emperor."

Julia ventured, "Unless he has bribed them into joining him."

We both looked at her, then I let out a soft chuckle. Julia really was a very clever young woman.

"There is that," I conceded.

Fronto said, "But, to return to the question of the war, what happens if Aemilianus wins? The larger army doesn't always come out on top, you know."

"That's true enough," I agreed. "But I don't know anything about Aemilianus other than what I heard from the Emperor."

Fronto gave me his knowing smile as he said, "I know a little about him."

"Of course you do," I smiled. "Is there anyone in Rome you don't know about?"

"Nobody important," he chuckled. "As for Aemilianus, I fear that things would be even worse if he becomes Emperor."

"Why?" I asked. "Is he a tyrant of some sort?"

"Far from it," Fronto replied. "But he's not from a rich background. His family are Moors, and he rose through ability. He's clearly a capable military commander, but we both know that anyone from a less than respectable background will be hated by the Senate."

I could not disagree with that. In my lifetime, I'd seen three Emperors who had come from unorthodox backgrounds. Macrinus, whom I had liked, and Philippus, whom I had hated, had both been from equestrian families. That meant they were wealthy and important, but not at the level of Senators. Neither of them had been popular in the Senate, and both had been overthrown, although Philippus had lasted a few years as Emperor before Valerianus and Decius had plotted to bring him down.

And the third case in point was Maximinis Thrax, a barbarian who had risen through the army ranks and had seized power by instigating a military coup. Despite his popularity with the soldiers and the ordinary people, the Senate had detested him for his barbarian background. He, too, had been overthrown thanks to a plot engineered by my deceitful patron, Licinius Valerianus. If Aemilianus came from a similar background, he would never gain the full support of the Senate. Even if he was able to defeat and kill Valerianus, other Senators would work to undermine him even while they smiled to his face and promised loyalty.

Fronto was right. There was probably no good outcome from the impending civil strife, but having Aemilianus as Emperor was almost certainly the worst of the foreseeable results.

While Julia tossed a few crumbs of bread to the birds who squawked and flapped as they competed for these small prizes, Fronto asked me, "What do you think Trebonianus Gallus will do? Is he really going to sit here and wait for Aemilianus to march all the way to Rome?"

I shrugged, "I'm not sure. When I first met him, I liked him. He was a confident and competent commander during the siege of Novae, and I thought he'd make a good Emperor. Ending the religious persecutions was certainly a policy I approved of. But since then, he's done very little."

Fronto pointed out, "There's not much he could have done about the plague. It's still rife in some parts of the empire."

"That's true," I agreed. "But I'm not so sure that he's as good a soldier as I first thought."

"What do you mean?"

I explained, "In Novae, he sat behind the walls of the fort. It's a strong place, and he had plenty of men to defend it. The Goths had no siege weapons, so they had little chance of breaking in."

"That's the whole point of forts," Fronto reminded me with his familiar smile.

"I know. But after the Goths had moved on, he initially refused to leave. He let Messius Decius march into a trap without offering any support."

"Some might say he showed good sense," Fronto argued. "By not joining the Emperor's army, he saved his legion."

I shook my head.

"I think that was due more to good luck than good judgement, unless you call being afraid of Cniva sound sense."

"From what you've told me of Cniva, I think it would be sensible to be afraid of him," Fronto countered, taking up the opposite view as he so often did. We had held this sort of debate many times, knowing that it helped us to analyse the detail of whatever we were discussing.

I nodded, "All right, you have a point there, even if it is unlike a Roman Governor to sit behind a wall when he has a chance to defeat a barbarian."

Before Fronto could object further, I went on, "And then, after the battle in the marshes, he withdrew to a fortified camp rather than support Decius's army."

Fronto said, "Again, what choice did he have? You said yourself that he commanded the infantry. They couldn't chase cavalry. The battle was lost whatever he could have done."

"Fair enough," I said. "But there is a pattern emerging. He sat and did nothing at Novae, he sat and did nothing when Decius was killed, and now he plans to sit and do nothing until Valerianus arrives to save him."

"So he's cautious?" Fronto mused. "That may be no bad thing in a commander."

"Except that, if Valerianus defeats Aemilianus while Gallus is sitting in the palace, who are the people going to hold up as their hero? It won't be an Emperor who skulked on the Palatine while others defeated his enemy."

Fronto nodded, frowning as he did so.

"I see what you mean," he breathed.

I drained my goblet of fruit juice, then sighed, "Well, there is nothing any of us can do now. I'm going to get some rest. Tomorrow, I'll deliver Gallonia's letter, and then all we can do is wait."

Chapter 31
Scapegoat

Two days after my return, I felt refreshed, the rigours of my long journey having been shaken off by good food, good company and plenty of rest. Seeing this, Fronto persuaded me to accompany him down to the *forum*.

"The city is on edge," he informed me. "News of Aemilianus' approach has leaked out, and the mob are demanding action. I'd like to hear what the Senate has to say about it."

I could not deny my own curiosity, so we strolled down to the centre of the city, Fronto wearing his equestrian tunic, and neither of us bothering with cloaks since it was a fine summer's day with a hot sun beaming down from a cloudless sky.

The *forum* was crowded, and the mob were indeed voicing their unhappiness. There were no signs that a riot was likely to break out, but there were many chants and shouts as people demanded to know what the Emperor intended to do. A few hundred members of the Urban Cohorts had been called out to maintain order, and their presence was keeping the crowd in check for the time being. The Urban Cohorts were not soldiers, but they were armed, and in their role as public enforcers of order, they had a reputation for violence which tended to dissuade most people from stirring up trouble. This being Rome, of course, riots were not uncommon, but things seemed to be under control as we eased our way through the noisy throng. The purple stripe on Fronto's tunic held the power to make people step aside, so we were able to edge our way fairly close to the doors of the Senate House. As usual, these doors were open as a nominal symbol that the Senate operated openly, but the guards who stood at the entrance would nevertheless prevent anyone entering unless they had been officially invited.

Even so, many Senators were normally only too happy to address the crowd when they left the building. They would step up onto the *rostra* in the public space and deliver a speech about whatever was on their mind. Sometimes these addresses were informative, while others could be extremely dull. Most were furiously heckled by the crowd.

Perhaps it was the angry mood of the mob, or perhaps it was the seriousness of the situation, but that afternoon the Senators remained inside the debating chamber. The Senate, it seemed, was locked in endless debate as to the best way to deal with the approaching rebel army, even though everyone knew the Senate had no power to achieve anything in a civil conflict. The Emperor controlled the army, so all the Senators could do was sit and make grand speeches which altered nothing except a few opinions within the Senate House.

And, all the time, every Senator knew that the current rebel leader could soon become their new Emperor. The uncertainty about who would rule meant that most Senators would make bland statements in case they said anything which could be construed as disloyal by whoever won the battle for the imperial throne.

"I can't say I envy them," I said to Fronto. "One wrong word, and they could find themselves accused of treason."

"Or rewarded for loyalty if their chosen man wins," he said. "But it's a gamble, right enough."

At that moment, the crowd stirred at the approach of someone new, coming from the direction of the palace. As people stepped back, I saw a group of *lictors* pushing a way through the crowd, holding up their *fasces*, the axes bound in bundles of rods which acted as a symbol of their authority. Behind them walked Fabius Successianus, wearing a formal toga over his senatorial tunic. He was striding confidently along behind the *lictors*, nodding to people in the crowd as he approached the Senate House.

People shouted questions at him, but he gave no answer, simply continuing his way towards the main entrance of the Senate House.

Fronto guessed, "He's coming with a message from the Emperor."

"I'd have thought Gallus would come himself," I murmured, unclear as to why a former Legionary Prefect was the one coming to address the Senators. "But I suppose loyalty like that is why Successianus has risen so far so quickly."

Fronto whispered, "Perhaps you are right. Maybe Gallus feels safer behind the walls of his palace."

"That's no way to rule," I frowned.

Successianus' eyes had been scanning the crowd as he walked, and he caught sight of me because I was at the very front. Immediately, he stopped, beckoning me to join him.

A hush fell over the people nearest to us, and I was very aware of the curious glances of hundreds of spectators as I crossed the cobbles to where Successianus waited.

"Scipio," he nodded. "I'm glad I saw you there."

"It's good to see you, Senator," I said warily, wondering why he had singled me out for this unwanted attention.

He told me, "I'm just going to address the Senate. The Emperor has issued orders for his army to march north to confront the rebels."

"Have the legions from Hispania arrived, then?" I asked.

"Not yet," Successianus replied, his tone suggesting that he believed they were not likely to arrive any time soon.

"But you still managed to persuade the Emperor to fight?"

Successianus' expression revealed nothing as he said, "The Emperor consulted with all his advisors, as he should do on such an important matter. The decision to march was his."

I gave a nod. Successianus was obviously destined for a career as a politician, having the ability to deliver that sort of line without laughing. What worried me was why he was telling me this before he had delivered the message to the Senators. I was hardly important enough to warrant that sort of preferential treatment.

Then he leaned a little closer, lowering his voice to a whisper as he said, "I'd like you to accompany me on the march."

"Me?" I gasped, almost taking a step backwards in shock. That was the last thing I had expected to hear. "What on earth for?"

Successianus, still with his serious face showing for the benefit of the crowd, said, "Because you have proven useful and resourceful. You may be able to help in some way."

I protested, "I doubt that, Senator. I've never been a soldier, and even if I had been, I'm too old to fight."

"Wars are not always won by those who carry swords," he said enigmatically. "Report to the Palatine tomorrow at dawn. I shall expect you."

And with that, he resumed his steady march to the Senate House, sweeping past me with all the self-importance of a man who had the Emperor's ear.

Fronto sidled up beside me, other members of the crowd shoving their way behind him as they tried to listen in.

"What was that all about?" he asked.

All I could do was shake my head in bewilderment.

"Buggered if I know," I said.

Naturally, I was at the palace by dawn the next day. I was tired of running and hiding, and I did not want an imperial arrest warrant being issued. So, with a wide-brimmed hat to ward off the sun, a cloak to keep me warm at night, and my battered old satchel slung over one shoulder, I trudged to the main entrance. There were Praetorians crowded around, blocking my way, but one of them turned and saw me, his long, pinched face breaking into a ghost of a smile.

"I'm told I'm to be your nursemaid again," Livius Mento informed me. "Come on, my lads are bringing horses for us. We can wait over there."

He led me to the other side of the paved road, taking up position beside a plinth which bore a more than life-sized statue of the Emperor.

"Do you have any idea what this is all about?" I asked him.

He shrugged, "None at all. I'm just following orders."

"Orders from Fabius Successianus?" I guessed.

"That's right. And I'm glad you turned up here, because I was told to go and fetch you if you didn't come voluntarily."

"That's what I don't understand," I said. "Why does Successianus want me here?"

Mento gave another shrug.

"I can't tell you that. But my orders are simply to keep you alive. That shouldn't be too difficult."

I grunted, "I suspect Aemilianus and his men might have something to say about that."

Mento fluttered one hand in a dismissive gesture.

"We'll worry about that when we meet them."

An hour later, mounted on a brown mare, with Mento's squad behind me, I joined the long procession of Praetorians who were accompanying the Emperor. I had caught a glimpse of Trebonianus Gallus when he emerged from the palace, wearing full armour beneath his purple cloak, and with a purple plume bobbing on his iron helmet. He gave a short speech which I could not hear but which brought a rousing cheer from the Praetorians closest to him, then he mounted his own horse and set off for the north.

Close beside him was Fabius Successianus who made a point of looking for me, nodding in satisfaction when he saw me.

We found the bulk of Gallus' army waiting a few miles outside the city, legionaries, cavalry and baggage train all prepared to march. So we headed north, the column stretching for several miles along the road, moving at the infantry's marching pace, with supply wagons rumbling slowly along near the rear.

"We are to stay close to the Emperor," Mento told me. "In case he wants to talk to you."

I could think of no reason why the Emperor would want to talk to me when he faced a battle for his life, but I followed Mento's advice, always staying within sight of the imperial entourage.

It was a slow, boring march, although I knew that the men on foot would not think so. They were going to war, and I could not help wondering how many of them would survive to make the return journey. What really concerned me, though, was the mood of the men. I had been with armies before, but these soldiers seemed in a grim, reflective mood as they marched their dust-covered way up the road in sweltering heat.

"The men's morale isn't good," I remarked to Mento that evening as we sat beside a small camp fire close to the tent his men shared. There was, fortunately, space for me because, technically, there were ten men in a squad. Mento, as Decurion, commanded the group which should have comprised eight soldiers including himself, plus a young recruit, usually a teenager learning the art of soldiering, and a slave to tend to menial chores like fetching water and cooking. Like many units, though, Mento's squad was under strength, and there were only the eight soldiers.

"I had enough trouble getting these seven lads as recruits," Mento told me. "As for a slave, we'd need to buy a horse for him as well, and we've never got around to it."

I understood what he meant. The Emperor's recruitment drive had been recent, and all of Mento's squad were young and inexperienced, not long having joined the Guard.

"Will there be fighting?" one of them asked nervously as we sat together.

"Probably," Mento said. "Just follow orders and remember your training, and you'll be fine."

"We'll win," said another, a broad-shouldered youth with a fresh complexion. "Licinius Valerianus is bringing fifty thousand men to join us."

"That's right," Mento nodded, not bothering to correct the lad on the number of troops Valerianus had promised to bring.

Then he looked up, pushing himself quickly to his feet as a figure stepped into the firelight. It was a Tribune, dressed in fine chainmail armour and with a gleaming helmet and wearing an expensive cloak around his shoulders.

"I'm looking for Sempronius Scipio," he announced.

"That's me," I said, rising to my feet.

"The Emperor would like a word with you," the Tribune told me.

I exchanged a look with Mento who gave a lop-sided grin.

"My orders are to stay with you," he assured me.

So we followed the Tribune to the imperial tent. Gallus could have slept in a bed in one of the many waystations, but he had chosen to sleep among his troops, although his tent was more like a marquee rather than the ridge-topped leather rectangles which most soldiers slept in. Deep inside this chambered pavilion, he was holding court in a large space draped with purple hangings, and sitting on a backless curule chair, with several senior officers sitting on less elegant stools in a semi-circle in front of him. Spaced around the leather and canvas walls stood slaves and Praetorians, ready to do the Emperor's bidding if called upon.

"Ah, Scipio," Gallus said when the Tribune had announced my arrival. "Successianus told me you wanted to come with us."

I glanced at Fabius Successianus who was sitting at the far end of the front row of advisors. He remained stone-faced as he returned my questioning look, almost daring me to challenge the Emperor's belief that I had requested to join the army.

I merely bobbed my head in the slightest of bows as I said, "Augustus."

Gallus told the assembled officers, "Scipio has been a great help to me in the past few months. He recently rode to meet with Licinius Valerianus."

Gallus turned his eyes on me, and I thought how much older he had become in the last few months. The strain of ruling, combined with the threats of plague, Persian invasion, Gothic raids and three rival claimants to his throne had clearly taken a toll. His face was thinner now, his hair greying, and the dark bags beneath his eyes remained prominent.

Yet there was still an air of command about him. In a stern voice, he asked me, "Valerianus promised to bring his cavalry, did he not?"

"He did, Augustus."

The corner of the Emperor's mouth twitched slightly, and his eyes narrowed as he demanded, "Then where is he? If he left within days of your departure from Moguntiacum, he should have reached Rome already. Yet here we are, north of the city, and there is still no sign of him."

I felt every eye upon me as I said, "I do not know, Augustus. He promised to come."

"You would not lie to me, would you, Scipio?"

I felt stung by that accusation, and I shook my head vigorously.

"Never, Augustus. I told you once before, I would always tell you the truth."

"Even though you are Valerianus' client?"

"Even so," I assured him.

I could sense the officers growing uneasy at this one-sided confrontation, but Successianus suddenly put in, "We know Scipio's worth, Augustus. He dealt with the problem of Mariades with incredible efficiency."

"And look what happened as a result!" the Emperor barked, thumping a fist to his knee. "The Persians overran Syria, and now I face yet another rival Emperor in the east."

"That was hardly Scipio's fault, Augustus," soothed Successianus. "Your army commanders in the east failed you."

I began to wonder whether I had been brought here as a scapegoat, but Gallus took a deep breath, visibly trying to calm himself.

"I am sorry, Scipio," he said softly. "But we need Valerianus. He promised you he would come, did he not?"

"He did, Augustus," I nodded, wondering how many times he would need this reassurance.

Successianus suggested, "We should send messengers north to find him. He may be close."

"Aemilianus is closer," the Emperor scowled. "He is now between us and Valerianus."

"Which is precisely where we want him," Successianus stated with confidence. "We shall be like a hammer and anvil. We will hold Aemilianus in place, then Valerianus will strike him hard."

Several of the officers nodded in agreement, although their tense expressions suggested they were not as confident about the future as Successianus was.

After a long moment, the Emperor gave me another reproachful look, then waved me away.

"You may go, Scipio. Pray that Valerianus keeps his promise."

I wasn't sure whether that was a threat or not, but what was very clear was that Trebonianus Gallus did not believe he could win the impending battle without Valerianus' help.

Chapter 32
First Contact

We ran into the rebel army less than one hundred Roman miles north of Rome. The news came from the mounted scouts Gallus had sent ahead of our line of march. Mento and I were close enough to see the riders galloping back to deliver their news, and the report rippled all along the line of march. Soon, orders were being shouted, and units left the road, extending into the countryside to form a battle line. Legionaries and the Praetorian infantry formed up into maniples, while the hired Auxiliaries were grouped in front and at either end of the main battle line.

The cavalry, relatively few in number, were stationed on each flank, and the scouts went out ahead again to watch for the approach of the enemy.

All of this took less than half an hour to organise, the soldiers' training having conditioned them to obey orders swiftly and efficiently, but the army looked pitifully small to my eyes. I had seen Roman armies before, and Persian ones too, come to that, and this force looked paltry in comparison. In all, I doubted Gallus had been able to scrape together more than twelve thousand men, and many of them were, like Mento's squad, raw and inexperienced.

Gallus sat on his horse, a magnificent black stallion, watching his troops take up their positions along the top of a low, gentle slope which led down to a narrow stream and a wide valley. There was a small village near the stream, and already the occupants were gathering up their belongings and fleeing westwards towards the hills.

I had passed this place several times on my various travels, but I had never really paid much attention to it. The village had some small fields, there was an olive grove on the far side of the valley, and a wide expanse of vineyards and pastures beyond that.

Mento informed me, "North of here, the land is owned by some Senator. It's a *latifundium* which is going to lose a lot of its value."

As so often with Mento, he delivered this information in a deadpan way which concealed any personal delight he might feel that a wealthy aristocrat was going to lose a lot of money. *Latifundia* were vast estates which were farmed intensively, the work being carried out by thousands of slaves. Owning land and earning a living from agricultural produce was viewed by many upper class Romans as the only way a proper Senator should earn profits. Of course, most of them had fingers in other pies, owning various types of business through their clients, but owning land was still what brought the greatest wealth. In the long-past days of the Republic, ordinary Romans had worked the land in small plots, but title to lands had gradually been hoarded by the wealthiest. If a Roman citizen farmer joined the army and died, his lands could be purchased. If drought or famine afflicted production so that farmers who owned small plots could no longer make a living, they could sell their land, usually for a knock-down price. In such difficult times, the only people who could afford to buy these small farms were the wealthy, and so rich men gradually accumulated larger and larger tracts of land, then had slaves imported to work the fields. This cheap and inexhaustible supply of labour allowed them to earn even more money from their investment. *Latifundia* were now the most common type of agricultural business, with most small landowners having sold their property long ago.

Mento, though, was now regarding the landscape with a soldier's eye.

"From a military point of view," he observed, "This is a decent enough position. Those hills to the west protect our right. Aemilianus can't advance down the road because it's far too narrow to allow an attack, so he'll need to come through the fields. That olive grove will slow him down and disrupt his formations. Then they'll need to get around the village which will mess them up again, and then cross the stream."

"So we should attack before they can re-organise?" I guessed.

"I'm no General," he admitted, "but that's what I'd do. I'd also put some archers in the village to slow the enemy down even more."

"I don't see any sign of that happening," I pointed out.

"Maybe the Emperor has other ideas," he said.

"You could ask him," I grinned. "Here he comes now."

Trebonianus Gallus had been riding along in front of his troops, speaking to each group as he passed them. At the end of the line, off to our right, he circled behind the Cohorts, then came riding back to where Mento and I waited behind the centre of the Praetorian ranks.

More than fifty men accompanied Gallus as he rode. There were Praetorians, Tribunes and his senior aides, including Fabius Successianus. All of them wore chainmail and carried swords. The Praetorians also had javelins and shields, and they looked suitably formidable.

Gallus curbed his black horse when he reached us, giving me another searching look.

"Aemilius Aemilianus is only a few miles north," he told me. "His army will be here soon."

I gave a nod, not sure what he expected me to say.

He went on, "But where is Licinius Valerianus? We have no news of him."

I was still unsure of what he wanted to hear. I had delivered his message, but he seemed to be harbouring a grudge against me for Valerianus' late arrival.

I said, "I do not know, Augustus."

I was developing a horrible feeling that Cornelia Gallonia's warning had been correct, and that Valerianus was going to attempt to seize the empire for himself. I briefly contemplated telling the Emperor this, but I decided against it. For one thing, I would have the problem of explaining why I had not passed on this information earlier. Perhaps it was my own cowardice that convinced me of the futility of relaying the warning now. I told myself that the only purpose it would serve would be to frighten the Emperor into turning back and running to Rome. That would gift control to Aemilius Aemilianus, but would still leave us with the prospect of facing civil war because Licinius Valerianus was still out there somewhere with his supposed forty thousand horsemen.

So, despite my mounting fear, I held my tongue.

Frowning, Gallus twisted in his saddle, turning to Successianus.

"Can we win if we stand here?" he wanted to know.

Successianus, always unflappable, nodded, "Of course, Augustus."

"He outnumbers us," Gallus pointed out. "Perhaps we should fall back to a suitable location and dig a fort."

Successianus replied smoothly, "That would not be wise, Augustus. To retreat and dig in would be seen as an admission of defeat. Besides, we will only know if he does outnumber us when we see his army."

The Emperor looked exactly like a man who knows he has been caught in a trap.

"Where is Licinius Valerianus?" he asked, apparently addressing the question to the sky.

He received no answer from either man or god.

So we waited. The soldiers took off their armour, ate food, fetched water from the stream, and rested. Mento and I did the same, although he made sure his squad took the horses to drink at the stream before he allowed them to eat anything themselves.

"Your horse can save your life," he told them. "Always look after it first."

Later, he and I strolled along the slope to look out over the field again.

Frowning, he said, "I think the Emperor was right."

"About what?" I asked, uncertain about his meaning.

"When he said we should fall back and dig a fort. If we bar the way south, Aemilianus would need to attack us, and we'd have a better chance of holding out until Licinius Valerianus arrives if we are behind a ditch and ramparts. That could make a difference when half of this lot are new recruits."

I recalled my conversation with Fronto when I had suggested that Trebonianus Gallus preferred sitting safely behind walls rather than taking risks. Building a fortified camp was something Roman soldiers could do very quickly, and it would certainly make our situation safer.

I suggested, "Couldn't Aemilianus simply by-pass a fort? He could leave a force to besiege us, then continue on his way to Rome."

"He could," Mento agreed. "But he needs to kill Gallus before the Senate will consider confirming him as Emperor."

I said, "Fabius Successianus seems confident we can win here."

Mento's long face twisted in a sour grimace as he sighed, "I wish I knew why. I see we still haven't fortified that village. It could act as a bulwark to hamper any advance, but we've left it unoccupied."

Once again, I silently questioned Successianus' motivation. Was he now working for Valerianus? Was he attempting to undermine Gallus so as to remove one claimant to the imperial throne?

I shook my head. Successianus was here. If we lost the battle, his own life was at risk. Would he really turn against his former comrade in arms in a way that might result in his own death? It seemed unlikely.

And yet the thought nagged at me all through the next few hours as we baked in the heat of the summer afternoon.

Mento said, "I suppose we have the advantage that Aemilianus' men are marching in this heat. They might be tired by the time they get here."

I suggested, "Perhaps they will stop and make camp themselves, then attack us in the morning."

Mento shrugged, "I suppose that will depend upon how keen Aemilianus is to fight. If he's in a hurry, he'll keep coming."

It turned out that Aemilianus was in a hurry. By late afternoon, I think most of us had decided that there would be no battle that day, but then the scouts came charging back across the low valley with the news that Aemilianus' own cavalry were less than a mile away. Soon, we could all see them as they reached the far side of the olive grove. And in the distance behind them was a faint cloud of dust marking the approach of thousands more men.

"Armour on!" came the shouted command. "Saddle up! Weapons at the ready!"

The men scrambled to prepare, but there was no real need for urgency. Aemilianus' scouts rode cautiously down the far slope, picking their way between the gnarled olive trees, then halted while a few of their number rode into the village. Once they were satisfied that Gallus had not garrisoned the houses, they rode back up the slope again. Some of them remained on the far slope, keeping an eye on us, but others rode away, no doubt to deliver the news of our location to Aemilianus.

Before long, more rebel horsemen came into view, spreading out to either side, creating room for the infantry. We heard the drums and horns before we saw the legionaries marching beneath their standards. As Mento had predicted, their formation was disrupted by the olive trees, but they passed through swiftly, then re-formed once clear of the obstacles.

I think every one of us was counting them as more and more men joined their battle line. Counting standards was the easiest way to do this, for each unit held its own long staff which held a banner nailed to a cross-piece. Each standard usually marked a Century of up to eighty men, so it was easy enough to estimate the size of their army. Our count kept increasing as more and more of them came into view, creating a pattern as each Maniple took up position facing us.

Five thousand.
Eight thousand.
Ten thousand.
Fifteen thousand.
Twenty thousand.

"Nearly twenty-five thousand," Mento said in his matter-of-fact voice. "More than I'd expected. He must have stripped the frontier."

"They are not all legionaries, though," I pointed out. "At least half of them must be Auxiliaries."

"They can still fight," Mento reminded me. "The frontier troops have seen plenty of action in the past few years."

I checked the position of the sun in the sky.

"It will be dark in a couple of hours," I said.

"There's still plenty of time for a battle," Mento replied grimly.

Then came the usual round of talking. Aemilianus sent emissaries to demand that Trebonianus Gallus step down as Emperor and cede the title. Gallus sent his own heralds who, naturally, refused on his behalf. Both sides knew that his life would have been cut short if he had accepted, because no Emperor would allow a rival to continue living. After exchanging demands, both sets of emissaries returned to their own army.

Mounted on my horse, I had a good view of the battlefield even though I was some way behind the leading ranks of soldiers. Looking across to the rebel army, I saw Aemilianus. Like Gallus, he had a host of riders following him as he rode up and down among his soldiers, delivering his speech to them. He was too far away to make out any details, but I could see the dark purple of his cloak over his armour.

"This is not right!" I exclaimed. "Romans should not be fighting Romans."

Mento muttered, "It's how things are these days."

He sounded old and cynical far beyond his years, but he was right. Ambitious men had long ago learned that whoever controlled the army could win the empire, and the soldiers had learned that they would be rewarded for helping their commander seize power. Once stable under firm rule, the empire had become like a damaged toy being fought over by squabbling children.

We were sitting on horseback, some thirty paces back from where the Emperor and his followers were stationed. I saw Gallus turn around to cast an accusing look at me. He was too far away to ask his question, but I knew what he was thinking.

"Where is Licinius Valerianus?"

I wished I knew the answer to that. Had he lied to me? Had Cornelia Gallonia been right all along? Was Valerianus merely biding his time, waiting to see who won? It was the tactic Uranius Antoninus, one-time Priest-King of Emesa and now a rival Emperor in his own right, had told me he would adopt in this sort of situation.

And then there was no more time to concern ourselves with Valerianus because the battle sprang to life. Aemilianus clearly wanted to deal with Trebonianus Gallus without delay. His archers ran forwards and began loosing volleys of arrows, and his cavalry charged up the gentle slope on our right flank, while others tried to circle around our left flank which extended beyond the road we were blocking.

Our own cavalry made a counter-charge, and the clash of weapons, the screaming of men and horses, and the clouds of mud and dust brought back memories of too many such sights I had seen in the past two years.

Then Aemilianus' legions were advancing, marching forwards in grim silence, a tactic often used by Roman armies to instil fear into their opponents. Most armies used horns, drums and cheers to rouse the spirits and bravery of their soldiers, but Romans had long ago developed the silent advance to intimidate their foes, telling them that they needed no encouragement to face and deal out death.

"Hold firm!" Gallus shouted, his Tribunes galloping along the line to relay the order. "Stand your ground!"

The rebels trampled the crops in the village field, then climbed the slope, facing little opposition. Gallus had few archers, and their arrows made little impact on the horde which was now advancing up the slope. Aemilianus' own archers continued to shoot, arcing their arrows over the heads of their infantry, forcing our troops to raise their shields over their heads. Some arrows came near us as ambitious archers attempted to strike Gallus himself, but we were far enough behind the front line to keep us relatively safe.

The tension in the air was incredible. I had to force myself to take a breath. I had seen battles before, but I had rarely been so close to the fighting, and I could feel the fear coursing through my body. I wore no armour, and I carried nothing more lethal than a small knife. Even with Mento's squad to protect me, I felt horribly vulnerable, especially because the rebel archers were drawing closer as they followed the legionaries up the slope.

More and more arrows came closer to the Emperor, falling down with considerable force despite the range from which they were being loosed. One dropped into the rump of a Praetorian horse, causing the wounded animal to rear, throwing its rider from the saddle. There was a metallic ringing as another arrow struck the helmet of a second Praetorian, but the men who formed the Emperor's personal bodyguard were seasoned veterans, so they did not panic, simply moving to fill the gap in their ranks.

But many of the soldiers among the infantry were not as hardened as the Emperor's protectors, and now they faced the toughest soldiers in the entire Roman army.

"Hold steady!" I heard someone shout from among the nearest Cohort. "Front rank! Javelins! Rear ranks, shields raised!"

This heralded the next phase of the battle. The rebels paused in their advance to hurl their own javelins, with Gallus' troops returning the favour. I heard the clash of metal tips striking armour and shields, and I heard the cries of men who were struck. Some in the rebel army fell, but not many, with a similar result on our side. The effect, though, was quite different. The rebels drew their swords, then broke into a run, charging up the last part of the slope, while our own army seemed to waver. Then there was a loud roar as men vented their fear and hate, and the two sides crashed together, shield to shield and sword to sword.

The Roman army had developed its tactics over centuries, disdaining the solid phalanx of men standing shoulder to shoulder. Instead, they fought with room for each man to move, and with support coming from the men behind. Thousands of individual combats sparked all along the slope, with men in the second row of each Cohort stepping in to help their comrades in the front rank. Swords flashed, men ducked, parried, lunged, swung their shields and tried to kill the man facing them before he could deliver a fatal blow.

It was both fascinating and horrible, but it did not last long. Morale, I knew, was an important factor in war, and Gallus' army was sadly lacking, while Aemilianus' troops, toughened by years of fighting barbarians, were supremely confident.

The break came far out on the right flank, where the superior numbers and skill of Aemilianus' cavalry had driven the Praetorian horsemen back. This created a gap, and the rebels charged in, smashing into the flank of one Cohort of Auxiliary infantrymen. The Auxiliaries broke and ran, discarding their weapons, the rebel horsemen charged on, and Gallus' entire line crumbled.

I do not know who gave the order, or whether any order was given at all, but some of our men turned to flee, desperately scrambling to escape from the rebel swords. Those who still fought were being forced backwards, the centre of our line bending inwards while the right flank continued to disintegrate as the rebel cavalry ran amok.

The Emperor's entourage realised they were in danger. Someone grabbed the reins of Gallus' black stallion, and then the whole imperial staff were turning to flee.

"We're beaten!" Mento shouted, straining to be heard over the din around us. "Follow the Emperor!"

We hauled our own horses around. They were already skittish thanks to the raging battle in front of us and the presence of other horses riding back past them, so they needed little encouragement to follow the rout. As we urged our mounts into a gallop, I twisted around to see that the infantry ranks had collapsed, and that many men were fleeing in our wake, while others had thrown down their weapons in surrender.

It had all happened so astonishingly quickly after the long tedium of the armies arraying themselves to face one another, and now we were racing southwards again, presumably heading for Rome.

But what then? With his army beaten, what could Trebonianus Gallus do if he wished to remain Emperor?

And why, I asked myself, was I following him?

Chapter 33
Fatal Results

I hoped that the coming of twilight might save us, but the glory of catching the Emperor was too strong a lure to dissuade all of Aemilianus' cavalry to let us go. Some of them must have stopped to plunder the bodies of the men they had killed, or to rob prisoners of any valuables, but Mento, risking a glance back over his shoulder, cursed, "There must be a few hundred of them chasing us!"

We had a good lead, and our horses were fresher than those of our pursuers, but I was still terrified. I clung to the saddle horns in front of me, the reins loosely looped around my hands, as I let the horse have its head. Up ahead, one of the Emperor's Praetorians fell when his horse stumbled on uneven ground, man and beast crashing to the ground with horrible consequences for both. The horse broke a leg, screaming its pain as it thrashed on the ground, while the Praetorian lay very still, either dead or unconscious. Nobody stopped to offer aid. We galloped on, racing into the diminishing light as the sun edged towards the western horizon.

"There's a town up ahead!" Mento called, trying to give his men encouragement. "We'll beat them to it!"

The town sat a little way off the main road. It had walls, although they were not very tall, nor substantial enough to withstand a siege by a determined attacker. I could see the tiny shapes of men's heads peering out over the ramparts as we thundered towards the nearest gate.

The riders ahead of us began to slow, and then I realised why.

"The gates are shut!" Mento hissed as he hauled on his reins to slow his panting horse.

We all reined in, our group clustering to one side of the Emperor's retinue, some horses milling around as men looked nervously back to check on the pursuit.

At the front of the crowd, the Emperor rode a little way forwards, looking up to the city wall above the barred gate.

"I am Trebonianus Gallus, Emperor of Rome! I command you to open the gates!"

His voice sounded high-pitched and anxious, carrying more than a hint of desperation. It was an emotion I could appreciate. In moments, the rebels would catch us, and then there would be a slaughter.

But silence was the only response to the Emperor's appeal. There was no longer any sign of anyone on the town walls. It was as if the inhabitants had closed the gates, then slunk away to their homes. The Emperor repeated his demand, but nobody answered.

As I watched, sweating and breathing as heavily as my horse after our gallop, I saw Fabius Successianus move his horse alongside the Emperor. Successianus was on Gallus' right, so close that the men's legs touched. Gallus, though, did not appear to notice. He continued to shout up at the walls, demanding that the gates be opened, his voice growing ever more frantic.

Successianus moved in his saddle, swinging one arm at the Emperor, then Gallus stiffened before letting out a strangled cough, then slowly toppling from his saddle. His magnificent black stallion snorted and tossed its mane, trotting away from where its rider had fallen to the ground. Gallus was gasping and kicking, but his movements soon stopped, and he lay on his back, very still, his eyes staring sightlessly up at the darkening sky. His throat was a dark patch, stained by blood.

Successianus, turning his horse to face us, wiped clean the dagger he had used to punch a hole through Gallus' neck.

"Take off his helmet, then remove his head!" he snapped at the closest Praetorians. "Quickly, or we'll all suffer!"

Two men jumped down, hurrying to the corpse. They yanked off the dead Emperor's helmet, then one of them hacked at the corpse's neck with his sword.

"Give it to me!" Successianus urged, reaching for the grisly trophy. Gripping Gallus' head by the hair, he eased his horse away from the town, moving to face the pursuing rebels who were now very close to us.

"Form up!" ordered one of the Tribunes, and the shocked Praetorians jostled to place themselves behind Successianus. Mento, though, kept his squad off to one side, perhaps preparing to make one last, desperate attempt to escape if Successianus' ploy failed.

"He's got some balls," I'll say that for him," Mento growled as we watched Successianus ride out to meet the rebels, holding aloft the proof of his betrayal.

The rebels had yelped in delight when they saw us trapped outside the town, but now they slowed, some of them spreading out as if to encircle us.

"Trebonianus Gallus is dead!" I heard Successianus shout at the top of his voice. "Hail Aemilianus Augustus Caesar!"

Our fate hung in the balance. The rebel cavalry outnumbered us considerably, and they might decide that they could gain even greater wealth and glory by killing us all. Then they could loot our corpses and take Gallus' head back to Aemilianus with a tale of their own bravery.

Successianus must have known this too, because his next shout stopped them in their tracks.

"There is no need for anyone else to die!" he bellowed. "The war is over!"

The sun had vanished beyond the distant hills now, but the sky was still just light enough to make out some details of the men facing us. They were a mixed bag, many of them probably recruited from Germanic or Gothic tribes, but few of them were keen to be first to tackle thirty Praetorians. They would win, but some of them would be killed or wounded in the process.

Successianus went on, "Take us back to Aemilianus. I will see that he rewards you for bringing him the head of his enemy."

"We could take it from you!" came a voice from the dark mass of rebels.

"You could," agreed Successianus. "But why risk losing your life when you have already won? Besides, we have information our Emperor needs to hear."

His claim of unity with these tough riders made little impact. One, wearing a fur-trimmed cloak and holding a sword in his right hand, called, "What information?"

"Information that may prevent him losing the empire he has so recently won," Successianus replied. "Now, let us ride back together. The Emperor must see that he has won, and he must hear our news."

For a long moment, I thought the rebels would decide to kill us anyway, but the man in the fur-lined cloak gave a nod.

"Very well," he said. "Come, then."

So we set off, retracing our desperate gallop, and leaving behind the headless corpse of the man who had been our Emperor. It had been a sudden and brutal ending to his reign, betrayed by the man he had trusted most in the world. And yet, I knew, if

Successianus had not killed him, all of us would by now be dead or prisoners.

We moved at a slow trot as the gloom gathered about us. Successianus took the lead, riding alongside the rebel commander, still holding Gallus' head in his left fist.

"He's a cool one," Mento sighed as we followed, all too aware that the men who had so recently been chasing us were now riding all around us, keeping us penned in.

It was full dark, with our way now lit by moon and stars, by the time we encountered the bulk of Aemilianus' army. They had moved a little way south of the battle site, and were busy digging a marching camp, their work lit by flaming torches.

Challenges were called and answered, and we rode on, heading into the large, almost empty rectangle of the camp. No tents had been pitched, only a handful of fires lit, and the place seemed eerily barren.

Over the noise of our horses, I heard Successianus call, "Sempronius Scipio! To me!"

Puzzled, I glanced at Mento who gave a shrug. Then he and I rode up to join the Senator.

He gave me a firm nod when I drew alongside him.

"You will tell Aemilius Aemilianus about Licinius Valerianus," he said. It was most definitely an order, not a question or a request. This, I realised, was the important news he had spoken of when convincing Aemilianus' cavalry to let us live.

"I can do that," I nodded.

"Good. Tell it well, Scipio. Tell him everything you know. Our lives may depend on your words."

His eyes were bright in the moonlight, but his expression remained as stony as ever as he added, "You have a reputation as being good at that sort of thing."

I muttered, "Let's hope my luck doesn't run out this time."

Successianus merely gave me another nod of encouragement.

Around us, the camp was slowly filling up. Mules and supply wagons were being led in, the cavalry were staking a claim for the northern part of the growing fort, and a few tents were now being erected in neat rows, lining up with the small flags which had been pushed into the ground to mark the places allocated for each unit.

My focus, though, was on the knot of men who were gathered around a fire near the spot where the *Principia* of any Roman camp would normally be located. We stopped some way short of this, then Successianus dismounted. The commander of the cavalry did likewise, while the rest of us waited.

Successianus turned back to look at me.

"Come with me," he commanded.

My heart was pounding as Mento and I followed him as he strode purposefully towards the men around the fire. They had all risen to their feet to face us.

"Hail, Augustus Caesar!" Successianus proclaimed as he drew near. He held up the head he still clutched in his left hand. "I bring you the head of Trebonianus Gallus."

It was clear who the new Emperor was. Aemilius Aemilianus may have been in the centre of the group, but he stood apart from them, their deference plain to see even in the firelit gloom. He was a tall man, with swarthy skin and bright eyes, his stature and complexion confirming his Moorish ancestry.

"Fabius Successianus," he said, clearly recognising the Senator. "I thought you had sworn loyalty to Gallus."

"As did we all," Successianus answered smoothly. "But my primary loyalty is to Rome, and it is clear the gods have favoured you, Augustus."

After saying this, he tossed the head towards Aemilianus' feet. It bounced and rolled, landing close to the newly proclaimed Emperor's boots. He glanced down at it as if to confirm that it was Gallus' head, then he idly kicked it to one side.

"Throw it in the camp ditch!" he ordered.

One of his aides bent, picked up the gory proof of Aemilianus' triumph, then hurried away.

Successianus said, "Augustus, there is important news you must hear."

Aemilianus cocked his head to one side in question.

"What is that?"

Successianus gestured towards me.

"This man is Sempronius Scipio. He was recently sent to Gaul by Gallus. He has news you must hear."

Aemilianus' hawk-like features turned to me, and I heard Successianus whisper, "Make it good. And make it loud. Let them all hear."

I cleared my throat, acknowledged Aemilianus with a nod of my head, then began, "Augustus, Trebonianus Gallus feared you so much that he sent me with a message to Licinius Valerianus, Governor of Gaul and commander of the army of the Rhenus frontier."

Once again, I found myself the centre of a great deal of attention. I still had no idea what Successianus' ultimate aim was, but all I could do was tell the truth as I knew it.

"Valerianus has raised a force of forty thousand cavalry. He promised to ride south to join with Gallus, but I heard from someone close to him that he actually intends to claim the Purple for himself."

There was a tense silence before Aemilianus asked, "And what do you think he intends to do?"

I said, "I do not know, Augustus. I do know that Valerianus has a great deal of support in the Senate, that he is an ambitious man who cannot be trusted, and that he claims to have a very large army."

"You do not trust him?" Aemilianus asked, seeming amused by my comment.

"I have known him too long to trust him," I replied.

Aemilianus' teeth flashed white in the darkness at this. He probably knew Valerianus as well as I did.

With an expansive wave of one hand, he said, "Well, we shall rest tonight, and tomorrow we will plan how best to deal with Licinius Valerianus."

Successianus and I were invited to join Aemilianus for a hasty and rather meagre supper while Mento and his troop were ordered to rejoin the rest of the Praetorians. The Auxiliary cavalry who had escorted us to the camp also went to rejoin their comrades, no doubt to relate the tale of how Gallus had met his end.

All around us, tents were being put up. The legionaries who had dug the camp's perimeter ditch and hammered wooden stakes into the top of the earth wall they had created, were now helping to complete the interior of the fort. Food and wine were being distributed, while the medical teams assessed and bandaged wounds.

Aemilianus was in an expansive mood. Considering his success in the battle, that was understandable.

"Gallus' troops have sworn loyalty to me now," he informed us. "There will be a formal parade tomorrow morning where the entire army will repeat that pledge before we resume our march towards Rome."

I could not tell whether he was being sarcastic or not. There had been so many Emperors in recent years that such oaths were easily broken.

Aemilianus must have understood this because he told us, "The Praetorians are here now, but the men of my own legions will be my guards tonight."

He obviously feared treachery, but Successianus nodded approvingly, "That is a sensible precaution, Augustus."

Aemilianus went on, "If it were not for the fact that Rome is so short of troops, I would disband the Praetorians and replace them with my own men."

"That has been done before, Augustus," Successianus agreed.

"I'm not sure I can afford to do it, though," Aemilianus confessed. Then, with a fierce smile, he added, "Although I'm not sure I can afford not to."

He was probing, but Successianus gave nothing away, simply saying, "I am sure you will reach an appropriate decision, Augustus."

Aemilianus mused, "Perhaps I could dissolve the current Guard and have them sent to various legions in different parts of the empire. Splitting them up might work. Then I could create a new Guard from among my loyal legions."

Again, Successianus nodded, "That might work, Augustus."

I sensed more than a little distrust between the two men, and I supposed that was understandable. They had been on opposite sides of the war only a few hours ago. But Gallus was dead, and Aemilianus had the backing of the army, so he remained outwardly cheerful in spite of the impending threat of Valerianus' arrival.

The new Emperor asked me several questions about my relationship with Valerianus, and about my recent trip to deliver Gallus' appeal for help. I was vague on my past dealings with Valerianus, but told the truth about my hurried visit to Moguntiacum, omitting only Gallonia's identity as the source of my information.

"Forty thousand cavalry, you say?" Aemilianus pressed.

"That is what he told me, Augustus."

"So he could have been exaggerating?"

"It's possible, Augustus."

"And does the Senate know of this?" he asked.

Successianus replied, "Only in broad terms, Augustus. They know that Valerianus promised to bring an army, but they do not know how large it is claimed to be."

Aemilianus' white teeth flashed again in the moonlight as he said, "So if I reach Rome tomorrow, I can have the Senate confirm me as Emperor. Then I can declare Valerianus as an enemy of the State if he does not acknowledge me."

It was a statement which required no answer. Whether it would end the strife was debatable, though. Valerianus was too dangerous to be left alive, and he might decide to stake everything on continuing the war.

If the new Emperor was thinking about any of this, he concealed it well. Ostentatiously, he covered a yawn with one hand, then said, "Well, it has been an eventful day. I think I will retire for the night."

The Emperor's tent had been erected not far from where we sat huddled around the camp fire. The men had worked by the light of the moon and stars, but that had not really hindered them as they were well accustomed to the art of creating a marching camp. Normally, the work would be completed before nightfall, but the late climax to the battle had precluded that.

Rising to his feet, Aemilianus said, "The camp will be woken at the usual time. That is only a few hours away, so I suggest you all try to get some sleep."

He headed into the vastness of the tented *Principia*, which I suspected had been looted from Gallus' supply wagons only a short time before. A handful of Tribunes and other aides followed him.

Successianus and I were allocated a small tent nearby, the two of us sharing the type of leather tent used by the legionaries. As we settled in, we could still hear the raucous sounds of men celebrating their victory, but those were soon silenced by the bellows of the Centurions who demanded quiet.

Successianus said softly, "It does not do to flaunt your triumph when your former enemies are sharing the camp with you."

"No," I nodded. "But I notice that there are legionaries standing guard close to our tent. I don't think Aemilianus trusts us."

In response, Successianus said softly, "He is right to be cautious. He trusts his own men."

I was incredibly tired, so I lay down on the ground, pulling a borrowed blanket over me as I used my old satchel for a pillow. Inside the tent, it was almost completely dark, but I was aware of Successianus' presence beside me, and I knew I needed answers to the questions burning inside my head.

I asked him, "How long have you been in league with Licinius Valerianus?"

I heard his breathing momentarily stop as if my question had caught him off guard, but his voice was perfectly calm when he replied, "I have been in contact with him for some time. That is not the same as being in league with him."

"So whose side are you on?" I asked. "I have it on good authority that he seeks the Purple for himself."

"A matter which you did not reveal to Trebonianus Gallus," he pointed out.

Mention of the recently murdered Emperor reminded me that Successianus had displayed no qualms about killing his former friend. No doubt he would dispose of me with the same lack of concern if he believed I was a threat to his plans, but I could not let this matter drop.

I said, "Gallus was a decent man. I don't know much about Aemilianus, but he seems to have the loyalty of the troops."

"Loyalty is fickle," Successianus said from the darkness.

Ignoring his remark, I went on, "I do know Licinius Valerianus, and I was not joking when I said I do not trust him."

Successianus was silent for a moment, then he said softly, "Gallus was a good Governor, but he lacked the resolve required by a good Emperor. He created his own downfall through his weakness."

Recalling my conversation with Fronto, I could not disagree with Successianus' assessment.

He went on, "If Valerianus really does seek to become Emperor, we have a decision to make."

I said, "I am loyal to Rome. I don't choose who should rule."

"But I am a Senator," Successianus reminded me. "Recently elevated, certainly, but that does give me some influence."

"Influence over whom?" I asked him.

He did not answer. Instead, he said, "Aemilianus is a talented man, and he might make a good Emperor. But the Senate will never fully accept him. He is, after all, from barbarian stock."

"So you are going to back Valerianus?" I guessed.

"I intend to do what is best for Rome," he replied.

I heard him move, and for a moment I feared he was about to use his dagger on me in order to silence me, but instead he shuffled to the tent's entrance flap. I heard him untying the cords which held the flap shut.

"Stay here," he told me. "I have things I need to do."

And then I was alone in the tent, staring up at the emptiness around me, and wondering what Successianus planned to do.

I was asleep by the time he returned. I woke to hear him fumbling in the dark as he sought out his blanket.

Sleepily, I asked him, "What is happening?"

"Nothing yet," he replied in a whisper. "Get some sleep. It will be dawn soon."

I was exhausted, but I could not get back to sleep. Successianus began to snore, while I lay awake, listening to the sounds outside our tent but hearing nothing out of the ordinary. Patrolling sentries marched past from time to time, mules brayed, and soldiers snored, but nothing disturbed the night apart from the distant bark of a fox.

I must have dozed again without realising it, because I was jerked awake by the sound of horns summoning the soldiers to the beginning of a new day. The leather tent was suffused with dim light as dawn broke, and both Successianus and I wearily clambered to our feet. I rubbed at the stubble on my chin, wondering whether I would have time to have a shave, but Successianus announced, "I must go to the *Principia*."

I helped him don his armour and, with nothing better to do, I stumbled along after him. The sky was light in the east now, and the camp was coming to life. Fires were being fed to heat water, and soldiers were busy pulling on their chainmail tunics. It promised to be another fine day, but there was an odd atmosphere, and I noticed many of the soldiers shooting expectant looks at Successianus as we walked towards Aemilianus' command tent.

There were legionaries on duty at the entrance to the huge marquee. Nearby, the Eagle standards of the various legions had been planted in the round, and the *signifers* stood beside them, guarding those sacred emblems which represented the spirit of each legion. Successianus stopped as he passed them, and his eyes focused on one in particular.

I stopped, following his gaze, and saw it was the standard of *Legio I Italica*, the legion he had commanded at Novae. So those men were here, having joined Aemilianus' army and marched on Rome to confront the man who had led the defence of Novae against the Goths. War, I reflected, brought about too many such situations.

"Is all well, Vinius?" Successianus asked the signifer who guarded the standard.

The man saluted him and barked, "The legion stands ready, Sir!"

Successianus nodded, then he caught sight of me watching him, and his stony expression softened slightly as a faint smile played around his lips.

Then he moved on, heading towards the main entrance to the vast tent. Here, a Centurion met him, a man aged around forty, his chest bedecked with medals which hung from coloured ribbons around his neck. This man was clearly a veteran, and he looked vaguely familiar. I supposed he must have been at Novae as well. I was close enough to see him meet Successianus' eye, then say softly, "It is done."

Successianus nodded, "Call the army to parade."

The Centurion stepped out, bellowing orders, and soon the horns were blasting again. Every man in the camp came quickly, forming up into their various units in the open space in front of the *Principia*.

Successianus waited patiently, and several Tribunes emerged from the Headquarters tent to join him. None of them spoke, but many of them exchanged nervous glances, and I had a horrible feeling I knew what had happened during the night.

I watched as the legions shuffled into ranks. The Praetorians were there, standing off to one side, and I noticed Mento standing in the front row, his face set in a grim frown. Like me, he must have figured out what was happening.

When the army was gathered, Successianus strode forwards to address the troops. His voice sounded confident and strong in the still morning air.

"Soldiers of Rome!" he shouted. "You have all done your duty to your chosen Emperor, but this has led us all to a dangerous position. All of you fought well yesterday, even those of you who, like me, followed Trebonianus Gallus. But the gods decided that Aemilius Aemilianus should be the victor, and we must all acknowledge that fact."

He paused, scanning their faces. Most of them looked confused, wondering why Successianus was addressing them instead of their chosen Emperor, but the men of *Legio I* were grinning happily.

Successianus continued, "Despite your valour, we are in grave danger. You will have heard by now that Publius Licinius Valerianus has come from Gaul with over forty thousand cavalry."

He paused again, letting that sink in.

He went on, "I do not need to tell you that we cannot face a force of that size in open battle. Nor can we sit here behind the ditch and rampart of our camp. Valerianus' army can blockade us in here, and he can ride on to Rome to claim the empire."

Again he surveyed them, and I could see that they, too, were beginning to understand.

"It is not right that Romans should fight fellow Romans!" he barked, raising his voice to emphasise the point. "No more honest soldiers need to die. There is only one solution which will save us, and I stand here in front of you to tell you that action has been taken."

At that, without any other signal, another Centurion strode out of the *Principia*, holding high the head of Aemilius Aemilianus.

There was a collective gasp, including some groans of dismay, but the veteran Centurion roared, "Valerianus! Imperator!"

The shout was instantly taken up by the men of Successianus' old command, and soon every soldier was joining in, proclaiming their new Emperor.

I looked all around, trying to gauge the reaction of the senior officers. Some of the Legates and Tribunes looked shocked, others resigned to what had been done. Successianus had made his choice, and the men of his old legion had clearly backed him.

As the shouting subsided, another cry was heard from the sentries on the ramparts.

"Cavalry! Cavalry to the north! Thousands of them!"

Heads turned, but our view was blocked by the earth rampart of our camp.

Successianus shouted, "Stand still!"

His cry was taken up by the Centurions, discipline holding the army in place.

Then came more shouts, following in quick succession.

"Cavalry to the east!"

"Cavalry to the west!"

"Cavalry to the south!"

Successianus commanded, "Open the gates!"

The gates were little more than tree trunks laid across trestles, but they were pulled aside, admitting the first riders. Twenty of them trotted in, spears held with their points to the morning sky.

Behind them rode a man wearing a purple cloak over his chainmail, a crested helmet on his head. As he drew nearer, I could not fail to recognise his plump cheeks and prominent eyes.

"Valerianus! Imperator!" came the acclamation again, the sound echoing all around the camp.

Horns blared a fanfare, swords and spears were thumped against shields to add to the bedlam, and I saw Successianus walk towards Valerianus, bowing his head in welcome.

I felt utterly dejected. There had been an inevitability about this, and I knew it was useless to rail against fate, but I could feel guilt gnawing at my soul. Cornelia Gallonia had been right all along, but I had made no effort to prevent her husband's rise to power. Now, Rome had yet another Emperor, and all I could do was stand there, fearing for the empire.

Author's Note and Acknowledgements

By the year 250CE, the period known as Rome's Third Century Crisis was well under way. Under attack from beyond its borders, the empire simply did not have enough manpower to protect its long frontiers. The Goths, a large confederation of Germanic tribes, became a real power around this time, and the invasion of Cniva was a dreadful blow to the empire. Not only did he sack two important cities, he ambushed the army of Emperor Decius, and displayed a talent for deception in persuading the hapless Titus Julius Priscus, Governor of Thrace, to open the gates of Philippopolis. He then lured Decius into a double ambush in the marshes near the village of Abritus, leaving the empire without a ruler. Not much else is known about Cniva, but I must confess that he probably did not have a son named Aoric who is a fictional creation of my own.

With Decius dead, Trebonianus Gallus, the most senior Roman commander left alive, was proclaimed Emperor. There has been much debate about Gallus' motivations and actions, but he does seem to have become Emperor by doing very little except surviving. Most of what I have written about him in this story is my own invention, although the story is based on recorded events.

There is no doubt, however, that Gallus faced unprecedented problems. He persuaded the Goths to leave, and he promised to pay further tribute, but he was unable to do so when the plague struck Rome. This plague is normally referred to as the Cyprian plague because our records of it come from the writings of Thaschus Cæcilius Cyprianus, Bishop of Carthage, who himself became a victim of the pestilence. The plague afflicted the empire and lands beyond for several years, but it is still unclear as to what disease it actually was. Some historians believe it may have been smallpox or measles, but the contemporary accounts describe symptoms which are more akin to a haemorrhagic fever such as Ebola. Whatever it was, it had a devastating effect on all parts of the empire.

While this was happening, there was unrest in many places. The rebellion of Mariades is reported, although details of how it arose and why Mariades suddenly fled to Persia are scarce. My own interpretation is almost entirely fictional. But Mariades did flee, and the Persians did attack, destroying the Roman army which had been sent to put down Mariades' rebellion. It was the ruler of Emesa, Uranius Antoninus, who rallied the people and threw the Persians back, although it must be said that the presence of plague in Syria may have contributed to the hasty Persian withdrawal.

Then came another Gothic attack on a vast scale. Their ships sailed down from the Black Sea to sack the Temple of Artemis, one of the Seven Wonders of the ancient world which has featured in previous Scipio stories. They also launched a major land attack across the Danube, but this was beaten back by Aemilius Aemilianus who appears in the historical records only briefly. All we can really say about him is that he was of Moorish descent and was a highly capable military commander. As happened so often, his troops proclaimed him Emperor after his victories over the Goths, and he marched towards Rome, then encountered Gallus' army. Whether there was a battle of any sort is a matter of conjecture, but something persuaded Gallus' troops to turn on him. His head was presented to Aemilianus.

Whether Aemilianus' army changed its mind immediately or after a delay of some days is not really known, but it cannot have taken long for Licinius Valerianus to draw near. Aemilianus' confrontation with Gallus took place less than one hundred miles from Rome, yet he had no time to complete the journey before word of Valerianus' impending arrival reached his army. The troops, unwilling to face Valerianus' superior force, decided to do away with the man they had so recently proclaimed as Emperor, and switched their allegiance to Valerianus instead, presenting him with Aemilianus' head as proof of their new loyalty.

In the Scipio stories, I have painted Valerianus as the villain of the piece. That is my invention, but it does fit quite neatly with the known events in Valerianus' life. I may have done him an injustice, but the dictates of storytelling require a dangerous antagonist, and this role has fallen to Valerianus.

As for his wife, Cornelia Gallonia, I have been able to learn nothing about her except her name, so her character as femme fatale in this story is entirely my own invention.

As for the character who played such an important part in the betrayal of Trebonianus Gallus, there is a brief historical record of a man named Fabius Successianus who rose to prominence under Valerianus. Very little is known about him except his name and his later role, so I have invented this back story for him. There is, as far as I can ascertain, no historical record of him having played any part in the events outlined in this story, but I needed a character, and he came in useful.

As always with this confusing period in history, records are scarce and often contradictory. Some historians might place specific events in a different chronological order, but I hope my narrative presents a reasonably coherent and broadly accurate timeline. It is, though, a fictional tale, although I have tried to place it against actual historical events.

As for Scipio, his dealings with the new Emperor Valerianus (normally known to us as Emperor Valerian) are not over. The Crisis of the Third Century still has more in store for both of them.

As always, my volunteer team of friends and family have been vital in getting this story knocked into shape. Moira Anthony and Liz Wright did sterling work on spotting the many typos in the first draft, while Stuart Anthony, Ian Dron and Stewart Fenton provided comments and advice on plenty of other aspects of the story I had bungled. Stuart also prepared the document for publication and came up with the cover design. My thanks to all of them for their invaluable help. Without them, the Scipio stories would probably never get any further than the hard drive of my PC.

GA
April, 2025

Other Books by Gordon Anthony

Most titles are available from Amazon in both paperback and e-book format. Titles marked with an asterisk are only available in e-book format from the Amazon Kindle store.

In the Shadow of the Wall
An Eye For An Eye
Hunting Icarus
Home Fires
Bloody April
A Walk in the Dark* (Charity booklet)

The Calgacus Series:
World's End
The Centurions
Queen of Victory
Druids' Gold
Blood Ties
The High King
The Ghost War
Last of the Free

The Hereward Story:
Last English Hero
Doomsday

The Constantine Investigates Series:
The Man in the Ironic Mask*
The Lady of Shall Not*
Gawain and the Green Nightshirt*
A Tale of One City*
49 Shades of Tartan*

The Sempronius Scipio series:
Dido's Revenge
A Long Shadow
Clash of Giants
The Poisoned Chalice
A Matter of Honour
The Conspirators

ABOUT THE AUTHOR

Born in Watford, Hertfordshire, in 1957, Gordon's family moved to Broughty Ferry in the early 1960s. Gordon attended Grove Academy, leaving in 1974 to work for Bank of Scotland. After a long but undistinguished career, he retired on medical grounds in 2008 without having received any huge bankers' bonuses.

Registered blind, Gordon had more time on his hands after retiring so, with the aid of special computer software, he returned to his hobby of writing and had his debut novel, "In the Shadow of the Wall" published in 2010. Gordon's books are now being read by a world-wide audience. As well as his historical adventure stories, he has ventured into crime fiction with some spoof murder mysteries in the "Constantine Investigates" series. He is also kept busy with speaking engagements, visiting libraries, schools and community groups to talk about his books.

In addition to his novels, Gordon devotes some of his time to raising funds for the RNIB. As well as visiting schools and social clubs to talk about his sight loss, he has self-published a charity booklet titled, "A Walk in the Dark", a humorous account of his experiences since losing his eyesight. The booklet is available from Amazon Kindle Store. Gordon will donate all author royalties to RNIB.

Now completely blind, Gordon continues to write stories and, in his spare time, attempts to play the guitar and keyboard with varying degrees of success.

Gordon is married to Alaine. They have three children and two grandchildren. The family lives in Livingston, West Lothian.

You can contact Gordon on Mastodon or BlueSky where his handle is @BlindGordon, or by sending an email to ga.author@sky.com

Printed in Great Britain
by Amazon